THE MORNING AFTER

Later, after they'd both showered and sat drinking coffee in his kitchen, she felt another wave of self-consciousness wash over her. The what-the-hell-am-I-doing-here-with-an-almost-complete-stranger? feeling of embarrassment. She leaned on the table and put her hands over her face.

"Are you okay?" Marcus asked.

"Oh, God." She smiled wanly at him through her open fingers. "What have we done?" She suddenly felt like crying. "What have I done?"

He reached over and peeled her hands off her face and, cupping them in his, kissed her fingers and grinned. His eyes were smoky green pools.

"It's just . . ." she paused, not knowing quite what to say or how much she should reveal, "just that, well, I haven't been with anyone for a long time, and I'm not used to it. I mean, we don't even know each other all that well!" She pulled her hands from his and grabbed her coffee mug.

"But we will." He gently stroked the side of her face. "We will . . ."

Fashion Slaves

Louise de Teliga

KENSINGTON PUBLISHING CORP.
http://www.kensingtonbooks.com

STRAPLESS BOOKS are published by

Kensington Publishing Corp.
850 Third Avenue
New York, NY 10022

All Kensington titles, imprints and distributed lines are available at special quantity discounts for bulk purchases for sales promotion, premiums, fund-raising, educational or institutional use.

Special book excerpts or customized printings can also be created to fit specific needs. For details, write or phone the office of the Kensington Special Sales Manager: Kensington Publishing Corp., 850 Third Avenue, New York, NY 10022. Attn. Special Sales Department. Phone: 1-800-221-2647.

First Trade Paperback Printing: October 2005
First Mass Market Paperback Printing: September 2006
10 9 8 7 6 5 4 3 2 1

Printed in the United States of America

For my mother Marie and my father Stan.

Acknowledgments

I would never have had the courage or inspiration to write this book without my teacher and mentor, Michael Levin. His UCLA classes and enthusiasm got me started on a journey that has changed my life.

My agent, Alison Picard, worked diligently with me on this manuscript and helped me whip it into shape. Thanks for believing in me, Alison.

Bucket-loads of thanks to John Scognamiglio at Kensington Books for making *Fashion Slaves* a reality.

Terry Kramer and Camilla More, my friends and sisters, you gave me so much encouragement and feedback; I don't know how I can ever express my gratitude and joy for your presence in my life.

Many thanks to my brother Mark and his beyond fabulous wife Jan, C.B. Harding (I still want to see you in a little cheerleader's outfit, jumping up and down and waving pom-poms at me!), Douglas Newton, Jamie Hacking, Carey More, Merv Asa-Dorian, Effy Young, Paul Fortune, Holly and Eric Montgomery, Simon Doonan, Heidi and Richard Sturges, Kathy Rhodes, Leslie Vaughn, and Mala Vasan. You've all been an inspiration!

And last, but certainly not least, Sweetie the sheared-mink-teddy-bear-love-magnet wonderdog.

1

She should have known she'd manage to screw this one up. There were clues, after all.

Wearing four-inch spike heels was the first idiotic choice. Mountain climbing. Her whopper-size ten-and-a-half feet squeezed into the needle-sharp pointed boots like one of the ugly sisters' gelatinous hooves into Cinderella's dainty slipper. Brilliant choice.

Josie trudged wearily up the hill through a forest of majestic firs, barely glancing at the pale sapphire sky and bloated white clouds floating above. A sheer, skim-milk sun trickled through the branches, illuminating fallen pine needles and cones and odd outcrops of brightly hued fungus clinging to ancient logs on the forest floor. When she reached a small clearing in the undergrowth, she flopped onto a rock, pulled off her boots, and massaged her swollen toes. Why did she always have to be such a pathetic fashion slave? Like anyone would ever see her here.

She watched a cow graze sleepily on a carpet of emerald grass dotted with white Alpine flowers. The soft clank of its bell infused the forest with an unusual calm. She took a deep breath of the almost palpable mountain air. Beyond exhausted.

Suddenly, out of the depths of the forest charged a group of small children, dressed in traditional Bavarian clothing. Perfect little faces. Alive with laughter, they skipped into the meadow, dancing around in circles until Josie felt nauseous watching them. Finally they fell in a giggling heap on the grass.

"Cut! Cut! That stupid goddamned cow keeps facing the wrong way! Its face is supposed to be toward the camera, not its goddamned ass! For Christ's sake do something about it! Where's its goddamned wrangler?" David Sarinen screamed. "And wardrobe! Christie! Pull up that boy's lederhosen! He's practically naked by the time he hits his mark! We're selling yogurt, not fucking kiddie porn!" he yelled from his perch behind a camera, which was mounted on a crane that raised and lowered over the mountain set.

"It's Josephine"—she flashed a big, fake smile at him, clambering over a plastic grassy knoll to fix the offending suede shorts—"or Josie."

"Whatever," he growled, "just do your fucking job."

She bit down on her lip. Obnoxious little turd.

Second clue: work with abusive director who's forgotten to take his meds.

Her assistant, Mala, ran in to help. "That jerk," she hissed. "You've been working with him for two years. You'd think he'd remember your name by now."

"A year too many," Josie mumbled, shortening the suspenders on the boy's shorts.

"You know, he used to be one of the best in the world. It can't be easy watching your career go down the plug hole. When I first met him he was on top of his game."

She'd heard he was a screamer. A total bastard with a Napoleonic complex. So, before her initial interview with him, she'd dressed in her chicest, low-cut Prada dress and her highest heels. His eyeline was level with her boobs. Exactly as planned. Turned out he was quite charming, in a bratty rock 'n' roll way. Tousled, highlighted hair. Ripped jeans, wife-beater tank, and the ubiquitous tats on his tanned arms. She told him he looked like Jon Bon Jovi. She got the job. It had been downhill ever since.

"What happened?" Mala asked.

Josie put one finger over a nostril, sniffed loudly, then tippled an imaginary drink down her throat.

"So now he's got to shoot this crap. We all have to. Let's face it, we're bottom feeders. We're scraping the depths of the advertising gene pool here. No wonder he's pissed."

"But Bo Benchley's starring in this!" Mala said, like it would make the pathetic copy writing become instantly brilliant because another mega star had been paid a fortune to hawk yet another cheesy product.

"Phw!" Josie snorted. "Bo Benchley. I hear he's a complete dickhead."

"What's a dickhead?" the little boy asked, eyes wide with innocence.

"Ooh." Josie glanced around, hoping his mom or the set teacher was nowhere in earshot. "It's nothing, Freddie. Just something you'll encounter lots of if you stay in this business, kid. Now run along." She patted his little blond head and propelled him back toward the other children.

"Back to One!" yelled Miles, the assistant director, shepherding the children to their beginning positions in the forest as the crew readied for another take. The cow's legs had now been tied to sandbags and covered with foliage, hopefully preventing another bad performance. It didn't seem too perturbed by this encumbrance, as a new roll of fresh turf had been laid down for it to chew on.

Josie stumbled off the set into the dark of the cavernous sound stage and made her way past the camera crew, trying not to trip over the masses of electric cords snaking all over the cement floor. She was starving, but the sight of congealing, grayish scrambled eggs and mummified greasy bacon on the breakfast table nearly made her retch. She'd kill for a decent cup of coffee.

She slipped out of the stage and into an elevator across the hallway. Leaning her head against the wall, she closed her eyes, drained at the thought of the tedious day stretching before her. Endless hours trapped on a plastic Alpine set, with a bunch of fat grips whose beer guts wobbled out over their jeans. And that jerkoff director. The glamour of it all.

The doors opened and she saw, to her dismay, that the top-floor cafeteria was closed. But she stepped out anyway. Her dour mood lifted instantly. Through the huge stretch of windows along one side of the building glistened the Manhattan skyline, sparkling in the early morning sun like a fabulous jewel. Postcard perfect. She strode across the room, pushed open heavy glass doors leading to a large walled-in terrace, and stepped outside.

A frigid wind whistled around her. She crossed the flagstones to the edge of the parapet and gazed across the East River, gulping in the fresh air, energized by the vision of power spread out before her. It always had that surreal quality, like a diorama in a museum, or a backdrop for a movie set. Except this was the real thing, not some spurious hack job thrown together in a dungeon in Queens, like the set downstairs.

Sometimes she still couldn't believe she lived here. A girl from the burbs of Sydney living in New York. Pretty cool. Okay, so maybe things weren't going as well as she'd like. An understatement to say the least. But she lived in New York, for God's sake. How bad could it be?

She was working. Advertising had been so depressed for so many months she was thrilled to finally have a job again.

She shivered and clutched her thin white shirt close to her. November. Winter loomed. Rubbing her arms to keep warm, she turned and crossed back toward the exit.

She pulled at the door. Wouldn't open. Another tug produced nothing. *What a complete weakling. Fat lot of good all those weight-training sessions did.* She pulled with all her might, rattled as hard as she could, but the door wouldn't budge. She realized, with mounting horror, that she was locked out. *Oh, shit.*

Oh, shit! It's bloody glacial out here! What'll I do? Panicking, she banged and rattled the doors, frantically trying to pull them open. Not an inch. Nada, nothing. *Shit.* She peered through the glass in hopes that someone might be inside, but she couldn't see any signs of life, and there didn't appear to be a security camera anywhere in sight.

Ohmygod! No one knows I'm up here! "Help!" she yelled out to the magnificent view. "Help!"

Third clue: lock yourself out. Freeze to death.

She imagined her stiff, icy remains being found days, maybe weeks later. They'd have to cut open her frozen black leather McQueen pants. Underneath they'd see she'd forgotten her mum's advice—"always wear good underwear, dear, in case you get run over by a bus"—she had on shredded knickers, and an ancient Vicki's Secret bra clung to her frozen nipples. That's what happens when you dress at 4:30 AM. *Shit.* At least she was wearing the most fabulous Louboutin boots. Which she'd charged the day before. Now she'd never have to pay for them.

Yeah, no problem. You'll be dead, you twit.

She rattled at the doors again but realized it was useless. Shivering, she raced over to the other side of the terrace, where a row of potted fir trees rimmed the parapet. Climbing onto one of the pots, she leaned over the edge to the street below and yelled out. It was a barren wasteland down there. The studios were in the middle of a vast urban slum. Great. Not even a drag queen hooker lurked below. They only came out after dark. She yelled out again, feeling the air icing her lungs, bringing on the asthma.

Calm down! Think!

A mass of vines, their leaves withering into dormancy, trailed over the edge and down the side of the building. She considered grabbing hold of the strongest-looking one and lowering herself down. But it petered out about halfway down the building. *So then what? Jump a floor or two? Yeah, right. What a pity I missed those "How to swing like Tarzan in the urban jungle" classes in the Learning Annex magazine. You just never know when they'll come in handy.*

Shut up and think!

She stared at the trees for a few seconds and figured maybe she could charge the doors and smash the glass with one. So she picked the smallest tree and set to work unearthing its roots from the wooden pot. The wind was howling now, whistling and eddying around, lifting dirt from the pot and throwing it in her face, up her nostrils, in her eyes.

Coughing and spluttering and barely able to see with all the grit and hair blowing everywhere, she dug away at the roots until she could feel them loosening. When she finally stood up and attempted to grasp the trunk, spiny branches scratched her face and she heard her shirt rip and felt a painful scraping on her right shoulder as she reached in toward the middle of the foliage.

She gasped and swore but didn't let go, determined to yank the fir out. Using one foot as an anchor on the pot, she tugged hard until she felt the tree freeing up. She pulled with all her force and found herself on her back with the tree on top of her.

"Aahggh," she groaned. She lay there for a few seconds, trying to catch her breath. When she managed to get up, her back ached and she was covered in dirt and there were blood spots seeping through her shirt.

She grabbed the top of the tree and dragged it until she was in a direct line with the glass doors. As she lifted the tree a huge gust of wind threw her off balance, whirling her around like a bizarre dervish. Finally righting herself, she looked toward the doors and found, to her amazement, that she was no longer alone.

In the doorway, tall and elegant in a dark suit and a black cashmere coat, stood Bo Benchley. A hunter green cashmere scarf slung nonchalantly around his neck added luster to a deeply tanned complexion. Smooth as silk.

"Oh!" she gasped, still clutching her spiny green dance partner. "Hi." *Ohmygod! It's him! And could I possibly look any worse?* She glanced past him at her reflection in the glass. *Nope. Not a chance of that.*

"Bit early to be lifting a Christmas tree isn't it?" he said with his celebrated resonance, an amused condescension spread across his large face. He was huge. She could feel the space around him disappear. He took a puff of a giant cigar and stared at her.

She shrank back, mortified, and tried to smooth her rat's nest of hair into place. Like it would make any difference at this point.

"Ahh," she squeaked, attempting a wan smile, "I ah . . ."

"Put it back," he boomed and, flashing her a final withering look, he grasped the door handle with a gargantuan paw, opened it with the greatest of ease, and swept back inside.

She lunged after him to grab the door in case it locked again and fell in a twisted heap over the tree. "Beautiful day, isn't it?" she groaned breathlessly.

Fourth clue: make complete ass of yourself in front of celebrity. Even if he is a total dickhead.

"What the fuck happened to you?" David Sarinen hissed, as she staggered back onto the stage. "You look like a bull dyke on acid."

"I do not!" Josie snapped. "I just got locked—"

"Been out in the parking lot picking up tricks? You look like shit."

"Thanks a lot," she mumbled, feeling worse than shit. She felt like she'd been beaten up. She shuffled painfully over to the production desk.

"Are you okay?" asked Arnelle, the producer, looking horrified. "What happened? Do you need a doctor?"

"I'm fine," Josie said sheepishly, "I just—"

"You don't look fine."

"She looks like shit," David Sarinen said, walking off toward the mountain set. "Why does everyone on this crew look like shit? Why can't I have a decent-looking crew for once? All I ever get lumbered with is this ugly bunch of morons."

"Have you looked in the mirror lately?" Arnelle muttered after him, rolling her eyes.

"Little rat," Josie said, examining the wreckage of her body. Her shirt was ripped to shreds and she had a large bleeding cut on the back of her shoulder.

"I think you ought to let the medic check you out," Arnelle said. "And I want to know what happened. You really do look like shit."

* * *

"What the fuck is with that getup? If that sweater were any tighter it'd fucking strangle you," said David Sarinen, as he spotted her sitting back on the fake rock twenty minutes later.

"I wish *you'd* put it on then," Josie said, although he had a point. The only thing she could find to change into was one of the children's spare Tyrolean sweaters. And it did feel like she'd bust out of it any second. The sleeves were so tight she couldn't lift her arms up and it barely came down below her bra, leaving a huge gaping area of midriff above her leather jeans. She sat up as straight as she could and sucked in her stomach so the roll of fat wouldn't show.

"Nice tits," he said, with a wriggle of his rodent nose.

She felt her jaw drop, but before she could think of a retort, Bo Benchley, flanked by an entourage of acolytes, entered the soundstage. A hush fell over the set.

"So where's my mark?" he boomed, to no one in particular. "Let's get this over with."

"Hi there, Bo." The director held up his tiny rodent-like hand to the enormous star. "How are you, man? Wow, you look great."

Bo Benchley puffed on his cigar and glanced down at the rodent for a nanosecond. "I am," he said and bounded up onto the mountain. The set shook as he pounded over the Astro Turf like a monster, leaving crushed fake edelweiss in his wake. His make-up artist and costumer chased behind him, ready to primp. He waved them away and stood for a few seconds, surveying the set with hooded eyes.

Josie, relieved he'd brought his own wardrobe stylist, hid behind a tree, pulling at her miniature sweater, and watched him. His protuberant belly, pushing over the top of olive green Ultrasuede lederhosen, was offset by spindly legs encased in knee-high yellow woolen socks with red and green ties around the tops, and a pair of green pointy-toed booties. A small boiled wool hat with a long bouncing feather perched jauntily on his monster-sized skull. He looked obscene, like some sort of perverted Austrian man-child. Not exactly a vision that would make one in any way crave a pint or two of yogurt.

"You look hilarious, Bo, just great," chortled rat-face Sarinen, sidling up beside him. He was about half Bo's height and he had to strain his head back to look up that far. Bo didn't lower his gaze at all. "I was thinking—"

"The first shot will be me with the cow," Bo thundered. "We need a close-up of my face next to his. Get the camera over here." He pointed to a spot. The crew stood in stunned silence for a minute, not knowing whom they should obey. "Well? What the hell are you slackers waiting for? Get on with it." He took a long drag on his cigar. "And keep those ankle biters away from me 'til I need 'em. Too damned noisy."

The children, mute since his appearance, were nonetheless herded off the mountain as the crew rushed around. To Josie's delight, David Sarinen shuffled off and sat down on the crane, looking humiliated.

Bo directed himself and the tethered cow in one take, then walked off the set. "Next shot is me with the ankle biters. And get a move on, slackers. I'm out of this godforsaken joint in two hours. You hear me?"

A few minutes later, as Josie knelt checking children's costumes, he thundered back onto the mountain. Giving her a vague glance of recognition, he made a couple of cheesy faces at the kids, an attempt to loosen them up, she supposed. She quietly slunk back to her plastic rock and watched as he shot a few takes with the kids. Bo yodeled along with the Swiss Alpine music and she had to admit he was a pro. Knew his lines, had it down pat. And he was funny.

The children, finally emerging from a sort of terrified catatonia, started giggling at the faces he made at them. He'd won them over, and they jostled for his attention, laughing and asking questions.

"You're a dickhead!" yelled one of the little boys.

"Really?" Bo said sweetly, Mr. Congeniality now. "And who told you that, young man?"

"She did," Freddie pointed at Josie.

As no convenient chasm opened up to swallow her into the bowels of the earth, Josie just sat there—and smiled at Bo.

Fifth clue: call superstar a dickhead.

"And what exactly are you planning for an encore?" Arnelle was apoplectic.

"Suicide?" Josie mumbled, feverishly throwing her equipment into a large black nylon bag. She could still feel her cheeks burning with embarrassment.

"You've already committed that, honey. What were you thinking? Bo Benchley is one of the biggest names in the business! You can't just go 'round calling famous actors dickheads!"

"Well, he is a dickhead."

"Well, duh. But did you have to say it in front of a child?"

"David Sarinen was swearing like a trouper in front of those kids!"

"So you think that makes it okay for you to do the same? Get a grip. We're lucky the studio teacher didn't shut us down!"

"Do you think I should go up there and apologize? Would it help?" Josie zipped up the bag and looked at her friend.

"I think you should make a quiet exit," Arnelle sighed.

"I'm sorry, Arnelle. I really am."

"Me, too, Josie."

Josie slung the bag over her shoulder and walked out, keeping her head high, although she felt like crap and she didn't know if she'd make it to the front door without crying.

Sixth clue: get fired. Before 11:00 AM.

Well, at least she had the rest of the day off.

2

Hamish Kent woke with a start and that moment of panic when he couldn't remember where the hell he was. He looked around. A limo. Yes, but where in a limo? *Oh, bollocks. New York again. I hate New York,* he thought. *Every bloody week I'm in New York.* He checked his image in both small mirrors on either side of the backseat. He ran his hand over his newly shaved head, pursed his lips, then smiled, almost grimaced, to make sure he had nothing wedged in his teeth from his first-class lunch.

"Are we nearly there yet, driver?" he said, pleased with the reflection smiling back at him. *Not too shabby at all,* he thought, admiring his Yves Saint Laurent suit and his navy and black checked Richard James shirt and matching tie. Utterly fabulous.

"Very close, sir. We're just heading down Lexington. Should be about ten more minutes," the driver shouted back at him.

Hamish wound down his window and shivered as icy air blasted over him. "Hideously dressed lot," he said, sniffing with disdain as the limo edged past throngs of pedestrians.

"What was that, sir?"

"Nothing, just admiring your gorgeous city."

"Thanks. I love the place," the driver beamed into the rear- view mirror. "You here on business, Mr. Kent?"

Oh, bollocks, Hamish thought, *here we go. A bloody chatterer.* "Yes," he replied, hoping that would be the last of it, but knowing it wouldn't be.

"Lemme guess. I'm a real pro at guessing what people do."

"Really," Hamish said, bored stiff. He looked for the button to close the glass partition separating them.

"I just know you're somebody famous," the driver yelled. Hamish perked up a little. "Aren't you whatsizname? Ya know, from that rock band?"

"I'm a fashion photographer," Hamish said, trying not to appear flattered.

"That so. Wow. All them beautiful gals. Lucky guy. Do ya do them Victoria Secret photos? What a great gig that must be. Or *Sports Illustrated.* Now them are some hot bods. What I wouldn't do to be a fly on the wall at one of them gigs." He looked hopefully back at Hamish.

"I'm here to do a shoot for *Vogue* magazine," Hamish said, repulsed at the mention of such publications. Sports. Hmph. And catalogues. Even worse.

"Oh," the driver sounded disappointed, "that's nice."

A silence ensued, and Hamish stared back out the window as they went past Bloomingdale's. He was thinking how awful the window displays looked when a woman in a grubby white shirt, black leather pants, and a long black coat caught his eye as she emerged from the subway, dragging a Gucci bag over her shoulder. Bedraggled, but interesting. Long blond hair, freckles. Pretty, in a sullen, over-the-hill way.

Their eyes met for an instant as she reached the edge

of the sidewalk, and a flicker of recognition washed over her face.

"Stop!" he yelled at the driver. "Stop the car!"

The limo screeched to a halt at the curb, sending yellow taxis flying in its wake and a chorus of horns into action. Hamish opened the door, climbed out, and stared at his old friend.

"Down on your luck I see, darling," he sniffed as they air kissed. "Can't afford the real thing these days?" He glanced down at the fake Gucci bag.

"That *would* be the first thing out of your mouth, wouldn't it?" Josie said.

"Get in, get in." He grabbed the bag and threw it in the back, almost pushed her in after it, then climbed in next to her. "What on earth are you doing in this hellhole?"

Josie couldn't believe it. Running into him after almost, what, eight years, give or take a couple. Long enough that she was flabbergasted he even recognized her.

"Well look at you," she said, leaning back into the seat and eyeing him up and down. "All tarted up and riding around in a limo, like a flash pimp."

"And you, darling," he eyed her back, "look like you've been trolling Eleventh Avenue. Like a bit of rough trade these days?" He flicked at the collar of her torn, filthy shirt and raised an eyebrow. His tiny mouth curled up at the edges. "You look hideous."

"Tell me something I don't know," she said, not at all fazed, even though she should probably feel mortified by her ghastly appearance in front of one of the world's most famous photographers. She was too tired. "I had a fight with a shrub."

"You don't strike me as the gardening type," he sniffed. "More likely you were asleep under a bush. With someone on top of you."

"Shut up."

"Are you living out of that faux Gucci, darling?"

"Not quite yet," she said, although at the rate she was going it might not be long.

"Which gutter can I drop you in?" he said, his gray button eyes glinting in a way that made her feel a taut hardness behind them that hadn't been there back in the old days.

"Oh, there's one down near Beekman Place I'm rather fond of." She gave the address to the driver and they headed off.

She knew she had hardened over the years as well. She felt a terrified cynicism insidiously edging through her the older she got. Every glance in a mirror these days produced another wave of despair she could feel slowly calcifying her. She wondered if her eyes betrayed her the way his did.

"You're looking rather good, darling, despite the filth," he smiled, as if he'd read her mind and was trying to appease her. Not that he was the type to appease anybody, if he could skewer them instead.

"Poverty must agree with me," she said, brushing at strands of hair that still had green flecks of shrubbery clinging to them.

"Filth agrees with you. Poverty is just a by-product of the filth."

"Getting philosophical in your old age?"

"Certainly not. Just richer. I'm so rich now, I can hardly stand it."

"Then by your theory, you must be pristinely clean as well."

"Oh, I'm a paradigm of cleanliness, darling," he said, and they both laughed.

They bantered back and forth for a few minutes until he asked her the inevitable and dreaded question, "So what are you doing here?"

She never quite knew how to answer that. "*Well, I was engaged to a psychotic trust fund millionaire who nearly killed me, so I ran away and tried to become a fashion stylist but ended up working on shlocky commercials and even that's a disaster*" sounded a little over the top to tell someone you haven't seen in a dog's age. Let alone a top-notch fashion photographer who'd most likely view your meager achievements with disdain. Especially looking like she did right now.

She mumbled something about the TV commercial and film end of things and was relieved to see they were right outside her front door.

"So, dinner tomorrow then?" he said, air kissing her cheeks as she clumsily retrieved her bag and climbed out. "Meet me at the Mercer at eight." And before she had a moment to protest, the driver had shut the door and she couldn't see through the black-tinted windows. So she pretended to act cool and sauntered into her apartment building, feeling the filth and poverty clinging to her like a highly unpleasant aroma.

3

"What fresh hell is this?" she mumbled as the doorman, looking slightly askance at the sight of her, handed her the day's mail. It was, as usual, a pile of bills.

"Are you all right, Miss Vaughn?" he said.

"Never better, Henry," she sighed. "Just peachy." She staggered into the elevator and slumped on the wall behind him, beyond exhausted.

"If there's anything I can do, Miss," Henry said, in an almost fatherly tone, as she got out.

"You are sweet, Henry"—she smiled at him—"but I'm fine. Thanks."

Inside her tiny flat, she threw the bundle of bills into the ever-increasing pile on her desk, went into the microscopic excuse for a kitchen, and poured herself a monster glass of red wine. She didn't give a fat rat's ass that it was broad daylight outside. She lay down on her couch and considered her fate.

It would have to be a day like this when she'd run into someone like Hamish. She couldn't possibly run into someone flashy when she looked halfway decent. Oh, no. That'd be way too good. Oh, what the hell. She gulped the wine and thought about him.

She'd first met Hamish in London in the early eighties, when he was a budding luminary in the photographic world, she one of the top models in the city. They'd been drawn to one another; she to his razor-sharp facetiousness, and he, she supposed, to a certain extent, her looks, although she knew she had never made it so far in that world just by her looks. She was never the most beautiful, never had the best body, or could be photographed from any angle and look good. She had gotten by on her personality. More than merely gotten by. She had done pretty well. She had been the one they'd take on a trip because she was fun and willing to do just about anything to get a good shot.

He had a crush on her, she realized, and he'd booked her any chance he could. They worked together nearly every day for months on end, a confluence of evil humor prevailing whenever they were in each other's company.

"Ahh, Josie," he'd say, "you're a girl who understands."

She figured he meant she got his sick humor. Which she did. But it was more than that.

He was smart. Really smart. Intelligence and humor were a magnetic combination for her. Unfortunately, the combination usually ended up being in tandem with other traits rather less attractive: drug addiction, extreme and violent jealousy, or some other twisted mind-set. Or simple unavailability. Hamish was married. And she was involved in an on- and off-again relationship with a loser cocaine dealer. Well, she didn't know at the time he was a cocaine dealer. But he always had piles of it on him, and she, for a while, found this amusing, as just about everybody did in those days. Plus it helped her stay thin. It didn't come naturally for her not to eat. She loved food.

She'd spent her teenage years either wolfing down gigantic servings of food or rationing out lettuce leaves and popping diet pills and diarrhea-inducing potions. When she left Australia at seventeen, she found herself with a fast-moving, club-hopping set in Paris, Milan, and then London.

It was a set populated by a particular breed of male, often from, or at least posing as if from, inherited wealth or some enormously successful business that afforded these men the opportunity to spend copious amounts of time and money preening themselves in front of girls barely weaned off high school cafeteria lunches in small towns in the Midwest. Or in Josie's case, Down Under. Girls who found themselves, by way of a fortunate bestowal of genetic pulchritude, thrust into the international fishbowl of modeling.

The Model Groupies, or MGs, as she and a couple of her friends called them, lived large. They drove fast sports cars (or, in Milan, shuttled round in old bombs driven by armed bodyguards, because of the increase in kidnappings at the time). They inhabited ultra luxe bachelor pads, or family manses with spectacular views. Their attire was classical and expensive—bespoke tailored suits, Hermes, Gucci before it sank and came back into uber vogueness; gold Rolex watches; pressed jeans with Lacoste T-shirts; or crisp Egyptian cotton shirts open low enough to display the ubiquitous tan, offset by a gold chain or two nestled in the chest hair; and loafers without socks. They also had voracious sexual appetites they hoped would be satiated by as much young pretty flesh as possible.

MGs befriended the top model agents in Paris and

Milan and knew when girls were arriving for photographic shoots and where they were staying. They would hang around hotel bars and lobbies waiting for the daily influx of beauty. They bribed desk clerks and got room numbers and made multitudinous calls to the girls' rooms. Usually they managed to lure a few of them out for an evening. Dinner, dancing, lavish amounts of champagne and cocaine and, with luck, sex. That is, if they were able to get it up at five in the morning coked to the gills, and the girl (or girls) hadn't staggered out pleading an early morning call.

Josie had been simultaneously amused and repulsed by the MGs. She'd go out to the dinners, the latest clubs, drink the bubbly, snort the coke, and sometimes go back to their playboy abodes (mostly just for the thrill of actually viewing and giggling at the ostentation and to snort more coke). But she had a detached humor about the whole scene and never allowed herself to be immersed beyond minor frivolity.

She never went out with MGs alone; always in a group, unless she'd been invited to La Scala for the opera, or some hot concert. Perhaps, she thought later, she had actually been smart enough to know danger when she saw it displayed as such flashy overindulgence. At least she'd escaped that much. Besides, she knew they weren't at all interested in her personally. She supposed they thought of her as some sort of plebeian misfit. It was merely what she represented. The accessory every model groupie needed dangling off his arm was, of course, a model.

There were stories of girls who had fallen for MGs, enamored with the lifestyle, the cars, the money, the exotic trips, and the drugs. Not many of them survived intact. Everyone in Milan knew the model who became involved with the most famous and wealthiest of the

Italian MGs, Carlo Cessari. He shot her while in a drug-induced haze. She died. He got off and continued his lifestyle untrammeled by consequences.

Some of them profited. There was a girl Josie had worked with who was flown from Milan to Africa to shoot a spread for a major fashion magazine, only to find, on her arrival in Kenya, that there was no photographer, no stylist, no make-up artist or hairdresser, and no clothes. She was met by the notoriously lecherous (and happily married) publisher and expected to share a tent with him on safari. She did. She later graced several covers of the magazine and became a hot commodity.

Most famous of the MGs was also the world's most prominent model agent. He was renowned for elevating girls who slept with him to the top echelon of his agency, pretty much a guarantee they would become big money earners. He sent teddy bears to girls he was courting, a sure sign he was ready to make them famous—and fuck them. He also sent girls who were willing to Saudi Arabia for weekends with wealthy Arabs. They would earn tens of thousands of dollars for a few days' "work."

Despite the plethora of sordid characters hanging round the business like oversexed leeches, for the most part it was run very professionally, and usually a great camaraderie existed among models, and between them and the photographers, make-up artists and hairdressers, fashion stylists, and magazine editors. They were a little team, a family, who would come together to create beauty and style and sometimes even art.

That was one of the reasons Josie loved working with Hamish. She admired his eye. His shots had a graphic and spatial purity she had never seen before. She enjoyed being a part of a creative process, using her face and body as a shape, part of the overall design. Maybe that's what he meant when he said she was a girl who understood.

Their flirtation had begun as a humorous dance around each other, neither of them brave enough to act upon it, until he booked her on a shoot in Greece. There, away from his crumbling marriage and her insanely jealous boyfriend, the dismal gray of London abandoned for the wild, tortured beauty of the Chalcidice peninsula, they ran out of excuses.

She could still picture the winding dirt paths and secluded, tiny beaches surrounding the new hotel complex where they were staying. A yachtsman's paradise, set among the turquoise coves of the northernmost part of the country, an area up until then completely untouched by foreigners. Developed by the local shipping magnate, a man whose immense wealth had not, unfortunately, given him a passport to the finer points of aesthetics in luxury, the complex was a garish, sprawling combination of a hotel, condos, and yacht moorings, all of them sparklingly new.

They had been the first guests, invited to shoot there, in exchange for a word or two, to be dashed off by the magazine editor accompanying them, about the beauty and exclusivity of this wonderful new resort. The beginning of the last vestiges of the area's natural splendor. Josie imagined that by now, more than fifteen years later, there was barely a tree left standing, barely any trace of the Macedonian influence that had permeated the entire countryside surrounding the hotel. The quaint innocence of fishing villages squandered and replaced by cheap concrete propitiations to the hoards of plundering visitors that descended each August.

They sailed on the magnate's enormous yacht, a vessel as aged as himself, the most beautiful fixture of the port he had created in his own honor. Crafted entirely of teak, immaculately maintained and staffed, the sails hoisted proudly as they toured the coastline, and worked—Josie draping herself around the yacht in an outrageous swimsuit or two—dined on seafood, drank copious amounts of local retsina, and giggled, quietly among themselves, about their ancient mariner host with his navy blue bobbled wool cap fixed permanently on his wrinkled brow. He pointed a bony finger toward his house, a blond stone edifice perched majestically atop the hill overlooking the port. An invitation, more an edict, had been issued to visit him for lunch the following day.

At the appointed hour, the motley array of creatively attired humanity that comprises a fashion crew—photographer, an assistant or two, models, make-up and hair, editor and assistant—all piled out of a rented minivan into the courtyard of their host's mansion. They'd spent the morning shooting in a small, classically Greek boat; Josie, swathed in black silk couture, lace veiled, blackened eyelids, rouge-smudged lips, poised statuesquely on the prow; an homage, Hamish said, to Greta Garbo in her role as Queen Christina.

Presenting themselves before the local royalty, they dragged politely around on a grand tour of his estate, his vineyards, and were fed and feted as exotic interlopers into his quiet existence. A quietness he obviously hoped would be shattered by many more of their kind in the near future.

That night, Josie and Hamish sat alone in the large hotel dining room, the rest of the crew having abandoned the resort for a more authentic meal in a real village. The magnate and several henchmen, the only other patrons, chatted quietly in a far corner. After a while, one of them approached the table and politely asked a bemused Hamish to follow him outside. He reappeared several minutes later, his eyes narrowed into slits of mirth.

"What was that about?" Josie asked.

"It appears, my dear Josephine"—he said, sliding in beside her, his voice regal—"that you have had rather an effect on our host."

"What?" she said, not getting it.

"Mr. Apatsos's assistant informed me," he said regally, "that Mr. Apatsos is very impressed by you. That Mr. Apatsos, even though he is well over seventy years old, is still very young at heart, and that indeed, all his parts are in excellent working order."

"Excellent working order? What? What is he—a car?" Her eyes rolled skyward. She glanced over at the billionaire's table. They were rising to leave. The ancient mariner looked over and smiled at them before tottering out.

"There's more," said Hamish jauntily. "Mr. Apatsos, he said, is a widower. He longs for the company of a beautiful woman—"

"You're joking!" Josie spluttered a mouthful of wine onto the table, coughing, to conceal her laughter. "You've got to be joking!"

"Mr. Apatsos would be very appreciative," continued Hamish, "if you would visit him alone one evening, or stay on after the shoot is finished. Mr. Apatsos would look after you very well. You could stay as long as you please." His voice cracked with a deep gurgling laugh.

"Just think . . . This"—he said, sweeping his arm in the general direction of the port outside—"could all be yours!"

She was crying with laughter now. "Eeuw. Yu-uck."

"Now, Josephine," he went on, "be serious for a minute. Think about it. He's on his last legs! A few months with you might push him completely over the edge. You could keep us all in the style we'd love to become accustomed to. You'd be The New Jackie O!" He gave her a lascivious wink.

"So what, pray tell, did you say to this chap?" she finally managed to gasp, between paroxysms of laughter.

"I told him to send a car at midnight," he said, completely straight-faced.

"You didn't! Did you?" She wouldn't put it past him.

"I did." His face had not the tiniest inclination of a smile.

"You bastard. I'll kill you!" she squealed, pummeling at him, laughing so hard she nearly slid under the table. "Pimp!" She grabbed for his arm as he tried to escape her onslaught.

She chased him out the open French doors of the restaurant, into the moonlit garden, both of them laughing until pain ripped at their sides, collapsing in a heap on the grass, underneath a large tree. She sat on him, pinned him beneath her, and pounded on his chest, both of them breathing hard now, still laughing, aware of the closeness, the heat of the other's body. Then he pulled her down toward him and kissed her.

"I'm still going to kill you," she whispered hoarsely, wresting her mouth away from his. She rolled over and lay motionless beside him, both of them gazing heavenward, silent, their thoughts absorbed into the indigo blanket of night. The rise and fall of their breathing, the beating of their hearts formed a rhythmic, nocturnal symphony with the musical creak of cicadas, the rustle of leaves in the soft breeze, the gentle lapping of water against the stone embankment of the nearby dock. They lay there for ages, engulfed by anticipation.

Finally, she turned to him, her eyes finding his through the gray flannel miasma of darkness, and began kissing him again. He moaned and pulled her closer, cupping her breast in his hand, his tongue now entwined with hers.

"We'd better go inside," she finally whispered. "One of Mr. Apatsos's spies might be watching!" But she kept kissing him, not wanting it to stop.

"C'mon then," he said after a while, pulling her off the grass. She stood up, jellied at the knees, and looked at him, aware that their friendship would be altered irrevocably from then on.

He grabbed her hand and led her, not inside, but away from the building, out across the lawn, toward the water. She felt the warm, salty breeze against her skin, the fine chiffon of her long skirt brushing against her legs as she walked, acutely aware of every physical nuance around her. The hot roughness of his hand as it gripped hers, the crunch of their shoes over the pebbles when they reached the embankment and jumped down onto the receding shoreline. They hugged close to the shoulder-height embankment as he pulled her along with him, the lights of the port slowly waning behind them. Eventually they reached a dirt path, barely discernable in the pale, silvery light of the half moon, and traversed it, both of them silent, concentrating, until it rose over some rocks and down to another tiny cove. Nesting themselves into a sheltered patch of sand in the hollowed base of a rock, they attacked each other with the abandon of wild animals, their moans floating into the antiquity of the Grecian night.

The phone jolted her awake into semidarkness. She must have been asleep for hours. Maybe she'd slept all night. What bliss.

"It's me," said her friend Priscilla. "I've got a hot one for you."

"Hot one what?" Josie said groggily.

"Guy, honey."

"Oh, no. Not another one."

"He's fabulous. Rich! Rich beyond belief! His name's Andy Wyatt, and he just bought Vive."

"Vive?"

"The cosmetics you slather on your mug every day. Now, get out of bed. We're going shopping."

"At this hour?"

"It's only two."

"Two?" she said, extremely confused. "In the morning?"

"Are you on drugs? It's two PM bonehead. Now wake up. I'll pick you up in an hour."

"No, P., wait—" but the phone clicked dead. *Oh, cripes. I'm so tired. All I want to do is stay here and sleep.* Josie painfully rolled herself up, sat on the edge of the sofa, and attempted to stretch, which induced gnawing pain in every muscle. *I feel like crap. Bruised dog meat. I must look like bruised dog meat, too. And she wants me to go shopping? Jesus.* She glanced over at the pile of bills on her desk. *I can't even afford bruised dog meat, let alone an excursion with P. today.*

Shut up! Just pull yourself together and stop being such a wimp! So what if you're battered and aching and you just got fired and have absolutely no prospects of any income in the foreseeable future. So what if those bills are not going to pay themselves. So what if you're overdrawn at the bank. It's only money! Now get up and get dressed, twit! You never know what will happen. Just look what has happened already today. Running into Hamish—what are the odds of that? So get up*!*

She staggered into the black-and-white-tiled bathroom, ignoring the many layers of badly applied glossy paint peeling down the walls like polished dandruff, yanked off her clothes and threw them in a pile, turned on the ancient shower, winced at her reflection in the small mirrored cupboard as she grabbed a handful of Advils and gulped them, climbed into the rust-stained bathtub, and drew around her the white terry cloth shower curtain, which had certainly seen better days, the giveaway being the malevolent black mold beginning to steal along its bottom edges. All the while she thought of Hamish. As the water cleansed the blood off her skin, an idea began to creep around her worn-out brain, and a zap of excitement shot her back to life for a few seconds.

4

Josie hadn't known Priscilla very long. They'd met at some charity function. One of those lunches frequented by women who spent half their lives wrapped in couture at charity events, and the other half primping for them. Josie had been roped into helping out with the mandatory fashion show the ladies feasted their eyes on while picking scornfully at their $500 cold poached salmon and arugula plates. Fashion—yum! Food (any food)—yekk.

She'd even forked out her own bucks for the pleasure, if one could call it that, of dining with *the* luminaries of the New York Social Stratosphere, before dashing backstage at the Plaza ballroom to help the models dress. Naturally, she'd been seated at a table in Outer Siberia. Even so, the gaggle of overly pampered women surrounding her barely gave her the time of day. She felt disheveled and completely out of place in her pret-a-porter Prada. And, despite her fascination with the hand-stitched Valentinos, Oscars, Diors, Chanels, and Herreras in suffocating abundance, not to mention enough Manolos and diamonds to cover an entire aircraft carrier or two, bored stiff.

She'd quaffed two glasses of Veuve before she'd realized—These women aren't real! They don't drink! They don't eat! They exist on the heady scent of their own wealth, and gossip.

The exception had been Priscilla. She had flounced in, extremely late, and collapsed opposite Josie in a flurry of air-kissed greetings from the other matrons. It became immediately apparent that she didn't give a hoot. About anything. Especially the pumped-up prima donnas at the table, who, despite Priscilla's baudy, devil-may-care attitude (five glasses of Veuve, the entire meal snaffled in an eye blink), showed her such reverence Josie couldn't help being mesmerized. She was wise-cracking, charming, and beautiful. The face of a plump, naughty angel with a wild flame of hair. Head to toe in green silk YSL. And the emeralds! Giant, dripping boulders slung down her bosom with careless abandon. Who *was* this fabulous creature! And what was she doing in the Outer Limits?

She'd introduced herself to Josie (as no one else had bothered) and proceeded to compliment and quiz her simultaneously. How lucky she was to come from Australia! How wonderful she had volunteered her services for such a worthy cause! On and on.

"Come and sit with me!" she'd cried to Josie, when she'd returned from her duties backstage. "What a fucking boring bunch of bitches!" she exclaimed, after the last of their table had departed. They ordered more bubbly and giggled until they were the only remnants of the lunch. Instant best friends.

It hadn't dawned on Josie who Priscilla was. Until she read her card. Her last name was Saunders. *The* Priscilla Saunders. With the billionaire investment banker husband. *The* Saunderses, who lived in arguably the best co-op on Park. Whose walls were slathered with one of the best modern art collections in the world. Whose friends were all famous artists or designers or celebrities. *Cripes. Why the hell does she want to hang around me?* Josie remembered thinking.

Spoiled as she was, though, Priscilla was so down to earth she could have been a fellow Aussie. She'd sprung from Bayshore, Long Island, into the city fresh out of college and landed herself a job as Richard Saunders's executive secretary. The rest was history. By her own account, she'd given Richard the most amazing blow jobs he'd ever had ("Honey, I can suck the chrome off a Carrera!" she beamed proudly). They'd married within six months. And then he started making serious money. So, now she lived the life of ten Rileys.

"What the hell happened to you?" she said, as Josie climbed into the back of the car and slumped down next to her. "You're covered in scratches."

"There's only one"—Josie felt her neck in panic—"isn't there? I thought I'd covered it up." She whisked out a mirror and examined herself while she related the morning's debacle. She looked horrid, and she felt about as much like going shopping as taking a trip to the gyno's.

"I should have stayed in bed today," she sighed.

"Nonsense, honey," Priscilla said, "I'll take you to tea. But would you mind coming with me to Pierre's first?" Josie knew what was in store. An afternoon holding P's hand while she shopped. *Great.*

"I know it!" Priscilla said, as they entered the chaotic foyer of the Pierre Parau beauty salon. "I just know it! I can feel it in my bones! Eleven goddamn years, and you know what he does for our anniversary?" She was almost visibly frothing at the mouth.

"What?" asked Josie meekly. They sat on one of the black leather benches placed around the sleek, wood-paneled rotunda.

"Nothing! That's what!" Priscilla fumed. "Not a goddamn thing! Except tell me I spend too much money! Too much money? How can I possibly spend too much money!"

Josie shrugged, wishing she had just a tiny fraction of the Saunders's fortune. The Amex bill she'd opened yesterday was of such tomelike thickness she'd nearly fainted. She didn't have enough money to pay it and had no idea how she'd manage to do so. She found herself in the ironic position of being surrounded by wealthy friends and living a life of supposed luxury on a rotting shoestring.

"We practically print fucking money!" Priscilla cried. Her words drew a few glances from the pretty girls behind the bustling reception desk. "He's having an affair, I tell you!" she moaned, almost on the verge of tears. Josie gave her a droll look.

"Oh, I know," Priscilla said, her eyes narrowing. "I know exactly what you're thinking. But this is different!"

Josie did think Priscilla was being rather hypocritical considering where they were sitting. Like most of the women who were his clients, Priscilla salivated over the exotically sensuous face of New York's most famous straight hairdresser, Pierre Parau.

"Nothing happened between us. It was simple flirtation!" Priscilla flicked nervously at her auburn locks.

Parau's sexual prowess was legendary. Many fashionable New York women enjoyed the odd quick fling in the privacy of his office in the salon, emerging with their designer clothes askew and their lipstick smeared, to the silent, ruthless mirth of Pierre's assistants, who made bets with each other as to which of his clients he'd slipped his reportedly staggering appendage. Pierre gave new meaning to the words "cut and blow-dry."

Josie knew of this because her regular stylist, Suzanne, had been Pierre's assistant for years and had endured such brazen advances—in other professions known more simply as sexual harassment—that she would request rooms on separate floors during their frequent business trips together, in the hope he wouldn't be bothered to locate her if she was farther than a hallway crossing away.

"I've never cheated on Rick! I swear it!" Priscilla barked. Josie noticed the girls behind the desk quietly twittering by now. "Anyway, I'm spending as much money as I possibly can on this party, just to piss the asshole off. You're coming, of course, and you're to bring this Hamish friend of yours. He sounds interesting and I want to meet him."

"You're such a fashion groupie," Josie rolled her eyes.

"I am not! I just like creative people. Is that a crime?"

"Priscilla!" Pierre's mellifluous, French-tinged voice flowed toward them. "How beautiful you look, as always." Priscilla fluttered her eyelids and smiled, as she rose and kissed his cheeks. He had a way of making women feel like the most beautiful of all earthly creatures. "And Josephine," he said, with a rapacious smile. "*Ravissant, comme toujours,* Empress," he whispered, as he grazed both her cheeks. *Yeah, right,* she thought, clasping her hand to her scratched neck.

Josie was one of the few women who had rejected Pierre's amorous advances. He had approached her soon after she'd split with her fiancé, Jonathon.

"You look more beautiful than ever," he'd purred, like he'd probably told at least ten other women that day. "What are you doing this evening?"

"Well, actually," she'd replied somewhat smugly, fully aware of his notorious reputation, "I'm leaving for London in a couple of hours."

"Oh, but that's incredible!" he'd exclaimed. "I'm going there tomorrow! We must have dinner!"

"Oh, you know, I'll be busy every night," she'd half lied, as she wrote out a staggeringly large check for her cut and highlights. "Perhaps we could have tea." She had figured she'd be safe at a tea. What harm could come over a cucumber sandwich or two?

In London, when she'd arrived at Blakes, the Kensington hotel favored by many famous travelers, hungrily expectant of a full British tea, she'd been shown not to the restaurant downstairs from the lobby, but into a suite of rooms she realized must be Pierre's. There was, however, no sight of the devastatingly handsome coiffeur. She'd quickly surmised, judging by the sounds of splashing water, that Pierre was lounging in the tub.

"I'll be right out, darling," he had called from some inner sanctum. "Make yourself at home."

Amused by his obviously well-timed ablution, she had sat, bewildered, in the pretty living room, and waited.

And indeed he was right out, in a white fluffy robe, with enough of his tanned, smooth skin slyly displayed, that when he sat down on the couch with such alarming proximity to her, she got a flash of his world-celebrated cock. She had gasped. Then lurched into a nervously twittering account of the day's events.

"You must come with me to Paris tonight, darling," he'd crooned, leaning, if it was at all possible, even closer to her. "I'm having a big party at the Ritz tomorrow evening." Josie, leaning politely away from him, had declined, explaining that she was only in London for a few days and was booked solid.

"Ah, but you must! So come tomorrow! I'll send a

plane for you." Another polite decline. She had wondered if he planned to order any tea. They had chatted banally of the inclement weather, the latest goings-on in London, and the construction and interior design of his new salon. By now she was uncomfortably squashed into the arm of the silk brocade couch, her torso leaning back over its edge.

At his insistence she had finally acquiesced to seeing him back in New York and managed to escape, tealess, from his white fluffy pounce. Obviously his idea of scones, jam, cream, and finger sandwiches was not at all the same as hers. She supposed that many women would have behaved very differently under far less auspiciously sexual circumstances, but at the time her heart was swamped in the murky depths of grief.

She wouldn't behave any differently now, she thought, as she watched Pierre charm his way around Priscilla's red Boticcelli-like curls. Pierre was one of those men who applied, like a baseball player, the law of averages to his favorite sport: the more times at bat equaled more home runs. Quantity over quality.

"So you'll trim me today," Priscilla was smiling at Pierre, "and then before the party, you'll send someone up to me, okay? But they'd better be good, or else you'll spend the evening fixing it!" she warned, laughing.

"Priscilla," he smiled coolly, "everyone who works here is good. Unless of course you'd prefer me to spend the evening 'fixing' you." His dark, almond-shaped eyes glistened at her.

"Oh, you're such a card," she giggled, blushing, but Josie sensed fury beneath the cheery grin and could tell her friend was miserable.

5

Antonia kicked at the sand, a cell phone glued to her left shoulder, cramped up to her ear, her temper rising. She was not a happy camper. Her British accent clipped through the ether with polite black rage. A stiff breeze blew off the East Hampton shore and whipped a luxurious ebony mane across her porcelain skin, stinging her ice-blue eyes.

"I don't care how you manage it"—she snapped, as she hugged her Dior parka close around her body to block out the chill—"that's your job. He wants to shoot in that house. If you lose that location he will be less than thrilled." She slammed the phone shut. "Idiot," she hissed, as she shoved it in her pocket, and strode back down the beach toward the misty figures in the distance.

Antonia ruled with an iron fist in a not-so-soft velvet glove. Agent to several of the world's top photographers, she ran their lives with the efficiency of a drill sergeant, pairing them with the best hairdressers, makeup artists, and stylists. She had the power to make or break careers. Those who displeased Queen Antonia were suddenly unavailable when her stable of photographers requested them having mysteriously disappeared, or were now working with a rival. Off with their heads!

She stopped before reaching the figures, turned into the wind, and watched the dense gray light wane over the Atlantic. Waves pounded the shore, matching her ferocious mood. She hated when things didn't run smoothly. Why the hell couldn't people just do what she told them to?

Keep calm. She breathed deeply, set her ruby mouth in the Mona Lisa smile she was famous for, and approached her star photographer, who was finishing off the last roll of film before the light disappeared completely.

"Beautiful, that's it, darling, just a hint of a smile, not too much, yes, yes more with the eyes, that's it!" Hamish coaxed the ethereal waif shivering at the water's edge in a red Valentino ball gown with a long, soaked hem that trailed nonchalantly into the surf. The shutter whirred away, capturing the hairdresser in frame as he ran and pushed the girl's wild tresses out of her perfect face.

Antonia surveyed her realm. The *Vogue* editor looked pleased, the make-up and hair people had done wonders on the girl, and of course Hamish was creating another genius shot. Perfect. Finally she could relax.

She turned her gaze on one of his assistants, Marcus, who was checking the receding light with a meter and reading off the changes to Hamish every few seconds. Delicious. Tall, with smoky green eyes and a sandy stubble grazing his chin, he had the tightest butt she'd seen in a long while. She shuddered when she thought about that muscular torso hidden under the layers of clothing. Marcus, sensing her stare, looked over at her and smiled. She didn't avert her gaze—quite the opposite. She pouted her red mouth even more and raised one eyebrow with a Come-and-Get-Me insouciance. She knew he would.

Antonia could help Marcus. His photographs were brilliant. Hamish had trained him well and he'd soon be ready to break out on his own. That's when he'd need her. And she'd be only too willing to take him on, push him out there and get him the big bucks, of which she'd happily take her 15 percent commission. Marcus would be her next project, her next star—and her next lover. It didn't bother her that he was more than fifteen years her junior. Why should it? She still looked great. Besides, who would want some old fart with saggy skin when you could have a young stud with energy to burn and a hard cock whenever you wanted it? So, they could use each other. No big deal.

If Marcus didn't make it to the top, which she very much doubted, she'd cast him aside for her next cause. This was big business, and no amount of hot sex could replace the thrill for Antonia of making lots of money. Also, she would never compromise the allegiance of her other photographers. She couldn't afford to have anyone in her stable who brought the rest down. She possessed the ruthless professionalism of a hit man.

And then there was Hamish. She would always be true to Hamish. He was the jewel in her crown. She'd do anything for him. He had started her off in this business, and she owed him for her success. None of her boy-toys would ever come between them. Nothing. She guarded his life with more care than her own.

They had an impenetrable bond, one that defied convention but was more powerful for both of them than any normal business relationship. They had, after all, been married once.

* * *

Hamish had swanned across her path nearly twenty-five years before. He'd been grazing the spread at some toff's literary party, when she was slaving as an assistant to the high-powered editor at a renowned London publishing house. She had spied him wrapping canapés in napkins and shoveling them in the pockets of his trendy black sharkskin jacket, creating bulges in the slim line. As she had advanced to make some snarky comment about his thievery and have him turn red with embarrassment, he'd twisted to her as if he had rearview vision, and, perusing her up and down with gimlet eyes, had said, "That frock of yours looks like a dog's dinner. But with *un peau de maquillage* you could be quite presentable," before resuming his brazen pocket stuffing, a fraction of a smile curling the edges of his pink lips.

Naturally, she had been the one to turn crimson. But had recovered snappily by telling him that if he kept ironing his poorly tailored jacket it would soon be so shiny he'd be mistaken for a wop waiter at a Golder's Green wedding and all he needed was some Brylcreem slicking his thinning hair to match the grease that was now oozing through his pockets. He had chortled with glee.

And that was the start of them.

He was studying philosophy at Cambridge, younger than her by several years (Antonia had conveniently forgotten this in the interim), and, armed with youthful, Bolshy cynicism, a wicked mouth, and a camera, he'd been hired to snap pics of the toff lit figure. A starving student with a penchant for photography and a thirst for success almost equal to her own, Hamish had wooed her with his evil wit. Theirs was a match of sarcastic bon mots aimed for their respective jugulars while ripping each other's clothes off and fucking brutally.

While she plotted her rise in the publishing world by sleeping with her boss and whomever else she thought would escalate her position, Hamish started shooting young models' test shots and gradually made his way into the fashion magazines. Somehow they made the mistake of marrying.

It was not long before she managed to claw and fuck her way to one of the top positions at the venerable publisher's, incurring the wrath of all others in her wake. She was proud of her reputation as a conniving bitch and thought of herself as a trailblazer in a staid industry.

By this time, Hamish was not only booking fashion editorial, but also beginning to lure the big advertising accounts. They were a successful couple with a failing marriage, business being far more important than each other.

Unfortunately, her star in publishing came to an abrupt fizzle when it was discovered she was demanding kickbacks from prospective authors (whose books subsequently flopped), as well as outrageously padding her expenses. She was fired unceremoniously and her career appeared finished, much to the delight of those she'd pissed off on her way up.

It was then that she begged Hamish to fire his agent, who she deemed a total incompetent, and hire her as the taker of his commission instead.

Now, they were both wildly successful. She had offices in London and New York and kept a tight rein on Hamish's life by only taking 5 percent of his earnings. She knew he was too cheap to ever leave her. And in their own fucked-up way they still held each other in high esteem. They were the Royal Team of the international fashion set, and they reveled in their own exaltation.

* * *

As darkness spilled over the sand like ink on a blotter, Antonia pulled her Dior snugly around her slim body, strode over to Hamish, and whispered in his ear, her eyes still hungrily perusing Marcus. She couldn't wait to maul him.

6

Josie sipped her martini and eyed him across the table. Nervous. How would she ever have the guts to ask him?

Hamish was batting on about his latest trip to the Amazon, or somewhere. His downturned mouth moved expressively around his words. It seemed small on his triangular face, as did his gray eyes. A strange face, hardly one to be considered good-looking. Almost ugly. But somehow attractive.

"So what's the name of this river again?" she asked, a halfhearted attempt to participate coherently in the conversation.

"The Casiquiare." He gave her a patronizing smile. "Have you been listening at all?"

"Don't look at me like that. I'm sorry, I'm just all over the place tonight. My brain's on vacation."

"Your brain's been on vacation for decades," he shot at her, downing the last of his cocktail.

"Ha-de-ha. Actually, I was considered a genius in my youth." She wrinkled her nose into a sneer.

"A genius in Australia. Hardly counts, does it? So what happened then? The drugs addle you?"

"You can talk. A Scottish genius. An oxymoron if ever there was."

"I never implied I was a genius. I'm way beyond that meager measure of intelligence. And actually I'm not Scottish."

"Of course you are! You were barely down from the heath when I first met you, laddie," she said, in an appalling Scottish accent. "And, laddie, that was nigh on sixteen years ago. You were lurking 'round Covent Garden with a camera 'round yer neck, trying to snap the likes of gorgeous Aussie models like me. Just a wee thing, ye were, with a sporan hangin' down off yer kilt—"

"That was no sporan, lassie."

She threw her head back in a throaty laugh, not at the joke, but at their mutual affinity for useless banter.

Their eyes met and she knew it was now or never. But how? How was she going to ask him? She took what she hoped was an unobtrusive deep breath.

"Look," she started, "I, ah, I was wondering." She could feel her heart racing. "I—"

"Wondering, darling? You mean you actually still have some kind of curiosity left in that shriveled old brain of yours?"

She took a large gulp of her drink. "Shut up. I was wondering, well, hoping, that perhaps maybe sometime it would be possible, I mean, that you might need a stylist occasionally. I mean, I know you probably have a stylist, or lots of them actually, but mayb—"

"Stop rambling will you! For God's sake, woman, get to the point. Am I to take it that you're asking me for a job?"

She nodded, too embarrassed to open her mouth again. The rambling thing always got the better of her.

A few moments of excruciatingly deadly silence nearly deafened her.

"Why not?" he finally said. "You can help me on this godforsaken campaign next week."

"Really?" she grinned, beside herself with excitement.

"Sure. It's a piece of piss. Even you won't be able to fuck it up."

"Thanks a lot," she said sarcastically, but she really did mean it. She looked at him and his eyes were glinting. He knew she meant it. Maybe he wasn't so hardened after all.

7

Sunshine drenched Manhattan. One of those crisp autumnal days on the upper East Side that brings the natives out in their new winter fineries; an exotic, endangered species parading festively along the avenues in self-opinionated splendor. Checking each other out.

The wrong shoe or tragic combination of an incorrect color match could either induce bitchy, snickering looks or strike fear into the hearts of that remarkably large sector of the New York populace whose existence is governed by fashionable correctness.

Josephine, nearly bankrupt from the outfit she now sported—a chocolate Alexander McQueen sleeveless cashmere and leather dress and jacket of such exquisite cut that she felt unearthly in it, the latest four-inch Christian Louboutin spikes stretching her calves into dizzying sexiness, her feet in searing pain—strode up Madison Avenue. Trying not to trip. Feeling the eyes follow her. An indication that she looked great. A pathetically superficial honor, she knew, but it allayed her increasing dread of losing her looks.

Each morning, in the mirror, she examined the latest development in the slow decimation of her youth. A new line appearing at the edge of her eye, a certain sagging around her mouth. The skin on her chest no longer moist and dewy, but freckled and sun damaged. Cellulite creeping down her thighs like molten lava down a volcano. The inevitable descent into middle age luring her face, her body into shadows of their former luminescence. She hated it.

And she hated that she was so vain. She could have a good laugh about it, but the maintenance was becoming hair-raisingly exorbitant. Botox, PowerPeels, collagen, Restylane; enough creams and potions to sink a bloody ship.

Not to mention the clothes. She had to keep up. It was her profession, after all, to look stylish. She couldn't be seen in some shlubby old outfit going to work. God, how could a girl survive?

The curse of living in a seething, catty metropolis was that, tediously, one grew older and lost one's looks. And if you hadn't made a shitload of money, or married rich, you were done for.

Josie definitely felt done for these days. She was poverty-stricken. Single. Aging at supersonic speed. And the thought of hooking up with some old fart simply for his money was beyond putrid.

She'd love to find a great guy. Not some maladjusted child. A man. No more diamonds in the rough. She wanted one already multifaceted and sparkling.

But what if she never met the man of her dreams? What if she'd missed the boat? Was her soulmate on another continent? Roaming around another city? Maybe she'd passed him in the street and never known it and instead fallen for some infantile excuse for manhood who had ended up torturing her.

What the hell was the matter with her? Couldn't she just grow up? And find a nice, solid guy who wasn't a junkie or an emotional pygmy? Her mother was right. She would look nice in a wedding gown.

But at the rate she was going there was a fat chance of that happening in the foreseeable future. She'd be like Miss Haversham on her cobweb-covered throne in a dingy apartment, waiting for Mr. Right to come breezing into her life.

She'd already been waiting an awful long time, and there was not the faintest glimmer of hope in the Mr. Right department.

Then there was the career. What career? Ever since she'd given up work to trail around the world on a supposedly wonderful journey with Jonathon, a journey that had lasted several years and had her in the many diverse roles of lover, mother, nursemaid, pathetic codependent, and—she cringed at the memory—occasional punching bag, her career had mostly disintegrated, never to be fully revived.

She was sick of drifting, feeling like her life and happiness were continually on hold for something or somebody to come along and ground her. Things had to change.

Drifting was no longer an option. She, not anyone else, was responsible for her own happiness. It was time to pick up the shreds of her life and move forward.

The fact that she'd plucked up enough courage to ask Hamish for work was, for her, a miracle. A leap in the right direction. Hope pulsed through her as she rounded the corner into the building and took the elevator to the elegantly minimal suite of offices in the penthouse.

She announced herself to the receptionist and sat skittishly, waiting for Hamish to show up. He had set up the meeting for her to see the clothing they would shoot for the advertising campaign, and to introduce her to Antonia Kent, whose muffled voice she could hear behind a sleekly polished ebony door.

Josie surveyed the office. Pale wood-paneled walls were complemented by the soft beige of linen, squishy down sofas, and the smooth beauty of limestone floors. A travertine marble coffee table, covered with the latest fashion magazines, sat in front of her. On one long wall was a collection of large black-and-white photographs, six in all, beautifully printed editions of each of Antonia's clients' work.

The only color in the room was an enormous bunch of long-stemmed crimson roses, about three dozen of them, tightly packed into a simple crystal vase sitting on the front desk, matching the crimson patterned silk cushions on the sofas. An iron floor lamp with a shade made of the same Fortuny fabric stood in the corner, diffusing the light into soft patterns filtered through the fabric design.

The receptionist, an androgynous-looking young girl with squirrel-bitten bleached hair, clad in a bright orange shirt, glossy with silver lipstick and fingernails, sat behind the bird's-eye maple desk—which looked like a Jean-Michel Frank design from the forties and was probably worth at least a hundred grand. Josie examined her face for signs of boss abuse; Antonia had a tough reputation. None. Cool as a cuke.

Josie admired the girl's calm. Regardless of the beautiful simplicity of the office, Josie felt like she was sitting in the headmaster's office. She flipped through a copy of *Vogue Italia* that she'd already read weeks before and tried to divert her attention from the butterflies in her stomach. Why was she so nervous? *She's only a woman,* she told herself, *a woman who struggles with life just like you do.*

She's Hamish's ex-wife, you moron. And his agent. She's

got a reputation as a world-class viper, and you're sitting in her pit. Oh. Right.

Just then the door to the office swung open, and out walked the most gorgeous guy Josie had ever laid eyes on. *Whoa, who the hell is that? Swoon material. Probably a male model. Oh, God, could you leap on that or what?*

He stood about six-three, with slightly greasy dark blond hair, a lock of which fell over the sexiest eyes. Sort of smoky looking. Well he sure smoked anyway. He looked over at Josie and smiled, a big, white friendly flash, and she thought she'd faint.

Before she had a chance to gain some composure and do something other than let her gob fall open and pant, Antonia sauntered out, a phone at her ear, dressed in cream Chanel. Talking at the speed of light in French and gesticulating with her free hand in a menacing fashion, she stopped in the middle of the foyer and gave Josie the once-over.

Josie felt like an animal in a zoo. Trapped and on display. Even Miss Trendy Silver Lips was now checking her out. Was she dribbling or something? Suddenly her chic little McQueen number felt like an old rag.

"*Oui, oui, d'accord. Très bien. A tout à l'heure, cherie.*" Antonia put the phone down on Jean-Michel's monument to cool, walked toward Josie, and frowned. "Who are you?"

"I'm Josephine Vaughn." She stood, smoothed a sweaty palm over the suddenly boiling cashmere, grabbed Antonia's perfectly manicured hand, and shook it firmly. Antonia's crimson nails matched her mouth and the roses on the desk.

"Yes. But who *are* you?" Antonia withdrew her mitt and glanced at it with disgust. Like it was covered in slime.

"I'm, ah, Hamish's, ah, friend," she managed to choke

out, "and you must be Antonia." She put on her best smile, trying to appear in control.

"Oh." Antonia sniffed disapprovingly. The hunk stepped toward the two women.

"I assume you've both met," Antonia yawned.

Met? Are you kidding? In my dreams. My wildest, wettest dreams.

"No," they both said in unison.

"No, we haven't," Josie giggled softly, then lowered her eyes. She felt weak at the knees.

"Marcus is Hamish's assistant," Antonia purred at him. Oozing more charm than an Indian snake wrangler with a flute could ever dream of mustering. Her full lips curled in a coy smile. "But not for long, huh, Marcus?" She flashed him what Josie could only describe as the most self-possessed, avaricious look she'd ever witnessed. Like a panther, or some other wild predator.

Marcus took Josie's limp paw and squeezed it in his large tanned hand. She could see the blond hair peeking out from the unbuttoned cuff of his shirt, the strength of his wrist. Even his hands had a godliness about them.

"It's a pleasure," he said in a deep voice with a hint of a Southern accent, and a smile that generated enough wattage to light up the entire Eastern seaboard. "I understand you're going to be working with us. I've heard a lot about you from Hamish."

"You have?" she said, surprised, finally coming up for air. She'd completely forgotten about Hamish.

As if summoned by magical powers of suggestion, the front door of the office opened and in staggered Hamish, sweating profusely, a heavy looking leather knapsack draped over his shoulder.

"God. What a bloody nightmare this city is."

"What on earth happened to you?" demanded Antonia. "You look like something the cat dragged in."

His close-shaven head was shiny with beads of sweat, which dripped down his forehead, into his eyes. He had on a deep charcoal Helmut Lang suit, and a finely pin-striped vest, beneath which was a plain white T-shirt that stuck to his chest like wet tissue paper.

"You don't want to know," he groaned, throwing the knapsack onto the couch.

"Try me," Antonia said.

"Hey, want some water or something?" Marcus asked, looking slightly uncomfortable, Josie thought.

"Yeah, thanks," Hamish sighed. Then he did a sort of double take. "Were you going to meet me here? I must be out of my mind. I don't remember anything any more." He gave an exhausted shrug. Marcus had already sloped off to the kitchen.

Hamish slumped onto the enormous couch and groaned again. "Stupid bloody cab driver. Couldn't find his way out of a paper bag."

"None of them can, darling. That's the Big A for you," Antonia said, standing imperiously over him, her blood-red nails planted firmly on her hips.

"The big Arsehole," Hamish said. "I finally got out somewhere on Third Avenue and had to walk miles."

"You got lost? How can you get lost in Manhattan? God you're hopeless sometimes." Antonia rolled her eyes.

He glared at his ex. "So, what's all this then? The meeting of the minds?"

"Hardly," said Antonia, with an almost imperceptible flash of her baby blue daggers and the Mona Lisa mouth at Josie.

Bitch. Josie smiled sweetly back.

"Hello, Josie, darling," Hamish said to her, raising himself up wearily. "Come with me." He led her down a hallway covered in more photographs, all fashion, all his.

"Don't mind her," he said, when they were out of earshot. "The Ex-Mrs. K can be—"

"A barracuda kind of sprang to mind."

"A piranha would be a more accurate description," he sighed. "Sorry. Have you been here long?"

"No, no . . . not long." *Long enough to know I'm in deep shit.* "Don't worry. I'm a big girl. I can take care of myself." *Not with that forked-tongued fashion slave. And as for Adonis. Forget it. Really deep shit. I might as well get the hell out of Dodge right now.* "But gosh!" she exclaimed, her eyes suddenly wide, her hands going up to her cheeks in a Macaulay Culkin–Edvard Munch–type scream. "I just remembered I left the iron on. Gotta dash. See ya!"

"Fuck off," he laughed, grabbing her by the waist, pinning her to the wall. She could smell his sweat. A familiar, acrid, salty smell that had her fighting to stay in the present. He kissed her, roughly, on the lips and then released her. She felt even more flustered. "We've got work to do." He led her into a room full of garment racks stuffed with clothing, and they went through each outfit together. "Heinous shit, darling, but we'll manage," he said. Just then Miss Silver Lips came in.

"Antonia wants to see you," she smiled at Hamish. He ducked out and left her with the clothes.

"You're leaving for Rome tonight?" Josie said, seated in Antonia's office a half hour later. "I thought we were supposed to start shooting next week."

"We've pushed it back a day or two," said Hamish. "*British Vogue* wants me to shoot Sophia for them, and this is the only time she's available."

"You don't say no to Sophia Loren," said Antonia. "Anyway"—she turned to Josie—"you've got loads to keep yourself busy. You're the one who should be worried about time. Can you pull it off?" she waved her hand at Josie patronizingly. Hamish pursed his lips, but she continued. "What showrooms have you called? I spoke to Ed over at KCD and he said he hasn't heard from you yet. You do know Ed, don't you?"

"Ah, yes," Josie lied. "But I was waiting 'til after I saw the clothes to call." *Why don't you style this yourself, bitch,* she seethed inside, knowing that Antonia was testing her deliberately, just to see how well connected she was.

"Ant, leave it off will you?" said Hamish, with a bored look on his face. "Josie knows what she's doing." Josie hoped he was right.

Marcus, silent since the onset of the meeting, looked at her now, a kindness emanating from that incredible face, and once again Josie thought she'd melt.

She pulled herself together. "I've put some accessories on hold. Shoes from Christian Louboutin and Jimmy Choo, and I've got shoes and bags from Gucci and Prada lined up too. Jewelry. I'll be fine." She looked at Antonia with a sweet "fuck you" smile. "Actually, I should have it pretty much finished by the end of tomorrow." *So back off, bitch.*

"Josie," Marcus said, "I'm wondering . . ."

Yes, yes, I'm wondering too—what it would be like to have you licking Reddi-wip off my inner thighs.

". . . as there's now a bit more time, if perhaps you'd be interested in styling some test shots with me on Monday or Tuesday? There's this great new girl at the Z. agency—"

"What a genius idea!" interrupted Antonia. "There'll be tons of stuff here to use—won't there, Josie? I'm sure you could use some photos for your portfolio. Oh, that's right, you don't even have one, do you? Marcus, darling, you're a genius!" She fluttered at him, ignoring Hamish. "I'll get Ricky on for make-up and Max for hair—they both owe me big favors. So does Studio 28 . . ." She was off, conniving and dialing.

Hamish was furious. Josie could tell because his eyes, narrowed into tiny slits, and his mouth, set in a thin, straight line, harbored more animosity than she'd ever seen in him before. She wondered if it was jealousy of Marcus. Or years of having to put up with his gorgon of an ex-wife's maneuvering.

Marcus looked sheepish, like he'd just realized he'd maybe blown it with Hamish. "I'm sorry," he said quietly to them both. "Is this okay with you?" Then to Josie, "I didn't mean to put you on the spot."

"It's fine," she said. "Antonia's right. There will be tons of accessories here, so you might as well use them. I'll get some great clothes to go with them, because the advertising stuff we'll be shooting is Yawnsville, isn't it Hamish?"

"It pays the rent, doesn't it?" he snapped.

"I didn't mean it like that," she sighed. "You were the one who said the clothes were awful!" She was suddenly exhausted. She sat down close to him and whispered, "Let's get out of here!"

They slugged back martinis in virtual silence at the King Cole bar in the St. Regis hotel.

"So you've finally met the Ex-Mrs. K," Hamish said.

"Boy. She is something. Is she like that all the time?"

"Oh, no. Not all the time." A wry smile turned up his teeny mouth at the edges. "Sometimes she's worse."

"Fabulous. What a piece of work."

"You'd better watch yourself, my girl."

"Oh, for God's sake. Why? I've only just met the woman. What's to watch? Besides, I'm working for *you*, not her."

His beady eyes glared coldly at her. "What?" she said. "What have I done? Oh, come on. I didn't mean to insult you in there." She felt irritated, and more than a bit confused. She couldn't figure him out. One minute he was trying to kiss her, then the next he was like this.

"Are you angry because I said I'd do the test shots with Marcus?"

"Don't be absurd," he sniffed.

"I won't do them if it's going to upset you." She leaned closer and pecked him softly on the cheek. He stiffened.

"Do them. It'll be good for you both. I have to go." He pulled out a wad of cash and threw some onto the bar. "See you in a week, darling." He air kissed her and strode off, leaving her completely nonplussed.

8

"Oh, God. He's early!" Josie slammed the phone down, trying to ignore the sense of impending doom. The doorman was sending him up. Mr. Wyatt. Mr. Blind Date. Mr. Hot Investment Banker.

"*Rich*!" Priscilla had chanted, when she'd told Josie about him on their shopping excursion last week. Like it was the only thing worth considering in a prospective mate. "Rich!" like it was a mantra.

Josie hated to admit it, but the money did tempt her. Not much. Enough to agree to yet another probable exercise in futility. If you're going to subject yourself to the torture of a blind date, you might as well get taken to a good restaurant. Anyway, he'd sounded really nice on the phone. Some kind of Southern accent. Very polite and quite funny. He'd practically begged her to go out with him on such short notice.

She ran around the apartment in a cleaning frenzy. *What a slob.* How much junk can you tidy up in ten floors' worth of time? Why on earth didn't she tell the doorman she'd be right down? *What an idiot. He'll take one look at this mess and walk back out the door. You're about to ruin yet another date. He's probably handsome too. And nice. And you've blown it. Fool.*

It was Saturday, and he'd only called her yesterday. A big no-no to admit she was available. But what did it matter? It was a blind date, for God's sake. Besides, she wasn't exactly overrun with suitors lately. Her dance card was full of glaringly blank spaces. So she'd pretended to grant him a total favor, only because he swore he was leaving town for a week on business, and would she please, please go out with him. *Yeah, right.* Now or never. *Heard that one before. Heard it all before.*

The doorbell rang. Great. She smoothed her deep rose velvet bustier dress and checked herself in the mirror. *Creased already. Damn. Well maybe he won't notice. It is one of Ralph's prettiest designs ever. Low cut without being vulgar. At least I never look vulgar. Or do I? Oh, shit. He's going to think I'm a bimbo slob with the messiest apartment in the city.*

Well, here goes. Bimbo Slob greets Mr. Right. Rich, handsome, funny Prince Charming, who takes one look at the hooves hanging over these Manolo mules and realizes he got one of the ugly sisters, not beautiful Cinderella. No way is the glass slipper going to fit this Big-Footed Bimbo Slob, he'll think, and walk back out the door.

She took a deep breath and headed for the foyer. The bell rang again. Closing her eyes for a second, a Zen moment, she reached for the door, opened it, took a look at her suitor, and nearly fell to her knees.

I'm going to kill you, she thought, as Neanderthal Man held out his hand. *Priscilla, I'm going to fucking kill you.*

Shut up!

He's probably a great guy. Just because he's wearing a mushroom-colored jacket of some highly suspicious-looking fabric and a gold chain around his neck, just because he has a strand or two of brown frizz blow-dried over his bald patch, just because he's gawking at you through those big gold-rimmed glasses tinted a pale shade of pink—a strong case against the seventies revival happening these days—doesn't mean he's a bad guy.

"Hi, Ah'm Andy," said monobrow, "Andy Wyatt. Wow. You're a great-lookin' gal." She laughed awkwardly. Astonished.

"Thanks." She smiled politely, trying to extract her hand from his viselike grip. "Come in." She remembered years ago her grandmother saying, "Well, dear, if it sounds too good to be true, it usually is." Boy was she right. "Would you like a drink?"

God you're vile. Always so critical. How dare you judge a person by his looks! But, then again, how can you not? It's all you've got to go on.

Oh, God, how am I going to get through the evening?

Stop it! Now!

Vegas goes Manhattan. That's it. A vision in Vegas mushroom.

Shut up! Be nice!

At least he's not wearing white shoes. He's not a total time warp.

He smiled, a big, overwhite toothy grin. "Thanks, daarlin', but I've got the car waitin' downstairs. If you're ready why don't we head on out for some fun!"

This is an investment banker? I-don't-think-so.

She noticed he was wearing a gold bracelet. And a humongous gold Piaget watch. About twenty grand's worth. And a big gold pinky ring with an enormous diamond in it. Hell, the guy was sporting more jewelry than a model on the Home Shopping Network. She grabbed her evening bag and shawl, a cut silk velvet, hand-beaded number that had been a gift from Jonathon, and followed him with dread out to the elevator. She felt like she was on her way to the executioner's. Dead woman walking.

What kind of investment wanker are you? She smiled wearily at him as Giovanni, the doorman, plummeted them into an evening of certain horror. *You're definitely not from around these parts.* No self-respecting New York investment firm would have this paradigm of the sartorially challenged hanging round its office.

Maybe this was just his weekend look. Maybe he wore Saville Row pinstripes and Hermes ties during the week. *Yeah, right.* He looked like he slept in those jewels.

"Beautiful weather we're having, Miss Vaughn." Giovanni smiled politely as his white-gloved hand maneuvered the gleaming brass elevator controls. She could tell what he was thinking, by the subtly obvious glance he'd thrown at her date. A withering "you're not good enough for her" type of look. The doormen were very protective of their tenants, or at least of Josie.

"Yes . . . beautiful," she said, her olfactory senses twitching. She wondered how many times a shift, how many times a week, how many millions of times a year for an entire career a doorman talked about the weather.

"Just gorgeous, ain't it," Andy Wyatt boomed, but neither she nor Giovanni responded. A suffocating blend of musk and something else had gripped their throats. Surely it wasn't Giovanni. She could tell he was appalled. It certainly wasn't her.

She only wore one of two scents: in summer, the light green tea aroma of Bulgari; in winter, Bois des Isles from Chanel. Wood of the Islands. She loved the sound of it. Tonight, though, she'd forgotten to wear either. But this stomach-churning brew her date was marinating in had her gasping.

Was there no way out of this misery?

She might have guessed, if she'd been working on more than a single scent-soaked brain cell, that he would, of course, have a white limo. *Oh God.* Parked out in front of her building. The pinnacle of embarrassment. The zenith of bad taste.

White limos in Manhattan are never from Manhattan. Bridge and Tunnel to the max. All she could hope was that they'd go somewhere anonymous. So much for a good restaurant. A Burger King would suit her just fine.

It cannot get any worse than this.

Somehow, though, she knew it would.

Please, God. Save me from my judgmental criticisms.

Deliver me from my evil thoughts.

Save me from this evening.

Please. I'll never do anything bad ever again. I promise. Please, God. Pleeese!

"Where are you from, Andy?" She sidled into the limo, trying not to inhale the noxious fumes permeating the maroon velour interior. She felt like she'd just stepped inside a floating bordello.

"Atlanta, ma'am," he said with a wink, as he smoothed his polyester jacket down. "Georgia, that is." Another wink shot through the pink glasses.

"What are you doing in this neck of the woods? I thought you Southerners didn't like it up north with us Yankees."

"Well, Ah don't really, but you know a fella has to make a livin'. Now, sugar, you don't sound like no Yankee neither. You're a Brit, aintchya?"

"Australian."

"An Awssi. Ya don't say." He grinned at her. The limo rolled off. Josie was speechless. How could Priscilla do this to her?

"Ah hope you like a good nosh up. Ah had the concierge of the hotel make a reservation at Coco Pazzo."

"Hotel? I thought you had an apartment here," she said, puzzled and full of dread at the mention of the restaurant. Talk about Front Row Center. She was sure to be busted now. Still, it was Saturday night. Most locals stayed away from popular places on Saturday nights because of the white limo crowd, of which she was now an official member. How depressing.

"Well, Ah do, kind of. It's in the Carlyle. That way Ah get the best of both worlds," he said. Josie opened the window so she could get some breathable air, and hung her head out as far as politely possible. She felt like a dog.

They chatted for a few minutes. She found out that he hardly spent any time in the city, or his "cottage" in Southampton; that he traveled most of the time; that he was an old friend of the president's; and that he wasn't an investment banker at all, more a T. Boone Pickens corporate raider type. He'd just pulled off a major buyout of Vive, the huge cosmetics firm. The news had flown around Wall Street and provided dinner conversation at the city's most illustrious tables. The deal had been brokered by Priscilla's husband, Richard's, firm, Whiterock. She also discovered that in fact he'd never even met Priscilla. *Note to self: Kill Priscilla.*

The limo slithered through the traffic and pulled up outside the restaurant. Several other cars and limos—all elegantly black—sat out front. She examined the entry for signs of anyone familiar. Not a soul. So far, so good. The driver opened the door, and Josie stepped hesitantly out, followed by her Southern escort. That's what she felt like, she suddenly realized: an escort. A girl plucked from the descriptive back pages of some weekly Tourist Guide. Beautiful Masseuse. Mistress of Pain. At your Service.

Oh, God.

She threw the shawl around her shoulders and Andy

put his hand lightly at the small of her back and guided her toward the entry. Josie had to admit he'd been a total gentleman so far. Solicitous and polite. She looked at him and smiled, thinking that maybe this wouldn't be such an ordeal after all, if she could only hold her vicious judgments about his appearance and his abundant use of colloquialisms such as "darlin'" and "sugar" at bay.

Josie glanced at a couple emerging from one of the cars and nearly swooned in total panic.

It was Jonathon, with his new young bride, looking about as smart and fabulous as a young Manhattan couple ever could, on a collision course with her and Dreamdate.

The twist in her stomach froze her solid. Paralyzed. She could feel the color draining from her cheeks as the pain welled up in her gut.

Jonathon. Scion of a heavy hitter industrialist, a Superpower of the City, newly married to the daughter of a socialite fashion designer. Josie had seen them, beautiful, smiling, and happy, in a slew of wedding pictures, lavishly spread across the pages of *W.*

Jonathon. The love of her life. The death of her self-love. So many images she'd hoped she'd successfully buried flashed across the screen of her mind in the nanosecond she stood there that she thought she'd burst. Overload. Images of ecstasy, horror and laughter, pain and frail hope, longing and failure, of the purity of love they had shared and finally abandoned for their own misguided, selfish ends. The ultimate betrayal of each other preventing their paths from ever crossing without malice and acrimony as escorts.

He stopped in front of her, long lashes framing milky aqua eyes, the sole freckle on the side of his pretty nose, the perfect olive skin encircled by the soft, wispy hair of a child.

A child whose parents' immense wealth had showered him with every material convenience but left him, like so many other heirs to great fortunes, with an excruciating poverty of inner strength. Their frequent absences in the name of procuring and plundering that wealth left a legacy of abandonment and loneliness so great that it could only be mollified by the consumption of death-defying amounts of alcohol and drugs.

Jonathon. Who'd detoxed so many times he could write the Zagat guide of Worldwide Rehabs. The human pincushion, he'd joked, about his very recent past when she'd first met him, six years earlier.

She'd heard through the grapevine that he was sober these days. A changed man. Unfortunately the change happened on a jagged graph while they were together and she never got to see the final reformation. She'd been a stepping-stone in his growth toward a semblance of normality.

"Josephine," he said, his eyes traveling the entire length of her body, then crossing to Andy, and then to the limo lurking like a white elephant behind them. Not missing a thing.

"Jonathon," she whispered, too stunned to move. Miraculously, in a town as small as New York, they had not encountered one another since The End. Two years of dread now culminating in a few seconds of horror. They'd have to meet now, of all nights.

"Nice shawl." He flicked the glowing butt of his Marlboro into the gutter, took his wife's hand, and strode into the restaurant.

Josie was barely able to step inside before the room started swirling. She couldn't remember much more of the evening except that she found herself in the ladies room, retching and sobbing into the stark white porcelain.

There was a furious banging on the door. "Are you ahlright, ma'am?" Andy boomed.

"Yes," she heaved, with the raspy voice of a bulimic. "I'll be out in a minute."

"Darlin', y'all been in there a dog's age. Can't I get you something?"

A gun. Let me end it all now. Just put me out of my misery. "No thanks. I'll be right out." She splashed her face with water and tried to cover up the bulbous red eyes and the running nose with make-up. It was no use. She looked a complete mess. She could now hear Andy talking to someone outside.

Doesn't matter. Pull yourself together, for God's sake. She took a few deep breaths and tottered out to the bathroom vestibule.

Jonathon stood there, menacingly close to Andy, another Marlboro clutched between his fingers, a picture of effortless elegance, despite a faint sway that bent his slight frame.

He wore a tuxedo jacket, undoubtedly Armani, over a charcoal gray cashmere polo shirt that was buttoned to the top; jeans; and black woven silk loafers with white socks. He only ever wore white socks. A sliver of a Dolce & Gabbana silk leopard print shirt and collar flopped casually out between the jacket and the polo. An odd Rock and Roll meets Park Avenue combination that somehow looked great on him.

"You mind your own goddamned business!" he snarled, his eyes narrowed in the hostile demeanor that possessed him when he'd had a few too many Absoluts. His vodka demeanor. "And who the hell are you anyway—her pimp? Nice getup," he sneered and flicked the double-stitched edge of Andy's mushroom lapel. The ash from his cigarette tumbled down its front. Josie wondered if it would melt. "Where's your furry hat, Superfly? Hee

hee heee," came the squeaky infectious giggle Josie used to alternatively roar with or cower at, depending on his state of inebriation. This was a middling-to-cower giggle, which meant he was near the edge of straight-out violence. So much for a changed man.

Neither of them had noticed her watching them. "Listen, boy, ain't it past your bedtime?" retorted Andy, like he had nothing to prove to this drunken fool. "Now be a good kid and get on back to that cute little woman of yours."

"Past *my* bedtime! What about you, Grandpa?" Jonathon chortled. "Time to soak those fake choppers, Grandpa, and dose up on that prostate medicine—"

"What's going on here?" Both men's heads swiveled at the sound of Josie's voice.

"Ah, here she is"—Jonathon purred sweetly, lurching toward her—"beautiful Miss Australia, Miss Innocent—"

"Jonathon, please—" she said, fear burning through her like it had a thousand times before with him.

"Well ain't this a cute casual Caucasian couple," he said, mocking Andy's accent. "Look at you—pretty in pink. Hee hee hee! A pretty pink pair. Hee hee. You were always good with color, now weren't you, Pookie?"

Josie let out a nervous laugh. Andy and she were remarkably well coordinated in tones of mushroom and rose. Andy's face had wrinkled into a scowl, his brow furrowed into a reddish caterpillar shape between his eyes.

"Jonathon. Please. Just go back to your table," she said, feeling the clench in her jaw, her knuckles, knowing it was totally useless. Reasoning with Jonathon drunk was like asking a two-year-old to give back a new toy. She knew better than to argue, but it had always proven more difficult to practice outside the dislocated comfort of an Al-anon meeting.

There was still a part of her that wanted to engage

with him. Unfinished business. The glimmer of hope that someday they'd be friends again, like they were in the first place. The sense of always wanting to make things right. Maybe then the pain and gaping hole of loss would go away.

Jonathon took a drag of his cigarette and eyed her up and down with the added viciousness that alcohol produced in him. "I just wanted to see the face of a murderer," he glared at her. "A murdering gold digger."

He took another drag and swayed toward Andy. "You'd better watch out, Grandad. She'll go for your jugular any chance she has. And your wallet. But then you'd make a good pair. A pimp and a murdering whore."

"That's enough, you drunken scum," snarled Andy.

"C'mon, darlin'." He grabbed her shaking hand and pulled her away from Jonathon.

"Darlin' is it?" Jonathon sneered, as she stumbled out of the vestibule, but she could hear the falter in his voice. She glanced back at him through a myopic wet blur, as they reached the end of the hallway. His head and body were stooped, and she could see tears on his cheeks.

"I'm so sorry," she said to Andy, as the limo slid away from the restaurant. "I'm really sorry." She felt mangled with shame and sadness. "I don't know what to say."

"Why darlin', you don't have to say a thing. God-damned punk. How dare he speak to a lady like that. Why, Ah oughta have his daddy read him the riot act!" he said, with disgust. Josie winced.

"You know him?"

"Ah've known Robby Cantero for years. Did some business with 'im a while back. Nice guy. Real gentle-man, but one tough mother to deal with." He poured two glasses of bourbon from the bar.

"Don't I know it." Josie sighed, taking the offered glass and gulping a mouthful. She hated bourbon, but she'd drink anything at this point. "So how come you knew that was his son?"

"Stupid punk doesn't know Ah helped him out a few years ago. Did his daddy a real big favor. Sprung his little boy from jail in some tiny town at the edge of Georgia. A word to our governor and that drug-addled kid was free to go, no questions asked. Ah'da punched 'im out back there if Ah didn't like his daddy!" He paused and took a slug of bourbon. "Aside from that, Ah've seen 'im in the social pages!" he laughed.

Josie, surprised at Andy's sphere of influence, and the fact that he actually read the social pages, knew he was probably wondering what the hell she'd been doing with Jonathon, and what Jonathon had meant by calling her a murderer. She wasn't about to tell him. He could find everything out in one phone call to Jonathon's father, if he was so inclined. What he'd get would be Robert Cantero's jaundiced opinion. Jonathon could do no wrong. It had all been her fault.

She looked over at Andy and gave him an exhausted smile. "It's a very small world, isn't it," she said, not really caring what he'd find out about her. She was just so tired of it all.

"Too small, darlin'," he replied, looking at her with the kindness of a father. Then he gave her a soft pat on the back of her head, and she knew somehow she'd made a friend.

The next day, Josie was too comatose and depressed to get out of bed. She didn't even have the energy to be angry with Priscilla when she called to get the lowdown on the worst evening in recent memory. Besides, the beautiful, fragrant arrangement of all-white flowers that arrived that morning had silenced any criticisms she might have left of Andy Wyatt. The man had a certain style—even if it wasn't at all apparent in his appearance.

"Don't let 'em get you down" the card said. She knew she couldn't feel much lower, so things had to be looking up soon.

9

Still feeling like she'd been run over by a Mack truck, Josie dragged herself out of bed on Monday morning and headed downtown to do the test shots with Marcus. When she got out of the cab in front of Studio 28, she stood on the sidewalk for a moment and took in her surroundings.

It was a grimy area on the lower West Side, right near the docks. From the outside, the building looked like a deserted warehouse, but she knew the dilapidated façade housed one of the biggest photography studios frequented by the fashion cognoscenti. She hadn't been here before and felt like an imposter trying to infiltrate the ranks of an industry she no longer belonged to. It had been years since she'd been one of the transient bunch who skimmed the globe at a pace so fast they barely had time to air kiss each other before flying off to a shoot in some exotic location, or the latest party in a far-flung center of style. It was completely different from the world of TV commercials. More stylish. And a lot more venal.

She found her way to a large dressing room, where her assistant, Mala, was busy organizing the shoes and accessories along a bench that stretched along one wall. On the other wall hung all the clothes she'd chosen from designers' showrooms. Wispy sheer dresses in fruit sorbet colors from next spring's collections.

A familiar laugh gurgled down the hallway and Josie peeked out to see Max, the hairstylist, mincing toward her with a young guy in tow, who carted a heavy looking Gucci suitcase.

"It's the Empress!" he screached. "Empress Josephine!" He ran and picked her up and twirled her around. "Antonia didn't tell me you'd be here! Jojo! How divine!"

"Maxi!"

He grunted as he plonked her back down. "Yes, I'm a tad heavier than the old days," she said, planting a kiss on his shaven head.

"Aw, darls," he said in his thick Aussi accent, "ya still look fuckin' amazing."

"And you look exactly the same," she laughed. Although he didn't. He'd aged and had put on quite a bit of weight, which she was glad of because she hated seeing extremely thin gay men. It usually only meant one thing. He was decked out head to toe in Prada. A fitted blue suit, blue silk shirt open to the waist, and retrolooking loafers. Sort of a modern-day lounge lizard look that reminded her of Andy Wyatt. Maybe Andy was ultrahip and she just hadn't realized it.

"Jeez," he said to his assistant, "look at those legs, will ya?" He pointed at her calves. "I don't know why you gave up modeling, darls."

"Hello!" Josie yelled. "I'm thirty-six! What would I be doing now? Depends commercials?"

"Aw fuck off!" Max gripped her cheeks between his

huge tattooed hands. "With a dial like this? Darls, this face could still launch a thousand ships." He pouted a kiss at her.

"Yeah, couldn't it?" came a velvety smooth voice from behind her. Josie felt herself blush.

"Marcus, you gorgeous hunk," growled Max, with a look of salivating hero worship and a lascivious glint in his eyes. "How are ya love?"

"Never better, Max." Marcus smiled that swoon-making grin and hugged Max, who looked like he'd be the one to faint this time. "Thanks for coming, I really appreciate it."

"For you, darls, anything. Anything your hunky heart desires," Max said dreamily. Obviously she wasn't the only one in complete awe. "Now don't ya think I'm right about The Empress? Just look at the old tart. She's still divine. Better than ever if you ask me." He gripped her cheeks again.

"Well, nobody asked you!" Josie snapped, pushing his big mitts away.

"Oh, yeah," Marcus said, his eyes smoking her, "you're much more beautiful than any of the pictures I used to see of you."

"Not bad for an antique is she?" Max grinned at Marcus.

"She's a classic." Marcus looked at her and she could feel she'd gone beet red.

"But still an old tart," Max said.

"Shut up," she said, relieved to see the make-up artist, Ricky, sauntering down the hallway toward them, swathed in beige cashmere and leather, his wrists covered in gold Hermes bracelets. He pulled a Louis Vuitton logo wheeled bag behind him.

"I'm here, dahlinks," he panted in a gravelly South American accent. "Did jou miss me?"

"Oh, look, the other old tart's here," Max said, then

stared at Ricky in disbelief. "Aw fuck! What've ya done now? Ya haven't had another winching have ya?" He rolled his eyes at Josie and Marcus. "Crikey! He disappears for a couple of weeks and now look at 'im. His dick's practically up where his mouth used to be. Ya dickhead."

"It's so cheap in Brazil, dahlinks," Ricky said, as he air kissed them all then pushed his face out so they could get a look. It was remarkably tanned and smooth as a drum. Definitely stretched to the limit.

"That face has seen more knives than a chef at Benihana. I reckon you and that cat woman—what's her name? The one who's had so much surgery she looks like a lion."

"Jocelyn Wildenstein," everyone said in chorus.

"Yeah, her—you and her oughta hook up. Couple of tired old pussies."

"Jou could use a leetle work yourself, dahlink," Ricky sneered and stuck his finger into Max's paunch.

"I'd love some suction honey," Max grinned. "Wanna start?" He thrust his pelvis at Ricky and wiggled it.

"That old thing?" Ricky wrinkled his nose in disgust. "Dahlink, it would be like sucking a thousand-year-old mummified monkey's cock."

"Donkey, darls. I'm bigger than a donkey."

"Some things never change." Josie rolled her eyes at Marcus. "Come see the clothes." They walked off, leaving the two old buddies insulting each other.

An hour or so later the model still hadn't arrived, but they hadn't really noticed because they'd been gossiping and laughing over cappuccinos and setting up their equipment. Marcus was in the studio getting the lighting right and Josie sat with the boys in the dressing room.

"So," she said to Max, trying to appear casual, "how well do you know Marcus?" She was dying to find out about him.

"Not as well as I'd like to, darls," he sighed. "I mean how fucking gorgeous is he? Have you *ever* seen a butt so tight? And those eyes. Ouch."

Ricky made a sizzling sound through his teeth. "Sscheee! Zat boy is hot!"

"Yeah," grumbled Max, "fat lotta good it is. I already asked him if he wanted a blowy. Wasn't interested. He's hitting for your team, love," he said jealously to Josie.

"You asked him if he wanted a blow job?" she said, incredulous.

"Course I did! Do ya think I'd pass up even the slimmest chance he'd say yes?"

"Well, I guess not, you slut!" She poked him in the ribs.

"I'm not a slut! I'm just very friendly."

"Speaking of sluts, dahlinks," whispered Ricky, winking at them and looking over their shoulders.

"Antonia!" Max cooed when he saw her. "How are ya, gorgeous!" He was up and hugging again.

Antonia's raven hair fell down over the large collar of a floor-length, black and white patchwork coat of some dubious furry origin. Her pale porcelain face barely peeked out over the top. As she took off her Jackie O.–style sunglasses, she revealed startling blue eyes encircled in charcoal eyeshadow. Her ruby lips and nails were the only color in the black and white spectacle. Showing from under the coat were extremely high-heeled black patent boots, which reached over her knees to meet a tight miniskirt. A black satin shirt fell casually open to reveal a hint of black lace beneath.

"Perfect, darling," Antonia replied, as she swept by Josie without even the vaguest flicker of recognition and gave a peremptory toss through the clothes. "Harumph," she sniffed. "Where did this stuff come from? Looks like the dregs of the collections."

She gingerly picked up a pink shoe with a red leather sole and examined it at arm's length. "And what is this?" she asked with disdain.

Josie thought she bore a remarkable resemblance right then to Joan Collins doing Cruella De Ville.

"Hello, Antonia. How nice to see you again. How are you?"

A pause while she waited for Cruella to respond. Not a syllable emerged from the bloodied lips. Not even a glance in her direction.

"That, Antonia, is a Christian Louboutin silk shoe," Josie finally announced with as much politeness as her humiliation and fury would allow. Cruella threw the shoe down as if it were a rabid animal about to bite her. Josie wished it would spring to life and attack.

"And the clothes, Antonia, in case you haven't noticed"—she pulled out a dress or two and brandished them in Antonia's face—"are from the best designers in the world. I was lucky to get them for a new photographer."

"Of course you were, darling," said Cruella, her right eyebrow raised. "You were lucky to get any clothes at all." She turned her back to Josie. "Well they'll do, I suppose," she said, with a dismissive gesture at the sherbet-colored racks. "But didn't you know Marcus wants to shoot in black and white? They're entirely too pale."

"Nobody told me," Josie said, gritting her teeth. "Anyway, what does it matter? Black and white comes down to good lighting, and I'm sure Marcus knows what he's doing. And besides, he absolutely loves all the clothes, doesn't he, Max?" Max stood in mute neutrality. *Traitor!* Josie glared at him.

Antonia turned and smiled at Josie. The sort of venomous smile a snake would have for a mouse. A "lick my boots" kind of smile. Which made Josie even more annoyed.

"And by the way, Antonia," she smiled back, "just exactly how many puppies did you kill for that coat you're wearing?"

Cruella's nostrils flared and the ruby lips pursed ever so slightly. With a flick of her mane she turned and stalked off, calling for Marcus, patent heels clicking furiously down the corridor, piebald fur flying behind her.

Cruella, to Josie's relief, had finally departed. The model never showed. Max offered to give Josie a trim and she relaxed in the chair as he deftly snipped her long blond hair. Marcus, aggravated, paced in and out of the room, and Ricky lay on a couch arguing passionately in Spanish into his cell phone.

"Every fucking day," Max rolled his eyes at Ricky as Josie watched his reflection in the mirror, "he and that boy toy of his fight so much you'd think they were splitsville, but they've been together for six years. And what about you, Jojo love? You got something hot on the burner?"

"Not a sausage," she said.

"Dryer than a nun's nasty, is it, darls?"

"Dryer than the Sahara."

"Reckon you should give Hunk-Face one. Why would ya wanna miss out on that? Bet he's got one bigger than a baby's leg. What I wouldn't give to get my mouth around it."

"God, you're disgusting!"

"Look! You're a new tart!"

She admired her new coif in the mirror. "Thank you, honey. It's fab!" She gave him a big hug.

"Crikey, what time is it?" Max stretched. "I'm so famished I could eat the crotch out of a low-flying duck. Let's get some grub in here."

So they ordered up lunch. Max took a stroll and returned with a case full of bottles.

"Let's get rat arsed," he said, popping open a bottle of Cristal Champagne and filling glasses.

"Might as well," Marcus said gloomily. "There's fuck all else to do. I'm sorry, guys. What a waste of everyone's time."

"Yummy. Cristal. My fave," Josie said, then looked at Marcus. She felt sorry for him. "It's fine, Marcus. We're happy just to be seeing each other again, aren't we, Max?" She picked up a glass and drank.

"Course, darls," Max said, already tossing back his second glass.

"Notting is ever a waste, dahlinks. I'm going to vork." Ricky took a glass of champagne, grabbed Josie's hand, and led her back to the dressing room. "You need a face to match that favuleus new cut, dahlink."

He pushed her down on the make-up chair, and before she knew it she was slathered in foundation. Her face was now a blank canvas and Ricky started to paint. It reminded her of the old days, when she had her face painted every single morning. When she'd been one of the celebrated and spoiled. It had been so much fun, she thought now, but it never really was at the time. It had all just seemed so normal, mundane in fact. Only in hindsight did she appreciate the extraordinary life she'd led. When it was too late, natch.

An hour later she'd been transformed into a different person. Soft cocoa smudged around her eyes made them appear verdant green instead of the normal hazel, her cheeks glowed with an amber crème blush, and her mouth was a voluptuous peach. She batted the false eyelashes at him and grinned.

"Voila!" said Ricky. "Jou look eencredible, dahlink! Max! Come!"

"Fucking gorgeous, darls," Max barked, as he staggered in with another bottle of Cristal and filled her glass. "Here's to old tarts!"

Marcus walked in and bent down beside her, examining her face in the reflection of the mirror. "Look at me," he said, taking her chin gently and turning her face to his. She felt a jolt of energy pass between them. Their faces were about three inches from each other. The urge to lean forward and kiss him was almost impossible to resist. "Beautiful," he said. "Now get dressed."

"Yes, darls, get dressed. Here! Throw this one on," Max said, tossing her a papaya-colored sliver of chiffon.

"I am dressed. And I am not putting that on."

"Aw, go on."

"Jes, dahlink, put it on."

"Aw, for fuck's sake, darls, we're bored shitless. At least let's have a laugh. It'll be like old times."

"I can't fit into this! Look at it! There's about a half yard of fabric in it. It's built for waifs, not big old broads! Besides, the old days are gone. Long gone."

"Aw, chill, will ya?" Max pouted. "So what the fuck else are you going to do? Go home and put on your old flannel nightie? Climb into bed and watch soaps?"

"Looking like that?" Marcus said. "What a waste."

"Oh, alright! But you'd better give me some more of that first." She pointed to the Cristal. She knew she'd have to be half tanked to relax enough.

"Yes, your highness." Max curtsied as he poured another glass for her and one for himself. He was already well on the way. "Now drink it, bitch, and get dressed!"

She gulped back the bubbly; stood up; and, without pausing, took her clothes off and tugged the slip of fabric over her head. Mala helped her pull it down over her body. She didn't much care if they watched. Any woman who has been a model has no qualms about undressing in the company of others. It's simply part of the job description. There's no time to be embarrassed about one's body. The body is an apparatus that moves in a way that sells clothes. That's all. It's what the model does or the way she moves after she's in the clothes that matters. Besides, everyone here saw naked bodies all the time.

She strapped on a pair of bejeweled Giuseppe Zanotti sandals, pushed a couple of gold bangles onto her wrists, and attached some long gold chain earrings. Then she stood back and assessed the look in the mirror with professional detachment.

"Stunning." Marcus stared at her like he was mesmerized.

"Now sit down, Empress, and let me finish your hair," Max said. As he teased it up, Josie drank more champagne, all the time feeling Marcus's eyes on her. She looked at him and smiled and felt a strange kind of power coming over her.

But maybe she was just drunk.

"Lean on the bench," Marcus said, aiming his camera at her. He looked through the lens, and moved around until he found a spot. "Put your head back a bit," he said. "No, chin down, a little to the left."

Josie wondered if she had a double chin, or her stomach was bulging through the tight chiffon. She sucked in. "Head up a little, that's it, beautiful." He started snapping away with the motor drive, and she started moving around ever so slowly. "See? You haven't forgotten. Beautiful. It's like riding a bike, Josie." He talked as the camera whirred and he moved around her. "Or having sex. I know by the look in your eyes right now you haven't forgotten how to have sex."

She put her head back and laughed and he kept snapping until the roll ran out. She felt exhilarated. And beyond attracted to him.

She changed into a long, pink bias-cut chiffon dress that clung to her curves like Saran Wrap and had a slit up one side that revealed her entire leg when she moved. Max and Ricky touched up her hair and make-up; then they moved into the all-white studio. She gingerly climbed up onto a set of white stairs that twisted around in interesting shapes.

Max filled everyone's glasses and made a toast. "The old trout is back in the saddle!" he drawled. "Here's to the Empress!" They all laughed and drank. He blasted some music on.

"You're glowing." Marcus held a light meter up to her face and the light box went pop! bleep! as it recharged when he took a reading. "Just glowing."

"I'm drunk," she laughed. "That's an alcoholic flush. I still don't know why you're bothering with this," she said to them all, sipping at another glass of champagne. Max and Ricky fussed over her hair and make-up like trainers in a boxing ring corner between rounds. "I'm old and fat and if this lighting isn't perfect I'll look like shit and in any case no one will give you a job if you flaunt pictures of an old bag around town and—"

"Oh, fishing are we? Jesus bloody Christ you're pathetic!" Max silenced her, poking her ribs with his comb.

"Ouch! Trawling, if you want to know the truth," she giggled.

"Shut up, bitch, and get out there."

"Vork it, dahlink!" Ricky squealed. They retreated to their out-of-frame corners, ready to pounce on a stray wisp of hair or a defiant bead of sweat, leaving Marcus and her alone on the stairs.

She oozed herself into the lens, moving her body in sinuous shapes on the stairs. A fan blew a soft breeze onto her and the chiffon went flying off her legs. She felt nearly naked, but she was really getting into it. Raw energy flowed back and forth from Marcus to her and back through the lens to him. A sexual osmosis.

They finished the shot; then she changed into another outfit. The boys fussed with her and fed her more champagne and pushed her back out onto the set. She was so relaxed now she was flirting outrageously with Marcus. Hell, she would have flirted with a brown dog, the amount of Cristal she'd guzzled. Plus, he was flirting right back at her.

"Am I being a complete slut?" she giggled, as she faced herself into the wind machine and let the dress fly up to the tops of her thighs. Marcus just smiled that irresistible grin and kept shooting.

"Course, darls," Max yelled over the music and the fan, "that's why we loves ya! You're pissed as a rat, darls!"

"You can talk," she slurred.

"Full as a boot," he said. "Isn't it fun? I love it."

"Me too, dahlink," Ricky said, smothering her lips with gloss. "Life feels better with Cristal." And they did a little dance with each other.

"Here!" Marcus threw another camera at his assistant. "Go up to the side of them and take some shots." The assistant climbed the stairs until he was parallel with them and focused his lens.

Marcus blasted the music even louder and they all wiggled and strutted on the stairs, with the wind blowing her hair and dress all over the place. She laughed into the lens as Marcus snapped away. Max grabbed her hand and twirled her around and she felt the red-soled shoes slip from beneath her and she and Max tumbled down the stairs over each other, screaming and laughing.

"Ow!" Josie squealed, as her head hit the bottom stair. Max fell right on top of her. "Get off me!" She tried to push him off, but they were completely tangled together. Max just lay there laughing. "You're killing me!" she squealed breathlessly. He finally pulled himself up and collapsed next to her, still laughing. She looked up and realized her dress was ripped and up near her waist. And she didn't have any panties on. "Oh, God!" she moaned and tried to cover herself.

"Too late, darls. The twat's been shot," Max gurgled and laughed until tears ran down his face.

Marcus ran over and picked her up. "Are you okay?"

"I guess," she giggled nervously, still shocked and feeling like she'd fallen off a roller coaster.

"Come and lie down." He carried her over to the couch against the back wall and sat with her. "Anything injured?"

"Just my decorum." She tried desperately to cover her crotch with flimsy shreds of mauve chiffon.

He leaned over and brushed her hair out of her face. "It's okay, it's only us," he whispered. "Nobody else will ever see." He kissed her and she realized he was drunk too.

"How gorgeous you are." He ran his hand down the side of her breast, over her waist until it touched the top of her thigh.

"Ohh," she groaned, embarrassed, but totally excited.

"Hey you two!" yelled Max from across the room. "Cut that out!" They jumped up, with the startled expressions of two naughty children with their hands in the cookie jar, and she feverishly adjusted what was left of her dress. "You sluts!"

"We're not sluts," Josie slurred. "We're just very friendly!"

10

Several hours later, on the other side of the world, a sharp gust of wind blew through the open windows, chilling Hamish Kent, who stood leaning on a small balcony with his back to the soft pink glow of early morning Rome.

In one hand he held up to the light a proof sheet of black-and-white photographs. In the other he had a magnifying loup pressed to the thick, shiny paper, his eye closed around it, studying his work. He shivered and tugged at the white toweling robe with its Hassler Hotel insignia embroidered over his heart, dropping the loup in the process. It bounced on the door frame, rose, bounced again, and fell through the wrought-iron railing down toward the Spanish Steps five floors below.

"Buggering bollocks!" As he turned and leaned over the balcony, his brand-new Cutler and Gross prescription glasses fell off the top of his head and followed the loup. They sailed down, past the middle-aged guests two floors below who sat arguing over their daily sightseeing schedule, past a honeymooning couple kissing passionately for the second morning of the rest of their lives together, and hit the pavement. Just in time to be crunched by a runner, who stopped, picked them up, and looked up to see what appeared, from the distance, to be a half-robed bald man with a dark scarf of some sort around his neck peering in his vague direction.

"Fuck! Oh, fuck! Bugger!" said Hamish into the miasmic blur below, stamping his foot, stubbing his toe on the railing. "Oww! Fuck!" He jumped and stumbled through the French doors, landing flat on his face onto the thick carpet. "Fucking hell!" he cried into the woolen fluff. His whole body ached.

The doorbell rang and he slowly pulled himself up, trying to ignore the pain and muscle spasm that twinged threateningly in his lower back. "Bloody hell!" He spat out carpet fibers that clung to his nostrils and mouth and hobbled, his left hand alternately reaching for his stubbed toe and his back, not knowing which hurt more. His right arm flailed out before him through the now unseen opulence of the room toward the door. "I'm coming!" he yelled as the bell rang again, "Oww, fuck!" He hit the wall near the entry hall. "Fuck! Fuck!"

"*Buon giorno, Signor Kent,*" bowed the waiter as the door opened. "*Come sta?*"

"Bloody awful!" Hamish snapped, flattening himself back against the wall, so the waiter could pass with the rolling breakfast table.

"Ees everything alright, Signor?" asked the waiter solicitously.

"Oh, yes, just fine and fucking dandy, Fabrizio—it is you, isn't it, Fabrizio?"

"Si, Signor," said Fabrizio, as he set up the table.

"I can't see a fucking thing, Fabrizio." Hamish hobbled back toward the hazy shape of the waiter. "My back's gone out and I've just broken my fucking toe. Everything's just bloody fabuloso!"

"Do you need a doctore, Signor Kent?"

"Oww! Gawd, I dunno." Hamish lowered himself painfully down on the chair Fabrizio had pulled out and guided him to. "I need some new fucking glasses, Fab, that's what I need. I didn't bring another pair with me. Can you imagine? A blind photographer. I'm not worth the price of a disposable fucking camera without my glasses! Oww, my toe. Is it bleeding, Fab?"

"*No, Signor.*" Fabrizio bent down, averting his eyes from his guest's shockingly exposed body to examine the offending digit. "It appears to be well."

"Jolly good then, Fab. Just get a hammer, will you Fab, and pound my aching bloody skull with it. Maybe that'll help the toe."

"*Che, Signor?*" The doorbell rang again.

"Oh, nothing," said Hamish dejectedly. "Answer the door, Fab, old boy. I can't possibly get up again."

"*Si, Signor.*" Fabrizio's short legs were already propelling him toward the door. Hamish heard a rapid conversation in Italian, nothing much he could understand, as he steadfastly refused to speak anything but English, even though he was in Italy at least five times a year. Fabrizio closed the door and returned, Hamish's broken glasses held gingerly in his white-gloved hands.

"Signor, your spectacles—"

"Oh, bravo, Fab, they found them! Bring them here then!"

"Signor, they are not well." Fabrizio offered the mangled frames to his charge.

"Not well? They can't be as not well as I am, Fab." Hamish snatched for them. The glass felt jagged in his hands. He attempted to place them on his face, which required careful maneuvering, as the frames were twisted into an odd shape. "A not well man in his not well glasses, eh, Fab?" he said jauntily. Fab would not disagree with him on this point.

Hamish peered out through the shattered lenses. It

was rather like a kaleidoscope. He looked up and several images of Fabrizio stood gazing down on him with polite disdain.

"Gawd. What a morning, Fab." He slumped down to the fractured vision of eight bowls of muesli, eight glasses of blood-orange juice, eight coffeepots, eight cups. "Oww," he moaned at his aching muscles. The pain not only squeezed at his back but wracked his legs, his arms, his neck.

His neck. He grabbed his hand to his throat, turning to his right, knowing there was a mirror on the wall.

Leering back at him were eight shaved-headed middle-aged men around whose necks were eight black leather collars embedded with large metal studs and spikes. The men's robes had fallen open and they wore black leather metal-studded harnesses strapped around their genitals.

"That'll be all, thanks, Fab," said Hamish, with dismissive aplomb, as he turned back to his repast and tried to find which of the eight spoons in front of him was the real one.

His body felt as mangled as his specs, but his mind worked feverishly. He couldn't possibly blow the whole day's work by an admission of literal blind stupidity to Sophia Loren's people. He dialed New York. Fuck that it was only after one in the morning there. Somebody's head would have to roll. And he was fucking sure it wouldn't be his.

Josie gasped at the sound of Hamish's contemptuous snarl hurtling over the ether toward them. Although she bolted up instantly, petrified, Marcus pulled her back down and cuddled her close, as garbled abuse flowed over them like an icy black cloud. They were in deep shit, now, she knew. But it was too late. How the hell did Hamish know about them?

Holding her breath tight and listening, she was relieved to hear it was some technical matter. Marcus had packed the wrong camera equipment. Strangely, Marcus seemed not the least bit perturbed by the situation.

"I'll check it out and get back to you, boss," was all he said before hanging up.

"What was that about? Aren't you in trouble?" she said.

"He does this all the time," Marcus yawned. "I packed exactly the right equipment. Something's gone wrong and he has to blame somebody."

"Really?" she said. "I've never heard him so venemous."

"Then you don't know Hamish," he sighed and got up. "Now I'll have to phone Antonia, who'll call him and fix things. It's always like this."

Josie felt queasy at the mention of Antonia's name. Couldn't she ever have a bit of fun without some hideous consequence? The hideous consequence in this case being a bitch named Antonia.

So, Marcus got on the wire to his boss's ex-slash-agent. Josie cringed each time she heard his voice. Sounded like Antonia was giving him the third degree. And not about Hamish. Marcus must've had a date with Antonia and had stood her up. Or so it sounded. *Christ. In two (okay, at least three) bottles of Cristal I've managed to fuck up my entire attempt at a new career by having sex with the ex-slash-agent's new squeeze and my old friend-slash-future employer's assistant. What a moron. What was I thinking? You weren't, twit . . . you were using Cristal's brain. It's those bubbles. They'll seduce you every time.*

Her memory was rather hazy past the fall in the studio. But it involved dinner with Marcus, Max, and Ricky round the corner at L'Odeon, where she barely picked at her steak frites and salad. Then they'd all walked back to Marcus's loft and drunk more champagne. God, no wonder she had a pounding headache.

Next thing she knew, the boys had left and she and Marcus were making out again. They started on his couch, and before long there was a trail of clothes into his bedroom. He kept telling her how beautiful she was as he covered her entire body with kisses. Their love-making was warm, languorous; the champagne had slowed them to a perfect velocity, as if they were under water. They both passed out soon after, until Hamish called. It had seemed like a fabulous idea at the time. Now she knew she was in deep shit. *Goddamned bubbles.*

Josie got up and started to dress. Her head throbbed. Hangover hell in full swing. But she had to get out of this mess. Now, before it got any worse. Could it get any worse? *Oh, yeah. Heaps.*

Marcus finally hung up from his inquisitor and looked surprised to see her buttoning her shirt. "Please, don't go. It's not what you think."

"It never is." She felt like a complete dolt.

"Ah, Josie," he sighed. "I'm sorry. I said I'd have a drink with her after the shoot, but, well, obviously I didn't make it. I had something much more important to do." He came over, hugged her, and stroked her hair. "There's nothing going on between Antonia and me. It's purely professional."

She looked up to him. "Look, this was not a good idea—"

"It's late. Just stay, will you please?" He leaned down and kissed her. "I promise I won't attack you." He kissed her again, and she felt her knees go to jelly.

"Oh? How boring." She finally managed to yawn and he led her back to his bed.

11

"Marcus. Are you there?" Antonia's voice clipped over the answering machine.

"Fuck," Marcus mumbled.

"Hrumph!" The phone clicked dead.

Jesus. Does this woman never sleep? She'd phoned him three times already since he spoke to her last night and it was only eight AM. Josie had managed a fitful sleep, but had woken, startled, when the first call came through about an hour earlier.

She had crept up slowly and tiptoed to the bathroom in a feeble attempt to quietly rinse her mouth out and apply just a smidgen of foundation so Marcus wouldn't get a fright when he saw, in the harsh morning light, an old broad with broken capillaries in her cheeks lying next to him. But on her way back she'd banged her toe on something and fallen onto the bed, yelping with pain. He had laughed and cuddled her until they both fell back asleep.

Ignoring the phone, Marcus curled against her and stroked her breast, teasing her nipple, kissing the back of her neck and her shoulder, then rolling her toward him and grabbing both her breasts, kissed her full on the mouth. She drew his tongue inside her, reached down and stroked him until he couldn't take much more without exploding. He grabbed at the table beside the bed for another condom, rolled it on and then entered her, filling her up until he could feel her shuddering, her soft moans escalating as he came with her, the force of his orgasm decimating everything beyond primal, reptilian brain waves.

Later, after they'd both showered and sat drinking coffee in his kitchen, she felt another wave of self-consciousness sweep over her. The "what-the-hell-am-I-doing-here-with-an-almost-complete-stranger?" feeling of embarrassment. She leaned on the table and put her hands over her face.

"Are you okay?" he said.

"Oh, God." She smiled wanly at him through her open fingers. "What have we done?" She suddenly felt like crying. "What have I done?"

He reached over and peeled her hands off her face and, cupping them in his, kissed her fingers and grinned. His eyes were smoky green pools.

"It's just . . ." she paused, not knowing quite what to say or how much she should reveal, "just that, well, I haven't been with anyone for a long time, and I'm not used to it." *And I feel like a slut* is what she really wanted to say. "I mean, we don't even know each other!" She pulled her hands from his and grabbed her coffee mug.

"But we will." He gently stroked the side of her face. She thought she'd melt again.

"But what about Antonia?"

"What about her?" He stopped smiling and looked down.

"She doesn't seem like the kind of person you want to piss off," she said, sipping her coffee.

"It's just business." He looked at her defiantly.

"I didn't mean just you. I meant she doesn't strike me as being someone one would want to get on the bad side of. She's vicious. And she already loathes me."

"No, she doesn't. How could anyone loathe you? You're so sweet."

She laughed and blushed simultaneously. "She does. And she's obviously hot as Hades for you."

He rolled his eyes. "It's none of her business."

"Right," Josie nodded. Feeling weird. And guilty. It wasn't just Antonia; it was Hamish too. "So we won't tell anyone, okay?"

He pulled her up out of her chair and gave her a big squeeze and a deep kiss. "Whatever you want, beautiful."

Right now she didn't know what she wanted. Except to keep kissing him. But there was a niggling feeling in the pit of her stomach.

"I'd better go," she said, grabbing her bag off the counter.

He walked her across the loft to the industrial elevator, took her downstairs, and hailed a cab.

"I'll have the proof sheets later," he said.

"Yeww, I was so drunk! They'll be awful!"

"No they won't," he laughed. "They'll be great."

"No they won't!"

He grabbed her and kissed her again, and then gently put her in the cab, like she was some kind of precious cargo. "I'll call you." He smiled and shut the door and waited till the cab pulled off before he went back inside. She didn't think he'd ever call her and she certainly didn't feel like precious cargo. More like extremely damaged goods. Her head was throbbing like crazy and she felt nauseous. What the hell. At least she'd had fun. Lots. She reckoned a hangover and a dose of guilt were a small price to pay for such amazing sex.

* * *

"When can I see you? You've got to take a look at these."

"Huh?" Josie could barely lift her head off the pillow.

"It's me." Marcus sounded excited. "You do remember me don't you?"

"Very funny." She yawned and looked at the clock. It was six, so she'd been asleep for about three hours. Her pillow felt wet, which meant she must have been drooling. *Wow! He called!*

"You look incredible," he said.

"Not right now I don't." She sat up and peered round the corner of her bedroom door to the mirror at the end of the hallway. Her hair was standing on end and she could see sleep creases on her face even from that distance.

"Having a blond moment are we, honey? The pictures, dopey. They're incredible."

"I am blond. Ergo, a blond moment is a normal occurrence. So they're good?" *He called me honey!*

"Beautiful."

"Really? I can't believe it." *He also called me dopey. Maybe he thinks I'm one of the Seven Dwarfs. So don't even go there.*

"You've gotta see them."

"When?" She yawned and stretched.

"How's now sound? We could get something to eat."

She gasped. "You mean like a date?"

"You got a problem with that?"

"Ah," she smiled, "no, none whatsoever." *Oh my God! He's asking me on a date!*

"Shall I come over?"

She glanced around her bedroom. It looked like a bomb had hit it. She couldn't face a cleanup right now.

"How about I come down there. You've got all the right viewing thingies."

"Viewing thingies?"

"You know, the magnifying glass thing."

"You mean a loup. Yeah, I have all the viewing thingies. On me. And I'm already halfway uptown. So how about it?"

"But it's a mess here!"

"I'm not coming to see the mess. I want to see you."

"Oh." She was shocked. "Well, I'm a mess too."

"Just give me your address, will you?"

She'd barely had time to shower and throw on a pair of jeans and a T-shirt by the time the doorbell rang. He stood there with a huge smile and an armful of pink roses. She couldn't believe he was real. That someone so gorgeous would be even vaguely interested in her was unbelievable. He put his arms around her, pushed her wet hair off her neck, and kissed her forehead.

"Mmm, you smell good," he whispered. She pulled him inside, slammed the door with her foot, and melted into him. He backed her up against the foyer wall, kissing her wildly as he tossed the roses and his bag onto the console next to her. She could feel his cock bulging through his jeans and it made her so hot she just had to put her hand on him and rub, like he was a genie in a bottle dying to be released. Well, she sure as hell knew what her first wish was going to be. She wished for that beautiful cock right in her mouth, and then inside her. She wished for him to come all over her. Okay, okay . . . so that was three wishes all rolled into one.

They worked their way into the living room and down on their knees, onto the carpet, their tongues never leaving each other. She couldn't believe what a fabulous kisser he was. She undid his belt and fly and slid her hand down his jeans. He was huge.

He did the same to her and she could feel her wetness slip all over his fingers as he stroked her. It was all she could do not to come right there. Their clothes somehow flew off in all directions.

And, before too long, all three wishes were granted.

Later, as they lay in bed drinking red wine, he showed her the proof sheets.

"Pretty cool, huh," he said, grinning excitedly.

"Wow. Is that me?" She giggled. "It doesn't look like me at all."

"See how beautiful you look? You're such a babe."

"Shut up!" she said, blushing. "It's amazing what a bit of spackle filler and some computer manipulation can do!"

"They haven't been retouched yet. That's all you."

"Rubbish! It's all lighting and really great make-up. Smoke and mirrors. But, Marcus, these are good. Really good."

"Your energy is just amazing."

"Ours." She smiled up at him. "Team effort, remember?" She put the loup down and drank some wine. "So, have you showed them to anyone else yet?"

"Only the guys at the lab." He picked up the loup and looked over her shoulder at the shots.

"Antonia?"

"I wanted you to see them first." He kissed the back of her neck.

"Good. Because I don't think you should show them to her."

"Why not?" He pulled her closer to him and smoothed her hair.

"One look at these shots and she'll know."

"So?" He nibbled at her ear.

"So?" She pulled away and turned to face him. "So, maybe she won't take you on."

"Of course she will. I'm good."

"I know, but you have to play the game."

"I don't care about her stupid games." He sat up and drank some wine, agitated. "And I need to show these shots around. They're some of the best I've ever taken."

"Marcus, she can make or break you right now."

"Bullshit. If she won't take me, there are plenty of other agents who will."

"Probably." She sat up next to him, took his glass, and had a sip. "But still. She is the best. And what about Hamish?"

"He doesn't give a shit about anyone, except Hamish." He took the glass from her and poured some more.

"He's giving me a chance, and I don't want to ruin it."

"But how would us being—oh," he said, "so you two were—"

"A long time ago." She felt embarrassed. "It was nothing, really. Just friends working together all the time. You know."

"I know." He drank, then handed her the glass again.

"So maybe," she said, staring into the glass, "I mean, this is really fun and all, but maybe we shouldn't do this again."

"Fun? So that's all you think of me? Fun?" He started tickling her and she coiled up, laughing and spilling wine as she tried to escape his grasp.

"Fun? So I'm just a boy toy for you!" He grabbed at her, torturing her with his hands.

"No!" she giggled. "I didn't mean it like that!"

"Oh! So now I'm not fun!" He kept tickling her, pinning her beneath him. "No fun at all, huh?"

"You know what I mean!" she squealed, struggling and laughing. He was kissing her neck and working down her body.

"This is no fun?" he growled, reaching her stomach. She stopped writhing about. "And this? What about this?" He was between her legs now. "You don't think this is fun?"

"Yes," she panted. "No . . . it's not fun . . . it's . . . incredible," she gasped. "And that scares me."

He lifted his head and looked up at her. "It scares the hell out of me too." He smiled, then resumed his task with cannibalistic fervor.

They had dinner delivered and stayed in bed eating, laughing, drinking wine, watching TV, and making love. Josie felt like she'd died and gone to heaven for a night. Only it felt real, honest, and normal. And she didn't want it to stop. They fell asleep, curled up next to each other, and she slept deeply, even though she wasn't used to having anybody lying next to her.

The phone jolted her out of a dream and she thought she'd have a heart attack.

"Darling," echoed the dry voice of Hamish. Her stomach lurched.

"Oh . . . hi!" she croaked. "Where are you?"

"In Rome airport, darling, waiting for my flight. Don't tell me you're still sleeping."

"It's six-thirty," she growled. Marcus put his arm round her waist and pulled her close. Her heart pounded even faster.

"What are you doing?"

"Uh." She froze as Marcus started kissing her back and stroking her. "Sleeping?"

"Later, darling, I meant later. I thought you might like to have dinner." It sounded more like a command than an invitation.

"Dinner?" She gasped as Marcus put his hand between her thighs. "Tonight?"

"No, next month!" he sniffed. "Of course tonight."

"Ahh," she panted. "Yes . . . yes . . . okay."

"Is everything all right?"

"Oh . . . yeah . . . fine," she wimpered.

"You sound strange."

"I'm a bit asthmatic, that's all."

"Later then," he said.

"Ahh . . . okaay . . . ah . . . bye."

12

After Marcus left Josie that morning, she was feeling the ambivalent guilt of an adulterer. She didn't know why she felt this way, but in her gut she figured it would all come crashing down. Dinner loomed. She couldn't get her mind around anything much all day and frittered time uselessly on the Internet. Kind of dreading the thought of facing Hamish at all. And then fighting herself about it. Why should she feel guilty? Hamish was just a friend, nothing more. She didn't owe him anything. And she certainly didn't owe that Gorgon ex-wife of his even the time of day.

"So how was Sophia?" she said, after she and Hamish air kissed each other and sat down in their booth.

"*Beyond*, darling! Simply *Beyond*," he said, fluttering his wrist campily. "She's absolutely fabuloso."

"So you got some great shots?"

"Divine, darling. But let's not dwell on Sophia. I saw some rather good shots this afternoon when I got back."

"Oh, yes?" *Uh-oh. Here we go.*

"Yes, darling. I'm sure you're aware of them?" He had that steely glint in his eye and his tiny lips were turning up at the corners.

"So, he showed you." She could feel the blush rising. "He wasn't supposed to. They were just supposed to be for fun."

"Oh, yes, I saw them all. They're divine," he said, brandishing his glass of Bordeaux in an authoritative manner, his gaze firmly on her now. "I told you—he's a talented lad."

In many more ways than you realize, she thought, a pleasurable twinge surging between her thighs.

"What did Antonia think of them?" she asked, then wondered why she was interested in anything Antonia thought.

"She thinks they're genius, darling. But then she thinks anything Marcus does is genius." Josie felt a strange pang at those words. "The subject she was rather less complimentary about," he added, smiling wickedly.

"Why? What did she say?"

"Oh . . . nothing much."

"What?"

"Really, darling, you don't want to know."

"Yes I do want to know!" she snapped. "God, you're annoying when you do that!"

"Do what?" he said, fluttering his eyelids at her.

"Ooh!" she rasped, wanting to throttle him. "Just tell me what she said!"

"Well"—he pursed his mouth—"I can't quite remember it all, but something . . . I don't know . . . something about . . . silk purses and . . . sows' ears, and some other allusion to . . . oh, now what was it again? Oh, yes, that's it . . . mutton dressed as lamb, if I recall."

He sipped at his wine as an evilly innocent grin slid across his face. Like that of a child who has just inflicted some form of brutal torture on its younger sibling and slipped from the scene of the crime before the howls of distress alert its weary guardian.

"You bastard," she hissed. Then she howled with laughter.

The phone message light was blinking furiously when she returned, exhausted, but amused by Hamish. She eagerly pushed playback, hoping to hear Marcus's voice. But he hadn't called, and her heart sank a little.

Instead there was a message from Andy Wyatt.

"Howdy, darlin'," his voice boomed, "your friend Priscilla has invited me to her little hoedown Saturdy naht and Ah was wonderin' if y'all would give me the pleasure of takin' you along. Keep me outa trouble. Ah'll be back in town tomorrow and Ah'll call you then. Until then, keep fit, stay well, and, shug, carry a big ole stick."

Ugh. She didn't want to go with Andy Wyatt. In any case Priscilla had asked her to bring Hamish along. So she had an out. But why hadn't Hunk-Face called? She wanted to hear his voice, feel his skin next to hers, his breath on her. She felt like an idiot. Still, she was going to see him tomorrow, on the shoot with Hamish, so maybe he didn't think he needed to call her. Whatever. She went to bed and snuggled up by herself.

13

Swaddled in her black alpaca Gucci coat, red cashmere scarf, and sharp Philip Treacy hat, Josie strode the next morning from her Beekman Place apartment uptown. She stopped at a deli on Fifty-eighth for coffee before crossing Fifth in front of Bergdorf's, said good morning to the doorman outside the Plaza, and descended the steps into the frostiness of Central Park.

Watery sun dribbled through the decaying remains of the few leaves left clinging to their skeletal hosts. She could feel the frost crunching beneath her boots, the spongy dampness of the auburn and gold carpet underneath the frost, the spike of cold air in her lungs each time she breathed in, and the knot in her stomach expanding the closer she got to her destination.

She passed by a couple of stoic ducks who'd obviously missed the flight down south, freezing their little bodies in dejected silence on the icy pond.

What the hell am I doing? Her pace slowed to a distracted stroll along the Mall toward the Bethesda Fountain, where the location van would be parked. *I'm using*

Hamish to try to change careers. And screwing his assistant on the side. What a fuckwit. Talk about self-sabotage.

Grow up! Be responsible for once! Stop spending more money than you make, don't go for the most dangerous guy. Try choosing the most stable for a change. And don't, whatever you do, drink too much Cristal in the presence of an absolute bona fide Hunk. And if you do, never ever stick your tongue down his throat. And if you find yourself—

"Aaah!" she jumped in abject fear as something grabbed her arm.

"Josie!" Marcus, dressed entirely in black, grabbed her and picked her up—no mean feat considering she must weigh a ton with all the alpaca wrapping her up like a big furry bear. Her hat fell off and coffee splattered all over their coats.

"You scared the hell out of me!" she yelled.

"You looked lost," he said, placing the struggling bear back down.

"Lost?" she said, grabbing through fallen leaves for her hat. "Lost? Are you in the habit of creeping up on people and grabbing them because they look lost? This is New York City!"

He pulled her to him and kissed her and then all her resolve of the last few minutes blew, along with the white clouds of their hot breath, into the freezing air.

"Sorry." He smiled down at her. She liked that he was so tall. Most of her boyfriends had been shorter than her, especially if she wore heels. *Boyfriend. Oh, God. Not that stupid word. Boyfriend.* A twitty junior high school term she felt way too old to use. And besides—she'd slept with him, yeah, so what—just cause she'd fucked some guy's brains out didn't mean he'd be elevated to boyfriend status. Or that he would deign to elevate her to girlfriend status. If they weren't working together, he'd probably never see her again. "Hello . . . anybody home?" He squeezed her back to the present. "See, you *are* lost."

"Got a lot on my mind," she pouted.

"Nervous?" He tilted his head toward the van.

"Nervous? Me? Never." She fidgeted with her coat. They turned and walked the final stretch of leafless overhead canopy before they emerged at the band shell not far from the van. He put one arm around her waist and took the sodden brown paper bag from her tenuous grasp. She noticed her gloves were wet. Ruined.

A homeless person lay in cardboard bedding on one of the benches. Marcus threw the coffee in a trash can next to the body. It didn't move at the sound. She felt awful, worrying about her stupid gloves when a human being lay there, freezing.

"So why don't we just march in there and tell them the truth?" He kissed the top of her head and squeezed her again. She liked that. The squeezing bit. And the kiss.

"What—just go in there and say, 'Top of the morning to you, Hamish. We're having hot throbbing sex with each other and thought you'd like to know.' Is that what you had in mind?"

He laughed. "How about, 'Hi, Antonia. I think Josie is the sexiest woman I've ever met.'?"

"Is Antonia going to be here today?" She felt her stomach tighten even more. "Fabulous." With Hamish they could have fun. He was so unaware of anything beyond his own realm, he probably wouldn't notice any lustful glances or stuff like that. But with Antonia there, it'd be hell. Worse. Lying under a cardboard carton in twenty-degree temperatures appealed more to Josie than spending a day with Antonia. She considered asking the homeless man if he'd swap places with her.

"Do you?" she finally asked, after a sullen moment or two.

"Do I what?"

"Mean what you said. You know. The sexiest woman stuff." She looked up at him, trying to gauge whether he was a good liar or simply a complete dolt.

"Absolutely." He kissed her again. *Oh, God. I could so keep doing this for the rest of the day.*

She hastily separated herself from him as they got to the van and a chauffeur-driven Lincoln Town Car pulled up.

The door opened and out stepped Hamish and Antonia.

"Darls, we were there, remember?" said Max, wielding his scissors perilously close to Josie's face. She jolted back from the hairstylist and bumped her head on the back door of the location van.

"Oww!" It was a tight squeeze, what with hair, makeup, models, and all the clothes shoved into the back of the motor home, while Antonia, Marcus and another assistant, and all the photographic equipment had commandeered the front.

"Ya can't fool us, darls." Max turned back to the young model sitting in front of him staring blankly into a light-surrounded mirror. "So ya might as well give us all the dish. What's he like in the sack?"

"Would you kindly lower your voice to a shriek?" Josie hissed. A narrow corridor divided the back from the front, but it wasn't exactly private.

"Ah, come on, darls. Tell us? Please?"

Josie could hear Antonia in heated discussion on her cell phone. Hamish and Marcus were outside scouting locations. That cute anchorman who lived two floors below in her building was reading the morning news on both TVs and the coffee brewer was making a manic noise up front. Thank God they hadn't been overheard.

She rubbed at the lump on her skull, ignored Max, and moved to the racks of garments, placing shoes and accessories with each outfit, while Mala steamed them and checked for any marks or loose threads.

"Dahlink, I bet hee's hung like a stallion," teased Ricky, brutally stabbing a blusher brush over the cheeks of a beautiful but vapid-looking teenager sitting at the mirror.

God. It was useless. They wouldn't let up, these two.

"Well you'll never get to find out," she said into the clothing.

"Don't bet on it, darls."

"Bet on what?" came a husky voice from up front. Josie's eyes narrowed threateningly at the two beauty queens as Marcus appeared in the doorway.

She looked at him, rolled her eyes, and cringed slightly. A sort of "help me!" gesture. "I need some coffee," she said and squeezed past his big frame.

"Ahh. Ahhgh." Excruciating pain ripped through Jonathon Cantero's skull. Nausea curled around his stomach. *Where the fuck am I?* He opened his eyes and tried to focus. He could see the faded colors of the antique Tabriz rug his mother had given him as a wedding present. He sighed, closing his eyes against the light, relieved he was lying on his own couch. *At least I'm at home.* Although he didn't remember how he got home, or even where he'd been.

Next thing he knew, his wife's poodle was at his side barking. *Fuck.*

"Are you okay?" He opened one eye and there was his wife leering down at him, an expression of frozen horror on her face.

He could tell she hated him right now. Not as much as he hated himself. "Guess I tied one on." He shrugged, not knowing what else to say. The dog licked at his face. "Don't, Chica." He pushed him away, thinking he'd throw up all over him.

"Well, that's obvious," Daniela said. "Come, Querido." She retrieved the dog, bent and picked up an empty Grey Goose bottle that lay at Jonathon's side, grimaced at the overflowing ashtray on the antique Japanese table in front of the couch, and then turned back to him, her eyes glistening with tears. She walked back across the room toward the kitchen. As she passed by the Regency mirror next to the archway, he could see her smooth little face crumpling like brown paper.

Fuck. He couldn't deal with this. Not right now. He lay back down again, feeling parched. Water. He needed water. And food. He should eat. No, he'd probably puke if he ate right now. Did he eat any dinner? He remembered he hadn't.

The hazy image of Reggiano's crossed his mind. That's it. They'd gone to Reggiano's for an early dinner, before all the social mountaineers had arrived. He'd promised himself that he wouldn't drink. But, then, what harm would just one glass of wine do, he'd thought. Just one. Daniela had given him that disapproving look when he ordered it.

He sat back up and attempted to stand, but his legs felt nonexistent and his head felt like molten lead.

Well, fuck you, he'd thought last night, looking back at Daniela's angry, flashing eyes. *You're becoming like the rest of my family. Like my mother, always critical, giving me looks. Like Josie ended up being. Well you can all fuck yourselves.* He could become president of the United States and his mother would still fucking disapprove. Malcontent bitch. Guilt monger extraordinaire.

So he'd ordered a martini instead. Just to spite her. And anyway, she was drinking too, wasn't she? She had wine. How could he possibly be expected to refrain when his own wife wouldn't?

He felt the clammy stubble on his face and shuffled over to the mirror. Hollow eyes stared back at him. Gaunt. He really should eat something. He could hear Dani crashing around in the kitchen and a wave of guilt and remorse and the never-ending shame came over him.

He crossed through the dining room, edging past the Ruhlmann table and chairs that had cost him an arm and a leg at Sotheby's, pushed open the swing door to the kitchen, and approached his wife. She had her back turned to him at the counter and he felt her stiffen when he put his arms round her and nuzzled at her neck. "I'm sorry," he whispered.

"You reek of liquor," she said, furiously slathering butter on a piece of toast. She evaded his grasp and took some orange juice from the fridge. She poured two glasses and handed him one, still not looking at him. "Do you want some breakfast? You didn't eat last night. You drank your dinner." She resumed her assault on the toast.

"No thanks," he mumbled, gulping the juice. "I'm not hungry."

"You should eat. Have you seen yourself lately?" She regarded him now, with contempt, he thought, as if she were his mirror. "You look horrible and thin and sick. Like a corpse."

"And you don't look like the woman I married," he snarled, shoving his empty glass in the sink and starting for the back door of the kitchen. "You look more like my mother every day."

"Where are you going?" She sounded scared. He crossed the foyer, threw on his overcoat, and picked his keys up from beside the beautiful arrangement of flowers on the console.

"Out."

She grabbed the dog, its leash from a drawer, and followed him, her pink slippers clattering on the parquet. "Then take Chica with you." She handed the mound of wriggling fluff to him. "He hasn't been walked yet."

"Great," he snarled. "Now you're throwing me out?"

"Ai!" she rasped back at him. "Stop being such an asshole!"

They stared at each other for a moment, strangers lost in uncomfortably familiar surroundings, and then he got into the elevator and staggered out onto Fifth Avenue.

Chica relieved himself on the first available tree, then took off toward the park. *God, why am I doing this? I'm in no fucking state to be walking a dog. Fuck women. Bitches, the lot of them. My life as a dog.*

"I wish I was you, Chica. Not a care in the world, eh, buddy." He leaned down to pat the dog and a wave of nausea nearly leveled him.

Chica somehow managed to drag Jonathon as far as the boathouse. Actually he'd hoped the cafe would be open, so he could get a coffee or some juice, or a hit of vodka to get him back into the land of the living. No dice. Too early. Not even the sidewalk vendors were out yet. God, he was parched. Just one drink would fix him up.

He shuffled along by the lake, Chica sniffing and peeing on every tree. Over by the fountain he saw a photo shoot in action. They always shot there, with the view of the city skyline in the background.

He wanted a cigarette and he realized he was cold now. Really cold. He didn't have gloves or a scarf on or the furry Russian hat he liked to wear when it snowed. His hair felt like an icy casing around his face, and his nose felt raw. He felt raw all over. He wanted to go back to bed, but he was afraid of having to face Daniela again. Her yelling and throwing things at him like she had last night. South American firecracker. She had some temper.

Perhaps he could bum a cigarette from somebody at the photo shoot. Anyway, he'd like to see if there were any famous models there. He used to know some of those girls, from the old party days.

He missed those days. When it had been fun to hang around the clubs and be totally, blindly out of it. Before it had taken him over. He didn't miss the coming down, or the aching loneliness when he was straight, so that the only alternative was to stay out of it, to never feel the pain. He still missed that feeling he got from the first hit. The needle in his arm and the boot into nothingness, into bliss, into his own world of infinite power. A power he never felt unless he was high.

He neared the edge of the square, feeling that ache again, the longing, like nothing could ever make anything right, so what was the point of it all.

And then he saw her. Josie. Standing with a bunch of people, fixing the models in their designer outfits. *Josie. Christ.* His stomach lurched again and he retched juice into a deadened flower bed.

How could he possibly run into her twice in one fucking week? Just when everything was going smoothly she had to show up and ruin it all. Ruin everything. So he couldn't think of much else except her. He wanted to run and hide, away from Josie, away from his wife and his family. But he found himself riveted at the sight of her, watching her move and laugh.

He leaned against a tree. Chica snuffled around him like a truffle pig. He didn't know if he could move. He felt weak. He kept watching Josie, the pain and the anger and the guilt mounting in him.

She'd ruined everything. Deserted him when he needed her most. He knew he'd been a bastard to her, but she'd been the one to leave him, gouge him for money. It was fucked. All fucked. She was fucked. He'd been right all along. She'd only liked him for his money. Why else would anyone like him?

At least with Daniela it wasn't money. She had her own. Not as much as he did, but she wasn't a bloodsucker. She was just insecure and fucked up in her own way, in the way that kids with famous or very rich parents are. He knew he could never match his father's successes, and in a way he resented his father for them. Because they kept him down. He never had to do anything, never could.

He wanted to see Josie. Tell her what she'd done to him. How she'd made him suffer. He stumbled away from the tree, toward her, almost giddy now. Lightheaded.

"Hey, Moonpie."

Josie blanched at the familiar voice, the nickname. She started shaking, could feel tears welling up. "Moonpie," he said, staggering toward her.

"Cover for me," she whispered to her assistant and slunk away from the group, hoping nobody would notice the disheveled character behind them. Max and Ricky were playing with the models' hair and make-up, and Hamish, who'd ignored her all morning, was cracking some joke with them while Marcus changed film and cameras.

Jonathon's face was gray and haggard. Her heart leaped. His eyes had that sunken, agonized look that she'd seen before, when he'd been in the lockup unit at the rehab in Connecticut. As if his personality and sanity had disappeared into the deep recesses of his corneas.

"Hi," she said, not knowing whether she should talk to him. But wanting to hold him, to take him in her arms and protect him. He looked so frail. "Oh, Jonathon," she sighed, reaching her hand out to him, terrified. "What are you doing here?"

"What does it look like I'm doing here?" he said, the hollowness of his eyes thinning into solid hatred. He leaned over and picked the dog up. "Walking my new wife's dog," he smiled, knowing this would hurt her more than anything.

"Oh," she said, patting Chica, not concentrating on the dog at all, but on Jonathon's ravaged face and her own bursting heart.

"Got a cigarette?"

"You know I don't smoke. I get asthma, remember? Or have you forgotten everything about me?"

He dropped the dog back down and then, feeling himself fade, slid to the ground in a heap.

"Oh! Jonathon! Oh my God!" Josie knelt down and shook him. "Jonathon! Wake up!" She slapped at his face. He groaned but didn't move. She put her ear to his mouth and could smell the stale alcohol, mingled with the remaining traces of Armani aftershave that he always wore, a smell that from the time she had first met him always made her feel like swooning. His smell.

All that time and all the things they'd gone through together, and how they were all lost now made her collapse onto the ground, her tears falling onto his unshaven mad face. A child's face. She sat there, rocking him in her arms and crying, unaware that the whole crew had turned to watch her.

Marcus came over. Pulling both her and Jonathon up, he managed to throw the slight body over his shoulder and carry it all the way up the stairs and over to the location van. Josie picked up the dog, who licked her face.

Jonathon's body hanging over Marcus's shoulders reminded her of when he first came to visit her in Sydney, during the infancy of their relationship. He had arrived at the airport in a wheelchair, his back out in self-described intense pain. He insisted on hiring a car and driver to ferry them around. The driver would carry Jonathon, who would hang over his shoulder smoking and talking incessantly, practically everywhere. If it hadn't been such a hilarious sight, it would have embarrassed her completely. Her friends and family had been simultaneously horrified and amused. They dubbed Jonathon "The Fruit Loop." He'd admitted much later on, when he got sober, that he'd been faking the pain so he could get drugs. Of course, he hadn't fooled anybody.

They reached the van and lay Jonathon on the sofa. Chica jumped in and sniffed at Antonia's impossibly high alligator pumps. *Wicked Witch of the West pumps,* thought Josie. Antonia was elegantly dressed in a form-fitting black-and-white houndstooth check suit. Her trademark ruby nails were wrapped around the ubiquitous cell phone.

Josie ignored her. She felt too flustered to explain, too worried and heartbroken.

"Are you all right?" Marcus asked, his eyes on Josie. Without replying, she went to the fridge and pulled out a bottle of mineral water, twisted it open, and took it to the slumped body of her former fiancé and forced some down his mouth. He spluttered, then swallowed more.

"Yeah," rasped Jonathon. "Course I'm all right. Thanks, man." He looked up at Marcus, then at Josie. "So who are you? Her latest squeeze? Boy, she sure gets around."

"Shut up, Jonathon."

"Who are you?" Marcus said.

"The prince of the fucking city, man," Jonathon mumbled.

"When was the last time you had a square meal?" Josie said, nervously shoving a plate of fruit on his lap.

"Here. Eat this." She'd gone into autopilot. It was the only way she could cope. Jonathon picked up a piece of melon and examined it. She noticed his hands and fingers. She had always marveled at how strong they were in comparison to the rest of his body. He was a mass of inconsistencies: A dichotomous amalgam of strong hands, slight frame. Huge dick, tiny feet. Kind and sweet when sober, bitter and mean and violent when strung out. Highly intelligent, yet completely stupid about his life.

She wasn't exactly smart about hers. They say water always finds its own level. She figured she must have been nearly on empty when she'd hooked up with him.

"You haven't poisoned it, have you?" he smirked, then slipped the juicy green flesh into his mouth.

"Very funny." She poured a cup of coffee and handed it to him. Her hands shook. "Would you like a bagel?"

"Why, Moonpie, sure I'd like a bagel," he replied, his eyes not so blank now. Josie nearly sank through the floor. She was sure her heart had stopped beating for a moment.

"Moonpie?" Antonia asked, putting her phone down. "How quaint." She smiled at him, her ruby lips a serene display of mockery.

"Yeah, Moonpie," he said dreamily, but his eyes darted angrily between the two women. "That's what I used to call her, back when she was rounder and sweeter, didn't I, Josephine?" He shifted himself up higher and addressed Antonia. "Not like now. Old and thin and bitter, hee hee. Just kidding, Pookie." He blew Josie a kiss.

Antonia actually had the gall to laugh. Marcus was silent. Josie glanced at him, embarrassed that he was there to witness this apparition from her past. Her very own incubus.

"Thanks, Jonathon. Always so fabulous with the compliments. Always so grateful."

"Oh, here we go. Get out the violins for the martyr. Poor little Josie. All the horrible stuff I put you through. Well, you sure squeezed me when it suited you."

"I only asked you to be fair," she muttered, horrified.

"Fair. You should talk about fair. Your idea of fair is kicking the shit out of someone when they're already down for the count." He stood up, unsteadily, his coffee slopping over the edge of the mug, and put the fruit plate on the table in front of Antonia, who had a look of complete amusement on her porcelain face. He slung himself down opposite her.

"Fair. Pff! Fair is for pigs with red fucking ribbons around their necks. Got a cigarette?"

Antonia opened her black YSL bag and pulled out a pack of Sobranies. Jonathon produced a Zippo lighter from his coat pocket and they lit up.

"Thanks. Jonathon is it?" She fixed him with her blue gaze.

"Yeah. Who are you?"

"Antonia Kent." She took a puff and leaned her elbows on the table, her hands at her chin, so she was closer to him.

"To what do we owe the pleasure of your company?" she asked. Josie could tell she was checking out the cashmere coat, the expensive jacket and shoes, the unusual gold Ebel watch with its green sharkskin band strapped casually around his strong wrist, and probably the waft of liquor as he came close to her.

"To the fact that he nearly cracked his skull open outside." Josie was unable to contain herself. "And that I, by some very strange coincidence, just happened to be standing right there." She cocked her head and stared at him. "Funny, that."

"Oh, Moonpie. You're not a martyr anymore, huh," he said very sweetly, then took a bite of his bagel and chewed it slowly. "Mm. Man, it's good to eat again." He took a sip of the coffee.

"No, Pookie, it appears you've graduated to paranoid schizophrenic status." He giggled and took another bite. "Don't fucking flatter yourself. I walk my dog—my beautiful wife's dog, that is—every single day."

"Jonathon." The knife felt wedged firmly in her ribs. The conversation was hurtling downhill at supersonic speed. She had to stop it. Before the blade twisted any further. "Look, we're trying to work here. I have to get back outside, to the shoot. You're welcome to stay as long as you want and eat as much as you like, until you feel well enough to go home." She tried to smile at him, but it felt forced and rubbery. "As long as it's okay with Antonia."

"Fine, darling. Make yourself at home." Antonia waved her cigarette around nonchalantly.

"Well, I might as well eat some more," he said. "Get my money's worth."

"Huh?" Josie said.

"So far I've eaten half a bagel and a slice or two of melon and a cup of coffee." He smiled at his audience. "That makes it, at three hundred thousand dollars, about the most expensive breakfast ever, I'd say."

She recoiled in horror. "Well, perhaps you should call the Guinness book of records! Take care of yourself." She stepped outside and slammed the door.

"So," she heard Antonia's smooth voice behind her, "where do you live, Jonathon?"

Josie, too angry for tears, stalked back to the fountain. Marcus caught up with her and took her hand, but she pushed him away, embarrassed, feeling like she'd been exposed, stripped naked.

"Don't ask," she said, in numb anticipation of any questions he might have, surely would have, about the painful shreds of her bond with the pathetic excuse for a man they'd just left behind. She felt as though Marcus had now witnessed, in blinding, vivid Technicolor, what a pathetic excuse for a woman she once was.

"I didn't intend to ask." He stopped her, turning her to face him with both his arms on hers, his smoky eyes looking kindly down at her. "It's none of my business. I just wanted to see if you're okay, and to tell you that I'm here if you need me." He let her go and they kept walking and she felt really stupid.

"Thanks," she managed to choke out.

She realized how little she knew about Marcus, beyond the feel of his skin and his mouth against hers and the unfamiliar sound of him breathing at night. In some ways she didn't want to know any more than that. It was too terrifying to reveal those things that had the potential for any sort of real intimacy.

Like spending months and years with someone and slowly finding out his idiosyncrasies; the annoying way he scratched himself when he sat watching TV, or belched in restaurants, or some other odious trait that grew to be unbearable; anything that didn't fit into the idealized mold she'd neatly squashed them into when she had first met him.

Although, she supposed drug addiction would be a little hard for anybody to live with and remain sane for too long. Walking out of your bedroom at three in the morning and finding your true love with a needle hanging out of his arm was rather tiresome, even for the most forgiving of souls.

"I'm sorry," she said, her head slumped down, unable to look at him. "He has this way of getting to me. Guess he knows me too well. It's been—"

"Nightmarish, I imagine."

"That doesn't even begin to describe it." Tears

pooled in her eyes. She looked down, trying to hide her face from him. When she looked back up, she realized he was studying her. She bowed her head again. It was too painful.

Maybe the superficial veneer was a lot easier to handle. That way everyone was always jolly and polite and there were no fights or acrimony when things got too uncomfortably close and dreams of the perfect guy, the perfect relationship, were shattered. Because she always ended up wanting way too much from men. More than they were capable of giving. This was certainly true of any of the guys she'd managed to attract so far, anyway. Although maybe with Marcus things might be different. Maybe she couldn't allow herself ever to fall for someone again. Not like she had before.

Getting close with guys had never brought her much beyond disappointment and the awful realization that she'd managed to pick yet another complete replica of her father, only more finely tuned, more developed in the fine art of abuse and self-destruction and endless low self-esteem. It simply didn't seem worth it, in the long run. She'd rather be on her own than with some emotionally distant loser in a designer suit, enveloped in all the trappings of wealth that only thinly masked the true horror of what their lives and minds were really like.

She finally glanced back up, and he was still looking at her, compassion in his eyes. He put his arm around her shoulder and gave a soft hug.

They reached the others, who were finishing the shot, the poor models nearly blue with cold.

"Oh, so you finally decided to return and do some work," Hamish said, with as much warmth as the wind-chill, as he casually shuffled through the stack of Polaroids he took before he shot each roll of film. "Who was that charming specimen? He didn't look like your run-of-the-mill homeless chap, with that Dior coat and the French poodle."

"He isn't," Josie said, a wave of grim hopelessness sloshing around her body.

"Luv, that was Jojo's old boyfriend," said Max, stuffing brushes into his Gucci carry bag. "That was Jonathon. Didn't he just get married to Victoire Santiago's daughter?"

"Yeah," she mumbled. Sinking even further.

"Oh, darls, that ugly twit couldn't power a twenty-watt globe. Not compared to you. And anyway, he's a cretin. You're much better off without him." He stroked the side of her face. "Jeez, ya sure can pick 'em, can't ya, love."

"Yeah, I'm brilliant at it. World's leading expert in cretinous men." *Oops. I've slept with two of the guys standing here! Who's the cretin?*

"What about that other one ya went out with, ya know, Godfrey or whatever his name was. He robbed banks for a crust, didn't he, darls?" Max was hooting now. "Can ya believe it?" He turned to Hamish. "He robbed more banks than Jesse James. Used to walk around the corner from his apartment in Hollywood, stick up the local bank, slip home through the back alley, and order in a pizza and a bag of smack with his earnings."

"Nice work, if you can get it," laughed Marcus.

Everyone was in guffaws now, even the models, as they struggled, shivering, into their coats. Everyone except Josie, who'd heard this story, all of it true, a hundred times before, had even dined out on it herself in more cheery moments.

"He didn't rob banks when he was with me," she snapped. "It was a long time after."

"She probably drove the getaway car," Hamish smiled wickedly.

"That's me. Gangsta's moll."

"I suppose that's the effect you have on men, isn't it, darling?" Hamish chortled. "Leave them ruined, fallen and broken in your wake; bank robbers and drug-addled shadows of their former selves."

"Thanks a lot." She collected a pair of shoes that were lying at the base of the fountain. "By the way. I'm having an opening party later. You're all invited."

"What opening? Whose?" asked Max.

"Wouldn't miss the opening of a fridge, would you, Maxi darling?" Hamish said.

"I'm opening a vein or two," she said. "Bring some wine and cheese. I hear it goes great with blood." She threw the shoes into a bag full of accessories and trudged dejectedly back to the van, hoping and praying that Jonathon had vanished.

That night the dream returned. The dream that had haunted her when she lived with Jonathon. Of sinking, silently sliding underwater and not knowing how to rise to the surface. Drowning. Always trying to scramble to the surface, to breathe, to survive, the water all around her, her long hair swirling through the bubbles like streamers in a breeze. And then finally getting to the top, gasping at the air, only to find she was lost at sea, alone with the wind and the clouds and the sun racing by at double speed, like a time-lapse movie.

She woke up gasping for breath.

The dream wouldn't leave her alone all morning. It nudged at the edges of her mind, seeping a profound sadness into her body. She tried to put it out of her mind. Like she'd tried for all her years with Jonathon.

Act as if. That's what they said in Al-anon. Act as if you're happy, as if you're not frightened, as if your life is perfect, and soon it will be. But she knew that to be a mere ruse, another form of the denial they so carefully pointed out was to be vanquished if one was ever to conduct a life of truth and sanity. Her life had fallen around her like a house of cards and she'd acted as if everything was normal, when in reality nothing could have been further from the truth. She'd wasted years acting as if. She didn't want to do that any more. She wanted to feel the pain, not simply mask it with some feeble platitude or the cocktail du jour.

By the afternoon, she'd driven herself half nuts. She finally went to the gym and worked herself out of her own head. She had to be up for the evening's festivities.

14

"So who is this Priscilla person?" Hamish relaxed into an antique paisley cushion on Josie's wheat linen sofa and blandly observed her apartment. "Is there any reason why I should know her?" He noticed the paint peeling off the corner of the ceiling, and the cheap-looking mantle over the fireplace, adorned with silver and tortoiseshell picture frames that contained what he assumed were family portraits; squalid displays of familial ties. He hated all that stuff. He didn't want to be reminded of his family.

"Not particularly," Josie said from the tiny kitchen, as she poured them each a glass of wine. "But she always gives great parties. They have an amazing art collection, and probably one of the nicest co-ops in the city. Plus, she is one of the most generous benefactors of the arts and she loves people like you."

It was his first visit to Josie's apartment. Her invitation had surprised him. He sensed that she'd been embarrassed to show him how she lived, and now he understood why. It was a rather shabby little place, although she did have some decent furniture and the color scheme was good. The couch was very soft and full of down. Not at all his taste, though. Much too antiquey and cozy. He preferred simple minimalist lines. Function following form; nothing too soft. The Zen look.

"People like me?" he sniffed.

"The creative elite, darling," she said, with an edge of sarcasm, handing him a glass, which he placed on an antique red lacquered Chinoise side table. Not bad, he thought, but not his style at all. She went to the window and unraveled a tortoiseshell bamboo blind, then pulled closed olive green sheer silk curtains that were trimmed in ruby and olive green fringe, mercifully blocking out the ugly view of the apartment building behind.

He had felt until then, sitting there in her softly lit apartment surrounded by the thick Manhattan night, rather like Jimmy Stewart in *Rear Window*, observing her neighbors conducting their endlessly dull lives. Although he supposed it might be amusing to watch the occasional carnal act, or some heinous crime of passion or domestic violence. Quite delicious, actually. And he could certainly get off if he knew somebody was watching him. Knowing his luck, though, his voyeur would be a bratty child or an old hag who'd call the police and he'd find himself, all kitted out in his leathers, being carted off to the local klink.

"She wants to meet you. She loves to mingle with the rich and famous."

"So what's she doing hanging around you? You're neither of those, darling."

"I guess it's my charming nature then, isn't it? I don't have to be rich or famous. I'm simply fabulous on my own. Unlike you." She poked her tongue out at him.

"Well, darling"—he gave Josie that condescending smile he had perfected over the years—"it's good to be recognized for one's body of work. That way one can behave like a total pig and still be adored."

"Adored? How do you know people still adore you? How do you know they ever did?"

She sat down next to him on the couch, crossed her long legs, and bounced a red satin Saint Laurent shoe in his line of vision. Her eyes had that mischievous look that he loved. He felt torn. He always did when he was around her. She was one of the few women who could tempt him. He had to stop himself. It would only lead to disaster.

"Darling, everybody loves me. Simply everybody," he said. "And if they don't it's their loss." She snorted at him.

"You're not actually planning on wearing that bit of fluff are you?" He was disappointed in her. He'd always thought she was beyond falling for the latest trend. Normally a picture of elegance, tonight she was done up in what appeared to be a bit of shriveled old aqua cut velvet. A long skirt, with a Chinesey-looking red silk top over it. He knew it came from Viago, the shop in London where style mavens and fashion junkies flocked to, and had definitely cost her a small fortune. But to him it just looked like shredded, colorful rags that had spent entirely too long in the dryer.

"What's the matter with it?" Her brow wrinkled. He smiled.

He glanced down at his Oswald Boateng suit and thought with smug pleasure how he'd been wearing Oswald's clothes long before the fashion press had got their carnivorous paws on the designer and made him a star. He made a conscious effort to stay way ahead of everyone else in matters of style and fashion. On his never-ending travels around the world he always found time to visit young artists' and designers' ateliers. It was his way of staying in the forefront.

"Nothing, if you like looking like an overpriced bag lady. You Aussies do fancy a bit of color, don't you?"

"Shut up. And drink up. We have to get going."

"I said we'd meet Antonia at Reggiano's for a drink first. It's on the way, isn't it?"

"Antonia! You invited Antonia? Why?"

"I didn't invite her. Your friend Priscilla did." Hamish curled his lips in pleasure at the sight of Josie's poor attempt to conceal her annoyance. He wanted to torture her. Make her squirm. Give her that edge. Then he'd feel better.

"She did, huh?" Josie kicked at his shin with her red silk shoe. Her green eyes flashed angrily at him. "You're lying, aren't you? I know you. You just wanted to see my reaction."

"Ouch! I did not!" he laughed. "I'm not lying. She received an invitation last week." He stood up and straightened his suit. "Come on then. We don't want to keep the ex-Mrs. K. waiting. She doesn't like it. She may not be as pleasant toward you as she has been in the past."

"Oh, what a pity. She's been such a shining beacon of charm already," she snapped, storming across the room. He watched her grab for her overcoat in the crowded hall closet, snatch up a red silk evening bag and felt himself smile when she slammed the door behind them.

"This place is always packed with the same tired, old faces," Josie grumbled, as they entered Reggiano's foyer a few minutes later and headed for the bar. "The same bunch of Euros who drag their faux aristocratic bones around the upper East Side every evening. It's so tedious." She was in a foul mood now.

"Darling, you're only saying that because you feel like an outsider here." Hamish scanned the room.

"What is with you tonight? You've done nothing but insult me since you arrived at my place."

"Darling, you know I'm only joking."

"Actually you're always insulting me." She scowled at him. He looked more pleased with himself than ever. His eyes shone like little gray buttons. His tiny lips had that curl to them.

"Oh, you can handle it, darling."

"What if I don't want to handle it?"

"Why would you want to spoil the fun? Why change now?"

"I'm not in the mood, that's why."

"Relax, darling." He signaled to the waiter and ordered two champagne cocktails.

"Just stop thinking and have a drink, darling. That'll make you feel better." He smiled that supercilious smirk. The one that got her blood boiling.

"You just love making people feel uncomfortable, don't you?" She glared at him. "It gives you a kick, doesn't it? You're sick, Hamish." She wanted a drink now.

"Now, there's a brilliant observation."

"And where's Cruella Kent anyway? She's late."

"Perhaps her broomstick isn't working," he chortled.

"God, what a pair you must have made. A couple of snakes married to each other." Josie tossed back a large mouthful of the bubbly.

"We did our best."

"What was your home called? Fork Tongue Palace?" She drained the glass.

"Who's doing the insulting now?"

"You were right. Why spoil the fun at this late stage?" She smirked back at him. "Seems like you were perfect for each other. So refresh my fading memory. Why'd you get divorced?"

"I can't really remember anymore, it was so long ago.

Let's just say that two snakes make a better working couple than a married one."

"Guess the venom needed to spread out a bit. Kill off the competition."

"Something like that." Hamish raised an eyebrow. "Ahh, here she is. The queen viper in person." He looked over Josie's shoulder and blew a kiss. "Hello, darling."

Although she didn't feel at all like greeting Antonia, Josie, wondering what black-and-white ensemble she'd be dazzled by, turned to face her nemesis. Actually, she'd never had a nemesis before. The thought was thrilling in a strange sort of way.

At Antonia's side, disturbingly handsome in a navy suit, pale gray shirt and tie, his arm entwined with a black lace and leather sleeve, stood Marcus. Josie felt her heart sink and her knees go weak when he looked at her and smiled. Her eyes darted away, back toward Hamish. A look of smug glee enveloped his small face.

"What's the matter with you?" Priscilla peered at Josie. "Your face looks like thunder," she hissed out of the corner of her mouth. "Pull yourself together . . . Calvin, darling! So glad you could make it. How are you?"

"You know I'd never miss one of your parties, Priscilla," Calvin crooned, as he kissed both her cheeks.

"Calvin, you remember Josie Vaughn, don't you? She stayed with us at the beach for a while last summer. We brought her to lunch one day."

"Oh, yes! Hi, so nice to see you again," said Calvin, although Josie could tell he had absolutely no idea who she was.

"Hi." Josie wanly shook the great designer's hand. Tried to force out a smile, but it didn't want to come. She stood in Priscilla's beautiful living room, surrounded by famous art and famous people, defeated and furious.

The walk over from Reggiano's had been torturous, and it had nothing to do with her impossibly tight red satin shoes. She really felt like the ugly sister tonight. Shoes she'd squashed her big feet into for pure vanity's sake. Again. An outfit she'd worn because she thought it looked hip, only to spy two other people in the same ridiculously shriveled velvets. Talk about fashion victim. Hamish had been right. How bloody annoying.

Hamish. She could kill Hamish, kill Antonia, and slice Marcus's head and balls off in one swoop of a machete. She'd lost them in the crowded living room the minute they had arrived.

"So, what the hell is the matter with you?" Priscilla dragged her by her arm into the kitchen. "Talk to me."

"Oh, nothing. I don't even know where to begin. Except I'm mad at you."

"Me? What have I done?"

"How come you invited Antonia Kent?" she pouted.

"Antonia who?"

"Oh, come on, P. You do know who you invite to these famous soirees of yours, don't you?" Josie made a sweeping gesture with her hand around the enormous kitchen, bustling with uniformed maids and waiters. "Or do you just pull names out from social pages of the latest fashion rags?"

"Oh, nice, nice. You're really in fine form tonight."

"Antonia Kent is the dark-haired witch I walked in with. The one in the Richard Tyler black lace and leather job you drooled over."

"Oh, her. Why didn't you say so?"

Josie rolled her eyes. "How come you invited her? Obviously you don't even know her." She could tell her voice must be raised, because a couple of the waiters turned to look at her.

"What's it to you? You must know her or you wouldn't have arrived with her."

"She's Hamish's wife."

"I don't get it. He's married, huh. I thought you were keen on him. There's no fucking way I would have invited him if you'd bothered to tell me he was married." Priscilla lit a cigarette from a flame on the stove and pointed it at Josie's face. "Honestly, Josie, when are you going to grow up and stop doing stupid things like dating married men?"

"It's not like that. He's not actually married to her. And I'm not dating him. She's—"

"For Christ's sake, will you make up your mind? Either he's married or he's not. In any case I didn't invite her. But who's that gorgeous boy she had her red claws firmly sunk into? Now that is a hunk."

"Tell me about it," Josie said, slumping against the marble countertop. She felt like sobbing.

"What is going on with you?"

"Oh, God, P., you're right. I sure do some stupid things. I'm a complete moron. I—"

Just then the Saunders's butler approached and whispered something in Priscilla's ear. Her eyes widened. "Oh, God. Let's get the guy as quietly as possible into the blue bedroom and call a doctor. Actually, don't bother. Doctor Gene's here tonight. Who is it, anyway?"

"We don't know, Mrs. Saunders," David said.

"Fuck. Here it is, barely even ten o'clock and I've got people passing out in my bathrooms. What do they think this is, Lot 61?" Priscilla stubbed out her cigarette and rushed out of the kitchen. "Sorry, Josie, hon, can we talk about this later? And, David, have you seen my husband?" She charged out of the kitchen.

Josie, curious as to the identity of the mystery flopster, followed in Priscilla's wake, inhaling her Boucheron perfume, ignoring the set of Warhol prints lining the hallway. Priscilla, she'd already noticed, was done up to the nines in the latest Christian Dior couture: a short dress of impossibly beautiful floral silk taffeta with a nipped-in waist and a long train that rustled behind her as she strode to the far side of the vast apartment through the back corridors, avoiding her guests in the front salons. Her red hair was curled into a soft French twist, with tendrils falling by her face, and nestling in her ample décolleté was that fabulous emerald necklace Josie would kill for. A pang of envy shot through her. She wanted this life, this wealth, a loving husband, the fabulous art collection, and the social recognition. All she had now was a sagging career. No man, no money, and no life to speak of.

Nothing was working out for her here. She felt beaten. Like she didn't belong anywhere. Homeless and lost.

"He's in here, Mrs. Saunders," David indicated, as they reached one of the guest bathrooms. There was a maid stationed outside, to ward off any other visitors. Priscilla opened the door, stepped into the cool of the white marble bathroom, and gasped. Josie looked over her shoulder. On the floor lay a young guy, with the sleeve of his crisp white shirt rolled up, his belt wrapped around his arm, and a needle hanging from the crook of his elbow.

"Quickly! Find Doctor Gene."

David scurried off.

"Let me see him," said Josie, pushing yards of silk taffeta train out of her way and kneeling down beside the slumped figure. She put her fingers to his neck and found a thin pulse. "He's still alive." She pounded on his chest and gave him the breath of life.

"You seem to know what you're doing," said Priscilla, with a certain admiration.

"I ought to. I've had some experience with these things, remember?" Josie replied. "Wake up!" She yelled and slapped at the gray, sweaty face. Very handsome. Soft dark hair pulled back in a messy ponytail, high cheek bones, and almond-shaped eyes.

"Yew, did Jonathon do this a lot? How gross." Priscilla grimaced.

"Only once—at the Royal Hotel. What a nightmare. If his father hadn't been spending thirty grand a month for that suite, I'm sure they would have booted us out. It was terrifying. He nearly died. So could this kid. Wake up!" She slapped his face again. "Who is he anyway?"

"Haven't the foggiest."

"God, Priscilla. Shouldn't you start checking your guest lists a little more carefully? I mean it's not like he could sneak in without someone seeing him."

"He's quite well dressed." Priscilla ignored her, leaning over the top of them, hands planted on her taffeta hips.

"Very. Charvet shirt and silk bow tie." Josie checked the label in the back of his collar. She'd recognize a Charvet bow tie practically blindfolded. "Lobb shoes."

"Not your average street corner junkie." Priscilla almost seemed impressed that someone so well dressed should OD in her guest bathroom.

"No. Probably just your average Park Avenue brat."

David returned with a man whom Josie assumed must be Doctor Gene, a balding, tanned man in his midforties wearing a dinner jacket and collarless shirt. She hated collarless shirts. They reminded her of car salesmen, or Hollywood agents. *Same thing, really.* The doctor pulled the needle out of the boy's arm. It had no other track marks on it.

"Not your average junkie at all," Josie said.

Doctor Gene and David picked up the boy and carried him across the hallway, into a bedroom crisply decorated in blue and white. They lay him down on a king-size four-poster bed adorned with blue and white linens, all starched to perfection. Josie loved this room. It felt like a seaside cottage on Nantucket.

They stood watching the motionless body as Doctor Gene dialed the phone and spoke rapidly to someone.

"My driver, Fred, is on his way up with my bag of goodies," he said. "We must get him over to Lenox Hill emergency room fast. Who is he?"

"I've never seen him before," Priscilla sighed. "David, who's on the door tonight?"

"Henry, Mrs. Saunders."

"Good. Henry's been here forever. He's probably seen a lot worse than this. Will you phone down and tell him we've got a minor problem—that one of our guests has had a bit too much to drink and that we're bringing him down on the service elevator?"

"Yes, Mrs. Saunders." David hurried out.

"Don't worry, Priscilla," the doctor said, "we'll take care of it. But we have to find out who he is. We can't just dump him there."

"Jesus!" Priscilla groaned. "How on earth am I going to do that? There's at least a dozen people I've never even met out there." She shot a sheepish glance at Josie. "What am I supposed to do—make an announcement? Or ask everyone as they leave if they're missing their junkie escort? What a fucking nightmare. I can't believe Genevieve got sick this week. There's always a drama when she's not around."

Genevieve was Priscilla's secretary, who normally took care of all her social matters. Her absence explained the disorganized guest list.

"He's not a junkie," Josie said. "He doesn't have any tracks on his arms."

"Well you'd know, sweetie, wouldn't you," Priscilla smirked.

Josie glowered at her and headed back to the bathroom to look for the kid's jacket. Not only could she not find a jacket, or wallet of any kind lying around, but there were none of the usual things she knew people used to fix up. No spoon, no matches, no bits of crumpled paper or plastic bags that held drugs. The only evidence she could see of the boy being there at all was a thin spray of blood across one of the white marble walls.

When she returned, the doctor was injecting the boy with a syringe of brownish liquid. "Fred! We've got to get him across the street," he ordered. "Now."

Fred looked more to Josie like a Mafia bodyguard than a limo driver. His skin was pockmarked, although cleanly shaven, and one side of his face was menacingly lopsided, as if he'd had a premature stroke and would get even with whoever had caused it.

They picked the boy up off the smooth, white bed, draped his arms over their shoulders, and pulled him unevenly between them to the door, his black velvet–slippered feet dragging behind him, head slumped down onto his chest.

"Thanks, Gene," Priscilla sighed, as she slumped down onto the bed. "Jesus. What an evening. And where the fuck is my husband? He's never here when I need him. I could rip his scrawny throat out. I just know he's been fucking someone lately. And I think I know who it is." She glared at Josie as she said this. Josie felt her jaw drop open and stared at her friend, shocked. Surely P. could not possibly think that she was Richard's lover? Surely not! She was about to respond, but before she had a chance, Priscilla turned abruptly away from her and said to the doctor, "What else have you got in that bag? I could use a little pick-me-up." She peered curiously into the depths of his black leather bag.

"Forget it, Priscilla," he laughed. "You've had enough help already this week." Josie wondered what exactly he'd been helping Priscilla with. She never would have suspected P. of taking anything more than an aspirin or the odd sleeping pill. But you never knew. Nothing would surprise her these days. Suddenly she felt more distant from P.'s surreal, perfect life than ever before.

She teetered back down the hallway, in the excruciating red satin stilettos, toward the sounds of laughter and music and the mirthful tinkling of glass, thinking she must have simply mistaken P.'s look just now. She decided it was time to enjoy herself, so she banished P.'s look from her mind. It was too preposterous an idea to even consider.

But the vision of that poor boy, and the memory of Jonathon several years ago, near death, made her feel very sad and heavy.

The party was in full swing. Josie paused at the entry to the main living room, awed at the beauty of it. The original ballroom when the apartment had been built at the turn of the century, it had fallen into disuse for over forty years, after the death of Sophie Van Horn, one of the great socialites of the Gilded Age. When Priscilla and Richard Saunders purchased the Candela-designed co-op from her granddaughter, Isabelle, it took them three years to restore the room to its former palatial splendor.

Glorimundi, the floral designers, had done an amazing job. Twenty-foot-high columns, overgrown with ivy and tendrils of jasmine, which crept over the delicate Adamesque plaster work on the ceiling, gave the appearance of an ancient fantasy garden. Gigantic urns of beautiful flowers, ivy, and votive candles edged the walls and softly lit columns of ivy and white flowers draped over the tables. The effect was breathtaking. An incandescent glow washed all imperfections from the guests' faces as they sat laughing, picking at food from the buffet in the dining room, or dancing to Samy Goz's orchestra.

Everyone sported their designer best. She spied

Hamish chatting to Faisa Nobowitz, the famously witty writer who never actually wrote anything after her first highly acclaimed novel, but lived off the kindness of her wealthy and influential friends. Faisa, her hair clipped extremely short, dressed in her regulation uniform of man's tuxedo and patent leather loafers, had an ebony cigarette holder dangling out of one corner of her mouth as she sucked on a glass of champagne and talked all at once, an art she had perfected over her many years as party guest extraordinaire.

"Amazing how perfect lighting gets a party going." Marcus slipped an arm around Josie's waist. She pulled away.

"So you're an expert on parties, huh?" she said, refusing to look at him, keeping her eyes firmly set on the room. "Figures. Seems you're quite the expert at a few things."

"What do you mean?"

"Try womanizing for starters."

"Josie, it's not what you think." Marcus grabbed her arm. "I've gotta talk to you."

"You don't know what I think." She pulled her arm away. *I think I'm a fucking fool. I think I'm going to jump from the nearest window.* She grabbed a flute of champagne from a passing waiter's silver tray.

"Josie! Please. We got some great news today! I've been dying to tell you."

"Leave me alone, Marcus." She gulped from the flute, hoping for relief. She felt betrayed by him, angry with herself for even hoping there would be anything significant between them. Now that Antonia had sunk her fangs into him there was no longer the slimmest chance of that possibility.

"Josie, I've gotta talk to you!" He pulled her arm again, harder now, so she had to turn. The champagne spilled onto the parquet.

"Now look what you've done!" She knew the hurt was showing in her face. He dragged her out into the hallway, away from the crowded room. She struggled in his grip. "Let me go!"

"Josie, will you just shut up and listen! Antonia sent the pictures off to Bezel and Crocket. They went crazy over them."

"Great, Marcus, great. I wish you all the best. Now leave me alone, okay?"

"Josie—they went crazy over *you!* They want *you!*"

"What the hell are you talking about! Let me go!" He put his hands around the top of her arms, pinning her to the wall. "Stop this! Let me go!" She kicked his shin.

"Ouch! Josie, for God's sake! Will you just listen to me? They want you for the Great Gams pantyhose campaign! They've been looking for someone for months. They want you!"

"Oh, what a load. Is that the best you can come up with? Try to flatter poor stupid Josie so she doesn't—"

"It's true, Josie. It's true! They called Antonia late yesterday, after the shoot. They said you had the best legs they'd seen so far."

"Is this your idea of some kind of sick joke?"

"Unfortunately not." Antonia's razor-sharp voice pierced the air.

"When did you slither out here," Josie said. Marcus took his hands away. They both turned to Antonia, who was enveloped in a flimsy lace dress with strategically placed panels of leather that barely hid her nipples and crotch. Josie hated to admit it, but she looked fantastic.

"Charming," Antonia said. "Is that any way to thank me?"

"Thank you? For what? Being a world-class bitch?" She drained the few remaining drops from her glass.

"For getting you a contract worth thousands of dollars." Antonia smiled. "Of course, Josie darling, I understand you feeling insecure about your looks. But don't worry, they're looking for an over-forty model."

"Over forty!" Josie felt her eyes widen in horror. *Oh Christ.* "I'm not over forty, for one, and secondly—how could you possibly negotiate a contract for me without even asking me first?" She felt red with fury.

"We tried calling you, Josie," Marcus said. "But your phone was busy all day."

We? So, you were with her all day, huh. No wonder I felt suicidal. Intuition.

"Well, of course, Josie darling"—Antonia took a small mirror out of her purse and plied her lips with ruby paint—"you don't have to do the job. But I wouldn't have thought you could afford to turn up your nose at over fifty thousand dollars."

"Oh." Josie tried to act casual.

"Well"—Antonia looked highly amused as she snapped her purse shut—"let's talk about it on Monday, shall we? Come on, darling." She fluttered her ice blue peepers at Marcus and put her arm in his. Marcus offered Josie a wan smile as he was pulled back inside and onto the dance floor.

Josie stood for a moment, in stunned disbelief at this new development, wondering if there wasn't some strange concoction in the punch. Everyone was absolutely bonkers tonight.

Suddenly she was starving, and she realized she hadn't sat down all evening and her feet were killing her. Maybe hunger was driving her nuts.

"I must be hallucinating," she muttered, as she turned back to the ballroom. "None of this has happened. I've just got low blood sugar or something . . ."

"Talking to yourself is a sign of madness, you know, shug," boomed Andy Wyatt's voice, from behind her.

"Oh, Andy!" She turned and smiled for the first time

that night. "I'm way beyond that. I'm certifiable. It's great to see you. How're you doing?"

"All the better for seeing your beautiful face, shug." He smiled, leaned forward, and planted a kiss on her cheek.

"You look great, Andy," she said, and she meant it. He had on a dinner suit and a plain black bow tie. Somehow even his frizzy hair looked sharper. He'd had it cut, she realized, and he wasn't trying to cover up his bald spot. He still wore the ugly pink glasses. And the pinky ring. But an elegant, slim watch peeped from beneath his French-cuffed left wrist, and she couldn't see any sign of the bracelet.

"Not even Ah can screw up a tuxedo," he laughed. She laughed too, and blushed, as if he'd read her mind and knew how judgmental she was about clothes.

"God, am I that obvious?" She winced. "Sorry. Don't take it personally. I can't help myself. It is my job, after all."

"Good," he said, taking her arm. "Then you can give me a professional rundown of the crazy fashions at this party, shug. Boy, have Ah seen some sights tonight."

"You, too, huh?" she said, thinking of the boy with the needle hanging from his arm and wondering who he was and if he'd make it through the night.

"I'm famished, Andy, what about you?"

"Darlin', I could eat a horse and chase the rider." He led her into the living room, skirted her around the dancing throng and into the dining room.

They filled their plates and sat down.

"Interesting crowd," she said, trying to make polite conversation. She always felt shy at parties, like she didn't quite know what to say beyond the most basic of superficial pleasantries.

"Ah'm not too good at these kinda things, darlin'.

Usually squirrel myself away with a business associate. That's the only reason Ah'm ever invited to parties anyhow—to cut some kinda new deal."

"Oh, surely not!"

"Well, shug, Ah sure as hell ain't invited for my looks, or this amazin' body," he laughed.

Pierre Paraux, the handsome and infamously well-endowed hairdresser to the rich and stylish, approached the table, a tall, model-slash-actress-type girl draped from his arm like a new handbag.

"Josephine, cheri, you look beautiful tonight." He leaned over and grazed her mouth with his full, sensuous lips. She could tell he was drunk. He seemed more languid than usual, if that was at all possible. Beneath his open-necked white piqué shirt Josie saw smooth tanned skin and a few dark chest hairs. Extremely attractive. Extremely bad news.

The girl radiated sex. Her long bottle-blond hair nearly hit the bottom of her very short dress and the top of her very long shapely legs. She wore a white Herve Leger elastic bandage dress so tight Josie thought she could detect individual pubic hairs peering through it. Her bosom popped winsomely over the edge. If the dress was any tighter it'd squeeze her organs onto the table. She reminded Josie of one of those old pens she remembered seeing as a child in the shape of a scantily clad woman. If you squeezed the bit in the middle, the top of the dress fell down and her pink plastic tits zoomed out.

Josie made the introductions, and at the mention of Andy's name the girl nearly genuflected. Josie thought her tits would explode out any second.

"Oh, you're that guy, the cosmetics mogul," she purred, dropping Pierre's arm and sitting right down next to Andy. "I'm so pleased to meet you." She crossed her legs in Andy's face. His eyes bulged.

"If this is your idea of squirreling yourself away in a corner with a business associate, I have absolutely no sympathy for you." Josie laughed at him. "C'mon Pierre, let's go cut up some rug."

"*Quoi*?" Pierre looked puzzled.

"Dance, cheri"—she grabbed his tanned hand—"let's go dance!"

"Enjoying yourself, I see," Hamish said. He'd appeared by her side at the bar the minute she stopped dancing. "Taken a shine to old Donkey Paraux, have we?"

"You got a problem with that?" She smiled. "You're just jealous."

"Pffh! Of that slimy frog? Hardly. Has-been hairdressers don't do it for me, darling."

"What's happened to you, Hamish? You used to be so much fun in the old days. Now all you do is sit around and knock everyone. You can't stand the thought of anyone enjoying themselves, can you?"

They were both silent for a minute. She stared at her red shoes and could feel her feet painfully inside them. She felt like throwing them away or, better yet, at him. She didn't understand him.

"You set me up tonight, didn't you?" She watched his lips curl up in satisfaction. "Well—mission accomplished, Hamish. You made me feel awful. Happy now?"

"Darling, that was hardly the goal of the exercise."

"No? Then what was? Explain it to me, please. I'm all ears."

"From what I've seen, darling, you're all legs," he said, his beady eyes shooting bullets into her. "And those legs have been in some very interesting positions lately, haven't they, darling?" He turned and walked off before she had a chance to respond, leaving her wide-eyed with humiliation.

"You're leaving so soon?" Priscilla said. Josie had plonked down next to her at one of the tables, to say good-bye. On Priscilla's other side sat Doctor Gene and a trashy brunette Josie had never seen before. On the other side of the table, Priscilla's husband, Richard, sat in deep conversation with Andy Wyatt. Priscilla had changed into another beautifully crafted Galliano, a cobalt blue chiffon slip dress that intensified her blue eyes. An antique sapphire and diamond choker had replaced the emeralds.

"I don't think I can take too much more drama. I'm exhausted." Josie slurped at another flute of champagne. "Did you find out about the boy? Is he all right?"

Priscilla glared at her, then shot her eyes toward Andy and mouthed, "Shh! Not now!"

"Oh! By the way, happy anniversary. No one gave you guys a toast," Josie tried to cover up, feeling her words slurring. She was drunk.

"Wow! It's your anniversary? Happy anniversary!" The blond bimbo who'd attached herself to Andy's side raised her glass.

"Thanks." Priscilla smiled blankly at her.

"How long have you all been married?" The girl purred in an overly cute Southern accent Josie knew hadn't been there an hour earlier.

"Ah, God—it's been way too long, hasn't it, darling?" Priscilla looked across the table to her husband. She wasn't smiling now.

"Not long enough, my beautiful wife," he replied. "Happy anniversary, darling." He raised his glass and blew her a kiss, but his eyes looked flat, like he was phoning it in.

"Happy anniversary!" echoed all the others.

"Well, thanks for a wonderful evening." Josie rose and kissed Richard, as he stood up. "It was very exciting."

"Exciting? Really? Well I'm glad you enjoyed yourself. You look beautiful tonight. I didn't see enough of you."

"You didn't see any of me," she laughed. "My two favorite moguls were otherwise engaged. Squirreled in corners making deals." She winked at Andy.

"How are you getting home, darlin'?" Andy stood up and took her hands in his.

"Oh, I've got a ride," she lied, her eyes going from him to the girl and back. "My pumpkin awaits. Bye, Andy." She giggled and kissed him full on the mouth, just to annoy the girl, then walked back around the table, leaned down to Priscilla, kissed her on both cheeks, and whispered, "Call me."

"Bye, hon," Priscilla said. Then almost inaudibly she whispered, "Not a word, okay?"

Josie nodded and left, without looking back for any signs of Hamish or Marcus and Antonia.

Downstairs a line of black limos idled along the block. Josie stepped out onto Park Avenue and hailed a cab.

15

"Don't be ridiculous, Josie." Priscilla's voice sounded pinched. Dressed in a black Gucci skirt, cashmere sweater, and high-heeled boots, she paced the floor of Josie's apartment. Josie lounged on her crumpled linen sofa in old sweatpants and a T-shirt, feeling rather crumpled herself. It was exhausting just watching P. "Of course he's a real doctor. He's got an office on Park Avenue, just two doors away from me."

"How convenient. What kind of doctor?"

"He's a holistic psychiatrist."

"Oh. Well I guess that explains it." Josie leaned back on the soft paisley cushions and took a sip of tea from a bone china cup. Her head hurt.

"Explains what?" Priscilla sounded defensive now.

"Oh, I don't know . . . he just seems sort of . . . quackish, if you ask me."

"Quackish! He's supposed to be the best in town!" Priscilla's red curls shook in annoyance around her pale face.

"Why is he making house calls to you? That reeks to me of quackishness, P."

"Well—nobody asked your opinion."

"Well—I'm giving it anyway. And what did he do with that boy, and who is he anyway?"

Priscilla stopped pacing and looked down at Josie. Her eyes filled with horror.

"He's in a coma," she whispered. "Oh, Josie, it's dreadful. He's in a coma."

"Oh, Jesus." Josie felt a chill rise through her whole body.

"It gets worse."

"Worse?"

"Apparently Gene gave him the wrong antidote."

"I knew it! Jesus Christ. See? That Doctor Gene is a complete quack. I told you so. Oh, fuck. That poor boy." She got up, took the cups into the kitchen, and shakily poured them both some more tea. "So did you find out who he is?"

"They're still checking. We couldn't find any ID at the apartment." Priscilla sipped from the white china, her face ashen.

"And you still haven't figured out how he got there? Nobody's called about him?"

"No. Even Henry, the doorman, doesn't remember seeing him."

"Well, Henry's about ninety in the shade, so that's no surprise. What about Richard? What's he saying about all of this?"

"Richard is being his usual endearing self." Josie watched Priscilla's face sag.

"Oh, Josie." She sat on the sofa and put her head on Josie's shoulder. "What am I going to do?"

"Do? There's nothing you can do, except pray. Oh, Jesus. What a mess."

"No—about Richard!"

"What about Richard?"

"He stormed out this morning! He said I'd made a

complete fuckup of the party and that this was all my fault. He said we should've had tighter security and that I was on my own to fix any problems that arose." She put her face in her hands and sobbed. Josie put her arm around her friend and patted her.

"I just don't know what's happened to us, Josie. He's just so distant these days."

There was a knock on Josie's door. "Who the hell can that be?" Josie said, annoyed. "Honestly. The doormen here are useless. Talk about bad security." Josie crossed her living room, marveling at the size. It felt like a shoe box compared with the Saunders's vast apartment. A baby's shoe box. Priscilla had bigger closets than this apartment. Well, at least it was hers. She felt lucky to have a roof over her head.

"Who is it, Josie?" Priscilla wiped at the running mascara from beneath her eyes with the hem of her cashmere sweater.

Josie opened the little peephole and peered through. Through the fish-eye lens she could make out the distorted image of a huge bouquet of flowers. She opened the door and practically snatched them from Giovanni.

"'For beautiful Josie,'" she read from the card, "'sorry we didn't see enough of each other last night. Your favorite mogul.' Wow, pretty nice, huh?"

"Mogul?" Priscilla eyed the enormous basket of fragrant pink roses and lilies suspiciously, then grabbed the card from Josie. "Why would Richard send you flowers?"

"Richard? These are from Andy Wyatt. He sent me flowers after that disastrous blind date you set me up on." Josie felt Priscilla's eyes boring into her. She put the flowers on the coffee table and stood back to admire them.

"A complete disaster," she went on, "and you hadn't even met him. As it turned out he's actually a pretty good guy, Andy. Not my type at all. I mean, the guy has a face like a foot! I could never kiss him. Yuk. But a nice guy when all's said and done and let's face it—he certainly had to put up with a lot of shit from me. It was a total nightmare running into Jonathon again. I was a complete mess. I locked myself in the bathr . . . What? What are you looking at me like that for?" Priscilla's face was pinched in rage.

"What?" Josie said again.

"It's you, isn't it?" Priscilla whispered. "It's you."

"What's me?"

"It's you Richard's been seeing."

"Get a grip! There's no way on earth I'd have an affair with one of my best friends' husbands! Or anybody else's husband for that matter! Get serious!"

"It all makes sense now." Priscilla picked up her Gucci bag and started for the door.

"Priscilla! This is ridiculous! I'm your best friend! You've flipped your bloody wig! Just stop this now!"

She turned at the door. "If you're lying to me you know I'll find out. And I'll ruin you in this town. I swear to God I'll make sure you never get another job here ever again. And not one goddamned date either."

"Oh, that'll be a big leap," Josie said. "I'm already unemployed and dateless. Jesus, P., I can't believe you're saying this to me. It's insane!" She put her hands on Priscilla's shoulders. "Please! Get it through that hard-boiled brain of yours—I am *not* sleeping with Richard!" She tried to hug Priscilla but was pushed away. They stood silently facing each other for what seemed like ages.

"Promise, cross your heart and hope to die in a cellar full of rats?" For a second Priscilla still looked furious, but the words made them both burst out laughing.

"Promise. On my life I promise." Josie crossed her heart.

"I'm sorry, Josie. I'm just nuts today. I've had about two hours' sleep. I think these herbal diet pills are giving me the creeps."

"You're stressed." Josie gave her a hug and kissed her on the cheek. "Go home and rest. Everything will work out just fine, you'll see."

But it wouldn't, Josie thought, as she watched Priscilla disappear into the elevator. It wouldn't be fine at all.

16

"Josie. You must go and see the ad agency today. And wear some very high heels and a very short, sexy dress." Antonia's voice sliced through the phone into Josie's eardrum early Monday morning. A voice that could cut through diamonds.

"Oh! H . . . hi, Antonia!" Josie rasped and rolled over to check her bedside clock. "You mean dress like a hooker?" She sat up straight and tried to sound sharp.

It wasn't even eight AM. *She's keen,* Josie thought, then wondered if Marcus was lying next to Antonia. A sliver of hurt and shame pierced the lining of her stomach.

"I mean dress the way you normally do, except sexy."

"Oh, okay." *Is she saying I'm not sexy? Bitch. What does it matter? She's calling about work.*

"Come by here first, and I'll brief you and Marcus before you go."

"To your house?" *Marcus is coming too? Oh, no.* Panic jolted the sliver of hurt, sending shock waves around her body.

"No, darling." Antonia sounded even more clipped now. "Here to the office. Some of us do work, you know."

"Oh." The sliver felt like a finely honed hammer clawing at her insides. "Y . . . yes. Well, uh, can't I just go there by myself? I, uh—"

"Josie, this is not a time to be unprofessional. Be here at eleven. Your appointment is at twelve." The phone clicked dead.

Oh, no. This can't be happening. But, yes, it is! "Fifty thousand smackeroonies! I could be out of debt!" She jumped out of bed and did a little jig. "Oh goody! I could be debt free!"

She grabbed her white toweling robe from behind the closet door, glancing down to see the red silk spiked heels lying where she'd thrown them on Saturday night. They reminded her of Hamish and suddenly she was awash with mortification again. He knew everything. He knew she'd slept with Marcus. Christ, the whole world must know. Well too bad. Too late now. But the mortification was more than just her sleeping with his assistant, as if that wasn't enough.

Now she'd have to face Marcus again, and how embarrassing would that be? She could never escape all the pathetic mistakes she'd made. They always came back to haunt her.

Get a grip! Things could be a lot worse! Maybe you'll have a job by the end of the day. A huge job!

She went into the kitchen to torture some coffee beans.

17

Legs lined the hallway. Hundreds of them, illustrated, painted, photographed, fashioned from plastic and from wood and steel, framed and on pedestals, all in perfect nubile fantasy shapes; a kitsch envoy transporting the visitors into a salon where even more legs decorated the walls. Long legs, shapely legs, legs with boots and shoes and slippers and spike heels gracing their feet. Some of them were in the air thrusting from skirts appearing out of the glossy white floor, as if the upper part of the torso had been buried beneath and was dangling from the ceiling into the apartment below. In the middle of the long, white oval room knelt a woman, dressed in thigh-high, spike-heeled black leather boots and a black leather corset, her breasts protruding menacingly from the laced-up front. On her back rested a heavy glass top.

"Wow," whispered Marcus.

Josie recognized the woman under the glass coffee table as one of Allen Jones's famous sixties sculptures. "What kind of whacko is this guy?"

"A shrine to the leg." Their host held out his arm with a proud flourish.

"This is truly amazing, Mr. Gottlieb."

"Marv, Josephine, call me Marv," he replied, sucking on a large cigar. He raised his face to Josie, or rather to her bustline. Her five-inch Giuseppe Zanotti stilettos lent her a towering advantage over Marv, who was vertically challenged to begin with.

She had a commanding view of the age spots that spread over his bald cranium and down onto his wizened visage. Enormous black-rimmed spectacles, like the ones Josie had seen in photographs of the famous agent Swifty Lazar, magnified his pale, cataract-rimmed eyes into watery fishlike bulbs.

His otherwise impeccable attire of a gray hand-tailored suit and crisp white shirt was marred by a flesh pink silk tie in the shape of a leg, replete with a black fishnet stocking and high-heeled red shoe. Its hideousness almost elevated it to the heights of sartorial eminence. Almost.

They'd been summoned to Marvin Gottlieb's Fifth Avenue penthouse after meeting with the advertising agency. There, she'd been told that Marv, the owner of Great Gams Hosiery, had gone apeshit over her legs, and wanted to meet both her and Marcus immediately. Fighting off her fear of being alone again with Marcus, she had shared an uncomfortable, speechless ride with him in Marv's limo as it had whisked them from the agency's SoHo offices uptown.

On arrival they'd been shown by a young woman into an opulent living room, completely overdecorated in the French Rococo style. The woman, Josie noticed with humor, was a caricature of the sexy French maid: short black uniform, starched white frilly apron and cap, black fishnet hose, and black high heels. The only thing missing was the feather duster. Josie immediately had an inkling of what she was getting into, but it wasn't until Marv shuffled them down the corridor of legs that she realized she was in the presence of a bonafide fetishist.

"Wow," Marcus's eyes were wild, "how long have you been collecting this stuff?"

"Longer than you've been breathing, son," Marv replied, in a throaty crackle. "Here, take a pew." He led them to a bar at the far end of the room. They perched themselves on pink leg-shaped bar stools and glanced at each other, then had to look away, no longer from embarrassment, but because they could hardly repress their laughter.

"What would you like?" Marv popped sprightly up from behind the bar and poured himself a shot of Jack Daniels. "J.D.? A martini perhaps?"

"Oh, no thanks, not for me. I never drink in the daytime," Josie lied.

"Just some water, thanks," Marcus said.

"What a pity. Bad for you, all this healthy living. My doctor keeps telling me not to drink or smoke these things"—Marv waved the cigar—"but I've been around a hell of a lot longer than him, so what does he know?"

He picked a leg-shaped glass from a shelf behind him, filled it with ice, siphoned in club soda, and slid it across the bar to Marcus.

"So," he said, magically appearing back beside them, "whadya think? Are you up for this?" His wrinkled, age-spotted hand swept around the room.

"Uh, up for what, Marv?" Marcus said, a confused expression on his face.

"Adding to my collection, boy."

"Oh, sure, Mr. Gottlieb. That'd be swell," Marcus replied.

"Swell"? thought Josie, who was beginning to think Marcus wasn't exactly the sharpest knife in the drawer. *Swell?*

"What about you, young lady?" Marv turned his fish-eyed gaze on her. "Are you ready for this?"

"Well, it all depends, Marv." She smiled, slid off the bar stool, stood back, and deliberately posed so that he could see all of her. "I mean, what is it that you want exactly? A mere hosiery model, or someone to fulfill your fantasy of the perfect leg?" She felt like a hooker selling a body part, but she was loving this. "I mean, I assume you want a mold taken?"

"So, you can think, too. Good, I like that in my girls." Marv looked her up and down. Not a lascivious or devious look, she realized, but one of pure business-like appraisal.

"And as well as the photographs and the mold, you'd like a drawing, just for yourself, for here, right?"

"Part of the contract," Marv crackled.

"Tell me something, Marv." She sat back down and crossed her legs. His milky cataracts followed every movement of every muscle in her legs. "Are you married?" She didn't know why she asked the question, or why she was acting like this, but somehow it felt right.

"My wife, God rest her soul, passed away three years ago. I miss her so much," he replied, and she watched as his eyes became even more misty and fishlike, although not for an instant did they leave her legs.

"Well, what did she think of all this? All this leg stuff."

"Oh"—Marv wiped a tear from behind his giant specs—"Helen was my inspiration, my driving force. We started the company together, you know."

"Really?" Marcus said.

"Fifty-nine years ago this summer." Marv swayed slightly. Josie wondered if the Jack Daniels was getting to him. "Come over here," he said. "I want to show you both something."

Marv tottered over to the far end of the room. He pressed a button and the wall slid apart to reveal a black stage of sorts on which rested a lone pedestal. A soft pink glow bathed the alabaster plinth. Marv stared lovingly up at the leg poised upon it. Golden light washed around the limb, stretched inside a golden swimsuited torso, which faded into darkness.

"This is my Helen," he said, stroking the back seam of the sheer silk stocking encasing the object of his love. "She was the first, the only." His fingers reached the thirties-style gold sandal and to Josie's amazement he knelt on the stair and kissed the back of the heel, right at the point it entered the shoe. "And you'll always be the best, my darling," he croaked to the leg.

"Look at her." He rose creakily from his position of worship. "Just look at her leg. Perfection, this leg. Notice the slim curve of the ankle, the gentle swell of the calf, the thrust of the kneecap. Oh, and her thigh! Her thighs were so beautiful they used to make me weep," he said softly. "I miss you, my darling. I miss your beautiful legs."

"I know how you feel," Marcus whispered, and Josie jumped when she felt his hand brush against the back of her thigh.

"Ah." Marv drew himself back to reality and turned to Marcus. "So you do have the bug. I thought so, the minute I saw those pictures of yours, boy."

"Yeah"—Marcus blushed—"yeah . . . umm . . . I guess I do."

"Well, even if you didn't know it, I'm telling you—you do," Marv said. "When I first saw those pictures and those legs I knew. I knew those legs of yours, Josephine, were as near to my Helen's as I've ever seen. And I knew whoever photographed them adored those legs. It was as plain as the seam in this silk stocking. I want you both for my new campaign."

"That's wonderful, Marv!" Josie could feel the elation rising in her, and it wasn't just the thought of the campaign, or the money. Marcus worshipped her legs! "We'd love to do it." She leaned over and kissed Marv on the folds of his wizened cheek. "And I'm very flattered you think my legs look like your wife's."

"Will you do me a favor?" Marv asked. "Will you just stand up there beside Helen?"

"Sure, Marv, I'd be happy to." Josie climbed the stairs until her feet were at the same level as the alabaster plinth. Marv stood, transfixed at the sight of her legs, his milky eyes going back and forth between hers and his beloved's.

"Perfection," he whispered, climbing the stairs. He knelt at Josie's feet. "Ah, perfection," he sighed, as he gently kissed the back of her heel, right at the point it entered the Zanotti stilletto.

18

It felt cold and clammy against her skin, like being slapped with wet fish. She stood, unable to move, in a swimsuit and a pair of four-inch pumps, watching the white-coated young man spread the white plaster over her legs, first the left, then the right, with meticulous professionalism.

"I guess you've done this a lot," she said, looking around the stark white room.

"Yes," he said, his hands sloshing up and down her legs.

"Ooh," she giggled at the tingling cold. "I bet you must love this. Slathering women's legs with Vaseline and plaster." The boy silently continued his task. "Is this all you do here? The mold man?" More silence. "Ooh!" she shivered again. "Is that what your business card says? 'Great Gams Corporation, President of Cast Making'?"

The boy looked up at her and she wondered if he would have preferred a career in undertaking rather than wrapping women's legs with cement. A solemn lad, with fine, dark hair slicked close to his skull; a pale, pimpled complexion; and a thin, Adam's-appled neck, he appeared a tad less enthusiastic than a dead sloth.

He carefully washed the plaster off his hands in a porcelain sink a few feet away from where she stood shivering. The small, brightly lit room had a very lablike appearance, with the exception of the product it produced. On the far wall, stretching from one end to the other, was a series of shelves, on which rested the plaster of Paris molds of Great Gams models of the past, each tagged and dated. Josie felt like a lab rat in a leg mausoleum. Another prototype on the hopeful route to the Great Gams Hall of Fame.

"Remind me never to break my legs," she said, feeling uncomfortable now as the whiteness hardened around her thighs.

"It'll be off in a few minutes," he said, his Adam's apple flinching vigorously.

Josie stood patiently, marveling at her good fortune. A week ago she was penniless. Now she was about to sign a contract that would end up netting her four hundred and eighty-five thousand, give or take a few. Nearly half a million! The initial fifty for the print ads had been renegotiated for point-of-purchase sale, billboards, worldwide television rights, residuals, and personal appearances, stretching her income into far more than she'd ever earned in her entire life. Josie couldn't believe this was happening to her. How fabulous! She couldn't wait to put her autograph on that dotted line.

"Is she cooked yet?" Marv's hoarse crackle woke her from her reverie. He shuffled into the lab, a cigar in one withered mit, the other brandishing a pair of golden shears. Today he sported another immaculate suit of navy blue chalk stripe wool and an even more vulgar tie than the one he'd worn when they'd first met.

"Another minute, Uncle Marv." The boy stood to attention, gulping his Adam's apple and rubbing his hands together nervously. Marv ignored him and shuffled up to the small platform where Josie stood.

"What a glorious sight." Marv smiled at the congealing whiteness of Josie's legs, which were starting to itch. "This is my favorite part." He shakily held up the shears. "Unveiling the mold that will send millions of women running out to buy a new pair of hose."

"He's your nephew, Marv?" Josie couldn't imagine two more disparate souls: Marv, passionate about his life's work and this boy obviously deadened by the mundane task he'd been assigned. The itch increased and she felt herself twitching, dying to scratch beneath the plaster.

"Grand nephew," Marv said, looking at the boy with something close to disgust. "He hates it here, dontcha, Solly? Well you gotta pay your dues, just like the rest of us Gottliebs. There'll be no free lunches for any of you young punks."

"No, Uncle Marv," Solly replied, his eyes downcast, his hands clenched at his sides. Josie felt sorry for the kid.

"Half of them think they can mooch around here and do nothing, just because the old man owns the company. They're all waiting for me to kick the bucket, isn't that right, Solly?"

"No, sir, no, not at all." The kid slouched over with, what looked to Josie, a mixture of anger and defeat.

"Then they want to sell off the company piece by piece, destroy everything Helen and I slaved for. Well, let me tell you, Solly—I'll make sure that doesn't happen! I'd rather leave my Great Gams to the dog's home than have you all fighting over it. Bunch of vultures, the lot of you!" Josie imagined lots of dogs running around in Great Gams hose.

"It's not that, Uncle Marv. It's just, just—" Solly's Adam's apple was convulsing furiously.

"Just what, sonny? C'mon, spit it out, kid!" Marv's face reddened and his hands started shaking.

"It's just that we think the way you run Great Gams is old-fashioned! All this, this . . ."—he indicated the room—"mold stuff, is so . . . so antiquated. No one runs a billion-dollar-a-year business like you do any more, Uncle Marv." Solly's eyes darted nervously around and he slumped down, sweating profusely from his outburst.

"And more's the pity they don't, Solly." Marv menaced the shears at him. "More's the pity they don't. Now get out!" he snapped, his ancient face quivering with rage. Solly practically ran from the white room. "Goddamned young punks." Marv turned back to Josie, who was shimmying around in her plaster cast, trying to control the itching. "I won't let them destroy this company!"

"Good for you, Marv," she replied, trying to keep still. Marv sank the shears into the bottom of the cast. She watched his eyes return to the softer, milkier hue they'd had when he'd kissed her heel the week before, but his hand was still shaking. She hoped he wouldn't spear her with the golden shears.

"This is the only way to run Great Gams," he said, as the plaster began separating from the bottom of the four-inch heel of her left foot.

"I understand . . . the hands-on approach."

"See? Only a woman can understand. Helen understood." Marv looked up at her, near tears. "But there's no women left in this company any more. We never had daughters and not one woman who married into the family wanted anything to do with it, can you imagine?"

"Really? What a shame, considering it's women's hose you make."

Marv let out a long sigh. The shears clattered onto the floor. His eyes widened at Josie through the giant black-rimmed spectacles and he crumpled into a heap, the cigar still dangling from his wrinkled lips.

"Marv!" she screamed. "Marv!" She tried to get down off the platform, an exceedingly difficult task with plaster casts holding her hostage. "Ohmygod! Marv!" The top of the plaster cut into her thighs as one leadened foot followed the other onto the floor, "Ouch! Ahh! Help! Help!" she yelled, realizing she couldn't even bend down to feel Marv's pulse. "Ow!" She put one solid block of plaster in front of the other and attempted to drag herself from the room. "Ow! Help! Help!" She hobbled spastically into the hallway, arms akimbo. "Someone! Help!"

"What the—" came a man's voice from behind her. Josie attempted a turn, but the four-inch, plaster-wedged heels wouldn't comply and she found herself sliding perilously.

"Ahhh! Help!" She fell at the man's feet. Her plaster casts stuck straight up toward him knocking him in the chest. "Ahh! Quickly! Help!" she cried.

"What the hell are you doing?" came the voice from above.

"What does it look like I'm doing! The Watusi?" She looked up at a well-dressed man in his midforties. "It's Marv!" she screamed. "Marv! He's in there! He's collapsed! Help him!"

The man sprinted toward the room where Marv had passed out, leaving her splayed like a beached plaster whale on the linoleum.

19

The next morning Josie caught a cab down to the Village, got out, and walked nervously into a diner on West Fourth Street. She scanned the dimly lit room and saw him, unsmiling, slumped against the wall, drumming the table with a fork.

Their eyes met and she felt sick to her stomach. She didn't want to be here at all. But she knew she had to be the bigger person. Had to clear the air. She sat down opposite him, not knowing what to say.

"Hi," Marcus said quietly.

"It's over," she blurted out, before she even said hello back.

"Us?" He looked quizzically at her, his soft green eyes devastating her once again.

"There never was an 'us'!" she snapped. But she for sure wished there had been, though. "Marv, the shoot. Over. He's had a stroke."

"Oh, no! Is he okay?" He looked genuinely concerned.

"I don't know. He's in the ICU."

"That's not good."

"No, it isn't. So I guess that's the end of that." She

felt like crying. Sitting there with him, knowing that nothing would happen now, either between them or with Great Gams. All hope down the tubes.

"Josie," he said and reached for her hand.

"Don't," she pulled her hand away. It was all too much.

"Josie, please. Don't do this."

"Do what?" Her voice rose involuntarily. "I'm not the one who's done anything. Except suffer from a case of bad judgment, yet again." She realized she was still angry with him, livid with herself. She looked up at him and felt her lip trembling.

"I've hurt you," he said.

"I've hurt myself."

"I'm sorry," he mumbled.

"Me too." She shook her head at her own stupidity. They both sat there for a while, silent. The waitress brought coffee.

"Look," he finally said, his voice soft, "I, uh, I'm really sorry." He sighed, looked down, and drummed his fingers nervously on the table. "I don't suppose we can, well, you know, just move on from here, and, well, and be . . . friends?" His eyes gazed up sheepishly. Manipulating her.

She froze. *How?* How could she possibly be friends with him? "I don't know."

"Please? Please, Josie?"

She took a deep breath. *Be the bigger person, remember? Well, I guess having a friend like him is better than not having one, isn't it? Is it?*

"I'll try," she said, attempting a smile.

He stroked her cheek and she wondered how on earth she would manage it.

20

Josie hated hospitals. The smells of illness and food so vile it made you feel nauseous always reminded her of her childhood, and the endless visits to her father's bedside. She was five years old when he rolled his souped-up Holden sedan while racing at a dangerous track in the Blue Mountains, outside Sydney. Rolled it eight times and nearly killed himself. The car door smashed his leg as it flapped open and closed with each roll and totally crushed one of his kidneys. She was too young to realize the gravity of his wounds, but every day when they left behind the motionless form of her father and walked through the sickly green hallways of Sydney Hospital, her mother and older brother would be sobbing. The doctors gave him twenty-four hours to live, day after day, for almost a month. He stayed in the renal unit for over nine months before they let him out. Nine months of almost daily visits left her with grotesque memories of hospitals, and every time she entered one she felt five years old again, wondering when Daddy would ever come home.

Those memory-charged odors hit her as she entered

Lenox Hill Hospital, just off Park Avenue. The last time she'd been there was to visit a friend dying of AIDS. The time before that she'd been in an ambulance with Jonathon, after he'd overdosed on heroin.

Fighting her urge to run, she walked through the glass foyer to the reception desk and asked for Marvin Gottlieb's room. In her arms she clutched two dozen yellow roses and a book. She thought Marv might like yellow roses, and she knew he'd love the book, if he didn't already have it.

She took the elevator to the third floor and followed the numbers until she found 331, and, rapping lightly on the door, let herself in. Although three days had passed since his stroke and Marv was no longer in the ICU, Josie blanched at the tubes and wires snaking in and out of his frail old body and the hostile beep of the cardiac monitor.

"You awake, Marv?" She tiptoed hesitantly to his bedside. Marv didn't move. She bent down and kissed the folds of his cheek. He smelled old, rancid. "I have something for you," she whispered, then gently put the book on his bedside table and looked for a container for the roses. She was surprised there were no other flowers in the room. She thought Marv would have lots of friends and business associates. What about his family? Why hadn't they sent him flowers? Poor Marv. She put the flowers in a sink in the corner.

"I even wore a very short skirt for you," she said, even though she knew he couldn't see or hear her. "Not that you need a thrill in your condition," she giggled. "But it must be very dull in here legwise, so I thought you'd enjoy a peep of the hottest news from the runways of Milan." She slipped off her coat and twirled around in a gray pinstripe suit and five-inch spike-heeled red patent leather shoes. She'd begged her friend in the Gucci showroom to loan her the outfit for the day, but she had to return it, as it was their only sample. "It's not your normal pinstripe suit, is it, Marv?" She smiled. The micromini had a slit in one side and the jacket had padded shoulders and a nipped-in waist. She walked closer to his bed and posed, hands on hips, legs strong. "Very eighties, don't you think? God, at the rate they recycle fashion these days, soon they'll be redesigning retro versions of outfits we wore yesterday!"

"It's called 'aggro-chic,' this look." She raised an eyebrow at the sleeping patient. "But I'm not sure who it's supposed to make more aggressive, me or the person looking at me. I must say, I do feel rather powerful in it. The new Amazon!" She did another twirl and was startled to see someone watching her. It was the man she'd nearly knocked to the ground with her plaster-casted legs on the day of Marv's stroke. He stood casually in the open doorway, a thick, silver-streaked head of hair framing the bemused expression on his tanned face.

"Oh," she said, embarrassed. "It's you." She smiled weakly. It was one thing posing around for Marv, who was completely non compos, but to be caught prancing around like an idiot in front of some strange guy was definitely not on. Especially when the guy was kind of cute. "Hi," she said, wondering what the hell to do now. *Act powerful! You've got the outfit—now go for it!* "I don't believe we've met." She held out her hand. "I'm Josie Vaughn."

"I know who you are." The man shook her hand firmly. "How's he doing?" He motioned his head toward the bed.

"Ah, well . . . I wouldn't really know, to tell you the truth. I just got here. Perhaps you should ask his doctor." The man walked past her to Marv's bedside. Josie noticed the beautiful cut of his charcoal suit and the rich blue of his shirt, elegantly offset by a yellow and blue Hermes tie. Mmm, not bad. "Ah . . . um . . . who are you?" she asked.

"William," he said, turning back to her, a surprised look on his face, like she was supposed to know who he was. "William Gottlieb." She noticed the brilliant blue of his eyes and his full lips. *Mmm. Attractive. Arrogant, definitely, but attractive.*

"You're Marv's son?"

"Grandson," he said.

"Oh! Sorry! Of course! You're much too young to be his son! Sorry!" *God, am I an idiot or what?* She checked his left hand for a wedding ring. None. *Mmm. Oh well, what's the use? He must think I'm a total moron, especially after my stellar performance the other day.* "Well, I'd better be going," she said. "It was nice meeting you." She grabbed her coat and struggled hastily into it.

"Did you bring those?" William Gottlieb pointed to the yellow roses in the sink.

"Yes, yes I did. I'd better get a vase for them."

"Don't bother. Grandfather's allergic to them."

"He is? Allergic to flowers? Oh! How horrible for him. I couldn't think of anything worse than being allergic to flowers, what a sh—"

"You'd better take them with you," he cut her off.

Stop rambling will you! Nerves. So much for aggro-chic.

"Yes. I guess so." She retrieved the roses.

"What about this?" He held up the book.

"Oh, that? I thought Marv would get a kick out of it, no pun intended, ha ha."

William read the cover slowly. He sighed and held it out toward her. "You can take this back too."

"Why, does he have it already?"

"I think we'd better talk," he said, giving her that "I think you're a moron" look again. "Have a seat." Josie obeyed and sat in a chair facing the bed, full of dread.

"My grandfather, as you can clearly see, is not a young man," William said, settling himself at Marv's feet on the bed, facing Josie. She squirmed and pulled at the hem of her micromini, wishing it would instantly grow four inches longer. She suddenly felt ridiculous in it. Mutton dressed as lamb. "Nor," he continued, "is he very well. For several years we've been worried about his state of mind. We don't think he's mentally competent to run Great Gams the way he used to."

"Who's we?" she asked, looking at his shoes. She didn't like his shoes. Black leather loafers with lots of fringes and tassels. Too busy. Not the shoes to go with that beautiful suit at all. His shoes made her think he was not to be trusted. Amazing how a pair of shoes can turn you off a guy. Or anybody for that matter. You can always tell a person by his shoes.

Don't be stupid! What a load! Shut up and listen!

"The family. The board of directors. We think he's got dementia."

"Really? He seemed sharp as a tack to me. But then what would I know? I only met him a couple of times." She shrugged, wondering why this man was divulging family secrets.

"My point is, we think Marv's judgment is way off. We've tried to dissuade him from making certain decisions in the company that we think should be handled by more competent, younger people."

"Why? Are your profits down?" she asked, suspicious of this man in his not-to-be-trusted shoes.

"Er, no, not at all, but that's not the point—" he shifted on the bed.

"So what is the point? Why not indulge him? He's obviously not going to last forever." *Why am I having this conversation with this person? It's none of my business what they do with their stupid company. Unless—oh, no. Here it comes. The old heave-ho.*

"We have to plan for the future, Miss Vaughn, and we think spending so much on advertising right—"

"So you're firing me as the new Great Gams Girl, woman, whatever, right?" She sat forward on the edge of her chair. William Gottlieb raised his eyebrow at her. *God, he's attractive. Shame about the shoes.*

"That's not what I mean, Miss Vaughn. If you'd give me a chance to finish—"

"Well, 'Mr. Gottlieb,'" she mocked him, annoyed now, "what exactly do you mean?" She could almost smell the panic thumping out of her. "I have a contract, you know."

"I'm fully aware of that. But it was a contract that my grandfather organized and signed. It hasn't yet gone before the board for final approval, and with my grandfather so ill, that contract will probably never get the green light."

"Why? Is it me? What's the matter with me? I know I've got a bit of cellulite, but my legs are pretty good considering—"

"Miss Vaughn, please!" William was agitated. "That's not what I'm suggesting at all."

"Please call me Josie. I feel like I'm in court, or something. Maybe I am. Look, I certainly don't want to appear desperate or anything, even though it may look just like that, but I don't understand what's going on here. Unless what Marv said the other day is true."

"What did he say?"

"That his family was waiting for him to die. That you were all a pack of vultures who wanted to carve up the corporation and ruin it."

"He said that, did he? Good old Marv." William shook his head and smiled. "It's not like that at all, really. But it's too convoluted to explain. Family stuff, you know."

"You're right. It's none of my business. Except for how it affects me, of course."

"Well, Josie"—he smiled at her—"I'm just trying to tell you that things might be very different at Great Gams if Marv passes on. And for the moment, you can assume that all bets are off."

"Oh." *So there it is. Dead in the water. Before I even had a chance to dog-paddle around the pond.* She stood to go, grappling with the yellow roses, the book, and her disappointment.

"And you can assume that I'm not passing on to any goddamned place," came a hoarse crackle from the bed.

"Marv!" Josie cried, overjoyed.

"Grandfather!" William leapt from the blue blanket as if electrocuted. They both stared down at Marv.

"My word stands as law at Great Gams, William. You oughta know that by now, young man," he rasped. Marv seemed bright as a button. His eyes twinkled blue.

"Grandfather . . . I uh . . . wasn't saying that. I—"

"Cut the crap, Bill. As long as I'm alive Josie is the new Great Gams spokeswoman, and that's final." *Spokeswoman? Mmm. Love the sound of that.* "And even if I do buy the farm, she's still got a contract, and we honor our contracts at Great Gams. Capice?"

"Yes, Grandfather," William said meekly, but he was smiling.

"Thanks, Marv." Josie bent down to kiss him, holding the roses back behind her, out of his way.

"Ouch!" The roses hit William in the face.

"Oops! Sorry, Mr. Gottlieb!" She giggled at him. *Naa na na na, I've got a contract, so there, Mr. Smarty Pants!* She almost poked her tongue out at him. "Here, Marv, I brought you these, but I heard you were allergic."

"Yeah, I am, but thanks." Marv smiled up at her. "They're beautiful. Just like you, young lady."

"And I got you this book." She held it out to him. He tried to peer at it, but without his giant black-rimmed spectacles, he was probably blind. "Oh," she said, "it's called *Footsucker.*"

"Oh, I know that book, it's a doozy," he cackled. "I could use a good laugh."

"Enjoy it." She kissed him on the cheek again. "Well, I gotta go. Got to get to the gym, keep these gams in shape! Bye, Marv. Bye, William." She gave him a sweet smile.

"See you, Josie," he smiled coolly back.

"Look after yourself, young lady," Marv croaked, as she turned for the door. "And Josie . . ."

"Yes?" She looked back at them both.

"The aggro-chic look's a kicker."

She laughed and walked out.

"Yes!" She shook her fists at the air. A nurse walked by and shot her a strange look. Josie knew she must look a sight—a six-foot-two woman in bright red stilettos shouting to heaven—so she tried to act a little more subdued, but she could feel the spring in her step and the tingle of excitement as she headed back to the elevator.

Of course, she realized her good fortune was contingent on Marv's staying alive. The minute he drew his last breath, which could be any tick of the clock, the contract would be considered the folly of a senile old lech, and his family would kick her out on her designer-clad butt quicker than she could spell D-I-O-R. For all she knew, the family could be helping Marv reunite with his beloved Helen a little quicker than he'd planned. Marv was a fighter, that was for sure, but how long could an eighty-two-year-old with a heart condition fight? Maybe she'd do a little research, find out about the Gottlieb family and what was really going on at Great Gams.

She turned a corner and reached the elevator bank, feeling stronger, more focused than she had in years. Pressing the button, she glanced back down the wide corridor she'd just stalked in her five-inch spikes. In the distance she thought she saw a familiar shape. She wasn't sure until the figure approached that it was Richard Saunders, struggling into a camel overcoat as he rushed closer to her.

"Richard!" she said, but he didn't seem to hear. "Richard! Hi!" She waved at the figure. He looked up in her direction for a second, then put his head back down and scurried past the turn to the elevator bank where she stood, farther down the hallway, and disappeared into an unmarked doorway. *Funny,* she thought. *I'm sure he heard me. Maybe he didn't recognize me in this outfit. Oh, well,* she shrugged, as the doors to the elevator opened and she stepped in. *He was certainly in a rush. I wonder what he was doing here? Maybe it wasn't even him.* The doors opened on the ground floor and she left the hospital.

Back down the corridor, in the room next to Marvin Gottlieb's, number 329, lay the comatose body of Juan Lopez. He'd been there for seven days, ever since he'd injected himself with a speedball at Richard and Priscilla Saunders's anniversary party.

21

Hamish Kent sucked in his cheeks, pursed his tiny bow-shaped mouth, and raised his right eyebrow. His steel gray eyes darted from toe to head of the figure standing before him. Brand-new Costume National shoes shone brightly black. The sharp gray silk and wool Dior suit felt thrilling, the charcoal vest beneath, an exquisite piece of tailoring. A symphony in gray and black, he thought, adjusting an anthracite silk tie around a pale silver cotton collar. "Perfect," he said to the figure.

He turned from the mirror, confident of his sartorial splendor. But he felt uneasy. A slight shift of the tectonic plates beneath the normally immutable foundation of the Kent empire had left him feeling shaky. Things were not as they should be.

He picked up his Prada satchel; threw it over his shoulder; and, with another glance back to the mirror to make sure his jacket was still hanging correctly, strolled out of his bedroom suite and into the foyer of his former wife's apartment. *No*, he thought, *I don't like this at all*. He felt threatened. Like his crown was askew, about to be snatched from his smoothly shaved head.

"Morning." Antonia swished excitedly before him. "What do you think?"

"I've seen wounds better dressed," he sniffed, perusing her red suit with utter disdain. Even if he liked it, which he didn't, he'd never tell her. Not bloody likely she'd get even the vaguest hint of a compliment from him today.

"I wasn't talking about my clothes," she snapped. "I was talking about this morning's 'Page Six.'" She waved a copy of the *New York Post* in his face. "Didn't you see it?"

"I don't read that crap," he sniffed again.

"Oh, really?" She stopped before the large black-framed mirror in the foyer. "What's the matter with this outfit?"

"You look like a telephone box, darling." Hamish's mouth curled up at the edges.

"Nonsense! It's vintage. From Gianni's last collection." She tweaked the ultrashort skirt and adjusted the buttons of the jacket. "I think it's fabulous."

"Just because the poor bugger was murdered, do you really find it necessary to prance around looking like a fire hydrant on stilettos? Have some decorum, for God's sake."

"Poor Gianni." She sighed at her bright red reflection and pouted her scarlet lips. "Such a tragedy. I miss him awfully."

"Bollocks"—he rolled his eyes—"you only met him once, and that was at that dinner *I* gave at the Ritz in Paris."

"That's not true. I saw lots of him here in New York."

"From the wrong side of velvet ropes, sweetie. Come on, stop primping. The car's downstairs. We'll be late."

"Judging by your glorious mood," she said, "I'd say, dear heart, that you have seen that article."

"I told you—I don't read that garbage." He felt his nostrils flaring with anger.

"That's strange. I wonder how it found its way into your bathroom. Walked in there by itself, I suppose." She grinned at him.

He managed to control his mounting fury. They walked out the large double doors of her apartment to a small vestibule and into the waiting elevator.

In the limousine, on the way to a meeting with an important new client, he slouched glumly in the corner as she gloated over the newspaper column.

"'It seems Antonia Kent, Uber Agent to the world's top fashion photographers has pulled off a triple coup,'" she read aloud. "'The raven-haired beauty has brokered a multimillion-dollar deal for Marcus Ashland, until very recently the assistant to her ex-husband and star client, world-renowned shutterbug Hamish Kent. Our sources tell us Ms. Kent will also be pocketing a hefty twenty percent commission of a very fat modeling contract for Josephine Vaughn, a former model–turned–stylist whose gorgeous legs will be stalking all over the place in shots snapped by handsome newcomer Ashland. Vaughn, a thirty-something blond bombshell, is being hailed as the new Great Gams spokesperson. As if all that money wasn't enough to please Ms. Kent's voracious appetites, the forty-three-year-old fashion plate has been seen digging her ruby red nails into the arm of the hunky twenty-nine-year-old Ashland at various soirees around Gotham in the last few weeks. No wonder she has such an enigmatic smile on her famed Mona Lisa mouth.'" Antonia carefully folded up the newspaper and pulled out her cell phone. "I could have done without my age being mentioned, but it's rather good, isn't it?" She grinned at Hamish and dialed.

"You're lucky they didn't print your real age," he snarled. "How'd you manage that? Another blow job?"

"What's the matter, darling? Feeling a little left out? A teensy-weensy bit jealous are we? Poor Hamish." She blew him a kiss. "Don't worry, darling. You're still on top. Uber Agent won't let you fall." She blew another kiss.

"Shut up. Of course I'm not jealous. I'm thrilled for you." He felt like clubbing his ex-wife with his Prada satchel. Not because of her affair with Marcus, but because he'd been up for the same campaign. It infuriated him that Marcus got the job. *His first job and he gets millions of dollars! What the hell was happening? Whatever happened to the concept of paying one's dues? Bloody Marcus. Fucking upstart.*

"Pru, darling," she purred to her secretary, "will you run out and get a dozen copies of today's *Post*? And call Glorimundi and send some flowers over to Richard Johnson. Did Marcus call? . . . Oh . . . okay. I'll be there in an hour." She snapped the phone shut.

"Who's Richard Johnson . . . your next lover? Next victim?" Hamish looked out the window into the sleet-covered mess of traffic. His mood matched the seething, icy cacophony.

"Don't be ridiculous. He's the editor of 'Page Six' and he's happily married."

"When did that ever stop you?"

"It never stopped you either, did it? You and Josie used to be pretty pally, if I recall."

"That was a long time ago, before—"

"Before we were divorced, darling." She glared at him. "And before your sexual proclivities—"

"You didn't seem to mind my being 'pally' with Josephine at the time, did you? Helped start your business."

"What on earth do you mean?"

"Stop acting dumb. You know perfectly well what I mean. When I returned from Greece with all that cash, remember?"

"Oh, that." Antonia waved her hand dismissively. "I would have got the money anyway, sooner or later."

"You got it a little sooner because of Josie . . . not to mention my clever maneuvering."

"I'm eternally grateful, Your Holiness," she said, pulling out a scarlet lipstick and a mirror from her Hermes Kelly bag. "Remind me to kiss your ring later."

He watched furiously as she examined her image with the smugness of someone who has nothing to prove. She drove him around the bend. It was time for him to bite the bullet and spring for a hotel or an apartment here, even though he loathed New York. There was too much work here to be silly about it. He hated spending money, but if he stayed with her any longer he'd go berserk. Antonia looked at him, her blue eyes glinting. "She still doesn't know, does she?"

"No, she doesn't," he snapped, "and I'd prefer it stayed that way."

"Isn't it comforting that we have no secrets? We know every single little thing about each other, don't we, darling?" She smiled as she finished rouging her pumped-up lips.

"You're a total nightmare." He sighed and looked back out the window. He wished she didn't know half the things she did. Their lives had been too enmeshed for too long. She had him twisted round her little finger, and there was nothing he could do about it.

The phone hadn't stopped ringing all morning. Josie wondered about the true commerce of a city whose residents appeared to spend an inordinate amount of time reading a gossip column in a local newspaper. She hadn't even had a chance to throw on her coat and run around the corner to get a copy of the *Post.* She was still in her pajamas at eleven-thirty, fielding calls from both friends and complete strangers, the former wishing her well, the latter inquiring about her availability for interviews, charity functions, and some blatant requests for her not-yet-realized earnings. She'd even been asked out on a couple of blind dates.

"I haven't even done the photo shoot yet!" she exclaimed to Priscilla, who was the first one to call, at seven AM, and read the article out to her. "Isn't this all a bit premature?"

"Hon, mark my words, you won't get a moment's peace for a day or two, at least."

Priscilla had been right. By about ten, Josie wished she had an unlisted phone number and now she was downright exhausted and her throat was hoarse from the incessant chatter. Still, she wasn't complaining. Far from it. She was thrilled at the attention and almost had to pinch herself to make sure this was all happening, that it wasn't just a figment of her overactive imagination.

She finally threw herself into the shower, dressed hurriedly in her new Marc Jacobs suit, and rushed out to catch up with the rest of the day. The sleet had burgeoned into large fluffy snowflakes, muffling the city's roar beneath a white blanket that threatened to suffocate it for at least a few hours.

Josie loved storms. Perhaps because she'd grown up on a beach, never seeing snow, she was seduced by its beauty and the smell and the feel of it against her skin. And she really loved that even New York had to bow to nature occasionally.

She missed the fresh air and the subtropical climate of Sydney, missed diving into the clear warm surf off Palm Beach, where she grew up. More than anything she missed the feeling of space and the startling, relentless blue of the Australian skies. She decided then that she'd go home in January.

Christmas was just a few weeks away, and it was now impossible that she'd be able to get away in time. She had two sets of photo shoots with Marcus, a television commercial, and several interviews lined up. She was even going on the *Today Show.* It was truly unbelievable.

Andy, whom she hadn't seen since the Saunders's party, had called and insisted on taking her to a celebratory lunch at The Four Seasons. She liked him, enjoyed his company, so she said yes. But hoped he wouldn't get the wrong idea and come on to her. Not in a million years would she be attracted to him.

He'd told her his driver would be downstairs waiting. She was relieved to see the awful white limo had been replaced with a sleek black Mercedes. She settled into the plush black leather seat and smiled out at the falling snow as they slowly edged along the white streets. *How cool is this!*

"You know you're being robbed, dontcha?" Andy swirled his bourbon and water. She was thrilled he drank at lunch. Now she didn't feel guilty ordering a glass of champagne. She looked around at all the well-known literary faces and the power brokers of the city, ensconced at their regular tables at the most famous of all New York's power lunch spots. She'd only eaten here once before, at dinner next door in the beautiful Pool Room. Now they were in the Grill Room. The place reeked of money and the electric excitement of wheeling and dealing. She spied Phillip Johnson, the celebrated architect who'd helped Mies Van der Rohe design the restaurant in the sixties. There was Tina Brown . . .

"Did ya hear me, darlin'?"

"Oh! Sorry. I must have drifted off. What did you say?"

"Ah said you're being robbed."

"Robbed?" She frowned at him for an instant. "Oh, the commission."

"Shug, that Antonia woman shouldn't be taking any more than fifteen percent."

"Yeah, I know, but I wouldn't have the deal at all if it wasn't for her, so what could I do? She kind of bamboozled me." Josie shrugged. She felt uncomfortable talking about money. Besides, what did Andy know about the modeling business?

"I hear she's a shark. You oughta think about getting a real agent."

"Well, it's not like I'm going to be doing too much of this stuff. I mean—at my age this is a one-shot deal."

"I wouldn't be too sure of that, darlin'." Andy smiled at her. "Let me help you. A manager type is what y'all need."

Josie gave him a quizzical look. "How come you're so interested in my career? Surely a busy mogul like you has better things to do than fuss over an agent," she laughed.

"Oh, Ah got a hunch, shug, that this is just the beginning for you." He raised his glass to her. "Here's to you, kid."

"Just what are you up to, Andy Wyatt?" Before he had a chance to reply, Anna Wintour, the famed editor of *Vogue*, walked up to their table.

"Hello." Anna held out her hand. "You're Josie Vaughn, aren't you?"

"Ah . . . yes, yes, last time I looked." Josie laughed nervously, absolutely gobsmacked that Anna Wintour would know who she was, let alone speak to her. The doyenne of the fashion world talking to her!

"I'm Anna Wintour. Congratulations on your new contract. I expect we'll be seeing a lot of you soon"—she smiled—"and I'd love to do a piece on you for *Vogue.*"

"That'd be f . . . fantastic," Josie stammered, barely able to breathe. "Great."

"Good. We'll be in touch." Anna turned to Andy, who had risen politely from the table. "And you, you wily snake." She kissed him on both cheeks. "You don't waste any time, do you?"

"Why, Anna, darlin', how can you accuse me of such a thing?" Andy smiled. "Josie and Ah are old pals, aren't we, shug?" Josie nodded meekly up to them both.

"You're an old rogue, Andy Wyatt." Anna laughed. "Have a very good lunch." She vanished.

Josie was so astonished by the morning's events she thought she'd keel over from shock. Indeed, she was so dazed that it wasn't until they were leaving that she noticed Andy was suavely dressed in a navy pinstripe suit and a Hermes tie.

It was as if her world had been turned upside down. Suddenly she was being courted and feted by the city's rich and famous, she was about to earn a great deal of money, and Andy Wyatt was tastefully dressed. She felt like Alice in the Looking Glass. Everything was back to front.

As he ushered her toward his waiting car, she finally remembered she had to ask him something. "Andy, what do you know about Great Gams?"

"What do you want to know?"

"Oh, business stuff, I guess. I haven't got the foggiest idea about business, but I'd like to find out what the company earnings are, what's going on there, that kind of thing." They walked down the stairs and reached the canopied entryway to the restaurant and she realized

Andy had his arm linked in hers. She smiled at him. "You see, I get the feeling that old Marvin Gottlieb, the owner—is that what you'd call him?"

"Something like that, shug," he laughed.

"Chairman, whatever, but the point is that I think his family's trying to push him out, one way or another, and if Marv goes, so do I."

"In sympathy?" Andy looked bemused.

"Of course not! I'm not a complete moron!" She explained about the scene in the hospital. "It's a privately held company, I think."

"Uh-huh."

"Family owned, actually. So how do you find stuff like that out? Do you have to snoop around? Or would they just tell you? The family, I mean."

"Well, shug, you could start with old Marv. He's the guy to ask."

"Go straight to the top. Yeah, that's what I thought."

"Great Gams, huh. Mmm. Good brand name, that." Josie could almost see the cogs turning. "Shug, you're a lot smarter than you think. I'll look into it."

"Thanks, Andy, and thanks for lunch."

"The pleasure was all mine. Speak to you real soon, kid." He kissed her cheek and helped her into the car. "Dave," he said to the driver, "take Miss Vaughn anywhere she wants to go, and stay with her for the afternoon. Ah won't be needin' you 'til six."

"Ooh, thanks Andy!" He closed the door and walked back inside the Seagram's building to his office. She looked up but could barely see the top of the landmark edifice through the low ceiling of fog and snow.

"Where to, Miss Vaughn?"

"Bergdorf's, Dave." She could feel a grin spreading. "I'm going to melt my credit cards."

* * *

Those cards were molten by dusk. She had leapt from the car at the 58th Street entrance to Bergdorf's and raced breathlessly to the second floor, where previously she could only salivate over the outrageously priced designer boutiques within the store, and her rare purchases had been off the deeply discounted sale racks.

Within minutes she had dropped over three grand on a pink wool boucle Chanel jacket, a required staple for every true fashionista (or so she justified her purchase). Her heart pounding feverishly with excitement, she padded down the softly carpeted hallway to the Zac Posen boutique, followed by an eager saleswoman who could obviously smell a true shopper from a mere browser a mile off. Josie knew the frenetic urgency to spend oozed out of every pore, a feeling both exhilarating and quite frightening, like a gambler on a roll, unable to stop. Still, she rationalized, as she forked out another two thousand on the most divine bias-cut liquid silk column in a shimmering gold, she could always return the items if she had buyer's remorse by tomorrow. *Yeah right.* She would swan out of Bergdorf's wearing that gorgeous gold silk frock in the flutter of a false-lashed eye if she could—the prospect of being viewed as a total nouveau-riche tramp was the only thing that held her back. Besides, she had more shopping to do.

While the saleswoman wrapped Josie's new friends (she always thought of clothes as beautiful companions) she sailed into the shoe department and asked to try on a few exquisite morsels. The nattily dressed salesman, sly enough to take advantage of her whopping feet, assured her there was very little to be had in size 11, then proceeded to bring out an array of confections so tempting that she had to have them all, lest, heaven forbid, she would not find anything to fit elsewhere. She knew he was scamming her, but she didn't care. A mere twenty-five minutes and seven pairs of assorted shoes later—black-beaded silk Manolo mules, gold Zanotti crystal-clad sandals, Gucci espadrilles wrapped in plum satin ribboning that clung seductively around her slim ankles, two pairs of her favorite Tod's loafers, and two pairs of Hogan sneakers—she came up for air, and another three and a half thousand smackeroos in the hole. By this time she had managed to attract stares from the other customers, who probably assumed she was some heiress on a daily mission, an idea she both loved and felt revolted by. She was, after all, simply an imposter with a newfound bank balance—a meager one at that—and an unhealthy addiction for the feel of superbly tailored fabrics against her skin.

She strolled out of Bergdorf's, followed by a slip of a boy laden down with her packages, and was elated to see Dave and the Mercedes idling exactly where she had left them. She tipped the boy generously, climbed aboard, and off they floated through the snowy streets, up Madison, to Barneys.

In another flurry of pure self-indulgence she charged a sheared mink bolero shrug in pastel turquoise, a stunning bustier and beaded skirt by the fabulous design duo Proenza Schuoler, a Stella McCartney suit, some beyond gorgeous underwear, and a whole bunch of cosmetics from the basement.

By the time she reached home, she estimated she'd spent roughly fifteen thousand dollars. It shocked her how comfortable she felt spending money. But, finally, it was her own money, and she could do whatever she wanted, and that was the most thrilling aspect of all. Still, she felt guilty, as if she had to hide the purchases from herself, as there was no one else to chastise her for her overzealous parting with cash. She thought of her grandmother saying to her as a kid, "Dear, a fool and his money soon go their separate ways," but didn't care. She hoped Andy Wyatt was right—that this frisson of publicity and the Great Gams contract was not the last she would see of nice, big fat checks in the mail.

She tried on all the clothes again, pranced around in front of her mirror, admired the cut, stroked the fabrics, strutted around in the shoes, and was happy that she'd been brazen enough to ask Hamish for work, as none of this would have happened without their chance meeting just a few short weeks earlier.

22

The next morning Jonathon Cantero, newly escaped from a two-week sojourn at the Country Club rehab in New Jersey, sat in his French limestone and green slate kitchen gulping coffee and smoking up a storm. The only vices still allowed. *How fucking boring.* Everything felt bland, useless, but he knew he had to toe the line this time. Not only had Daniela threatened divorce if he didn't stay straight, but worse, much worse, his father had threatened to cut off the money. *Fuck. Cornered like a rat. Can't a man just drink and drug himself into oblivion now and then without the whole world yelling Twelve-Step AA shit at him? Fuck 'em all.*

He flicked through the morning's *Post*, stopping at the "Page Six" column, which for some dumb reason was on page twelve. His eyes nearly popped from their sockets. "Josie Vaughn," he read, "she of the skyscraper legs and newfound fame as the Great Gams gal of the year, may already be broadening her horizons. The dazzling blond Aussie was seen lunching at The Four Seasons yesterday with none other than buyout czar and Vive cosmetics king Andy Wyatt. Could another contract be in the works?"

"Fuck that bitch!" He threw the newspaper onto the floor in disgust. "Who the fuck does she think she is?" He stood up, lit another cigarette, ignoring the two that already spiraled smoke from the Hermes ashtray with dogs painted on it. He wanted to kill her.

He paced the length of the kitchen, sucking as hard as he could on his cigarette. Josie had cared once. But she couldn't compete with the booze, and she finally got it and left him.

That's when the fucking fun and games had started. *Bitch.* Well now that she had some money, maybe she'd give back what belonged to him.

The phone rang. He ignored it. He knew who it would be. Christ, could he stand another dose of guilt? Well, he was fucked either way. If he didn't speak to the Terrorist she'd give him shit, and if he did she'd give him just as much. *Fuck.*

He finally picked up.

"Did you see the *Post*?" His mother's nasal Long Island drawl was almost too much to bear first thing in the morning. He needed to be medicated to hear her. Just one little boot would do it.

"What about it?"

"Page Six. You didn't see it?"

"Yeah, I fucking saw it. So what?"

"Don't use profanities around me, Jonathon. I'm your mother and I will be treated with respect."

"Sorry," he grumbled. "You got anything else to talk about? 'Cause I don't fucking want to talk about that cunt."

"Jonathon!"

"Sorry."

"Maybe you should talk about her. You never talked

about her after the incident. Maybe you need to deal with this. Have you discussed her in your meetings?"

"Mom, I don't want to talk about her, okay? That shit is way in the past." He could feel his jaw tightening, compressing his brain.

"Well you never dealt with it, did you? It's not good to stuff your feelings, Jonathon. In my therapy classes—"

"Oh, here we go." He wanted to reach down the phone line and strangle the whine out of her voice. "A couple of night classes on drug addiction and now you're the expert. A little knowledge is a dangerous thing, Mom. You're not my shrink. So butt out."

"Have you been going to meetings? You have to go to meetings if you want to stay sober, Jonathon."

"Mom, I just got out yesterday! For Christ's sake, cut me some fucking slack!"

"There you go with that foul language again. You should have stayed the full month in rehab, or even longer. We've been through this so many times before. You stay a week or two and think you're cured. You'll never be cured. It's—"

"I know, Mom, I know, it's a disease. Dis-ease. I just want everyone to fucking leave me alone! Get it, Mom? Leave me fucking alone!" He could feel the vein on his forehead throbbing. He felt like he'd explode.

"Don't speak to me like that, Jonathon."

"Mom—I don't want to speak to you at all. Get it?" He slammed the phone down. So hard it smashed the keyboard. "Fuck! Fuck you all!" He picked up the phone, yanked it from the jack, and threw it across the kitchen, where it slammed against a mirror, smashing it into a thousand pieces. "Fuck you, Josephine!" He grabbed the newspaper, ripped out the 'Page Six' column, screwed it into a ball, and set fire to it with his Zippo lighter. "I'm gonna fucking get you—"

"What are you doing?" his wife inquired from behind.

Oops. Busted. He cringed as he turned to her, a sheepish grin on his face. "Ahh . . . redecorating?"

Daniela's eyes narrowed. "Don't ever mention that woman's name in my home again," she barked, in her gravelly South American accent. "And clean that mess up." Then she turned and stomped out. He stood there, deflated, as he listened to the clopping of her tiny slippers on the parquet floor fade into the back of the apartment.

23

It all looked so dull, so disappointing, so . . . so . . . what. Josie sighed and stood back from the wall of the Great Gams boardroom, where the layout drawings for the new ad campaign had been hung.

"Dazzling," she said. *Shut up. They're paying you a fortune, so just shut up! Let them slather you in shit, cover you with feathers, who cares? Just take the money and shut up!* She sighed again and gazed sullenly around the room. Her eyes met Marcus's for an instant. *Help! Do something!* She glared at him, but his eyes were blank. *Geeze, you look about as sharp as a pound of wet leather this morning.*

"Anything the matter?" William Gottlieb said.

"Umm. Well, it's just, you see, um," she floundered, then looked disconcertedly at him, the two ad agency guys, and finally Marv, who sat in a wheelchair, his feeble appearance offset by the gaudiness of yet another "leggy" tie and a determined twinkle in his eyes. He smiled at her and nodded almost imperceptibly, a tacit look that told her to go for it.

She took a deep breath. *Here goes, it's now or never,*

speak up or forever be banished to the annals of boring advertising. "If I saw these layouts in a magazine, I'd turn the page without even a glance." There was a gasp from the creative director.

"Why? What's the problem?" Chip Farouka, the agency account executive, rose up in indignation.

"The problem is . . ." She took another deep breath and looked to Marv again for support. He winked back at her. "Well . . . they're not quite as exciting as a nun's sex life. Apart from that, nothing I s'pose." The gasp was louder this time. "Perhaps I have no idea what I'm talking about, but these layouts are coma inducing." She thought Oliver whatever his name was, the art director, was going to bean her, or thrust the pencil he was furiously twitching deep into her eyeball.

"Keep going." Marv smiled.

She stood up and gestured toward the boards. "I mean, what is this? What *is* this? Me getting out of a station wagon in a suburban driveway with a bunch of groceries? Last time I looked that was on the wanted list for the most insipid look of all time! And this one!" She pointed at another of the layouts. "In a supermarket with my two-point-five kids, snot dribbling from their adorable little noses and a shopping cart full of groceries—What are you trying to sell here—toilet cleaner? Birth control? I certainly can't tell." *I've done it again. Shot my mouth off. Fuck. Will I never learn?*

"But that's our demographic for this line of hose," Chip said curtly. "These are the women we're aiming at and this is what these women relate to."

"It's called 'Slice of Life' advertising, Josie." Oliver snorted at her like she was a complete moron.

"I know what 'Slice of Life' is." She glared back at him. "But I also know that it's so bloody passé it's more like 'Slice of Death' these days, and if it wasn't—this campaign would surely be the last nail in the coffin." Oliver's pencil snapped in his fingers. *Oh, cripes, I've really done it now.*

She paced round the conference table, running her fingers through her hair, trying to calm herself. Why? Why was she so antagonistic?

"I'm sorry," she sighed, "but I just have to tell you this. I know what your demographics say, I know who your customer is. But she isn't me. I'm not a housewife, and I don't live in the burbs, so why pick me as your spokesperson?"

"Well, that's the burning question, isn't it?" William smirked at her. "Bottom line is, though, you're just a model, not the 'voice' of our company." He held up his fingers in inverted commas when he said 'voice'; one of the most annoying gestures on the planet. "And as long as we're paying you, you'll do what you're told. Or, Ms. Vaughn, if you'd prefer, we'll cancel your contract." *Jerk,* she thought, but she felt terrified now.

"Now hold on a goddamned minute, all of you." Marv's crackled voice silenced them. "Let's just calm down, okay? You farshtunkene a-holes are not helping my old ticker none, I tell you."

"Sorry, Grandfather." William looked angrily down at his loafers, a pair more fringed and more obnoxious than the last, Josie noticed.

"Sorry, Marv." Josie felt like the asshole now. "Look, all I'm saying is that there must be some way of making these a little more lively, more interesting, something that makes a housewife, or working mom, if that's who you're aiming at, want to run out and buy Great Gams. They know their lives are boring. Can't we at least make what they do every day seem a little less mundane? Shouldn't we be leading them into a more exciting place instead of underlining what they already know and despair of?" Josie gesticulated passionately. "Where's the glamour? Where's the fun?"

"You got a point, kid," Marv said, raising himself shakily out of his chair.

"Grandfather, don't—"

"Can it, Bill, I'm fine. Need to pace when I'm thinking, just like Josie here." He tottered up and down the length of the room, stroking his chin, then stopped at Marcus. "And what about you, young man? You haven't said a word. What do you think about these boards?"

Marcus slowly got up, smiled at Marv, and sauntered over to the wall. "You know, sir," he said, his husky Southern drawl making him seem more laid back than he surely could be, Josie thought, "I think"—he examined the six storyboards more closely—"I can make these work."

"You do?" Josie asked incredulously. *Are you mad? Or really as dumb as a bag of hammers?*

He looked at her and smiled and she thought she'd melt all over again, even though he was making her furious. "Yeah, Josie, I think with the right angles and the right styling, we can make this look pretty good."

Great, Josie shrugged. *What was the point?* William was right. *Shut up and do what they want. Take the money and sprint.* She slumped down on the edge of the table and looked at the boards again. *What is Marcus on? These are pure shit.* She drummed her fingers on the table, looking for some clue in the drawings.

"Okay, but I'd like to do the styling, get all the clothes, and oversee the prop styling as well. That is, after all, what I'm best at." She looked over at Marv, who was still doddering around in front of her, and gave him her most innocent smile. "And just think of the money you'll save on stylist's fees!"

"You do that, kid." Marv winked at her. "Now can we all shake hands and get on with this?"

24

Priscilla looked bloody awful. Worse than awful. Josie had never seen her like this. Normally perfectly groomed and glowing with health, today there was something feral about her. Red curls, knotted like a bird's nest, clung damply on her forehead. Her eyes, dangerously wild and smudged with remnants of old mascara, gave her the appearance of a rabid raccoon on crack. Josie couldn't help staring at her friend's reflection in the wall-to-wall mirrors of her gigantic dressing room.

"Are you okay?" Josie had to step over a chaotic trail of men's clothing to get near Priscilla. It looked like Richard's entire wardrobe had been dragged out of his closets and hurled furiously across the room.

"Rose!" Priscilla screamed. "Get in here!"

Josie was horrified. "What's the matter with you?" If it wasn't crack, it was certainly some other drug.

"What's the matter with me?" Priscilla snapped. "It's all fucking disintegrating." She glared into the mirror at Josie. "My body, my face, my mind—and now my fucking marriage."

"Oh, honey." Josie reached out and gave her friend a hug. Priscilla felt rigid.

"He won't fuck me, Josie," she sobbed. "We haven't had sex in over a year."

Josie didn't know what to say. Except for Marcus—what a mistake—she hadn't had sex in nearly two years. Still, she wasn't married. Probably never would be. And maybe, she thought, looking at P., it wasn't such a terrible thing to be eternally single.

"Oh, P.," she sighed. "It's not that bad. You're beautiful. Maybe he's just going through something."

"Going through something? I'll tell you what he's going through! Another woman's pussy!" She sobbed and drew back from Josie. "And just look!" She opened her silk robe. "I'm grotesque!" She stuck her large breasts out.

Josie felt her eyes bulge. She heard a gasp from behind and saw Rose's face in the mirror, aghast.

"Would you wanna fuck this?" Priscilla wailed at them and put a hand between her legs.

"Let's get this cleaned up, Rose," Josie said, embarrassed beyond belief. She and Rose, heads to the floor, gathered up the piles of clothing.

"God, I'm sorry," Priscilla moaned. "Sorry. It's these diet pills I've been taking. They're making me nuts. And I've gained five pounds!"

"So, stop taking them," Josie sighed. "God, P., I'm really worried about you. Why are you taking diet pills? You look fine."

"They're herbal diet pills. Doctor Gene gave them to me."

"That quack! What are you—nuts?"

"No! He's supposed to be the best!"

"Best what? I bet he's not even a real doctor. And by the way—whatever happened to that boy he nearly killed?"

"He's fine!" Priscilla waved her hand dismissively. "Allergic reaction or something, that's all."

"Well, who was he?" She handed a pile of clothes to Rose, who skulked timidly out of the room.

"I have no fucking idea. Some idiotic work associate of Richard's."

"He works with Richard?"

"Richard fired his ass after that little trick he pulled. The kid's a total junkie. Rick told me he'd given him too many chances; then he comes over here and ODs at our party. Nice, huh?"

"Oh, so maybe that's why I saw Richard that day in the hospital." Josie still felt puzzled. Why did Richard ignore her? And that kid was no drug addict, or at least not a junkie who shot up. Something didn't make sense. She looked over at Priscilla, whose eyes looked even wilder than before.

"Fucking asshole. How dare he ruin my night! Now help me Josie! You've gotta help me find the cunt Richard's screwing!"

Josie felt her skin crawl. When had Priscilla become so insensitive? Was it the pills? Or was she yet another casualty of extreme wealth? The more time she spent around the truly rich, the less she liked them. Money enveloped them in careless self-absorption. Well, certainly the few really wealthy people she had known, anyway. She wondererd if Jonathon would have been so fucked up if he'd come from a poor family.

"I've been through every goddamned pocket and I haven't found a thing!"

"Is that why you called me here?" Josie felt annoyed. Like she had nothing else to do. "To help you get something on your husband? P.—you need to get a grip. You're acting like a deranged housewife."

Priscilla turned and shot her a venomous look. "What the hell would you know?" she growled. "You haven't got a clue when it comes to men! You couldn't find a husband if you were the last woman on earth! No man will ever want to marry you. You're a slut!"

Josie dropped the clothes and fled out of the room, down the long hallway to the foyer, pressed the elevator button furiously, and tried to catch her breath.

"It's you!" Priscilla screamed after her. "I know it's you! You're a fucking slut!" She came running down the hallway. "Get the fuck away from me and my husband, slut!"

Josie turned and faced Priscilla. "P., wait! This just isn't fair! You're out of control! Those drugs have addled your brain! I would *never* sleep with Richard! I don't even find him attractive!"

"I don't find him attractive!" P. wiggled her head and mimicked her cruelly. "Little miss goody-two-shoes doesn't find him attractive? You're a fucking liar, and you're going to be fucking sorry, cunt!"

She grabbed the Archipenko bronze statue from a console and hurled it at Josie, who managed to duck. It flew by her and hit a huge vase of flowers on the opposite console. The entire foyer flooded with water and floating blooms. Where the hell was the elevator?

Josie held her breath and tried to stay calm, too scared to turn her back to Priscilla in case she attacked her. P. stood and glared at her with witchlike evilness. It seemed to take an eon for the elevator to finally arrive, and when it did, Josie tried to smile at the doorman as she stepped over the sodden flowers toward him, but her heart was pounding and she had broken out in a cold sweat.

"Fuck off out of my life, bitch!" Priscilla screamed her parting shot as the doors closed.

25

"Jeez, love, can ya believe it?" Max flourished his hairdryer at Josie's mirrored reflection. "I told ya so, didn't I? Didn't I tell the old tart she looked better than ever, Ricky?"

"Jes, jou deed," sniffled Ricky, who lay swathed in a taupe cashmere blanket on the sofa behind them, filing his nails and sulking after his daily tiff with his boyfriend.

Max looked no less subdued than last time she'd seen him; the shaved chest still peeked from a red open-necked shirt, and the slim anthracite silk Gucci hipsters clung so tightly around his groin that his wedding tackle could be appraised with a single glance. Not that he'd ever get married. Not that she would either, she thought, remembering Priscilla's tirade. It had been two days since and she hadn't heard a word from P. She felt angry. Hurt. Still in shock at P.'s accusations.

"You're fuckin' famous, love!"

"Hardly. And in any case, I could do without the fame bit."

"Cut the crap, darls. I saw how you gloated when that

hunky male module recognized you in the kitchen just now. Ya fucking love it!"

"I did not!" Josie blushed.

"Ah, for Christ's sake, ya nearly stuck ya tits in his face!"

"I did not!" she squealed again but was drowned out by the sound of the dryer.

It was true. She was thrilled but totally embarrassed by all the attention she'd been getting since the Great Gams press junket had kicked into gear. She'd been interviewed on morning TV only yesterday; had done two spreads for fashion magazines; and, now, finally, they were back at Studio 28 to shoot the actual campaign.

She and Marcus had come up with a plan to alter the tedious layouts. Just a slight variation, sort of cheating, really, that would give the shots a hell of a lot more edge. The ad agency and William Gottlieb would throw a fit when they found out, but they had both agreed it was worth a try.

"So how's things going with the dragon?" said Max, as he turned off the dryer.

"Shhh!" She knew exactly who he was referring to. "Will you lower your voice to a screech please? Okay, I guess—what can I say? She got me this gig. I can't whine too much, now can I?"

"Aw, come on, darls, ya must be seething now that Hunk-Face is sticking his gorgeous shlong in her and not you." He deftly combed her hair through.

"Shut up! God, you're appalling." She still felt like a cretin for having slept with him, still felt an enormous attraction toward him, but knew nothing could ever come of it now. Antonia had rarely left his side in the past few weeks, jealously guarding him like a mother hen. Only not many mothers had sex with their progeny.

"I'd have knifed the bitch by now," he said, smoothing her hair with his tattooed hands.

"Why does that not surprise me?" She squirmed. "Aren't you finished yet?"

"Nervous, darls?"

"Yes—about you, nosy!" She poked her tongue out at him, stood up, checked her image in the mirror, then moved to the racks of clothes.

With the help of Mala, she dressed in a suit similar to the one she'd worn to the hospital to visit Marv; aggro-chic with the miniest of skirts. She strapped her feet into the highest steel-heeled stilettos ever and stalked out to the studio. Eager to get this over with, or at least started.

"Aren't you forgetting something, darls?" She turned to see Max waving a packet of Great Gams at her.

"Oh, yeah, might help to wear the product, mightn't it?" She giggled.

They hadn't told the agency they were shooting that day. They'd scheduled the exterior shots for a few days later. The driveway, the supermarket, the office shots were all to be done in the presence of William and the agency guys.

Today they were shooting her in razor-sharp, sleek clothes and the highest of heels on a plain background, with the camera close to the floor below her, making her legs look about fifty feet long. Then they'd plant the shots onto the backgrounds the agency had asked them to shoot, using computer graphics. They knew William would hate the clothes, the image, so they'd planned two shoots. One for them and the one they were supposed to be doing.

She felt as nervous as hell. *God,* she thought, *what if we're wasting all this—basically for test shots? It's costing a fortune . . . out of our own pockets! I must be out of my head . . . I've done it again . . .*

"Well"—she smiled lamely as she stood before Marcus—"here goes nothing."

"Ready?" Marcus flashed that incredible smile back at her and she tried not to melt. Especially since Antonia sat behind him, chicer than ever in a black-and-white Galliano suit and the same steel-heeled stilettos Josie's feet were scrunched into. Cell phone glued to her ear, abusing some poor sod in German, but her eyes not missing a thing in the room.

"Hang on, you can't start this auspicious event without a cocky!" yelled Max, emerging from the kitchen with a bottle of Cristal and several glasses on a tray.

"Aw, Max, give us a break! It's only eleven!" Josie objected.

"Good! We'll be as smashed as rats by lunchtime, darls!" He poured the champagne, handed it around, and made a toast. "To more of this for all of us. Cristal for breakfast! Cristal for lunch! Cristal forever!"

"Ha!" Josie downed the bubbly. "I can just see the gossip pages: 'Great Gams Legs of the Year spokeswoman legless by lunch.'"

Antonia lifted her glass and gave Josie the full benefit of her bright red Mona Lisa smile and her hard blue gaze before taking the most delicate of sips. Josie stared back at her for an instant, trying to ignore the chill in her veins.

26

"Darlin', how 'bout lunch?" Andy's supersonically loud drawl nearly broke Josie's eardrum.

"Huh?" she rasped, grappling with the phone, trying to pull it away from her ear, her heart savagely thrusting itself *Alien* style from her chest, from the shock of the ringing. "Ah, hi, Andy," she tried to say, but something like the remnants of a tube of Crazy Glue plastered around her lips prevented her from getting out more than a hoarse gurgle. She wiped the dribble from the edge of her mouth and attempted a vague recollection of her whereabouts and how she'd managed to get there. "What time is it?"

She still felt drunk. Definitely legless. The only thing she could feel was the hammering throb in her head. She could swear there were at least three serrated bread knives sawing through the swollen remains of her cell-decimated brain.

"It's nearly nine. You not up yet, darlin'? Busy gal like you should be out there grabbin' the bull by the horns."

"Aah," she bleated, "yes, well, ah, I think I tried to take the bull by the horns last night, but . . . uh . . . I got trampled." She took a swig from the water bottle beside her bed. At least she was home.

"A bull, huh. What kinda bull?"

"Ow . . . uh . . . his name was Cristal . . . but his pals Absolut, Veuve, and Grappa came along for the ride."

"Holy cow! That wasn't no trample, sugar. That was a full-on stampede. Some of that fizzy stuff will fix you up."

"Ah . . . the sound of plopping and fizzing would kill me."

"That bad, huh? Darlin', y'all need help."

"Betty Ford?" She sat up and winced as the knives increased by ten. Her loaf must be sliced into neat little grooves by now. Half-baked.

"Nothing that a hair of the old bull that gored you won't cure, shug," he boomed back so loud she had to hold the phone even farther away from her ear.

"Oh, no," she moaned and took another gulp of water.

"C'mon, get up, Ah'm takin' you to a slap-up lunch."

"No way."

"Ah'm not takin' no for an answer. Besides, we got business to discuss."

"The only discussion I could have right now would be with a large white porcelain bowl," she said, her stomach somersaulting at the mere thought of food.

"Baloney. Young gal like you should be feelin' fine after a shower and a couple of Bloody Marys. We got a meeting at one."

"Meeting?" The knives sawed down even harder as pure panic set in.

"Ah gotta friend Ah want y'all to meet, shug. Now get that cute ass of yours into gear and Ah'll pick you up at twelve. You got plenty of time."

"Twelve? Oh, no, Andy! Please! Plea—" But the phone had already clicked dead.

* * *

Mauritzio greeted them with the sort of charm that made you feel like you were his sole patron, the most important person in the entire world. Josie, eyes hidden behind the biggest, darkest sunglasses she could find, even though it was gray and raining out, hung limply from Andy's arm as their host ushered them through the garish new surrounds of his famous eatery to their booth.

"My God! Even if I didn't have the worst hangover in the history of the human race I'd need these shades," she muttered after he'd left. "What on earth possessed him? This place looks a cross between a Louis Quinze brothel and the circus on acid."

"You haven't been here since he moved?" Andy seemed surprised.

"I'm not quite the gourmand you mistake me for," she said, fighting the urge to crawl under the table and pass out. "Besides, I've neither the wallet nor the clout to eat at Mauritzio's more than once in a blue moon. I hear it takes six months to get a reservation since he reopened—unless one is a seriously heavy hitter, like you." She squeezed out a wan smile and slumped into the back of the extraordinarily high banquette, thinking the green hue of her skin probably offset the bright purple velour rather well.

"It's still the best eats in town. Worth every darn cent, if you ask me. Anyways, Ah woulda thought a beauty like yourself would be in the company of seriously heavy hitters all the time."

"I'm not that kind of girl." She was nettled by his assumptions. Maybe it was just that she'd feel nettled by anything that required more than monosyllabic answers today.

The waiter came and left with an order for a stiff and spicy Bloody Mary and a bourbon. Andy leaned forward slightly, examining her more closely than he had a right to, considering her condition. "Are you going to take those off?"

"You couldn't stand the shock. It's not a pretty sight."

"Ain't much could shock me. Let me see the pinks of your eyes, shug, and then we'll get down to business."

"I'm warning you . . . my eyeballs have been seared and there are bags the size of your home state beneath them," she said, slowly removing the glasses. The glare nearly made her faint.

"Jesus H." He withdrew in mock horror. "What the hell you been up to?"

"I wish I could remember. Now what's with this business stuff?"

"First things first, darlin'," he said, as the waiter returned with their cocktails. "The most important business of the day is to fill that tummy of yours up with the best vittles money can buy."

"And then?"

"And then we have a little jaw with mah pal from CAA to discuss your future."

"CAA? Today? Are you out of your mind? Look at me! I'm an absolute wreck!" She wanted to die right there on the spot.

"You look jest fine. Now drink up, darlin'. We got a whole lot a ground to cover. Cheers." She swigged at her drink, hoping it would bring even the faintest relief from the pounding headache and the parched interior of her mouth. But immediately she knew if she didn't get to the toilet right away, the purple velour and Andy's suit would be sprayed with projectile vomit. Her eyes bulged as she stood, hand covering her clamped lips, and tried to make a dash for it, but her passage was impeded by the arrival of a short, bespectacled man who smiled at her and held his hand out in greeting.

"Hi, Josephine, Carlton Barlow," said a voice attached to the hand, for she couldn't look the poor man in the eyes, not with scarlet froth desperately trying to extrude from her gob.

"Mmm—mm," she gulped in reply, then scampered like a wild goat from the table.

27

Hamish Kent also had a bit of a problem that morning. Except it wasn't his head that felt like it had been hacked into verminous shreds. Not that his brain was in absolutely tip-top form, but at least he could remember where he was when he opened his eyes.

The problem was his body. He realized he'd gone a bit too far this time. He'd woken to find his hands and feet still bound with black leather tubing to the posts he'd begged his master to tie him to ages before. His torso and limbs stretched in excruciating obeyance over the large round wheel, and if he lifted his head a fraction (a difficult task, due to the black leather balaclava strapped tightly around his face and neck), he could almost see the welts covering his chest. Fuck it hurt. But he'd been a very bad boy and had needed severe punishment.

He lay back for a moment, reveling in the agony, but also sensing something was wrong. No other sounds or the usual groans or chastising commands could be heard from any of the other rooms. He realized he must be alone. Where was his master? How long had he been here? They normally took him off the rack after an hour or so, but it felt like he'd been tied up a dog's age. He tried to look around, but it was almost pitch black. A lone shaft of light from a tiny barred window high on the wall to his left was all he could see by. *Bollocks.* Surely it couldn't be daylight.

It was certainly on the dank side down here in Hellfire. A putrid stench filtered through the leather. He couldn't believe he'd been left here all night. Usually they chucked him and the others out well before dawn; a bunch of excrement-sodden masochists thrown into the gutter of West Thirteenth Street, left to stagger in pain back to their daily grinds, their clean little "normal" lives. He'd met bankers and accountants, CEOs of multinational corporations, all skulking down the stairs into the exclusive bar at Hellfire, eager to be escorted into a dungeon and whipped and tortured to atone for their excessive existences.

"Mmm mm!" he tried to yell, but the zipper closed tautly over his mouth prevented any real projection in the sound department. "Mmnmm!" He struggled, which brought more agonizing shots of pain to his arms. *Buggering bollocks.* Where the fuck was everybody? "Heelph, theelph thme!" His muffled squawk only fogged up the leather mask, which now felt decidedly raspy and damp from his hot breath and sweat. He could feel the panic edging through his exhausted muscles.

Well, this is a first, he thought. *Claustro-fucking-phobic after all these years of begging for restraint. Who'd have thought it. A little torture is one thing, but a chap doesn't exactly relish the thought of being left on the fucking rack for an entire night.* He had work to do. A plane to catch. A fashion spread to shoot. "Ggrrrrahh." He made his best attempt at a scream. "Grraaaahh!"

Nothing. Nada. The fuckers must have closed shop and forgotten him. *Stupid bastards.* Still, what else could one expect from a bunch of moronic hulks covered in black leather and tats and pierced in every fucking orifice? Their brains must be fucking pierced into shrunken idiocy. Well, he certainly felt whipped into shrunken submission, except he figured by now he might be an inch or two taller from an all-nighter on the rack.

It dawned on him that any hope of getting off the contraption might be at least a whole day away. The place didn't open until ten at night. *Oh, fuck.* How could they have forgotten him? "Grrraaahh!" he howled again, more in frustration than for help. He struggled, tugging and pulling at the rubber ties, swearing and screaming from the pain as he tried to rip himself free. But the exertion was too much and he passed out.

He didn't know how long it had been before he heard the heavy footsteps and voices outside. "Thelpth! Helpth thme!" he gave a feckless wail. His mouth was parched and every muscle in his body screamed.

"Aw, Jesus. There's another one down here, Riley." A masculine bellow neared as a flashlight shone around the room, then finally hit his eyes like a burning laser. "Christ—what sort a fuckin' joint is this?"

"Mmmm," whimpered Hamish. "Thelph me, pweeth."

"Shut up, yer fuckin' deviant," said the man, as he untied his hands and feet. "You deserve to rot here with the rats eatin' away at yer scrawny little carcass."

Hamish fell off the rack into a twisted heap on the cold cement floor. "Get up, asshole." A boot landed excruciatingly into his groin. "Get up and show us yer kisser." Hamish tried to sit up but his body shook and quivered from the shock and cold. "Aw, jasus," the voice said in a rough Irish brogue. "Yer really fucking pathetic ain't yer." The man lifted Hamish up, threw him over his shoulder, and started out of the dungeon.

"Auww," Hamish groaned, his naked body flaccid yet rippling with pain. He could vaguely see the back of the man's dark trousers and the heels of his sturdy black boots as they stomped along the same long black corridor he had minced down in hungry anticipation the evening before.

"Shut up, dickhead. Yer bloody lucky we came back for a second look."

Blinding daylight scorched his eyes and he was thrown into the back of a van and a door slammed shut behind him. "Auww," he groaned again.

"That's it, O'Malley," came another voice outside, "just the two of 'em in there. Let's get the fuck outta here. This place gives me the creeps."

"Bit close to the bone, eh, Riley? Fancy a bit of a lashin' yerself, do yer?"

"Fuck off," came the reply, as the vehicle lurched, throwing Hamish across the floor and slamming him into something soft and fleshy.

"Aahh!" he screamed.

"Aahh!" came a scream in reply.

In his fright, Hamish managed to brace himself and sit up. The leather hood still clung to his face, but he could make out through the eyeholes another body sitting rigidly next to him in the dim light of the turbulent vehicle.

"Thoo are thu?" he asked.

"What?" came an irritated reply.

"I shaid—thoo the thuck are thoo?"

"I can't understand a word you're saying," the man replied, leaning over and unzipping his mouth. "Now what did you say?"

"Who are you?" panted Hamish through the slit. "What the fuck is going on?" He painfully reached behind his head and tried to undo the rest of the mask.

"Oh, wake up, you stupid pervert," came an exhausted reply. "We've been busted."

"Don't call me a fucking pervert, you depraved cocksucker," replied Hamish, tugging at the hood. He felt like his face would lift off with it. "What do you mean—busted?"

"What kind of moron are you? We were raided, shit-head. There was a raid last night and everyone fled. I guess a couple of us got lost in the sauce. Christ, didn't you hear it?"

"Well, I must've been taking my beauty sleep. What's your excuse—dick get stuck in your mouth, sweetie?" sneered Hamish, as he finally ripped off the balaclava and turned to his happy companion, who sported a grubby toweling diaper and a baby's bonnet.

"Shut the fuck up."

Their eyes met across the semidarkness. Hamish, who'd recently taken to wearing contacts on his evenings "out" on the town after the debacle in Rome, realized one of them was missing. But even with one blind eye he thought he could recognize the face of his fellow Hellfire member. He peered closer. The man peered back at him, obviously recognizing him too.

"I know you," Hamish said.

"No you don't," the man snapped, turning away. "We've never laid eyes on each other. Never. Got it?"

So they sat in glum aching silence all the way to the police station.

That evening sergeant Jimmy O'Malley sat at the kitchen table of his small Bronx apartment, sucking back a Guinness and talking to his wife, Rose.

"They're all fuckin' nuts if yer want my opinion. I mean—what kind of twisted mind must a man have to want to be beaten and pissed on in a stinkin' dungeon? One of 'em was on a bleedin' rack, Rosie, with a leather hood over 'is 'ead. It made me skin crawl, it did. Had to carry the little shite out, I did." He sighed; shook his head, which made a lock of ginger hair fall down over his pale blue eyes; and stared for a moment into the black depths of his ale before taking another pull.

"Both of them rich as Croesus, would yer fuckin' believe it," he continued after a minute. "Got their fancy lawyers down the station, bailin' them outa trouble, hustlin' them both into separate limos. It's like they got everything in the whole world, so's there's nothin' left but to be weird as all fuckin' get out. I just can't understand these rich fuckers."

"Yeah, love, I know exactly what you mean," replied his wife, who was finishing putting a layer of mashed potato on the top of a hearty shepherd's pie. "They're all as mad as snakes. Even 'Herself' has taken a turn for the worse in the past few weeks. I really think she ought to be locked away." She put the baking dish in the oven; stood up; and, wiping her hands on her apron, said, "Do you know what she did last week?"

"'Course I don't bloody know, woman."

"She flashed me."

"Flashed yer? Like naked flashed?"

"Full frontal naked, if you please! Nearly shocked the living daylights out of me. There she stood in her huge dressing room, five times the size of this whole flat, screaming about her husband. Then suddenly she opens up her fancy silk robe and asks me and her friend if we'd want to fuck someone as ugly as she is!"

"I don't fuckin' believe it!" Jimmy couldn't help wondering what the woman looked like naked. "Well, was she?"

"Was she what?"

"Ugly."

She slapped him across the cheek. "Cheeky bugger!" But she sat on his lap, took a sip of the Guinness, and kissed him.

"No, for your information she isn't ugly. She's actually rather beautiful in an overblown sort of way."

"Bet she's not a patch on you, Rosie." He hugged her and kissed her back.

"Poor Mrs. Saunders," she sighed, stretching her back and reaching for the ale.

"Eh? What's her name then?"

"Oh, for God's sake!" She stood up, annoyed at him now.

"No, no, my love, that's not what I meant. What's her name again?"

"Then what do you mean? You want to go calling her up do you? Want to see her naked do you?"

"No, lass"—he rose, towering above her—"don't be daft. It's not like that at all. I mean I want to know her name is all."

"I've worked with Priscilla nigh on five months. You ought to know her name by now," she said tartly. "Some cop you make, don'tya, not remembering the name of his own wife's boss."

"Well tell me again," he replied, somewhat abashed.

"Priscilla," she sighed, shaking her dark curls in disbelief. "Priscilla Saunders. Got it through that thick skull of yours?" She slumped over to the sideboard and took out the dinner plates.

"Saunders, d'you say?"

"For the love of God—yes! Saunders."

"Kent and Saunders were their names—them perverts we threw in the klink this morning," he said, standing like a big hulk next to her.

"Saunders?" Her eyes widened.

"Richard Saunders."

"Oh, sweet Jesus." The plates fell onto the bright green linoleum, smashing into white shards.

28

"Why are you doing this?" Josie leaned against the enormous mahogany desk and coldly scrutinized Andy's eyes in an attempt to detect the duplicity, the lie he must be concealing. As if his (or anyone else's, for that matter) presence in her life in any sort of beneficent capacity could not be possible, or true. And as if she'd be able to see it in his face, just like that, or get him to admit his conspiracy against her with one grudging stare. She knew how pathetically naive this was, but she couldn't help herself. She didn't for a moment suspect Andy of being any different from the norm. "Why are you being so kind to me?"

He leaned calmly back in his aged leather wingbacked chair with an expression of benign amusement, which irritated her, made her even more suspicious.

"You know why," he said, after a long pause, during which she'd managed to regret her puerile endeavor at hostile self-protection and rip her glare from his face out to the panoramic vista of the East River behind him. Losing herself, her nerve. She felt she didn't belong here, in the stratospheric realm of high-powered commerce. It made her giddy with a confusing dichotomy of greed and inadequacy. "You're a very smart woman. Ah'm sure, by that look of yours, you got me pegged."

She glanced back at him, expecting to see the pearly whites flashing condescendingly at "the little woman" before him. Instead, his normally jovial countenance had been replaced with earnestness. It jolted her.

"I'm sorry," she said, fidgeting with the hem of her jacket. "My judgments . . . can be . . . rash and . . . superficial."

"Your judgments ain't wrong," he replied, his pale eyes burning through the new Paul Smith glasses he'd purchased with her the day of her embarrassing encounter with the CAA agent. He'd refused to allow her to be ill, had dragged her from the restaurant on an afternoon shopping spree, during which he'd insisted she style him head to toe in whatever she saw fit. It had nearly killed her trying to be professional when she felt so vile, but she liked him for being so obstinate with her. Not letting her off the hook. Naturally, the pink and gold glasses had been the first thing to go. She hadn't let him off the hook either.

"You should learn to trust your instincts more. Rely on the gut. Ain't never wrong, not if you listen properly."

"Is that what you do? Your business is run on instinct?"

"That—and a few spreadsheets, a floor full of lawyers, and bushels of bean counters," he laughed, then reverted to his seriousness. "Now, of course y'all know Ah'm a businessman. Ah'm as hard bitten as they come. Ah don't normally go 'round helpin' folks out for the hell of it. But when Ah can be nice to someone Ah like . . . why that makes me happy. Real happy." He loomed toward her now, as if to assert his power, but his eyes betrayed him. She smiled, feeling strength rush back into her veins.

"So your angle here is . . . ?"

"C'mon, you already know that. You've known it all along, I'd guess. Hell, it's already been hinted at in that gossip column. We want you for Vive. New campaign. New product. New woman. We want a woman, not some silly little girl. A real woman. A woman who's been around the block, seen a few things. Has a few lines on her face. But can still send a man into a frenzy. And you're that woman."

"Love the sound of that!" she laughed. "That's all I've ever dreamed of—sending men into frenzies!" She stood up and walked to the gigantic ceiling-to-floor window, feeling his eyes on her. "Of course, I knew what you were thinking all along. I mean I'd have to be a complete dolt if I didn't. But it wasn't my business to say anything until you offered. And naturally I just adore the sound of another contract and another nice big fat check or two." She looked down at the city beneath them. It seemed miles below, like they were floating on some cloud of unreality.

"Nice view, ain't it?" He swiveled his chair around. "Get some of my best ideas lookin' outa this window."

"I can't look down." She stepped back, feeling that fear, like she'd fall or be pushed off the cloud, back down to reality, to earth. She didn't feel like she was on earth right now. More like she was on some strange planet.

"Only ever look up, darlin'."

"Your motto?"

"Somethin' like that."

"So what's your other angle?" She turned to face him.

"Ouch." He gave a pained expression. "You just don't quit now, do you?"

"Would you?"

"You got me there." He stood up, very close to her, and, for a terrifying moment, she thought he'd try to kiss her, but, to her relief, he held out his hand. "Are we friends?" he boomed.

"Y . . . yeah . . . I guess so," she said, embarrassed by his forthrightness but more because of her silly assumption. "Yes, of course."

"Good. 'Cause it's about time you started trustin' me. Ah ain't out to get you." Mortified, she looked away, back down to the ant farm below.

Why am I such a jerk? Why can't I just accept this man and his generosity?

"Ah'm offering you a major contract here, and all you can think of is that Ah'm gonna screw you somehow." An awkward hush engulfed the space between them, and she thought she'd keel over, through the plate glass.

"Oh, God, Andy . . . I'm sorry . . . you see it's just that . . . that—"

It's just that I can't trust any man ever again. Don't you get it?

"It's okay. I understand. No need to say you're sorry. Now, you gonna shake on this?" He offered his hand again. "Or you gonna stand there all lily-faced and let a great deal slide right by you?"

"But why, Andy? Why me? Why not some supermodel or famous actress?"

"Like Ah said before, darlin', it all comes from here"—he pointed to his stomach—"gut instinct."

"Thanks . . . I don't really know what else to say . . ." She held out her hand, took his, and looked him straight in the eyes. "Thanks."

"Course, it all has to go before the board. Then there's all that market testing stuff they do, but Ah got a hunch on this."

"I really appreciate everything you've done for me . . . the agent . . . just giving me a chance . . . all this—despite the fact that I've nearly thrown up on you twice now!" She giggled at him, still not believing anything that was happening.

"And Ah thought you Aussies could drink." He shook his head and laughed.

29

They huddled around the computer screen, mesmerized by the images being contorted and re-created.

"Amazing," Josie said, as the graphics editor totally erased her figure from a supermarket scene and filled in the blank space so perfectly she couldn't tell she'd ever been there at all.

"So which shot do you want to drop in there?" He looked back to her, then to Marcus. "This one?" He pulled up a shot of her in a tiny red slip dress and sky-high, gold strappy Giuseppe Zanotti sandals.

She noticed how the glare from the screen edged the angles of Marcus's jaw and profile as he carefully inspected the images. The way his eyelashes fluttered slightly with concentration, the way his long fingers with their clean white nails absently moved over the stubble on his chin, grazing his lips.

All she could think of was leaping on him. Straddling him. *Stop! Don't be so fucking shallow. He's not for you.*

"Hello? Anybody home?" Marcus was tapping her shoulder.

"Oh! Sorry!" She jumped. "Sorry! What?"

"I said—what do you think?"

"Think?" She ran her fingers nervously through her hair and looked down at the floor, flustered. When she looked up he was smiling at her and she could feel the red in her cheeks.

"About this!" He pointed at the screen, almost laughing. "Come on! Wakey wakey!"

"Wow."

Before her a giant woman—herself—marched down a supermarket aisle, her long legs dwarfing the products. "Supermarket Superwoman!" She leaned closer and examined the shot. "It's . . . fantastic . . . but . . . something's not right." She frowned. "Can you move her—me—forward?" The image moved an inch closer to them. "I'm not sure . . . is that it? Maybe it's that outfit. A suit's probably better . . . nobody wears a red silk slip dress to the supermarket—"

"Nobody's fifteen feet tall, either," Marcus said, "so does it matter?"

"Oh, yeah, course it does. We want to give the image of power . . . like if you wear these panty hose nothing will get to you, not even shopping for dog food after a nightmare day at work. I think definitely a suit for this one . . . we can use the red dress for the night scene in the city."

They stayed glued to the screen as the editor pulled up all ten shots of her in different outfits and placed them side by side. "That one!" they said in unison when the last picture of her appeared. She leaned forward, half closing her eyes, checking the proportions, the way she stood, her face, and finally that her legs looked absolutely flawless.

"Can you lose the crow's feet?"

"He can lose anything, can't you, Ed?" Marcus said, leaning in. She could feel his eyes at the same level as hers, close to the screen, his face almost brushing hers.

Oh . . . my God. She took a deep breath and tried to concentrate, tried to ignore him and the rush of adrenaline that had her heart racing. *Be professional! Stop! Now! Please don't make a complete fool of yourself. Not again. This guy is bad news. He hurt you. Just because he's the hunkiest guy on the planet doesn't mean you should act on your pathetic urges.* It *will* never *work.*

Then suddenly his hand was on her thigh, gently. She flinched and nearly leaped from her seat but somehow managed to stay put. Her eyes flickered to the side and caught his for an instant before she stared intently back at the screen.

Never—got it?

30

Marv's skin formed slack folds around his jaw; his mouth hung open, quivering slightly; and his eyelids flickered in an R.E.M. spasm. Josie hated to wake him. She looked around the room, his "leg parlor," or whatever he called where they now sat in sleek black leather and chrome chairs, surrounded by limbs and high-fashion heels. Not knowing quite what to do. Why had the nurse just left her there? Surely she was supposed to be with him at all times. What if he had a seizure or something?

She placed the manila envelope on the Allen Jones coffee table, rose, and slowly circled the oval room, marveling at the collection of legs. She stopped when she reached the far end, where she knew his wife's leg stood on a pedestal behind the sliding panel. For some reason she felt an urge to take another peek at the old man's object of desire. Just as she reached for the button, she heard a dry cackle.

"Oh!" She jumped and pulled her finger back.

"Ah," said Marv, as she turned toward him, "what a dream . . . what a dream." He sat up in the chair and adjusted his tie, another leg adorned with shocking pink floral hose, a garter belt, and a high black sandal that laced around the ankle. She wondered who on earth made them all for him. "And how are you, my dear?"

"Fine, Marv, just fine. Yourself?" She hustled back and rounded the table to face him.

"I could sure do with a drink." He smiled at her.

"What would you like? A tea? Water?"

His milky eyes looked vaguely in her direction; then he reached to a small leg-shaped table beside his chair and grabbed his glasses. When he had them secured on his face, his eyes darted around the room. "Where is the old battle-ax? She around?"

"Haven't seen her."

"Good," he whispered. "Then you can get me a J.D. on the rocks."

"Marv, I'm sure you're not supposed to—"

"Balls!" he croaked. "I'm not supposed to do anything now except be an old fart. To hell with them all—just get it for me!"

"Anything you say, Marv." She went to the bar and poured him a glass leg full. "By the way . . . how did you know it was me, if you couldn't see me?"

"I could tell by the way you walk." He pulled a stubbed-out cigar from the inside pocket of his pin-striped suit and lovingly sniffed it. "I can always tell a woman by the sound of her feet, always could. I could smell you, too. Bois des Isles. Always loved that perfume. Bought it for Helen in Paris . . . from Miss Chanel's atelier . . . 1939, I believe it was, just after we left the old country." He placed the torpedo between his ancient lips, creakily leaned forward and grasped a leg-shaped lighter off the table, lit up, took a long draw, and melted back into the chair.

"So, you want another look at my Helen, do you?" he said, as she handed him his leg full of bourbon.

"You're a treat, Marv." She laughed in amazement. "You must have eyes in the back of your head."

"You don't live this long without learning a trick or two." He took a large swig and sighed. "Ahh. Bliss. There's not much I need to feel good these days and I'm not allowed any of it. What the damn difference is a stogey and a drink going to make at this stage? They're all out to get me. Denying an old man his last few pleasures. Quickest way to kill someone off, that's for sure. I'm dying of boredom here."

"Oh, Marv." She sat down opposite him. "It's not that bad. You've got all this." She waved around the room. "And your business, your family—"

"Family! Don't talk to me about family! Did you meet Eva Braun yet? Assholes deliberately got me the ugliest nurse in the whole tristate area. Oy, what a face. She's got a mug like a dropped plate of gefilte fish. And her legs! Did you get a load of those things? A hippo would be embarrassed to stand on those wharf piles! Oy."

He had a point. She'd imagined his nurse would be some cutie with long legs and white fishnets encasing a beautiful set of pins. She could just see Marv hiring a nurse solely on the grace of her legs. Instead, she'd been greeted—if that's what one could call it—by a woman with a dour, Teutonic disposition and an obvious propensity for capacious amounts of fatty victuals.

"And you," he said, still riled up, "even you've disappointed me now. You, of all people."

"Me?" She stiffened.

"You haven't joined forces with the rest of them, have you?"

"The rest of who?"

"My goddamned family! Did they put you up to this?"

"Up to what? What have I done?" She felt anguish gushing through her.

"They're out to destroy me, I tell you. Bore the old

man to death, then take over the company. They got to you, didn't they?" He sighed. "What a goddamned sight! How could you do this to me?"

She looked down at the soft gray wool of her Marc Jacobs suit, thinking he must have lost the plot. Paranoid delusions. Maybe William was right. Maybe he was senile after all. She looked back up at him and smiled weakly but she knew her face was awash with confusion.

"How could you?" he whispered, pointing a bony finger to her legs. "How could you hide those from me? They're all I've got left."

"Oh, Marv!" The penny finally dropped. "I'm sorry!" She clasped her hands over the knees of her trousers, as if to hide the offensive garment from his view. "Sorry. It was freezing out and I had a lot of running around to do. I—"

"Ask for my car next time—anything—but never come here in pants again. Never. Hear me?"

"Yes, sir."

He sighed and leaned back, then took another slug. "I know I'm being an irascible old goat, but I've earned it. Paid my dues. I'm sick of being the nice guy. They can all go to hell."

"You really think your family is against you?"

"They're out to get rid of me, one way or another."

"Really?"

"In a box, preferably. I'm in the fight of my life and I'm not going down. Not while I've still got a pulse."

"Oh, Marv, let me help." She raced to him as he shakily stood up.

"I'm fine, I'm fine." He waved her away and shuffled over to the bar, ducked under the gate, and refilled his glass.

She followed him over and sat on a leg stool. "I mean I'd like to help you. With your family."

"Now, don't you worry about old Marv." His eyes

twinkled milky blue at her. "I'm doing okay. Just need a good game plan is all. Drink?"

"Love one."

He poured another leg full of bourbon. "They're trying to have me declared incompetent."

"Incompetent! You? You could run rings round the lot of them, from what I've seen."

"Senile. Can you believe it?" He handed her the drink. "After all I've done for them. Well, I've still got the controlling interest. If they don't stop with this senile crap, I'll dump the lot, just to spite them. Cheers."

"Cheers." So it was true, she thought. William really was out to get him. She took a sip. "Ah," she shuddered. "You know"—she fingered the hem of her jacket—"William hates me. For some reason he's got it in his head that I'm his enemy."

"He thinks you cost too much."

"Did I?"

Marv tilted his withered skull to one side and looked at her. "Probably," he cackled, "but I think you're worth every dime."

"Well, he's about to hate me even more."

"Is that so?" His eyes lit up.

She walked back to the table and picked up the manila envelope. "I wanted to show you these." She slid the photographs out. "You might hate them, but, well, Marcus and I think they're pretty hot. They're not at all what William and the agency had in mind, but we just wanted to try something different, a bit more . . . sharp . . . new . . . fun."

Butterflies leapt around her stomach as she watched Marv pick each shot up and examine it closely through his thick lenses. If he hated them, Marcus and she would have wasted their money. Thousands of dollars down the toilet. *Oh, God. What have I done? A bundle spent on ten shots. What a fucking moron I am. Ten useless test shots.* She closed her eyes, unable to bear it, waiting for him to fire her. Finally, she couldn't wait any longer.

"Well?" She stared at his wizened face for some kind of clue.

"I've never seen anything like these," he said, still peering at the shots. "Not in all my years have I seen this kind of style."

And . . . this would mean . . . you like them? You hate them? Do I still have a job? She broke out in a cold sweat and slugged back the rest of her drink.

"Sensational."

"Really? You like them?"

"Love 'em."

"Oh, God, I'm so relieved, you have no idea." She jumped off the bar stool, ran around the back of the bar, and gave him a big hug.

"I'm sure my grandson will hate them," he said with glee, through the mounting haze of cigar smoke. "Goody."

"So you're with me," she wheezed, "Marcus and me, on this? You'll back us up?"

"One hundred and ten percent." He took another draw on his cigar, chuckled, and swigged from the glass leg.

"And what is this?" came a stern voice from beyond the curtain of smoke. "What is going on here?"

The corpulent white form of the nurse loomed before them. Marv and Josie froze like two guilty children caught in some nefarious act. "Mr. Gottlieb! It is verboten!" She snatched the cigar from his mouth. "Und this!" She picked up the glass and shook it at him. "Poison, Mr. Gottlieb! You will not drink! Alcohol is verboten!" she roared. Nurse Ratchet had nothing on this babe.

"Hilda." Marv picked up the other glass and defiantly took a swig. "My friend and I are having a little party—so you just mosey on back to your room." He waved his hand dismissively at her. "Go on. Out."

"No! It is my duty, Mr. Gottlieb. You must obey!"

"Out. Get out you nosy old bag! Leave us alone!" He booted at her vast shin. "Out!"

The colossal white shape reversed back into the haze. Josie wondered why she didn't hear wide-load beeps. "I will tell your grandson, Mr. Gottlieb, und your doctor!"

"Good, Hilda, you do that. And Hilda"—he reached forward and grabbed the stogy from her, took another long drag, and blew it in her large round face—"you're fired!"

"You cannot fire me! Only your grandson can fire me."

"Then why don't you go stay at his house? I'll call and tell him to expect you." A mischievous grin corrugated his leathery skin, giving him a wicked, elflike appearance. "Josephine, my dear"—he shuffled back to the bar and gazed milkily again at the photographs—"I think it's time we honed our stilettos."

31

"What'll it be?"

"Glass of milk," Jonathon said, lighting up a smoke with his camouflage Zippo. He loved his Zippos. You could light up in a hurricane and they'd never go out. He knew Joe wouldn't rat on him, even though smoking was banned these days. "Don't look so surprised," he said, at the flicker of a rise in the bartender's right eyebrow. "Can't you tell?" He blew a cloud of smoke up and offered his sweetest grin. "I'm a whole new man, Joe."

"Lunching with your mother today, Mr. Jonathon?" Joe said, swiftly placing a highball down on the bar and filling it with milk.

"You've known me too long." He sipped at the white froth and grimaced. "Gotta put on a good show for the Terrorist."

"Indeed, sir."

"How long have you known me, Joe?"

"Your family has been coming to the Cosmopolitan for twenty years, Mr. Jonathon," Joe said, wiping and polishing the pristine appliances behind the long mahogany bar. He sure ran a tight ship. *Had to,* Jonathon thought, *or people like us wouldn't drop thousands every year in dues.*

"More than half my life." He sucked his cigarette like it was his last. "Figures. Eaten more meals here than I ever did at home. Do you know, Joe, ever since I can remember—although most of it's a blur these days—but I mean when we were kids, my parents never ate at home. Never. Always ate out. Not even one meal with us unless we were out with them. They still don't. I don't think my mother's stepped foot in her kitchen since they split this time."

"On the outs again, are they?"

"Third time this year, can you believe it?" He liked his chats with Joe. He was a good guy, a guy who cared. Joe'd looked after him a few times, when he'd been real down and dirty. Got him home safely, never said a word to his folks, and wouldn't take a tip. That's the kind of guy he was.

"I'd believe anything in this town," Joe said.

"Yeah, he strolls 'round the corner from the house to a suite at the Carlyle, has his clothes delivered and they bicker by phone for a few months 'til they realize they want to bicker in person 'cause there's no one else who'll put up with their shit. Drives my brother and sister and me nuts when they're apart, 'cause then we gotta listen to the Terrorist whining, and my dad, well that's another whole story. He just closes the store. Can't get through to him at all."

"No accounting for love." Joe smiled and adjusted his bow tie in the mirrored back wall, which was his signal he had another customer.

Jonathon saw an elegantly dressed, dark-haired woman perching herself on a stool halfway along the bar from him. Good-looking woman, probably one of the members' wives. His mom probably knew her. And where the fuck was the Terrorist anyway? Late, as usual.

He was starving for a real drink now, just sitting here. The least she could do if she wanted him to stay sober was arrive on time for once in her life. Still, he'd been sober for three whole weeks now, a fucking miracle, and for once he didn't want to blow it. Things with Daniela were tough enough without him liquidizing his brain and shooting it back up his arm. He took another sip of his milk, almost retched, and lit another smoke with the end of the first one.

"Excuse me," the woman said in his direction. "I know you, don't I?" She stood up and advanced and he swiveled his head to see whom she was addressing. Nobody else there. She sat at the stool next to him. He noticed she had a killer set of legs and the highest heels he'd ever seen. Even his mother didn't wear heels that high, and she practically had the mandate on the highest heels, she was so tiny.

"Probably," he said. "I'm here twenty years now. You've probably watched me grow up, like Joe here." The woman flinched slightly.

"I'm not that old, darling," she sniffed, in a sharp Brit accent. "I believe we met quite recently." Joe raised an eyebrow in disgust.

"Oh, yeah." Jonathon had no clue who she was. Hell, he'd been fucked up for months, years, it was hard to remember everyone he came across. Anyone, for that matter. He hoped he hadn't slept with her or anything dumb like that. *Na,* he thought, looking at her more closely, *too old.* She looked like a younger Joan Collins with sharp blue eyes and bright red lips. Jesus, that's all he needed—the Terrorist to arrive in time to see him squirming his way out of the fallout from another drug-hazed incident—with a members' wife, no less.

"In the park. Early one morning, with Josie Vaughn." *Oh, Christ, even worse.* He felt his pulse start racing. *Fuck.* He sucked so hard on his smoke he thought it would disappear in one hit.

"What of it?" he said, feeling the acid from his stomach ulcer kicking into gear. "I'll be frank with you, Mrs—"

"Kent." She pouted her lips at him. "Antonia Kent."

"Kent," he said, a vague recollection of the name nudging around his memory. "Well, Mrs. Kent, let's just put it this way. If I ever hear her name again, it'll be way too soon for my liking."

"You already told me that once before." She smiled at him. The kind of smile a guy could think was a come-on if he'd had a few. "And I agree with you, wholeheartedly." She picked up the glass of champagne Joe had put down in front of her and took the tiniest of sips. Her blue eyes iced into him for an instant and he remembered, sort of, that morning when he'd collapsed in the park. Well, he remembered her legs and heels, anyway. And those eyes.

"Listen, I wasn't exactly in tip-top form that morning," he said, ashamed to have to talk about anything he'd done lately.

"No, you weren't, were you?" Jesus, maybe he had fucked her. *Throw me a bone,* he thought. *Give me a clue, a morsel of what I said—anything.*

"Are you a member here, Mrs. Kent?"

"Oh, no, but strangely enough, I'm dining with someone here—a member, of course—who is not at all thrilled about your ex, either." She smiled that strange little smile again. *Christ who do you think you are—The Mona fucking Lisa?*

"Yeah? Well get in line," he said. "Look, I really don't want to talk about her, okay?" He pulled out another Marlboro and lit up. He'd had about enough of this woman. She was too nosy. He felt his teeth gritting. Now he'd kill for a shot of Stoli.

"Propping up the bar again, Jonathon?" His mother's nasal drawl was almost music to his ears.

"Very funny, Mom." He turned away from the strange woman and leaned out to kiss his mother, who brushed his mouth with her cheek.

The familiar smell of her Chanel Number Five wafted around him. With her immaculately coiffed blond hair and daytime uniform of a suit, probably from the latest Valentino or Chanel couture; high heels; and serious baubles around her neck, ears, and fingers, she looked, as always, perfect. Nothing in her appearance had been left to chance. Nothing at all natural about her. Perfect, in that way New York women of a certain age and economic surfeit always accomplish with such polished deftness.

He both liked that about her and detested it. Everything had to be perfect with her. And yet she was so screwed up. Why couldn't she just be a real mom?

"And who's your friend?" she asked, eyeing the woman up and down. Perfect on the outside, except for that voice of hers, which gave her away big time.

"We just met," he said, rising, not wanting to get into anything about Josie. Not here, not with his mother.

"Antonia Kent." She slid her red manicured hand lightly around his mother's soft-pink nails. "You must be Mrs. Cantero." That annoying smile again. Like butter wouldn't melt.

"Kent," his mother said, "that rings a bell. Kent."

Aw c'mon, Mom, let's go. He closed his eyes.

"Are you new here?"

"No, I'm meeting Priscilla Saunders, and actually I'm meeting her—"

"Ah, the Saunderses." His mother was suddenly interested. "Whiterock. My husband knows him. I haven't met her."

"Mom," Jonathon said impatiently, "please, we have to get going. I have an appointment."

"Well, you should, Mrs. Cantero, because as coincidence would have it, we all have something in common." Antonia rose up, towering over his mother in her stilettos. "As a matter of fact, I was just saying to Jonathon that we'd met before, with—"

"Ahem." Joe was adjusting his bow tie. "Mrs. Kent, I believe Mrs. Saunders has arrived."

"Excuse me, Mrs. Kent, but we really must be going. We're late." Jonathon steered his mother away from her. "Have a great lunch. Thanks, Joe." He gave a gratified wink to him. "See you later." Joe winked back. *Saved the fucking day again, Joe.*

"Will you stop with the pushing, Jonathon," his mother said, pulling her arm away from his grip. "What's with you anyway?"

"Can we just eat, Mom? I'm starving."

They sat in the wood-paneled dining room with its heavy velvet drapes and old masters adorning the walls. He liked coming here; it felt like home, even though it reeked of tired and musty old formality. The food was always pretty good, though, for a club; basic stuff like steaks and chicken pot pies. Which he knew his mother would send back and bitch about at least twice, like she expected it to be Le Cirque or something.

"So, who is that woman?" his mother said, looking around and smiling at a few of the other patrons. "I know that name. Why'd you drag me away from her?"

"I dunno," he lied. "She was weird." Christ, he'd love a drink. He was relieved when his mother didn't reply. Instead, she fished a gold compact out of her Chanel handbag and examined the paint on her face. "You look gorgeous, Mother," he said, "perfect as always. Now, can we please order?"

"Oh, so that's Priscilla Saunders," she said, angling the mirror. "The redhead. Mmm. Pretty, but she could lose a few."

"Mom! Will you put that thing away!"

"You can see her; she must be straight in front of you."

"Mother!"

"Antonia Kent. Antonia Kent. It's gonna drive me crazy. I know that name."

"Mom, I'm warning you. Put your goddamned compact away and pay attention to me."

"And what could we possibly have in common?"

"Okay, that's it," he hissed. "You wanna find out about her? Fine. Then go over and ask them. Go join the other two harpies and pick at a few carcasses. I'm outa here. Thanks a fucking lot for lunch, Mom. It was fabulous, as always." He threw his napkin on the table and stood up.

"Jonathon! Watch your language! People are looking at us!"

"Language?" he snarled. "Language? Is that all you care about? 'Cause if it is, I suggest you take a few fucking voice lessons, Mom." He stormed out of the dining room and headed back to the bar.

32

The Great Gams lobby gleamed white and silver, an original sixties minimalist design that was totally cool again. "I can handle this," Josie muttered, as she started up the curved flight of white terrazzo stairs. "I can handle anything. It's all going to be fine." She tried to ignore the nausea mounting with each step up to the conference room. "I can handle this." *Oh, God, who am I kidding? I'm toast.*

"Josie!" She looked down over the stainless steel railing to see Marcus at the entry. "Wait!" He sprinted across the white terrazzo floor, past the curved reception desk, and up to her.

"Hi!" He leaned down and kissed her on the mouth.

"Hi," she said, pulling away, embarrassed. *Oh, God, help me handle this.* She didn't know if she felt relieved or more agitated seeing him.

"Showtime, huh?" He patted the black leather portfolio of shots under his arm.

"Yeah, showtime." She breathed in.

"Nervous?"

"Me? Nervous? Never!" She tried to laugh, but a sort of groan came out instead.

"That bad, huh?"

"Oh, no. Not at all. We've got it all sewn up. He's gonna love the shots and we'll be able to do the second shoot any way we want, isn't that right?"

"I sure as hell hope so," he laughed.

"How come you never seem nervous?"

"I don't see the point. Whatever happens, happens, you know?"

"God, I envy you. All I can think is they're gonna throw me out on my ass. He's looking for any excuse and we're handing it to him on a silver platter."

"Oh, we'll get around him. You already said we had Marv on our side. Besides, if it doesn't work out, it doesn't work out." He shrugged. "There'll be other jobs."

"Not for me." She sighed and leaned back on the rail. "I'm already past my 'sell-by' date."

"Yeah, right," he laughed. "What about your contract with Vive?"

"That's a pie in the sky right now. How'd you know about that, anyway?"

He smiled that gorgeous smile at her. It was almost too much to bear. "Oh," she said, "don't bother telling me. Come on." She started up the stairs again.

"She's pissed at you, you know."

"Oh, God, what about now?"

"That you've signed with another agent."

"Another agent?" She stopped again and looked up at him. "Antonia's not a model agent! What is her problem? I don't know, I just can't put a foot right with that bitch." For the first time he looked uncomfortable. "Oh, sorry. Look, I am sorry, Marcus, but you may as well know what I think."

"That's been blatantly obvious all along. And you

shouldn't jump to conclusions about her. She's not that bad."

"Well, you have to say that, don't you? You're the one who's got to fuck her."

His jaw hardened and he looked down at his shoes for an instant before saying, "Let's go," and starting up the stairs.

Oh, God, she thought. *I've gone and done it again. Me and my big mouth.*

"Oh, Marcus. I'm sorry. That was way out of line."

"Stop saying you're sorry all the time. You know you don't mean it."

"I do so mean it!" She ran up the stairs after him. "I really am sorry! Ahhh!" Her brand-new Rene Caovilla shoe slipped on the shiny terrazzo and she went flying. "Aaaahhh!" she squealed, as she tumbled into a heap at the bottom of the stairs.

"Josie!" she heard Marcus yell. "Are you okay?" He was instantly at her side, helping her sit up. "Are you all right?" He hugged her.

"Yeah, I think so," she gasped, but everything was swimming and her whole body quivered like Jell-O.

"Here, let me help you." He gently pulled her up. "Anything broken?"

"No, of course not." She stood. "Ow. Oww!" The pain shot through her left knee. "My knee. It's okay. I'm okay . . ." She put her weight on it and the pain shot through again. "Ow!"

He picked her up, threw her over his shoulder, walked her back up the stairs, and marched along the corridor to the boardroom. "Ahh," she flinched. *Oh, God, I probably weigh a ton. How mortifying. First I offend him and now I'll probably put his back out. And my skirt feels like it's up my ass, which means that my panty hose with the giant hole in the top must be too. And they're not Great Gams either. Shit.* She fought back tears, more of humiliation than pain.

"Let's have a look." He lay her down on a long, white leather daybed. "Where does it hurt?"

"My knee, it's only my knee." She felt like a total moron. "I'm sure it's nothing."

"You may have pulled a ligament," he said, touching it.

"Ouch! Well that's my punishment, isn't it." She tried to laugh.

"Don't be sill—" He was looking wide-eyed at her. "Oh my—"

"What? What is it?" she cried, patting her face with her hands. "What?"

"Your, uh, tooth." His eyes were glued to her.

"My too—oh, no!" She felt the gaping hole in the front of her mouth and the razor-sharp stub of tooth that remained. "My cap! My cap's gone!" She attempted to stand, and ignoring the shooting pain in her knee, she hobbled toward the door. "Quick," she cried, "quick! We've gotta find it!"

"Sit down!" He picked her back up and practically threw her onto the daybed again.

"I can't let them see me like this! Let's leave before it's too late and—"

"Shut up, will you and just calm down. I'll find it, okay?" And he was out the door, scanning the floor as he went.

Her tongue rasped over the ghastly stump in her mouth again. "Oh, God, why?" She slumped down over her knees and covered her face with her hands and tried to hold back the tears. The last thing she needed now was red bulbous eyes and a runny nose.

"Ahem."

"Uh!" She sucked her breath in and she felt her

lungs about to explode. A pair of ugly alligator shoes with tassels and fringes came into view between her fingers.

"Anything the matter, Josephine?"

"Mmm, mm." She shook her head up at William Gottlieb and gave the nicest smile she could without opening her mouth.

"Mmm." She gave the saccharin-sweet tight-lipped smile again and pointed jauntily toward the door. William turned to see Marv's shrunken frame appear in the doorway.

"Morning, all," he cackled and hobbled in with the aid of a cane that was, of course, carved and painted in the shape of a woman's leg with a high heel supporting it. *Ah, Marv,* Josie thought, *what a treat you are.* "What's that young man doing out there? He's on his hands and knees in the middle of the stairs. Nearly tripped over him."

"I'll call him in, Grandfather." William stalked out.

"And what's the matter with you?" Marv scowled at Josie. "You look like you've seen a ghost."

"Hi, Marv," she mumbled, with her hand over her mouth. "Had a bit of a fall out there." She couldn't look him in the eye but instead pointed at her feet. "New shoes, you know?"

"You all right?"

"Well, my knee hurts a bit, not much, just a little." She shrugged up at him, still with her hand planted over her gob. "May I borrow your cane for a minute?"

"Sure." He gave her that quizzical wizened gaze of his. "Anything else hurt?"

"Mm-mm." She shook her head and curled her lips up in another natty smile. He didn't look convinced.

"Let's have a look." He shuffled over and handed her the cane as he bent down and peered at her knee through his horn-rimmed glasses. She took the leg-cane and stood painfully up and tried not to grimace.

"I think you ought to get that seen to."

"Mmm."

"I mean the tooth, not the knee."

"Oh, Marv." She didn't know if she should laugh or cry. "What am I going to do?"

"Just go see Irma and let me handle this. Now—are you ready yet, William? And where are those ad boys?" he said, as William and Marcus entered behind him.

How on earth does he do it?

Marcus winked at her and gave a thumbs-up. "Will you excuse me for a minute?" she muttered and hobbled toward him. He passed the tooth into her hand and she almost ran, even with the pain shooting down her leg, into the hallway.

"What now?" she heard William sigh, as she managed to squeeze by the phalanx of ad agency execs marching self-importantly to the boardroom.

"Quick," she panted to Marv's secretary, Irma, "I need some glue."

"What kind of glue?" Irma said. She was a woman of an indeterminate age who must have been a real looker in her day.

"I don't know," Josie said, "anything you think that could fix this"—she held up the cap—"back in here." She opened her mouth.

"Oh," Irma said, not at all riled, "you're in luck." She got up and walked into Marv's office. She had a fantastic pair of legs and she wore her skirt right at the knee, and high pumps. Marv's dictate, most likely. She returned with a tube of denture glue. "Here. This should do the trick."

"Marv wears dentures?"

Irma shot her an "I-can't-believe-you're-asking-such-a-dumb-question" look.

"Ah, yeah, well." Josie snatched the tube. "Thanks Irma, you're a gem."

* * *

"Nice of you to finally grace us with your presence." William glared at Josie after she sat back down. "Can we begin now?"

"Sorry," she mumbled in reply, still unsure of the strength of her new fang. Still, if that stuff worked for Marv, then it should work fine holding one measly tooth. Her leg throbbed now, and she could feel her knee swelling, but she wanted to get this over with.

"So," William continued, "I hear you have a surprise for us. I must admit, I don't much like surprises, but if you think you're onto something we're all ears. What is it?"

"They've done something sensational with those boring layouts of yours is what," Marv said, pulling out a cigar and giving it an unlit suck. "Show 'em, kid."

Marcus opened up the portfolio of graphically enhanced photos and spread them along the length of the boardroom table.

The agency guys hovered over the shots, with obvious distrust mingled with the fear of committing themselves to any one point of view. God forbid they offend the client. But which client should they be trying to please? William, or Marv? Not only that, but they had to swallow the horror of an insult to their creative pride if the shots were fantastic, which, Josie thought, they were. *They're dying to condemn these shots purely on that basis.* She breathed in and closed her eyes.

"They're different," William finally said, after picking each shot up and examining it closely. "Certainly different."

"Don't know how they'll read in the Midwest," said the marketing director. "They might be offended. She's practically naked in this one. Bit suggestive for our market, don't you think?"

Josie almost giggled at his interpretation of her in a

tiny bright red slip dress, her legs towering over the Empire State Building. Cradled on one hip was a naked baby.

"Who cares?" Marv said. "They're sensational. Let's shock 'em for once."

"She looks like she's been impregnated by that thing," mumbled the creative head.

" 'That thing' is one of the most distinctive pieces of architecture in the world." Marv stood up. "It represents this fine country's power and dominance. Not only that, but it's where we had our first office."

"So you want to say she's been fucked by America's power and dominance? Or by our first office?" William smiled. He had a point.

"Wiseacre," Marv said. "It means she's above it all. We want to show that women, especially mothers, can rule the world. That even one of the greatest symbols of global capitalism pales beneath her."

Go Marv! Josie smiled at him, revealing her newly glued tooth.

"Looks more to me like one of the greatest symbols of global capitalism impaled her, I gotta say," the account executive said, looking to William for encouragement.

"It'll never fly in the Bible Belt," said the marketing director, emboldened by the account exec's comment.

"Screw the Bible Belt!" Marv slammed his fist onto the table. "Boring bunch of farts. Most of them lust after this kind of stuff in private, then go off and act all pious and shocked in front of their preacher, who's been having affairs with his parishioners for years."

"Grandfather!"

"Shut up! I'm telling you we oughta go with this. It's about time we had some kind of campaign that people actually sat up and noticed. So what if we offend a few deadbeats! Think of all the new sales we'll generate.

Speaking of which, what were our sales last month, Bill?"

"Grandfather, that's not the poi—"

"Flat. Same as the month before and the month before that. And that is exactly the point. Gotta rock the old boat sometimes. A few passengers may jump ship, but a lot more may come on board."

"It's a very big risk, Marv," the account exec sighed.

"Yeah, well I haven't seen you guys taking any risks lately. You've been coasting on my buck for way too long. Get with the program, guys. Start doing some goddamned work for a change. Those layouts of yours are buried in the eighties. Even I know that and I'm almost older than the lot of you put together!"

"May I say something?" Josie said.

"Go ahead, sweetheart." Marv winked at her. She wished he wouldn't do that.

"Women these days are getting younger and younger as they age, if you know what I mean. A grandmother no longer looks like a little old lady in a floral dress. She doesn't sit at home knitting. Today's fifty-year-old is hip, attractive, and wants to fight getting old to the last minute. She's not giving in easily. Make her feel young! I already told you—don't remind her of her boring life—give her something to look on as fun. A fantasy she can relate to—"

"If you think every woman's fantasy is being fucked by the Empire State Building you're insane."

"Well, some of them might prefer the Chrysler Building," she said to William, her heart pounding. He was not amused by that one. She poured herself a cup of coffee from a silver thermos, added some cream, sat back, and sipped it, trying not to look nervous. Never let 'em see you sweat.

"We're running with this." Marv sat back down. "And

that's all there is to it. You should be thankful. All you clowns have to do now is come up with a killer logo. Remember that Maidenform campaign back in the sixties?" They all looked blankly at him.

"I dreamed I painted the town red in my Maidenform bra!" William finally said. "I remember that. The woman was on a giant ladder painting Manhattan red."

"That's the one. Get some fun into it! Grant the old man one of his few last wishes, will you, Bill?" He looked at his grandson and smiled in such a sweet way that even William smiled back. Maybe it was the thought that Marv didn't have too much longer to go, Josie thought. Surely he wasn't that callous.

"Sure, Grandfather," he said. "We'll run with this. You might be right. It just might push us into a new arena."

"Yes, that's absolutely true," the account exec whinnied. "This could really charge your sales. You'll be up there with all the top designers—"

"Put a sock in it, you yes man," Marv cackled at him. Josie started giggling. William let out a chuckle. The account exec laughed, and then everyone joined in. The whole room filled with laughter. Maybe it was the release of tension for the ad agency guys. For Josie it was relief and elation. They'd done it! She looked at Marv, blew him a kiss, and laughed some more. His eyes opened wide and he laughed so hard back at her she thought he might cark it right there.

And then she realized everyone was looking at her and laughing. They were all nearly hysterical.

"Oh, no. It hasn't fallen out again, has it?" She felt herself turn bright red.

"Don't you know not to drink hot coffee with fresh denture glue?" Marv laughed.

"Course I don't!" She started laughing again. "How do you think this'll sell in the Bible Belt?" She grinned at them all. "I look like somebody's inbred cousin. I'll go down a treat in the Blue Ridge Mountains."

They all roared with laughter. She glanced over at Marcus and he was just staring at her, a soft smile on his face. She gulped. They'd done it.

33

As she stood in line at the post office grappling with a load of packages, Josie felt an overwhelming sense of loneliness. Post offices always did that to her at this time of year. Made her acutely aware of how far away she was from her family, and that she wouldn't be swigging back champagne on Christmas morning before surfing in the baking Sydney heat. In fact, she didn't have a clue what she was doing yet. Only eleven days away and she hadn't thought to make any plans, and no one had asked her what she was doing. She looked around at the predominately male line and thought that most of these guys were probably as lonely and distant from their families as she was, although probably for very different reasons.

Her cell phone rang and she dropped half her packages trying to grab it out of her bag.

"You wanna go for a ride, shug?" She thought the whole post office must have heard Andy's deep roar.

"You offering any candy, old man?" She giggled and tried unsuccessfully to gather up the dropped packages.

As soon as she got one put back on the pile another would slide out and hit the floor.

"Sorry, little girl, only got caviar."

"Boy, you can pick me up anytime with an offer like that." Another package hit the floor. When she stood up again she realized half the post office was watching her. She blushed.

"Where you at, little girl?"

"In line at the post office."

"Post office! Good God almighty woman, what the hell y'all doin' there?"

"Being a good little girl and sending my folks presents. It's Christmas, remember?"

"Hrumph. Where are you? Ah'll pick you up."

"In the Village. Bleecker Street."

"The Village? What the hell you doin' all the way down there?"

"Well I've got some very exciting news, Andy," she whispered loudly. "There are these places down here called shops. Real shops, with nice things to buy! I realize this may seem strange to you, but there is actually a whole area of the city that exists below Park Avenue and Fifty-Third Street. Amazing, isn't it?" The man behind her snickered.

"Ha de ha. Wait there. Ah'll be down in twenty."

"Miracle of miracles, but I may actually be finished by then. What have you got planned, anyway?"

"Top secret. Ah could tell you, but then Ah'd have to kill you."

"You sure you can find your way in the wilds of downtown? Could be pretty scary for a small-town boy like you."

"Ah may have to kill you anyways, keep talkin' like that."

"I'll be here. See ya." She flipped the phone shut and another round of packages fell off the pile.

After she finally dumped the boxes and bought a gazillion stamps, she stood at the desk in the outer lobby, endlessly pasting pictures of the virgin and child onto cards while she watched out the window for signs of Andy's car. She wondered what he wanted. Maybe he didn't want anything, just some company. It was a lonely time of year for a single person in a foreign city. Although she supposed he'd be going back to Atlanta to see his family. It occurred to her that she didn't know much about Andy, if he had any family or anything like that. Maybe he was an orphan. *Poor orphan Andy. Yeah, right.*

A guy minced over to use the pay phone just next to the bench. Underneath his black duffel coat he wore a navy blue and white striped sweater, tight black trousers, and knee-high boots. The addition of a goatee beard, shaved head with a nifty cap placed strategically over the tip of one ear, both ears pierced with thick gold earrings, gave him a strong resemblance to a sort of effete pirate.

"Hello, Brian," he said into the phone, "this is Brad." A moment of silence ensued.

"Brad, from last night." More silence. "You know, Brad. Brad who you were supposed to be meeting half an hour ago." His body tensed at another moment of silence. Josie continued with her task, her ears straining to catch the conversation.

"What do you mean you don't remember?" the pirate cried out. Josie shuffled ever so slightly toward the phone booth in the next moments of silence and resumed her stamp pasting, keeping her head low, trying for the most inconspicuous position she could manage and still eavesdrop.

"Oh, come on," he continued, "you seemed to know who I was last night in the backseat! You sure seemed to like it." Another silence.

"I was on top, remember? You loved it!" His whole

body shook. "I just can't believe this! It was only twelve hours ago!" Josie could hear his breathing getting faster.

"So what does this mean?" he cried. "You're not coming?"

Josie's cell phone jarred the next aching moment of silence. The pirate jumped with horror at finding her less than two feet from him. Their eyes met for an embarrassing nanosecond and she instantly wished she could vanish and leave him alone with his humiliation. Too late for that.

"Tell him he's an asshole," she said, grabbing in the darkness of her handbag for the phone. "You can do better than that."

"Did you hear that, Brian? You're an asshole. And I hope it's really fucking sore." He slammed the phone down. Their eyes met again. "You're right. I can do better than that."

"Merry Christmas." She smiled at him, opened her phone and stuck it to her ear, threw her letters in the slot, and walked out.

"What have y'all been up to—makin' the goddamned stamps?" She laughed at Andy as she shut the phone and climbed into his car. It was strange to see him behind the wheel. Like he didn't belong there.

"Hi there," she said, pecking his pockmarked cheek. "You won't believe what I just heard."

"Rent boys talking about last night's escapades," he smiled, pulling out from the curb.

"How'd you know that?" she said, stunned.

"Shug, Ah know you think Ah'm just some rich hick from the South with no clue—"

"That's not true! You're one of the most sophisticated—"

"Rednecks. A real sophisticated redneck. Ah know that's what y'all think of me."

"No I don't! I don't think that at all about you!" But

it was true, she thought, looking ahead through the windscreen. Until now that's exactly what she'd thought of him. Until now she didn't even know he could drive. She felt like he could see right through her, her artifice, her phoniness. He'd busted her. Again.

She sighed, embarrassed. "I really don't know anything about you, Andy." She examined his profile as he maneuvered through the Sixth Avenue construction. "Do I?" She realized she selfishly hadn't wanted to. Beyond the obvious—the wealth, the power. Those were the things that he displayed, so that's all she'd seen or, to be truthful, been interested in. She felt awful.

"My brother was gay," he said after a while.

"Was?"

"He died six years ago." His eyes did not stray from the view ahead, but she detected a slight clenching of his jaw and a tightening of his grip on the wheel.

"Oh, Andy." She closed her eyes. "I'm so sorry." She didn't need to ask how.

"That's why Ah moved to New York. He wouldn't come home. Didn't want to embarrass the family. He said it'd kill Daddy. Made me promise not to tell 'im."

"And have you?"

He shook his head.

"But what do they think? How did you explain his death?"

"They weren't close. Hadn't talked in years. My daddy's a pretty tough ol' bird. Stubborn as a mule."

"Why didn't they talk?"

"Teddy never would fit in with anything Daddy wanted for him. Wouldn't go to college, wouldn't join the practice, that kinda stuff. Ran off to Paris, tried to become a writer."

"Your dad's a doctor?"

"Lawyer. Oldest law firm in Atlanta. Five generations."

"What's so wrong with wanting to be a writer?"

"Nothin'. Unless you're a Wyatt from Atlanta. And unless all you do when you're in Paris is drink and pick up boys in drag bars."

"Oh," she nodded, sort of understanding. "But . . . so . . . what did you tell them? About his death."

"He had pneumonia. It all happened pretty fast in the end. Asked not to be revived. He was sick of the fight. Daddy just didn't know about the three years of illness before that."

"But what about your mum?" Surely a mother would want to be near her dying son.

"She came up a few months before he went. He was pretty wasted by then. She just sat there day after day and held his hand. Tried to get him to take walks. Wheeled him round the park." His voice was shallow and soft now, like she'd never heard it before.

"And she's never told your dad?" He shook his head again. His jaw clenched even tighter.

"Ah guess he knows. He won't mention Teddy's name, walks out of the room anytime we do."

"Oh, Andy. That's awful. To carry such secrets around . . . it's just . . . awful. Your poor mother."

"She hasn't been the same since."

"They must be very proud of you," she said, then felt stupid, as if that was some consolation for having your family decimated by disease and secrets.

"Oh, Ah'm the golden boy who did everything right, everything he was supposed to. Trouble is, it wasn't never enough for Daddy. Nothing ever was. They never doted on me like they did Ted. He was the baby. Ah was the responsible one. Ah still don't count."

"Oh, Andy! This is terrible!"

"Oh, shug. Ah didn't come and get you for some ole misery tale," he laughed. "Ah wanted to show you something."

She'd been so shocked by this conversation she hadn't noticed that they'd circled around and were heading back downtown.

"So. Whadya think about that, shug?" He pointed up through the glass.

In the pale glow of fading winter sun the lights of Times Square twinkled merrily back through the windows at them. Her eyes followed the line of his finger.

"Oh my God!" She felt the blood rushing to her face. "I can't believe it!"

There she was. Fifty feet high, or so it looked. Her legs stalking over the Sony TV screen in the center of Times Square. It was the shot with the slip and the Empire State Building and the baby. "Ohmygod! I didn't think they were running these 'til next year!"

"Went up yesterday." He smiled at her proudly, like it was his product she was hawking.

"But how'd you know! They didn't tell me anything about this!"

"Not bad for a redneck, huh." He looked her smack in the eye.

"Pretty darn good." She laughed back at him, then looked away. She didn't quite know what was happening here, but she felt something was. A twinkle of hope, of promise, a tiny spark ignited and taking flight.

"C'mon. I think a little celebration is in order, don't you?"

"Absolutely!" She leaned her head out the window for a last glimpse of her alter ego as he sped off.

34

"It's *hideous*, darling. Truly hid," said Hamish Kent to his ex-wife and agent, Antonia. They stood at the corner of Fifty-third and Broadway looking down to Times Square. "I mean, really." His small mouth pursed in disgust. "Can't somebody think of something even remotely original for a change? She looks like she's being screwed by the Empire State Building. How tedious. Now where the hell is our car?"

"I think it's fantastic, darling." Antonia smiled that supercilious pout that made his skin crawl. "The shot, not the subject. I mean her legs look all right, I suppose—pity about the face—but just look at the quality of that photo. The lighting is superb. Marcus is simply genius, darling, you have to admit. Genius! Thinking up that idea and getting it through the ad agency. What a clever lad."

"I taught him everything," sniffed Hamish, who was in no mood for gushing about bloody Marcus. "Idiot driver's probably off watching a peep show over the road." He stomped off down Broadway.

"Course he's not, darling. I told him to pick us up at

four. It's only three-thirty." She fished her cell phone out of her Hermes Kelly bag. "And just because your meeting was a washout, do you really find it necessary to attack your former protégé? You should be proud of him," she said, attempting to traipse along beside him and dial simultaneously.

"I'll leave the 'attacking' of him to you, dearest one," he replied, "as you appear to be doing an extremely good job of it." He stopped and felt his mouth curl up at the sight of his former wife hobbling after him in a pair of four-inch heels and the tightest of skirts, which ended just below the knee, making it almost impossible for her to move. "And why you dragged me up here for this pathetic excuse for a meeting, I'll never know. It's about time you started doing a bit more homework, dearest. I've got better things to do than waste my time with a bunch of morons who have no idea who or what they want and no decent budget to shoot." He started walking again.

"Oh, like getting arrested in an S&M club, darling?" she called after him. He could hear the clicking of her Manolo's growing faster as he quickened his pace a little more. "That's such a fabulous way to wile away time, isn't it?"

"At least I don't parade my conquests around in public like some aging Svengali in stilettos, sweetie." He was fairly striding by now.

"You could hardly parade around in those charming little leather jobbies of yours in public, now could you, darling?" Her tiny steps clopped furiously after him and he smiled through his anger at her discomfort, reached in his pocket, and grasped the camera he always carried with him. "Really, darling. Talk about a 'fashion slave.'" Her voice tinkled with shrill laughter at her own pathetic joke. He felt his mouth tighten.

"At least I'm not a fashion victim," he snorted, walking even faster, just to annoy her. "At least I don't put myself through torture every day in a feéble attempt to look good."

"No," she said, "you just beg someone else to do it for you in a dungeon—don't you, darling?"

People on the sidewalk were staring at them now, he noticed with some glee. He knew he wasn't the one who looked bad. He could envision her right behind him, staggering down the street in his wake. A cool-looking man in a Dior suit with a tragically overmadeup woman tripping over herself to catch up. "I certainly don't need a dungeon when I have you around to give me grief." He smiled at a passerby.

"Grief!" she yelled. "You want to talk about grief, sweetie? You've done nothing but give me grief for years now!"

"With the amount of money I earn for you, you should be thrilled to put up with a lot more than a bit of grief."

"The amount of money you're earning me is diminishing, sweetie—at an ever-increasing pace."

"Well, if you weren't so busy opening those scrawny thighs of yours for that walking phallic symbol, perhaps you'd be devoting a bit more time to business and getting me more work. That meeting was a complete farce. How dare you subject me to that sort of crap. Your job is to protect your clients from excrement like that!" He reached the corner and the light turned red.

"The truth is, darling," she said breathlessly, catching up with him, "that you're slipping. Your star is waning and Marcus's is on the rise and you can't stand it. You're jealous and you can't stand it."

"What I can't stand is an over-the-hill nymphomaniac posing as my agent in order to pick up a new stud every month. You owe everything you have to me, sweetie, and don't you ever forget it," he snarled and stepped off the sidewalk.

"And I'm sick and tired of bailing a has-been masochistic misogynist out of the pitifully sick cock-ups he keeps making in his private life! I'm not your nursemaid, Hamish. I'm an agent. That's it! What you need is some serious therapy!" She stood there glaring at him, her ruby pout twisted in anger, her perfectly manicured hands planted firmly on her black and white pinstripe skirt. He hated her now more than ever before.

"What I need, my darling, is a new agent. Someone who thinks with her head, not her smelly old pussy."

"Fine," she yelled and stepped onto the street after him. "If that's the way you want it, that's just fine by me!" Her heel caught on the sewer grating and she tripped headfirst into the street. Her Hermes bag splattered its contents all around her. Hamish, grinning, snapped several frames off with his tiny camera, backing up as he snapped, thrilled to see her falling, hoping it was just the beginning.

He didn't see the black Mercedes swerve to miss him. He didn't see Josie inside watching from the open window with absolute astonishment as her old friend Hamish Kent took pictures of his ex-wife sprawled in the middle of Broadway, her stockings run, her heel broken, and her chin dripping with blood.

"What kinda asshole would take pictures of a woman in that position!" Andy shook his head as he turned the corner to evade hitting Hamish. "Goddamned ass!"

Josie thought Antonia looked pretty good in that position, but she didn't let on to Andy. Instead she shrugged and wondered what could possibly be happening between the two Kents.

Andy whisked her off to Petrossian for, natch, caviar and champagne and oysters and more champagne 'til they were both giggly. They strolled up Madison Avenue, to Fauchon, where they stood at the bar and sipped the best, creamiest cappuccino in the city. Josie loved that he knew and liked the little places she treasured as well.

They crossed the street and she became nervous because they were now at The Carlyle, where he lived. She was scared he'd make a pass at her. And also sort of wishing he would. It was all too confusing. What would she say if he asked her upstairs? On one hand, she'd love to see his suite of rooms—she wondered if he had decent taste, or at least enough sense to have hired a good decorator—but she certainly didn't want to be in any kind of uncomfortable situation with him. She liked him too much to want to reject him.

To both her relief and slight annoyance, though, he didn't ask and instead they went into Bemelman's Bar and had yet another glass of champagne. And she realized she must have it all wrong. That he didn't fancy her any more than she him. Maybe he was hitting for the other team and simply viewed her as a friend, a companion, which was fine by her. Normally her gaydar worked perfectly, but with him it was impossible to tell. And what did it matter, anyway?

So, she relaxed and had fun. She made him laugh with her witty observations of the other patrons' clothes. She could usually guess what nationality people were and what they did for a crust, just by the way they dressed. Of course, most of the people here were either tourists—easy to spot—conservatively dressed for a Midwesterner's night on the town, or people like her and Andy—well-heeled uptown types popping in for a drink and to listen to Bobby Short sing his classics. But they were early and soon she realized she had to go home and pass out. Those bubbles were getting to her again, and Andy was starting to look more attractive with each sip. Cripes.

She had to cut and run before she made a fool of herself.

So he put her in a cab and climbed in next to her, as he had to pick up his car where he'd left it. And all the way to her apartment she felt squeamish, from both all those bubbles and anxiety. Was she supposed to invite him in? She really wasn't up for it. And even if she was, she was way too tipsy. So, when the cab pulled up, she kissed him lightly on the cheek and ran inside like a giddy schoolgirl.

35

The light hit her face at an angle suggestive of a ray of late afternoon sun, golden and full of romantic promise. It glanced off the curve of her cheekbone and flashed into her eyes, illuminating their pale green intensity as they focused on something far away.

"Hold it right there, yes, beautiful, darling, that's it," Hamish said, as he pressed the motor drive of his 35-millimeter camera into action. She moved slightly each few seconds, altering her line of sight and her mouth fractionally. "Gorgeous, darling, divine," he gushed. The frames whirred by in quick succession until the roll was completed.

"Haven't you got it yet?" Josie straightened up and stretched. "I feel like I've got lockjaw."

"Whining already?" Hamish sniffed at her. "I would have thought you'd be a bit more humble in your dotage, darling."

"I'm not whining! I'm just stiff! I've been sitting in one position for nearly two hours!"

"Must be the rheumatism setting in, sweetie. A woman of your age has to be careful."

"Shut up!" she laughed.

"Don't laugh, sweetie, you'll crack that fabulous Vive cement poor Ricky spent hours spackling and filling all those lines with."

"Very funny. God, if I'd known earlier you'd still be like this after all these years, I'd have bowed out."

"Like hell you would have. Snub a chance at a million-dollar contract? You? Darling, if I told you to lick my boots for a hundred you'd be on your knees with your tongue hanging out in a flash." He curled his tiny lips up at her.

"Do you hear this?" she said to Ricky and Max, who were once again fussing over her. "I request him for this shoot out of the kindness of my heart and what do I get? Abuse and more abuse. Nothing but abuse."

"You didn't request me. My fabulous new agent"—he pronounced *agent* like the French, *arjant*—"got me in with your pals at Vive."

"I did too request you. Your fabulous new *arjant*," she repeated his word, "merely sent your book over, darling."

She loved holding it over him for once. "Of course you're absolutely right. Let's face it, I'd lick sidewalks for this contract!"

"What else would jou lick, darlingk?" Ricky purred at her, as he patted her face with a giant powder puff. "What have jou already licked for this test?"

"Yeah, darls, inquiring minds want to know," Max said, pulling a strand of hair delicately over one of her eyes, examining the position with his left eye closed, and then changing it again. "You been nibbling on the big cheese?"

"God, you're disgusting!" She jumped up and put her hands around his neck, ready to throttle him.

"Well, you're certainly pretty friendly with him, darls. So just how big is the Big Kahuna's Kahuna?"

"Maybe you should ask him yourself, Maxi, darls." She smiled sweetly.

"Yeah, like how's 'G'day, Mr. Wyatt, Mr. Big Cheese, how big's ya shlong?'?"

"Why Maxi, darlin', it's a monster. What else would the Big Kahuna have?"

Max swiveled round to see Andy standing right behind him. Josie roared, blushing. For once Max was at a loss. "Yep, Maxi, darls," Andy continued, "it's so darn big it terrifies even size queens like yerself."

"Ha!" Max grinned, bright red. For a second Josie wondered just how big it actually was and felt a tingle between her legs before she shoved the thought away. The fact that she was having thoughts like that about Andy shocked her. She felt herself blushing more. But Andy was proving more and more approachable every time she saw him, more normal. Who'd have thought that the head of a multinational corporation would even know what a size queen was?

"You actually managed to embarrass the infamous Max!" she laughed. "I don't believe it!"

"So how's it going, kids?" Andy sauntered over and picked up one of the Polaroids resting on the table. His manner was relaxed, but she knew this was a strictly business visit. "Y'all finished?"

"Another roll, and we should have it, Mr. Wyatt," Hamish said, "provided the old boiler doesn't start whining about her aching joints again."

"She looks good for an old gal, don't she?" Andy said, examining the Polaroids closely. "Pretty darn good." He winked at her.

She smiled back. "Amazing what a bit of Vive can do."

"Turns old sows into silk purses, darling."

"Thanks, Hamish. Remind me to put an antiabuse clause in the contract—if I get it, that is." She winked back at Andy. She still couldn't believe all this was happening. The Vive contract in her sights!

"These are great, Hamish." Andy stopped and studied Hamish's face for a second. "Ya know," he said, "you just look so darn familiar. I'm sure we've met before last week. I just can't figure where."

Josie blanched. She didn't want to tell Andy it was Hamish whom he'd seen five days earlier snapping his fallen ex-wife, and she hoped he wouldn't recognize him. Why she would want to shield Hamish she couldn't decipher, but she figured it was an old bond she still felt. Plus when she'd heard about Hamish and Antonia's parting of ways, she had been pleased and only too happy to recommend him for this test shoot. She had to think of something quick, though, to get Andy's attention away.

"Didn't you meet at Priscilla and Richard Saunders's party a while back?" she said.

"Oh sure, sure," Andy smiled. "That's it. Say, have you heard?"

"Heard what?" Josie fiddled with a hairbrush and sat back in her chair, relieved.

"About Priscilla?"

"I haven't heard anything from her." Josie shook her head. She felt really bloody sad at the loss of her friendship. "She's nuts right now."

"That's for sure. She's in rehab."

"Rehab?"

"Richard told me. Poor gal's hooked on some new diet pills. He says she went bananas—started throwin' things at him and screamin' all the time. Wild stuff. He had to have her taken away."

"She did that to me too! That hideous Doctor Gene gave them to her. I knew he was a quack. Well, no wonder."

"Wonder what?" Andy said.

"Why she thought I was having an affair with Richard."

"You, darling? An affair with Richard Saunders?" Hamish sniffed. "Hardly likely he'd want to have an affair with you."

"Thanks a lot!" Josie felt insulted. "What's so unlikely about it? Not that I am or ever was, mind you, but why wouldn't he?"

"I have it on very good authority that your Mr. Saunders likes 'other' kinds of extracurricular activity." He picked up his camera and started focusing on her again, that smug little curl turning up the edges of his mouth.

"Likes a suck of the old saveloy, does he?" Max had regained his normal composure.

"Oh shut up, Max," Josie snapped. "You'd say anybody was queer. According to you everyone's gay. You don't even know the man. Well, let me tell you. Richard Saunders is the farthest thing from gay I've ever seen. Aren't I right, Andy?"

Andy shrugged. A very noncommittal shrug, like he didn't want to go there.

"Darling," Hamish said, "Richard Saunders is very far from the image he presents to the rest of the world. That much I know with absolute certainty. Now would you stop frowning and start concentrating? That furrow between your brows is truly unattractive. Miracles we can perform, but surgery is out of the question today. Now smile. That's it." He resumed snapping away, as Josie relaxed her face, but her mind whirred along with the motor drive, simultaneously curious about and repelled by how and what Hamish knew about Richard Saunders. *Mind your own business,* she thought and pouted just a little more until the roll ran out.

36

"I do not have an eating disorder." Priscilla pulled her auburn curls straight off her face and glared at the man behind the desk. "There is nothing wrong with me," she said between gritted teeth.

"Mrs. Saunders, Priscilla," he replied in a gentle tone, "you are in here for abusing diet pills and tranquilizers. You didn't eat your lunch, nor dinner last night. We think that constitutes—"

"All that constitutes is that the food here is total crap! And they were herbal pills prescribed by my holistic doctor! You can't possibly expect me to eat that disgusting slop!" She pounded her fist on the table. "I'm absolutely famished! Can't I have something sent in from a decent restaurant?"

"I'm sorry, Mrs. Saunders, but it's against the rules."

"Oh, for God's sake! This is absurd!" She stood up. "What kind of place is this anyway? I don't belong here! There's nothing wrong with me! Don't you see? It's my husband! He's trying to get me out of the way!"

"Mrs. Saunders, you are exhibiting an unusual amount

of rage and paranoia. I can only recommend that you stay for the full thirty days."

"I'm not fucking paranoid! I'm starving and angry at my husband! He's the one who needs help! You'll see!" She turned and stormed out of the doctor's office, out of the cottage, and down the snow-covered hill toward her room in another cottage at the other side of a small winding road.

"Fuck you all." She bundled her cashmere wrap around her and shivered in the cold. "'Golden Valley, the finest, most luxurious rehab in Connecticut.' Ha, what a fucking joke. What a dump."

She'd kill for even McDonald's right now. Surely a Big Mac wasn't outlawed. Still, those stiffs had even taken away her mouthwash when she'd checked in five days before. Who'd have even thought of it containing alcohol! And that wasn't even her problem! "What do they think—I'd be bothered giving it to some pathetic alcoholic in this joint? Oh, sure!" She stomped over the thinning snow. "That's it! I'm outa here. And, sweet husband of mine, you'll be getting your marching papers as soon as I leave this hole. You and that tramp—ahh!" She tripped over a hidden rock and landed on her rump. "Oh, Christ!" She shook the snow out of her face and hair. She sat there and blubbered, unable to cope.

"You okay?" came a soft voice behind her. She looked up to see a thin, almost pretty, dark-haired man. "C'mon," he said, pulling her up, "you must be frozen." She grabbed his arm, noticing the softness of his cashmere jacket.

"Thank you," she said, still sobbing. "Thanks so much." She wiped at her runny nose with her black wrap.

"Here," he said, pulling a white handkerchief from his pocket and handing it to her. She smiled through her tears and wiped at her eyes and nose again. "This place sucks, doesn't it?" He laughed hollowly. "I always try not to let it get to me, but sometimes it really just sucks the big one."

"You've been here before?" He had a familiar look about him.

"Home away from home." He shrugged and gave that soft, hollow laugh again. He pulled out a box of Marlboros and a lighter. "Wanna smoke?"

"Oh, sure, why not. Haven't smoked in years, but I feel defiant enough in this shithole to take it right back up again."

"I hear you," he said, giving her a cigarette and lighting them both. "C'mon, let's get out of here. It's freezing. I hate the cold, don't you? I'd rather be anywhere but in the cold. I shoulda gone to that rehab in Antigua, you know, the one Eric Clapton started. I would have been warm there."

"How come you know so much about rehabs?" She examined him now, curious. He was very well dressed: expensive jacket, cashmere sweater underneath, jeans, and those black Gucci hiking boots she'd nearly bought a pair of the other day. His face was way too thin, but there was a softness, a vulnerability in it, and he had large, soft, almost aqua eyes and the longest eyelashes she'd ever seen on a man. His dark hair hung wispily about his face. He looked almost feminine, but his hands were large and strong, and there was a certain arrogant nonchalance about him that told her he wasn't gay.

"Same answer as before," he giggled, not at all embarrassed. "My homes away from home. What about you? This your first time?" They started down the hill again and she drew on her cigarette and felt like a schoolgirl when it made her dizzy.

"Yeah," she said, "and I'm getting the hell out of here as soon as possible. Like now."

"What're you in for?"

"Nothing really," she said. "Diet pills."

"Diet pills?"

"Herbal diet pills, can you believe it? Herbal pills that my holistic doctor gave me! They made me crazy for a few days, but I'm fine now. Fucking quack. I'm gonna have him skewered when I get back to the city. Him and my ever-loving husband, who so kindly dragged me out to this hellhole."

"Don't you hate that? That intervention thing really sucks. I ran away this time."

"Ran away? How?"

"When we got here. My father and his driver brought me out, and when the limo stopped I made a run for it."

"You did?" Priscilla almost laughed, wondering who this strange guy was. "Where to?"

"Oh, just out in the woods. Thought I'd scare them. You know—crazed addict on the loose in New Canaan. Gives these jokers something to talk about."

"And then what happened? Did they catch you?"

"Tried to. I hid behind trees and crossed the little stream over back there. But then I ran out of cigarettes and it was freezing, so I came back. Then they locked me up in building C."

"What's building C?"

"That new one over the hill back there." He turned and motioned toward an ugly modern building that didn't fit in with the rest of the complex, which was made up of quaint New England saltbox cottages and a grand-looking main hall, where the meals were served. "It's for the dangerous ones, the loonies, the suicidals."

"So you're a dangerous, suicidal loony?" she said, fascinated by his casual demeanor, wondering if he'd attack her or something.

"Na. Only when I go on a binge. Don't worry, I won't bite. Not now—I'm doing the thorazine shuffle, hee

hee." She laughed when he did a tiny jig in the snow. Then he stopped and sighed. "I hadn't been locked up like that before."

"Was it scary?"

"They take your belt and shoelaces so you won't try to strangle yourself, and there're cameras everywhere and a central nursing station, where they watch you all the time. Scared the shit out of me."

"Oh," she said, not knowing what else to say to this poor guy. It was like the whole place was full of people whose lives were hanging by very slim threads. She'd noticed it at mealtimes; the looks of despair and vacancy, like their souls had disappeared into a void and they were desperately trying to find them again. For the first time in ages she felt profoundly sad for someone else instead of herself, and it made her feel guilty and selfish. "How awful."

They were at her cottage now, a slightly dilapidated building that housed six people, not in any kind of splendor, not at all what Richard had told her it would be like, that's for sure. "This is me," she said. "You want to come in for tea or something?"

"Thanks, but I've got to get my head shrunk in five minutes." She could see the pain beneath his thin smile.

"Well, thanks," she said, "for helping me back there. My name is Priscilla, by the way."

"I know. Priscilla Saunders, right?"

"How'd you know?" She was shocked. She'd hoped it was a secret, her being here. "Was it in the papers or something?"

"No. My mother had lunch with you a few weeks ago. That was what started me off again."

"What?" she said, confused. "What do you mean?"

"My mother. I believe she sucked your brains about my ex."

"Your ex," she replied, no clue what he was talking about. Maybe he really was loony.

"Josephine. Josie Vaughn." His eyes hardened when he said her name.

"Oh, yes! My God! So that woman is your mom?"

"Nancy Cantero. Aka The Terrorist."

"Oh, so now I recognize you! You were Josie's fiancé! I've seen pictures of you!"

"The ever lovely Josie," he said sarcastically. "That was me."

"Oh, don't get me started on her. They really will lock me up."

"You too, huh," he said.

"That tramp is doing my husband. I swear if I ever see her again I'll tear her eyes out. I'm gonna get that bitch for ruining my marriage."

"Well," he smiled, "you've met just the right guy today, Priscilla. 'Cause I know exactly how you can."

She smiled. "Really! Your mom told me about you guys, but I wasn't sure at the time. Maybe I won't check out of here right now. Maybe I'll stick around and keep my new friend. Hey, what's your name? I don't even remember your name."

"Jonathon. Jonathon with two *o*'s."

"Well, hi, Jonathon. Like I said. Maybe I'll stick around with my new friend, Jonathon with two *o*'s, and we'll think of some fun ideas together. How's that sound?"

"Sounds cool." He giggled and did another little jig. "I'll see you later!" And he tripped off back up the hill, smoke from his cigarette billowing behind him in the frosty air.

37

"Oh my God!" Josie gasped, "Oh my God!" She flung the morning's newspaper down onto the kitchen table, knocking her mug of coffee flying. She was hyperventilating and wheezing so much she didn't notice the coffee spilling over her and the shattering of the porcelain on the black and white linoleum floor. She got up, flung herself in the direction of the bathroom, and threw up.

She knew the bubble had to burst sometime. It had all been too good to be true. But this was way beyond what even she could have conjured up in her most wildly pessimistic nightmares. Pain surged through her, perfection in pain, like that from the most finely honed sword slicing through her vital organs.

She finally stumbled back to the kitchen and picked the paper back up again, not believing it was there, in black and white for the whole city to read over breakfast.

"Josie Vaughn, the Great Gams Gal and spokeswoman, isn't perhaps as clean-cut as the image she'd like us to believe," it read. "Sources report she had a major falling out with her ex-fiancé, Jonathon Cantero, and sued him for a half million dollars in damages over what her lawyers termed 'Tortious acts' in their relationship. However, our source has confirmed that the money was not for 'damages,' but to pay her to abort his child after their rancorous split. Perhaps that billboard of her straddling the Empire State Building isn't so far off the mark."

"How can this be here? How can they print this? This isn't possible," she whispered, then practically crawled back to her bed, curled up, and wept.

For two years she'd been fighting to bury the pain and guilt of what had happened between Jonathon and her. Of what she'd done. Their breakup had been totally harrowing. Actually, the whole relationship had been full of trauma. It was like that rhyme "when he was good he was very, very good, and when he was bad he was horrid"! Jonathon was so sweet when he was sober. And if he had one or two drinks he was fine. But there was some invisible line of alcohol consumption that when crossed brought him to violent behavior.

She had spent the time with him walking on eggshells, never knowing how he would act, whether he would be sweet and funny and affectionate, or drink and become a raving maniac. The knot in her gut was constant. She still did not understand why she stayed with him for so long. He gave her two black eyes and fractured her nose. And still she stayed. Her self-worth had diminished to such an extent that she believed that if she loved him more, that if she behaved better, that if she hid the alcohol, or watered it down, he would change. She had truly become insane. Insanity became normality. She thought that he was her last chance at love. That she had to make the relationship work, because she'd never, ever meet anyone else.

There were times when his violence was so extreme

she would have to hide—under beds, outside in bushes, locked in bathrooms—hoping he would pass out before he found her. Why, why had she stayed? What had possessed her? Was it the money? The lifestyle? And what kind of life had it ended up being anyway? Ghastly. Trapped in a shell of wealth and loneliness. But she had loved him. And she now understood that she had needed to go through such horrifying trauma in order to grow.

She finally got the strength to leave when he fell off the wagon for the fourth time, after nearly two years of sobriety. She had told him she loved him but she simply couldn't go through such stress again, or it would kill her. And had left his place and sublet a friend's apartment, sad, broke, and barely able to function. He went on a drunken rampage and would call at all hours, screaming obscenities and threats at her.

Then two weeks later she realized she was pregnant. She had forgotten to take her pill. And that's when things spiraled totally out of control. Dealing with him and his family became her worst nightmare. And now, here was the gut-wrenching anguish again, back to haunt her.

38

Josie stayed in bed for the next four days, not answering the endless ringing phone, not even checking the messages, not eating, not showering, not wanting to ever leave the apartment. She watched the snow fall in thick, heavy flakes and considered what it would feel like to be blanketed by them until she could no longer breathe, until she became as frozen as the ground.

Nothing could ever be the same now. She'd known she'd have to pay for what she'd done at some point. But she'd shoved away the guilt, barricaded it behind walls of self-justification, always blaming someone else for her fuck-ups. And this, her biggest one of all, was now in the public domain.

On the fifth day there was loud knocking on her door. She didn't answer. The banging increased and she heard Giovanni, the doorman, calling for her. She shuffled to the door, still in her coffee-stained bathrobe and dirty pajamas.

"Miss Vaughn!" he called. "We want to see that you are all right in there! Please open the door!" He banged even harder.

"Of course I'm all right, Giovanni," she lied. "Now will you just leave me alone?"

"I have your mail, Miss," he said. She opened the door wide enough to reach her arm out and take the mail, but he pushed the door open. Standing next to him was Marcus.

"I thought you'd done something stupid," he said, after he'd invited himself in against her objections and made her a cup of coffee.

"Of course I've done something stupid." She slumped opposite him in the living room. She didn't want to get too close—she must stink—and she looked like pure shit. "Didn't you read about it? Hasn't everybody?"

"You know what I mean. I've been worried sick about you. You could have returned my calls."

"I haven't exactly been in the mood for a chat," she sighed, opening a letter with the Great Gams logo on the envelope. "I knew it. William must be so thrilled."

"He's not thrilled at all. They spent a lot of money on us, remember. He took a big risk."

"You know about this already? They haven't 'terminated' your contract too, have they?" She felt worse now, like she had a plague that affected everyone she came in contact with.

"Ah . . . no. No they haven't."

"Oh, I see. So you've come 'round to tell me that you're reshooting with a new girl, is that it?"

"No! I came here because I care about you."

"Oh, yeah," she said, "you care about me so much you ran off and slept with someone who could further your career at the first possible opportunity."

"Can we not get into this, please?" His gorgeous face hardened. She didn't care anymore if she offended him. She could give a rat's ass about anything right now.

"And how is the delightful Antonia, anyway? She must be overjoyed to see me humiliated in the press."

"Overjoyed? She's going to lose a huge commission if your contract is canceled."

"Oh. Yeah." She hunched up in the chair, feeling vile.

"Look, you've got to fight this thing, Josie." He stood up. "What they said about you is libelous. You can sue that pissant rag."

"I don't care about the stupid rag."

"But this is your livelihood! You've got to care. If you can get them to at least retract their statement, maybe you can save the contract!"

"I suppose," she sighed. "But really Marcus, right now I don't have the energy. It's hopeless. I'm hopeless."

"No you're not! You're fantastic! You're one of the smartest, most creative people I've ever met. Now stop feeling so sorry for yourself! Get up, take a shower, swallow a handful of Prozac, and get dressed. I'm taking you to lunch. How long has it been since you ate anyway? You look like a—"

"Don't go there. I know how I look. Like absolute shit."

"Aw, c'mon, Josie, stop it will you?" He pulled her up out of the chair. "It's not hopeless! We'll fight this together, okay?" He looked her in the eyes, but she looked away from him, embarrassed that he was seeing her like this. "We'll come back from lunch and get you a lawyer. And we'll find out who's spreading these rumors about you. Now, off you go!" He slapped her butt and pushed her in the direction of her bedroom.

"Rumors?" She turned to him, wide-eyed with fear. "You mean there's more than one? What else have they written?"

"Just get ready, will you?" he said, looking at her rather sadly. "I need to talk to you."

39

"We had no choice." Marv looked solemn. "I'm sorry, my dear." He sat in a Louis Quinze fauteuil in his rococo living room, dwarfed by gilt furniture and Impressionist art adorning the walls. "It wasn't just the first article. That we could have fought on your behalf. After all, what business is it of theirs, of anybody's, really, what happened in a relationship that ended. Although that first one has caused the most problems. We've been picketed, you know, by the right-to-lifers."

"I know."

"But when those other tidbits started appearing, about you having an affair with that Whiterock man"—he pulled the cigar from his mouth—"and the other stuff, all of it just malicious hearsay, I'm sure." He smiled at her, like a father would. "And then came the pictures of you fallen-down drunk with your dress up at your waist. That was the final straw. It just got too much for the Great Gams image. I hope you understand."

"Yeah, the fallen woman couldn't possibly be a pitch person for something as wholesome as women's undergarments," she said sarcastically. "Maybe you'd have thought differently if I'd been wearing Great Gams under that dress."

"Would have been a kicker," he chuckled, then sighed as his milky eyes rested on her face.

"I'm sorry, Marv. You didn't deserve all this scandal." She fidgeted on her tiny gilt chair and wished she could figure out how to beg without being too pathetic. "So the billboards are coming down?"

"Not yet," he smiled. "Sales have skyrocketed in the past two weeks."

"Skyrocketed?"

"Seems a bit of scandal is good for business," he cackled and lit up again.

"But, Marv"—she squirmed—"if that's the case, why have you canceled my contract? Why are you asking for all the money back?"

"Not all of it. You've been paid handsomely for the work you've already done. But we've gotta play the fence both ways. We can't be seen condoning your, ah, behavior, but at the same time it's great for us."

"That's just marvelous. You get to make millions from some nasty gossip about me and save money by getting out of paying me. Really good ethics. I thought you were different, Marv. I thought you cared."

"I do care, my dear. But my hands are tied. The board has overridden me on this one. Believe me, if there's anything I can do to help, I will. But for now this is the way it has to be."

"But what about the picketers?"

"We'll deal with that. And I'm prepared to help you out on that front. We'll put a security guard with you at all times until this blows over."

"You mean until you've finished with the billboards." She stood up, furious and more humiliated than ever.

"This is business, Josie. We have to milk it for as long as we can. Now you make sure to keep in touch, and, really, if there's anything you need, just call. I'm always here for you, you know that, my dear." He creakily rose and shuffled to her. "Kiss?" He smiled sweetly, and seething as she was, she didn't have the heart to say no. She leaned over and grazed the age-spotted folds of his dry cheek.

"You take care now," he said, his milky eyes staring up at her through the thick, black-rimmed glasses. "You know I'm rooting for you."

"Yeah, thanks," she said and walked out. *Yeah, sure. So much for begging. So much for having to return money you've already spent.* She didn't know what she was going to do now. A dive off the nearest skyscraper seemed like the best option at this point.

40

Melvin Shernofsky leaned back in his black leather chair and hooked his thumbs around his mauve suspenders with pictures of black and white chessmen woven into them. His shirt, also pale mauve, with a white collar and cuffs, was adorned with gold cufflinks in the shape of lions' heads, with eyes of emeralds. His deep pink silk tie had a gold tie pin with a matching gold and emerald lion.

While his clothing screamed "nouveau-riche shark," his face, etched with soft lines, and his thick silver hair gave the impression of a kind, fatherly figure, someone who'd take you under his wing and protect you. For a price of course. Seventy thousand, to be exact, in Josie's case.

It had been nearly two years since she had first walked into the offices of Freedman, Shernofsky, Gruffman, and Groinz and sat, petrified and distraught, before the sartorially sleek attorney and explained her predicament between embarrassed sniffles into a white linen handkerchief. Two years, which seemed like about two minutes now that it was all surfacing again.

"I bet you hoped you'd never see my face again"—he smiled at her—"but of course it's always a pleasure to see you."

"I'm sure it is." She laughed for the first time in what felt like a dog's age, remembering how his eyes had lit up on her first visit, when she'd mentioned the Cantero name. She could've sworn she'd seen dollar signs in them and heard the "katchink!" of a cash register.

"So, my dear, what can I do for you?" he asked, but the glint in his eye told her he had a very good idea already.

"Have you read the gossip columns lately?"

"You mean the scurrilous articles about you? And, by the way, congratulations on your new career."

"Ha! So much for that—it's over already, because of those articles. My panty hose contract has been canceled and now they're asking for most of the money back."

"Did you bring the contract with you?"

She handed him a manila envelope. "The termination notice is also there, as well as the newspaper articles. I thought all this was behind me, and now it's come back and bitten me on the ass, and it hurts like hell. I can't take this. It's exhausting." She sat silently while he read the documents, wondering how many dollars were ticking away each minute she sat there, and how she could possibly afford it.

"For a start"—he put the papers down—"those articles are libelous and you should sue them."

"Even if some of it is true?"

"Which part?"

"You know which part," she said.

"The settlement you got from that family had nothing to do with you terminating a pregnancy."

She could feel her lower lip trembling and the tears welling up. "But then how can he bring it up now? I thought part of the settlement was that we never talked about it to anyone, especially not the press. And, by the way, the only people who knew the term 'tortious acts' were us and Jonathon and his family and his father's lawyer, what's his name."

"Howard Skyles."

"Yeah, him." She always wondered what it would be like if she'd taken the other path. The baby would be over a year old by now. She'd never know if she made the right choice. "And if I fight the press, they'll easily find out about the doctor and, then, well, then—"

"So, you don't want to sue?" He looked at her as if she were mad.

"I don't know what I want to do. I just want it all to go away. I'd rather sue him than a newspaper."

"There's no way of proving how that information was leaked. Forget it. I can send a letter to Skyles threatening action if any further infringement of the privacy clause happens, but he'll have a chuckle at that." He leaned back in his chair again and smiled. "You could always leak some stuff, too, if you felt like it. Those 'tortious acts' would make for very good gossip and it'd shut him right up, if it's him blabbermouthing. He and his family have a lot more to lose than you."

She was stunned at this. "Surely you're not suggesting I buy into this degenerate mudslinging?"

"Josie, he beat the crap out of you! You had two black eyes when we first met."

"Don't remind me."

"Lots of my clients would have a field day."

"I'm sure they would. But I haven't the slightest interest in having any more of my private life all over the tabloids."

"What about the other article about you having an affair with Richard Saunders?"

"Complete lies, all of it. I think his wife planted that

story. I thought we were best friends, but she's obviously got it in for me."

"And the photos?"

She shuddered with embarrassment at the thought of them. "Obviously they're real. I just had no clue they'd been taken." She didn't believe Marcus hadn't known about them, although he claimed his assistant had taken them and kept the roll of film.

"Hmm. Listen, it's in your best interest to defend yourself. Your career has been threatened, your personal life torn to shreds and you should fight back. Now, you know I really only handle matrimonial law, so, when you've decided what you want to do, I'll hand you over to an associate."

When you've decided what to do. Those words rang through her ears, an echo of what he'd told her when she'd sat there last time. And she'd decided at the very last minute and even then she'd never be sure. How could she decide now? Although this was not a life-or-death decision. Or was it? It was her life now she had to look after. Except right now she felt like dying.

"And what about the contract?" Screw the press; she needed the money more than vindication in a stupid gossip rag.

"They have an out, unfortunately. This term 'moral turpitude' allows them to cancel if you behave in any way that is contrary to their image. Which is a very broad out. Probably can't do much about it, I'm sorry to say."

Great. She leaned her head onto her hand and her elbow onto his desk. Just great. She was washed-up, in debt, and fried. "I don't know what to do." She saw the tears falling onto the polished mahogany. "I knew I'd made the wrong choice back then . . . I knew I should've k—"

"Listen, if you'd kept that baby you'd still be tied to

that psycho addict and that family. They didn't care about you. They only cared about themselves and what it all looked like on the surface. They tried to get rid of you, like you didn't exist. You made the right choice. Stop torturing yourself. It's too late for guilt now. What's done is done and there's no turning back. Think of now. Now is the only thing that matters. And now is the time to look after Josie. Not some lost dream that would have ended up a nightmare."

She took a tissue from the box on his desk, wiped the tears from her cheeks, and hoped her mascara hadn't run. He was obviously used to clients crying. "You're right," she sniffled. "I know you're right. It's just . . . it's just that—"

"That you're a good girl and you're full of guilt about everything. By the way, did I ever ask you what religion you are?"

"Protestant, or Episcopalian as you call it here. Why?"

"'Cause the amount of guilt you drag around, I'd swear you were Jewish, or at least a Catholic!"

She laughed. "C'mon," he said, "it's not that bad. You can sue and at the very least get a retraction and probably some sort of settlement. Think about it, Josie, and call me. But don't leave it too long. Okay?" He stood up and patted her gently on the back of her neck as she rose.

"Okay," she said and shuffled to the door. He showed her out through the maze of hallways to the grand marble lobby and bank of elevators.

"Chin up, kid," he smiled. "You've been through worse than this and came up smelling sweet. Don't forget that."

"Thanks, Melvin." She stepped into the elevator, thinking she'd never smelled worse. Her malodorous past had caught up with her.

41

Josie hadn't heard from Andy. He'd left a message the day of the first piece in the newspaper, but when she'd finally pulled herself out of her aching depression and phoned him back, he'd left town, according to his secretary. Since then she'd left two other messages, neither of which had been returned. She figured there wasn't any place on earth where he couldn't get messages and concluded that he was obviously avoiding her.

She wasn't really surprised, then, when she scurried into Bergdorf's two days before Christmas and saw him strolling the first floor with a blonde on one arm and loads of shopping bags on the other. More hurt and disappointed and ashamed.

She supposed he'd been disgusted by the articles. How could she blame him? She was now the official social pariah of the moment. The drunken scarlet woman who'd had an abortion for money and an affair with one of the city's most powerful men, married, of course, to one of the luminaries of the social world—her best friend, no less. According to the press, that is, and although everybody pretended not to believe what they read in the tabloids, they all secretly did, she had now discovered. She ducked from view and hid herself at the perfume counter, shaking, nervously spraying herself with some disgusting potion the saleslady had thrust upon her with cloying politeness and promises of how fabulous this new fragrance would make her feel. She felt like vomiting.

Having purchased a flacon of the stinker out of sheer pressure and the need to keep her head low, and wondering which of her poor friends she'd inflict such a present on, she figured by now the coast was clear. No such luck.

"Josie!" boomed Andy, as she turned. They stood right there in front of her. Andy in a camel cashmere jacket and navy blue muffler over a sensible-looking suit, and the girl, whom Josie recognized as the bimbo in the white Herve Leger bandage dress from the Saunders's ball.

She gave Josie an unctuous smile with a collagen-enhanced pout, outlined in brown, smothered with pale gloss on her inner lips. Her brown eyes, surrounded by wads of thick black mascara and eyeshadow; the floor-length sable coat; her single-process platinum blond hair, trailing down one side of her face in a faux Veronica Lake wave, all shrieked "Bridge and Tunnel." She clung to Andy with long, fake, French manicured nails. Poor Andy.

"Andy!" Josie feigned surprise. "Hi!" She didn't know what to say next. How can you say "Why haven't you called me?" when a man has another woman on his arm? Even if she looks like a complete slut. How can you say that anyway? Instead she kissed him on both cheeks.

"You remember Heidi, from the party?"

"Sure, nice to see you," she lied. *Heidi Ho.* With this chick on his arm he should be wearing that old mushroom leisure suit and the gold chains. She looked down before he could tell what she was thinking. "Last-minute shopping?" she said to the packages.

"Sure thing, darlin'. Where you headed?"

"Oh, I'm driving up to my old friends Hailey and Simon Oakes's home in the Berkshires tomorrow. Should be a laugh. They've got about a dozen people coming and it's all snowed in and there's—"

"Ah mean now, shug. Wanna have lunch? We're on our way to Daniel."

"Oh, that's really sweet of you but I've already got plans and so much more shopping to do. I'm way behind, and there's so little time." *Not if hell freezes over is what I really mean.*

"Shug, Ah'm sorry Ah didn't call you. Ah've been—"

"Away, yes, your secretary told me." *Get me out of here!*

"Busy, shug, but Ah really want to talk to you about—"

"Look, don't worry about it, Andy, I understand. The Vive thing, well I never really thought that would happen, it was just a lark, and especially now, after all the press and stuff. It's fine," she mumbled. "Look I gotta dash. It was great seeing you. Have a wonderful Christmas." She kissed him again lightly on the cheek. Shaking Heidi the Ho's hand, she said, "Merry Christmas! I hope Santa looks after you!" and ran off into the crowd before he had a chance to say any more. She realized the girl had been wearing the same revolting perfume she'd just bought, and she threw it in a trash can as soon as she hit the corner of Fifty-Seventh and Fifth, then stumbled through the throng of Christmas shoppers, down Fifth, in tears.

42

It was great to get away from the city and be with old friends who couldn't care less about the tabloids. But Josie felt fragile and miserable. She cried herself to sleep the first night she arrived in the Berkshires. And dreamt again of drowning. Of feeling powerless, unable to bring herself up for air. But when she woke, she could hear the rushing of the tiny stream right outside her bedroom, and the stillness of the countryside, and she decided she'd try to forget everything about the past few horrific weeks and just enjoy herself.

She took long walks in the snow with Hailey and Simon and the numerous dogs and other guests, curled up by the enormous fire in the main hall of their beautiful, rambling stone house; ate and drank heaps; read; and slept. By the end of the first week she felt somewhat rested and revitalized.

But she felt a deep emptiness inside, a numbness that turned to pain and anger when she thought of Marcus, and, strangely, Andy. Although she wrote that off as being upset about the Vive contract and how he really hadn't bothered to contact her and tell her in person it was off. He was just as shallow as he pretended not to be.

"Oh, darling," Colbert Constable, the famous interior designer and the only other remaining guest, said to her one night after she relayed, with great humorous detail, her encounter with Andy in Bergdorf's. "That's all those rich tycoons want. A young floozy who'll go down on them at the snap of their fingers. They just want tons of blow jobs. They're too lazy to have real sex. It takes up too much time and effort they could be using to make more money."

"And let's face it, who wants to be giving blow jobs all the time?" Hailey laughed. "Once a week I get down on the creaky old knees and do my wifely duty, but any more than that, oh, please!"

"You still blow Simon once a week?" Colbert sniffed. "The lucky dog. I'm thrilled if I get one a year." He took a sip of his single malt whiskey and stared into the fire. "Anyway, Josie, darling, it's a well-known fact that tycoons usually have teeny dicks. That's why they have to achieve so much. Believe me, I've seen quite a few in my time, all of them pathetically underendowed." He wiggled his pinky finger at them in disgust.

"Penilely challenged? Is that what we're supposed to say these days?" Josie giggled, but she did wonder what Andy was like.

"Now that I wouldn't mind so much," Hailey said. "Simon is so enormous I nearly gag to death."

"And you're complaining?" Josie said. "Shut up, for God's sake, before I throw myself into that frozen stream outside."

"Oh, sweetie," Hailey said, "don't be so depressed! Marriage isn't all it's cracked up to be, you know. Sometimes I feel like strangling him, he can be such a pain in the ass. Although after thirteen years I must admit I have no clue what I'd do without him. But look at you! You're still gorgeous! You'll find someone, I know you will!"

"I dunno," Josie sighed. "I just feel like I've made so many stupid choices and mistakes, I don't know if I'll ever meet someone great. I feel like I'll be alone forever. I'll be like Miss Haversham, sitting in my wedding dress, covered in cobwebs until I die. And flat stone broke, the way things are going."

"Oh, darling, we'll look after you if you ever get in trouble, you know that." Hailey hugged her. "You can always come and live here."

"Yeah, this place will become the old, broke singles' rest home," Josie said. "We'll all be creaking around on our walkers, still dishing."

"Dish 'til you die, honey, that's what I always say," Colbert said, as he dusted ash from his American Spirit cigarette off the shawl collar of his Etro paisley quilted cashmere smoking jacket.

They heard Simon stamping his boots at the mudroom door, where he'd returned from his office in one of the outer cottages. "Who are you dishing now?" he said, as he entered, handsome and rugged in his worn cords and thick Aran sweater.

"Why you, darling, of course." Colbert smiled as he stood up and delicately pushed the fire around with a poker. "We've been discussing how huge your willy is. And when Hailey's tired of it, I'd love a go at it, darling."

Simon rolled his eyes. "This fax came in, Josie," he said, his mouth pursed slightly.

"A fax? For me? How would anyone know where I am?" she said, then wailed when she saw what it was. "Oh, no! Not another one. They're trying to crucify me!"

"GREAT GAMS GAL CAUGHT IN MILLION-DOLLAR SEXCAPADE WITH GREEK TYCOON THREE TIMES HER AGE," said Colbert, leaning over her shoulder and reading the tabloid heading. And accompanying it was yet another picture of her from Marcus's photo shoot, fallen down on the bottom of the stairs, drunk, and laughing. It was taken from above so one could see right up between her legs. Mercifully that part had been fuzzed out, but it didn't leave much to anyone's imagination.

"What a load of tripe. Any Greek tycoon three times your age would be about a hundred and twenty by now. Ooh, do tell all, darling," he cooed, "sounds simply divine."

"I can't take this anymore!" Josie wailed. She grimaced at her reflection in the mirror. "It's you," she said to the puffy-eyed moron staring back at her. "It's all you. You've got to change." She paced around the tiny stone bathroom, then stared out the mullioned window at the snow-covered fields beyond the cottage. The view was breathtaking.

Change. But how? She knew what was wrong with her. Two years of therapy had ground that out of her. But knowing your patterns was one thing. Being able to change them was something else again. That was work. "And you're too dumb and lazy to work." *Stop! Stop being so negative.*

"Please, God, if you're there, I beg of you, help me. I'm desperate." She sat down on the closed toilet and wept again. "I know I'm a flake and only pray when things are really bad and I should be praying when they're good as well, but I promise I'll start. I just don't know where to turn. You must help me. I need a miracle! I know I need to change the way I'm thinking, because the way I've been thinking doesn't work. It's never worked. I've been greedy and superficial and stupid."

She took a few deep breaths and tried to calm herself. Finally, she said, "I'm asking you now. Please guide me. Tell me what it is I need to do."

"What you need is to grow some balls and stand up and fight for yourself," said a man's voice from beyond the bathroom door.

Josie gasped and leapt up, her heart pounding. "Who's there?" She felt mortified. How long had he been listening?

"It's me. Marcus."

"What the hell are you doing here?" She stormed out of the bathroom. "How did you get here? Why are you here?" Her heart pounded just a little harder and she could feel the knot in her stomach squeezing even more the minute she saw his face. He looked pale, not as fit or robust as she last saw him, but still devastatingly handsome.

"Colbert told me you were here."

"Colbert?"

"He's done all my mother's houses. He's been a family friend for years. Look, Josie, I thought I—"

"Haven't you done enough damage? Can't you just leave me alone?"

"I came to try to help you, Josie."

"Why? Guilt?"

"Maybe." He sighed and slumped down onto the edge of her bed. "Yes. I feel bad. You're one of the sweetest, kindest people I've ever had the good fortune to meet."

She stared at him in disbelief. He tugged his black down parka off and yanked at the collar of a gray flannel shirt, pulling it out from the neck of a charcoal cashmere sweater. She waited, fighting the urge to say something offensive. He looked at her with those smoky eyes and she could see the sadness in them.

"I know I hurt you," he said. "And I came to tell you

that I'm sorry. I don't blame you for being angry. What I did was shitty. Really pathetic." He shook his head and looked down.

She could feel the tears welling up again. The pain, the loss, not just from what he'd done, but from all the other things and relationships and stupid situations she'd put herself through. It wasn't him at all, she realized. What he'd done was just another manifestation of her own self-loathing.

"But I promise you, I didn't sell the tabloids those pictures of you. I didn't even know they existed till they were there in the paper."

"I just don't know if I believe that, Marcus," she said, wiping tears from her eyes. "I don't know who or what to believe anymore."

"I really care about you, Josie," he whispered. "And I don't know how to make it right. Perhaps it never will be. But the least I can do is try to help someone I . . . I . . . someone I love."

Love? He loves me? Me? She felt her eyes widen.

Oh, God.

"I'm sorry," he said. "I'm so sorry." She sat down on the bed and he enveloped her in his arms and they sat rocking each other gently.

"It's okay," she blubbered.

"I'm not seeing Antonia anymore." She pulled away from him.

"What's happened?"

"Nothing, really, I just don't know what came over me, that's all."

"A severe case of avarice?" She smiled.

"I've been a prick."

"The silly part is you didn't need her. You're good enough to make it on your own. If anything, she's probably hurt your career. She's a cow."

"But you're the one who told me to play the game!"

"I didn't mean you should play it that well," she smirked.

"I can't believe I did that . . . I just can't believe it. It was like I was possessed or something."

"Don't beat yourself up. She dangled success in front of you. And you fell for it. Big deal. Look, I just happen to be the world's leading expert on avarice and doing something you regret for the rest of your life. At least you only slept with someone. I . . . took a life . . ."

"So that's true?" He looked surprised.

"In so many words, yes. I mean, I can and have justified what I did every which way you could imagine. But basically, at the end of the day, I had an abortion. And his family gave me a settlement. So you want to talk about whoring yourself? I reckon I beat you hands down." She leaned forward on her hands and examined the carpet. She couldn't look at him. The shame of her venality was too great.

"I don't think many people would blame you. He was a complete asshole to you, from what I hear."

"You can't begin to know. You don't want to know."

"You sound like Hamish," he said, putting his hand on hers. "I do want to know. Tell me. I love you, Josie. I want to know everything about you."

She sighed and smiled up at him through her wet lashes. *Trust your gut,* she felt herself saying. *Just trust your gut. Isn't that what Andy does? . . . Oh, Andy.* She took a deep breath and got quiet. *Listen to your heart.*

"Look, Marcus." The words came out of her mouth like someone else's. "As much as I'm attracted to you, I just don't think we should attempt to be anything more than friends. It'd never last. We're in different places in our lives. You're on the way up, and I, well, I don't know what the hell I'm doing, except struggling to stay afloat right now." She knew she could never be with him. For starters, she still didn't really trust him. That, plus she didn't think he was really very bright. *How can you be with someone who isn't going to stimulate you mentally?*

He smiled down at her and hugged her again. "I understand. I've blown it."

"It's not that," she sighed. "Yeah, you kind of blew it. But it's something else. I can't explain it. Except that it just doesn't feel right. I'm sorry, Marcus."

"Then at least let a friend help you make the float easier," he said. He kissed her on the forehead. What the hell was she thinking? Was she doing the right thing? Turning down the most handsome guy she'd ever met? Was she nuts, or what? *No. You're finally listening. He's not the man for you.*

"Marky! Honey!" Colbert suddenly appeared in the doorway, a crimson cashmere shawl swathed over his smoking jacket, a red fez perched jauntily atop his thinning silver hair, an American Spirit in one hand and a glass of scotch in the other. "Thank God you're here!"

"For Christ's sake! Doesn't anybody knock around here?" She rolled her eyes.

"Josie, darling, we only want to help," sniffed Colbert. "That's why I asked Marcus up here. To help you, darling."

"But there's nothing to do! My life as an aging panty hose pusher is finished. Kaput. So near, and yet—so what? All I need to do is lie low—disappear for a while—and this will all blow over. End of story. It's not like I'm some sort of megastar."

"You could be. That's why it's worth fighting," Marcus said.

"Nah. Who am I? I'm a nobody. And quite honestly I'm happy to remain that way."

"What—broke and lonely? Is that really what you want?" Colbert said.

"No, of course not," she snapped. "But I just don't

want to make things worse than they already are. Not that it's possible at this stage."

"Well if you've got nothing else to lose, then the only way out is up, isn't it, darling?" Colbert smiled. "And we really do want to help you."

"Really?" She smelled a rat. "You're up to something, Col, aren't you?"

"Yew! Please! Don't call me Col. It sounds like some hideous Aussie nickname," he sniffed.

"It is, darling." She sniffed back at him. "So out with it. What do you want?"

"Please let me help you, Josie," Marcus said. "It's the least I can do."

"But why? Why do you want to get involved in my sordid mess? I need to take care of it in my own way."

"It's my party and I'll cry if I want to, cry if I want to, cry if I want to!" sang Colbert, wiggling his slim hips against the door frame. "Oh, get with the program, honey. We love you! How long have we known each other?"

"Long enough for me to think you have an ulterior motive, Colbert."

"Ooh, she's a suspicious bitch!" He wrinkled his nose up at her, then winked at Marcus.

"Well—don't you?"

"Oh, come on! Hon-ey! What do you take me for?" He smiled ever so sweetly and batted his eyes at her.

"A conniving, manipulative 'inferior decorator' who wants to get back at someone, if I know you at all," she laughed. "Come on yourself, honey, cut the crap! It's me you're talking to. Who is it you can use me to get to, huh? And how can I possibly help you if you won't tell me? You'd better spill the beans about whatever's lurking in that evil brain of yours, shug." She felt a funny sensation at her use of the word *shug*—Andy's word. *Oh, Andy. I'll never see you again. Your dick's in Bimbo World.*

"Oh, all-right!" Colbert snapped and rolled his eyes. "If you must know"—he sucked on his American Spirit and curved his hand elegantly in the air in front of his face—"it's Richard Saunders."

"Why do you want to get at Richard?" She frowned.

"Well, for a start he owes me a hundred thousand dollars. But, oh! Honey! That's the least of it! . . . Well, I'm sure you've heard what's happened?"

"About Priscilla?"

"She had it coming, darling." He leaned against the door frame and waved his cigarette around again, "I mean, how spoiled and useless can a woman be? Don't get me wrong, *J'adore* Priscilla!" He pursed his lips and took a sip of the scotch. "But let's face it—she has absolutely no grasp on reality these days or she would have seen what was going on. I mean, really! You can't hide those things forever. Sooner or later it's got to come out, hasn't it?"

"What are you talking about? Her addiction and the rehab thing?"

"Oh, darling! Don't be ridiculous! That sweet young boy of his, Juan, is in such a state. He's inconsolable! That unconscionable bastard just dumped him and left him in hideously deep pooey water without so much as a single floaty, let alone a paddle! And now I'll never get paid for the work I did on that love nest! To think he just let him rot in the hospital like that. After all that time and with all that dosh of his. He's an absolute shit!"

"Love nest? Young boy? Do you understand a word of this, Marcus?" She turned to him in absolute shock.

Marcus shook his head and shrugged.

"Are you actually saying that Richard is . . . has a . . . is . . ."

"A fag, darling! Yes he's a big fat fag! A dyed-in-the-wool homo, darling!"

"But he can't be!" She was astonished. "He's my best friend's, well, my former best friend, I guess—her husband! It's not possible! They've been happily married for eleven years!"

"Ho-ney! Get with the program! Come on! He's as camp as a row of pink tents! A huge pillow biter!"

"Really?" She grimaced. "Reeeally? I . . . I uh, this is . . . shocking! Oh my God! Poor Priscilla! No wonder she's insane!" She stood up and paced around the bed a couple of times, trying to let it sink in.

"You know," she said after a minute, "Hamish said something funny a few weeks ago at the Vive test shoot about Richard . . . what was it? . . . not fancying me because he had other proclivities. Maybe he knows about this."

"Well!" Colbert smirked. "It takes one old Queen to know another, doll." He wiggled his hips again. "And let me tell you, in all honesty he has hid it well, I must say. But the tiger is about to leap out of the tank."

"Wait a minute . . . just hold on a second . . . now you're saying Hamish is gay too?"

Colbert merely rolled his eyes at that one, like he couldn't believe she was such a naive twit.

"Is he, Marcus?"

Marcus smiled. "That is one twisted mother."

"But I had an affair with him! He kissed me just a few months ago! A real kiss! A big, fat, juicy, wet, tongue kiss! He nearly jumped me!"

"Oh, yeah, he tried that on me, too." Marcus shrugged again.

She grimaced and shuddered at what she had done all those years ago, although it had all seemed so real, like he really did love her, for ages.

"He's completely confused, Josie, that's all. A real sicko," Marcus said.

"A total fuck-up, that old Queen," Colbert added, with glee in his voice.

"And you, Marcus? Don't tell me you're gay too!"

"Don't be absurd, darling!" Colbert snapped. "I and every gay man in Manhattan only wishes! No, darling, little Marky-poo here is as straight as Cupid's arrow, sadly." He cast his eyes down in mock wistfulness.

"There is a God after all," Josie laughed, looking Marcus right smack in those big smoky eyes of his. *Don't even go there . . . you've done the right thing.* "So Hamish is . . . bi . . . is that it?"

"I think he's a lot more far gone than that, darling," Colbert said. "He's into some weird shit, from what I hear."

"Oh my God!" Josie stopped pacing. "The boy. The boy at the ball! That must have been him!"

"The very same one, my sweet," Colbert sniffed. "Poor darling is beyond distraught. That billionaire bum bandit practically raped him. He was only sixteen! Four years he had poor Juan on a string! He's told me the whole story and now I'm personally out for blood. And my money of course."

"Naturally," Josie said, shooting him a look of disdain.

"What?" he asked innocently. "A gal has to make a living you know. Ain't no one else gonna keep this tired old broad in furs and jewels."

"You got a point." She smiled at him as she resumed her pacing. "But I don't get it. What does Richard Saunders being gay have anything to do with my situation? Except maybe his wife has spread some pretty nasty rumors about me because she thought I was having it off with him. But I really don't see the correlation."

"Well, that's why we've come to figure this out," said

Colbert. "I thought maybe we could join forces. It's time to do unto others as they've been doing unto us."

"You mean like the Golden Rule?" asked Marcus.

"Knowing you, Col, I'd say it's quite the opposite," Josie said.

"Stop calling me that heinous name!" Colbert cried.

"Still," she kept going, "maybe you're onto something." She sat at the head of the bed, behind Marcus, leaned back on the headboard, and closed her eyes.

"You're not going to sleep now, are you?" Colbert said.

"Shh! Quiet! I'm thinking!"

"I'll alert the media."

"Shut up!" she hissed. He did.

Gradually an idea started to form.

"You know"—she finally opened her eyes—"this could be fun. We could have some real fun here." She drummed her fingers on the bedspread and smiled. "And we just might pull it off!"

"Pull what off? Ooh, do tell, honey!"

43

The next afternoon, in a very popular downtown eatery, Antonia stood grinning into the bathroom mirror. She licked the red lipstick off her teeth, smoothed the straight black silky mane that hung down way below her shoulders, and took a deep, calming breath. *Mmm, yes, you're Gorgeous with a capital "G."*

She liked her new hair extensions. Very Now. Or were they still? Only yesterday, right after she'd left Pierre Parau's brand-new salon on Fifth Avenue, looking as "ne plus ultra" as anyone else on this minuscule island ever had or would, she'd overheard some young fashionistas in Barneys saying that curls were back in. A sliver of doubt had crept into her brain. But she quickly dismissed it. She was way too fabulous to be bothered with such trifles as shop girl gossip.

She turned away from the mirror. *I'm walking, no,* she thought, *slinking is the word for me. I'm slinking, in my new YSL black leather dress and these fabulous six-inch spike-heeled snakeskin boots, into this date. He won't be able to resist me!*

She slid into the banquette, smoothed her hair again,

and curled her mouth up in that soft Mona Lisa smile she was famous for. And waited. She hated that he was almost always late. But he was worth it. She had been fantasizing about his body and hers entwined and glistening with sex for the past twenty-four hours, ever since he'd called and asked if she'd meet him. It was all she could think about, although she knew, in the back of her mind, she was in trouble because of it. A man usually never obsessed her like this. It was power and money that normally got her hot.

But this guy was different. The things he could do with that tongue of his were truly miraculous. He'd brought her to heights she'd never even dreamed of before. She closed her eyes and imagined what it would be like in a couple of hours, having his tongue caressing her again. And again and again. Talk about afternoon delight.

"They say a nap at lunchtime gets the juices flowing for the rest of the day." His smoky voice permeated her reverie. She opened her eyes deliberately slowly and as sensuously as she could.

"My juices are always flowing," she said, looking up to Marcus and giving him the best of her Mona Lisa smile.

Antonia was still seething that both Marcus and Hamish had left her stable. Marcus she could kind of understand, because although he was a complete and utter ingrate, she knew she could seduce him into returning, but Hamish leaving had been inconceivable. It was worse than a divorce. He had no right to dump her. Silently, she had grieved the loss, of both her best and oldest client, and her best friend, but publicly she was prepared to go for his jugular. She wasn't about to lose face.

"I've been thinking of you," Marcus said, after he sidled into the booth, opposite her.

"Really?" She gave him the benefit of her sweetest

smile. "Have you missed me? Do you want to come back? I haven't heard you've signed with anyone else yet."

"Not yet."

"Why don't you come back? You've been a very bad boy. I'd have to punish you severely," she said, pouting and leaning across the table at him as she put her hand and crimson nails on his beautiful hands. *Oh, those hands.* She longed for them to hold her. She felt him twitch, but he didn't move his hand away. She stared into the green smoke of his eyes and pushed her leg out until she could feel the pointed toe of her Blahnik boot on his leg. He didn't move an inch. *Mmm. This is going to be easy.*

"I'm thinking about it," he said, as she slid her toe up farther between his legs, "but there is something I'd really like."

"Mmm. What's that?" She felt the tip of her shoe reach his crotch. He smiled at her. His hooded eyes made her melt. She wanted to reach out and grab him.

"I want the Saint James account."

It took a major effort for her not to flinch. "But that's Hamish's account." She purred and pouted and pushed her toe a little farther in.

"I know. But I'm good enough for it and I want it."

"He's under contract. There are lots of other big accounts we can get. We have plenty of time to build something fabulous." She wiggled her toes and smiled again.

"You're a very resourceful woman. I'm sure you'll find a way to get me Saint James. I gotta go," he said, pushing her toe out from between his thighs and standing. "Give me a call when you've got it secured." And then he turned and walked out, not seeing the look of absolute mortification wipe the Mona Lisa smile off her milky white face.

* * *

Uptown, in another overpriced, packed-to-the-gills-with-socialites eatery, Josie sat opposite Hamish and wondered exactly how perverted he actually was. How could she not have known? She'd suspected, for sure, but she hadn't ever allowed the thought about his effete manners to trail longer than a humorous dig. Oh, the bliss of denial!

"Why you wanted to meet in this hellhole I certainly don't know," he sniffed at her.

She grinned, knowing that the upper East Side made him feel rather less than his normal superior self. Or at least that's what she was hoping. She wanted him to feel uncomfortable.

"Just look at all these faces. Winched up until they're about to snap, most of them."

"Stop whining," she said. "It makes us look sooo much younger, being in a place like this."

"Well I know you didn't get me here to talk about plastic surgery, darling, so what's on your mind?" He sipped at his San Pellegrino and bore into her with his steel gray bullet-like eyes.

God, talk about getting straight to the point. "Oh, uh, nothing really. We haven't seen each other since the Vive test shoot . . . and I thought it might be good to catch up." *This isn't going to work,* she thought, feeling her palms getting moist. *He's way too smart to fall for it.*

"I suppose you think I planted that story about the Greek tycoon in the gossip rags." He stared coldly at her again.

"Well . . . now that you've brought it up," she said, as sweetly as she could. "After all, you were the only one there."

"I assure you it wasn't me," he said imperiously.

"Really?" She gave him a sickly sweet smile.

"Of course not, darling. I'd never do that to you. I adore you—you know that."

Yeah, right. She wiped her hands on her navy Chloe skirt and said innocently, "Well, who else would spread such a nasty lie?"

"Oh, please, darling! It was fifteen years ago. Can't you just forget it?"

"I thought I had," she said softly. "Until now. This whole thing has ruined my chances with Vive, I've lost my account with Great Gams, and now they want their money back! I don't know what to do, Hamish!"

He was silent. Now he couldn't look her in the eye. *Good,* she thought, as she watched him fiddle with his food. *I hope you feel dreadful.*

"Well, darling," he finally looked up at her with that sweetly evil curl to the edges of his mouth. "Let's face it. You were a complete slut in Greece."

"I was not!" she shouted. "Nothing happened—except with you!"

"Will you lower your voice to a screech, please?" he said, looking around to see if anyone else had heard her outburst.

"Nothing happened between Mr. Apatsos and me! For God's sake—he was over eighty!"

"But, darling, you stayed on there for days after the job finished." His eyebrow raised up at her.

"*So?*" *Oh, God.* This wasn't going at all how she'd planned. *He* was the one who was supposed to feel uncomfortable, not her. "I was totally exhausted from traveling so much . . . And the room was comped for another week! You could have stayed on too, if you'd wanted." She had always wondered why he hadn't. She had wanted him to. "I had one dinner with the old man—at the hotel, and that was it. The rest of the time I just swam and read and slept and ordered room service. But I told you all this years ago!" She drew herself up and tried to breathe deeply and keep calm. And then the penny dropped.

"You organized it," she said, her mind turning over the events from so long ago, her fingers drumming on the table. "So, how much did they pay you?"

"What?" He looked at her quizzically.

"How much? You pimped me, didn't you? How much did they give you, a million? Pounds?"

"Don't be ridiculous. You're hardly worth that much—"

"I thought you were my friend. I used to think you were more than that. A lot more." She glared at him, realizing he didn't give a rat's ass about anyone except himself. "You sold me, like some chattel. And then left on the next plane. Isn't that right?"

"What difference did it make to you?" he asked, with a flatness that was scary. "You just said you didn't fuck him. So you had a nice vacation. What's the problem?"

"I just can't believe you'd do such a thing."

He took another sip of his water. "Oh, wake up, sweetie."

"Great! So you're a sociopath as well as a pervert." *Oh, fuck. Now I've blown it.*

His eyes flickered. "Well I certainly didn't tell those rags about it." Just like that, like he was completely innocent. It took all the strength she had not to lean over and hit him.

"Then who?" She wanted him to say it.

"My beloved ex," he said, "has always adored the tabloids." *Good,* she sighed, *now I've got you back on the right path.*

"Oh, Antonia. Well, she certainly is a piece of work. Do you know what I heard yesterday? That she's got the Saint James account for Marcus. Isn't that amazing?"

"But that's my account!" His beady eyes narrowed. "I'm under contract with them!"

"Oh! Well, she's told them that you're pulling out, from what I hear." She tried to be as ditzy as she could without pushing it too far. "Course, I could be wrong. Maybe it isn't the Saint James account. Maybe it's something else. I don't know. Something."

"That stupid cow doesn't know who she's messing with," he hissed. "And she's going to wish she'd never met me if she even thinks about stealing my best account away. That fucking ankle."

"Ankle?"

"She's about three feet lower than a cunt."

Josie giggled. *Gotcha.*

"Oh, I'm sure I got it all wrong, sweetie," she said sarcastically, rising up. "And Hamish?"

He looked up at her.

She punched him as hard as she could in the eye and walked out, her fist smarting with pain.

44

Josie hesitated. She knew she'd have to swallow her pride and face him if she wanted to put her plan into action. Maybe she was being too bold, trying to reach too high. But she had to put her fear behind her, if only for a short time, and at least give it a shot. She picked up the phone and dialed Andy's office.

As she walked up the stairs of The Four Seasons, apprehension and fear engulfed her. What the hell was she doing? And why had she agreed to yet another lunch? The cellulite was expanding at an alarming rate.

She could feel a few sets of eyes on her as the maitre d' escorted her across the floor. It was strange and horrible to be recognized because of some heinous tabloid press. She held herself high and looked straight ahead.

"Why, darlin'," Andy boomed as she neared his booth. He rose, came round the table, and hugged her. "'Bout time you surfaced." He grazed her cheek with his mouth.

"I guess so." Her heart fluttered at the feel of him near her and she breathed in the soft freshness of his

Czech & Speake aftershave, which she'd made him buy the day they'd gone out shopping. She realized at that moment how much she'd missed him. His warmth and humor and caring. Even the funny way he spoke. And she realized, too, that she was terrified. She pulled away and they sat, just looking at each other for a few seconds. Then she had to look away, because although she was smiling, she thought she might cry.

"I have a proposition for you," she blurted out.

"Oh, yeah?" He raised an eyebrow and grinned at her.

45

Juan Lopez examined his shoes. Not a spot on them. Shiny and clean. He adjusted his Charvet tie and shot his cuffs. He looked at the back of the doorman's head as they rose higher and higher. He had a few dandruff flakes on his collar. Juan felt like brushing them off. Instead, he tried to ignore the pounding of his heart with each floor they rose.

"Thank you," he said, as the doors opened onto the beautiful foyer. "Showtime," he whispered to himself.

"Good afternoon, sir," said the waiting maid, as she escorted him into the magnificent living room. "Mrs. Saunders will be with you shortly. May I get you anything?"

A half hour later, Priscilla wailed, "Oh, hon! Can you ever find it in your heart to forgive me?" Josie crossed the parquet foyer and gave her a big hug.

She had to forgive her friend, even if she had been an evil, spoiled bitch. "Don't worry about it. I'm sorry you have to go through this." She stroked Priscilla's hair.

"You're sorry! I've been appalling to you!" She took Josie's hand and led her into the living room, where Juan sat, sipping tea, looking flustered, like a deer caught in the headlights of a truck.

"This poor kid has told me everything! He was a virgin! I just can't believe it!"

"I'm sure this must be really difficult, P," Josie said, as she sat down and poured herself some tea. "It's truly shocking and I'm sorry for you. But we'll get through this, all of us." She felt empowered after her lunch with Andy—strong, and clear about where she was headed. Except for one thing: Andy himself. "We just need to make a plan, is all. I'm big on making plans this week."

"A plan!" Priscilla cried. "I'll give my bastard of a husband a fucking plan all right! I plan to shred him alive and feed him to the dogs!" *Fat chance,* thought Josie, glancing at the two Yorkies on the sofa.

"We can ruin him," Juan said softly.

"But can you prove you've had an affair with him?"

"Ahem." Rose, Priscilla's maid, coughed, as she cleared up the tea service. "Mrs. Saunders, may I say something?"

"What, Rose?"

"I think it might be of interest to you, ma'am. You see, as you may remember, my husband is a policeman."

"Yes, Rose, of course I know that."

"Well, a couple of months ago he . . . uh . . . he . . ."

"What, Rose?"

"He arrested Mr. Saunders, ma'am. In a sex club. A gay sex club. With a teenage boy. There are photographs."

"Juicy," said Josie.

"Why the hell didn't you tell me!" screamed Priscilla. The dogs quaked. Rose collected the tea tray and left the room, her jaw set with the repressed anger subordinates are required to hide from untenable employers.

46

Marv looked even older, more withered and fragile than when Josie had last seen him. He emanated a certain sadness now, perhaps the sadness of those who know they don't have much more time left, but are not yet ready to leave.

He had a male nurse now, who carried him from his wheelchair onto the sumptuous lounge in Andy's outer office. Josie figured he couldn't be too pleased about that.

She had deliberately worn the shortest skirt she could find in her closet. "It's so good to see you again, Marv." She sat next to him and patted him on the knee. He had on a very elegant bespoke suit in navy, a blue striped shirt with white collar and cuffs, and shoes that shone so black they were like mirrors. But something was amiss. "Where's your tie?"

"Whadya think this is, Scotch mist?" he rasped and showed the top of his aged cranium as he glanced down to the conservative red and blue Hermes job that hung around his tiny wrinkled neck like a sad noose.

"But I love your ties!" she said. "They're so much fun! What happened?"

"Oy! I got bored. Everything bores me these days."

"That doesn't sound like the Marv I know," she said, in an overly perky tone that made her own skin crawl. "How's William treating you?"

"Guess," he said, swiveling his head in the direction of the monolithic pumped-up nurse.

"Oh," she said, nodding her head, "I see."

"Honey, you ain't seen nothing. They're killing me. It's murder," he said, pronouncing it "moider." She'd never heard him sound so defeated and bitter.

The door to Andy's inner sanctum swung open and he bounded out with his arm outstretched toward Marv. "Sorry to keep you, Mr. Gottlieb," he said, leaning down to the frail old man before him. "It's a pleasure to meet you, sir."

"I'd like to say the pleasure was all mine," Marv rasped in reply, "but I'm too old and tired to get much pleasure from anything these days."

"Oh, Marv!" Josie said. "Come on! Things are not that bad, surely!"

"Worse," he said morosely.

"Well," Andy said, "let's get you comfortable, sir, and then we'll have ourselves a little powwow. Cigar?" He reached into his top pocket and slid out two Romeo Y Juliettas. The milky sadness in Marv's eyes lifted slightly as he reached out his withered paw and took the offering.

"You can wait outside," he said to the nurse, before any reprimands were offered. The hulk obeyed and disappeared.

"Now, how 'bout a J.D., Mr. Gottlieb?" Andy said, smiling beneficently, as he sauntered over to an antique Chinoiserie cabinet and took out a bottle of bourbon.

Marv practically leapt at the suggestion. Josie could

see him straighten up and a small smile animated his wizened face. "Damn fools, my family," he cackled. "Don't know a thing about life. Never did." He practically grabbed the glass from Andy and swigged it back in one go. Andy topped him up without even asking.

"Well, sir, if it's okay by you, we'd like to become your new family, so ta speak."

"You and this lovely young lady?" Marv's eyes were positively twinkling now. *Like before,* Josie thought, smiling up at Andy. *I like this!*

"The both of us," Andy said. "We want to buy your family out."

"Praise the Lord," Marv cackled. "I couldn't think of a nicer way to stick it to those ingrates." He sat back in the couch and took a deep draw of his cigar. "Ahh," he said, "bliss."

Josie and Andy looked at each other, a conspiratorial look, pregnant with hope and a certain shyness.

"So," Marv interrupted them, "when are you two kids getting hitched?"

47

Richard Saunders had never really reconciled himself to the fact that he was gay. He thought of his behavior as a passing fancy of sorts, something that took him by surprise at times, even shocked him at others. But he really didn't think too much about it. He was entitled to do as he pleased.

He still loved his wife, and although things had not been going at all smoothly in the past few weeks, what with her addictive and crazy behavior, he'd stick with her. He was pissed that he had to go into therapy with her now she was "in recovery." Like he had time to blink, let alone sit for an hour twice a week and try to analyze their marriage. Fucking boring and a waste of time. She was the one who needed the help. He was just fine. With all the money he gave her she ought to be kissing the ground he walked on.

His car pulled up behind hers at the Eighty-Seventh Street entrance to her shrink's office. The Guggenheim Museum loomed above the street with a rondular grandness. He reminded himself to donate some more money to the Gug. It was about time he had his name on a wing or something on one of these goddamned museums. Hell, he forked out enough dough every year to these joints, just so his wife could chair all those social events she said they had to attend, just to keep up with everyone else. Like he gave a shit.

His wife stepped out of her black Mercedes at the same time he alighted from his. She was wrapped in a sable cape that he had no remembrance of seeing before. She spent money like a drunken sailor. She turned and looked at him with a face like a sheet of ice. *Christ, what now?*

"You're late," she snapped, as the doorman ushered them into the lobby of the prewar building.

"And you're in a charming mood," he replied, as they strode across the marble foyer and into the waiting room of the office. "This is sure going to be a barrel of laughs."

"We'll see who's laughing soon, dear," she said, giving him a glare like he'd never seen before. Maybe she was flipping again, and he'd have to lock her back up.

"Richard," Priscilla said, as soon as they were seated next to each other on the couch, in the presence of Dr. Antony, "I wanted to ask you something."

"What, dear?" He turned and smiled at her, knowing his tone was more than patronizing.

"Have you had fun fucking Juan Lopez for the past four years? Is his asshole tighter than my pussy? Juicier? Tastier?"

"Ahem, good afternoon to you both," said Dr. Antony, his eyebrows raised.

48

"It didn't go well?" Josie asked, from the cream silk sofa she had curled up in. She felt as nervous as Priscilla, but she could barely concentrate on what Priscilla was telling her. The meeting with Marv that morning had completely thrown her.

"It sucked." Priscilla paced around her enormous living room. "He denied it all. He said Juan was a conniving little gold digger who had it in for him ever since he got fired from Whiterock, and that he could prove that Juan had been embezzling money."

"Do you think there's a possibility that's true?"

"I don't know." Priscilla stopped, shook her head, then threw herself down in an overstuffed fauteuil. "If I know my husband at all—which is dubious at this point—he'll have covered his tracks extremely well. And quite possibly have manufactured damning evidence against Juan, even if the boy is completely innocent."

"So now what?"

"I told him I was getting a lawyer."

"How'd he react to that?"

"He said that if I thought I could get a nickel over our prenup agreement to think again. That he'd ruin me."

"He said that? In front of your shrink?"

"No. After. When we left." Priscilla's jaw started to quiver and the tears rolled down her cheeks. "I just can't believe this is happening," she whimpered.

"But what did the shrink say about all of this? I mean, surely he must see Richard is lying?"

"Oh, the usual stuff—'it's obvious you two have some issues you need to resolve'—that kind of bullshit."

The phone rang. Priscilla shakily picked it up. "Yes?" she sniffled. "Oh, oh yes. Umm." Her eyes darted to Josie and she put her fingers up to her mouth. "Well, I guess you'd better send him up." She put the phone down and looked guiltily at Josie. "Oops," she cringed, "I forgot to tell you. I told Jonathon Cantero he could come by this afternoon. Sorry."

"You what?" Josie stood up, shaking, her stomach immediately hitting maximum churn action.

"He just got out of that hideous place! I feel sorry for the guy."

"But you already told me he was the one who called the tabloids about me! How could you do this?"

"I thought it was about time you two sorted this out. I just forgot to tell you, that's all."

"Tell me? How about asking me? Did it ever occur to you that I never want to see him again? That it's just too painful?"

"Stop yelling at me!" Priscilla was crying now. "I'm sorry! It was a mistake! You can hide in my bedroom if you want!"

"Hi, Moonpie," came a familiar voice behind her, and Josie turned to see him, her heart leaping with fear and sadness.

"Hi," Josie said to Jonathon, with that sinking feeling

one has when seeing the person one dreads seeing the most and can't avoid it; knowing that the only thing that will come out of the encounter will be an overflow of pent-up emotions and heartbreak. But she remained frozen into the sofa like an overgrown cat with rigor mortis.

There was an awkward pause while everyone tried to assess the situation and the damage it may incur on each of them.

"Hi, sweetie." Priscilla got up and hugged him. He appeared to be frozen too, because Josie didn't see him respond. His arms hung at his sides like a rag doll. She remembered that posture. It was the wounded "how-could-you-do-this-to-me?" child pose that Jonathon had perfected into an art form.

"So you set me up," he said to Priscilla, when she released him from her overfriendly grip. "I shoulda guessed you'd do that." He reached into the pocket of his black cashmere jacket and pulled out a packet of Marlboro reds. "Mind?"

"No, course not, and, Jonathon, it's not what you think. I didn't do it deliberately. Josie stopped by and I forgot the time."

Josie looked at him and remembered the stab of rejection she used to feel when he slipped into his passive aggressive mode. He'd be sweet one minute and cold and distant and disapproving the next. And he'd make her feel, or maybe she'd made herself feel, his moods were her fault. So she'd constantly overextend herself in a pathetic bid to win his love. Walking on eggshells, never knowing what he'd do or behave like next, so gradually she sank deeper and deeper into her own morass of insecurity and bottomless, unfathomable fear.

She had thought he was her last chance. That she

had to make the relationship work, because nobody else would ever love her.

Now she couldn't believe she had been that person, a shell of an excuse for a functioning human being. Not functioning at all, really, but living on raw nerves, as if she'd been sucked into an alternative universe and left her emotional self-worth behind.

She looked at Jonathon and realized she was happy now. He no longer had her entrenched in the black hole of his alcoholic persona.

His pretty face, the big soft eyes no longer melted her heart and her defenses. She felt free of him for the first time, and that sudden perception somehow made her love him even more.

So she sat there and smiled at him, grinning like a Cheshire cat. *Free at last!*

"What's so funny?" he said, his soft, high voice flattening in suspicion. The same voice that had whispered so many false promises. Although she still believed he had truly loved her—as much as he was capable of love.

"Nothing," she replied, smiling again. "It's good to see you Jonathon. You look well." She could feel her heart racing, still, like it used to, but it felt different now. It was more an exhilarating quickening of her senses, grounded in self-value and faith. She felt her smile widen even more. And she could see the discomfort it caused him. "It's really good to see you," she repeated. And it didn't feel forced. She meant it.

This apparently unnerved him even more. It was the opposite of what either one of them would have expected; her being calm. But she genuinely did feel calm. *This is a miracle,* she thought, *a true miracle. Thank you, God!*

He was speechless. He sucked on his cigarette and eyed her leerily. She could tell his mind was racing several steps ahead, to the outcome of this little *tableau vivant*, and trying to figure how he could come out on top.

"So what do you want?" he finally said, strolling over to the couch facing hers and sitting himself down with a forced nonchalance.

"Nothing," she said, tilting her head in her best coquette pose and shaking it softly. "Nothing at all."

"That'll be a first," he said.

"Probably," she laughed.

"She doesn't want anything! Did you hear that?" He turned to Priscilla, who had cozied up in a huge armchair, as if trying to disappear.

"Alert the press," Priscilla yawned.

"Might as well," Josie said. "You two have been doing quite a bit of that lately, haven't you? You must have a direct hotline to Richard Johnson these days."

"Here we go," Jonathon rasped. "I knew this 'sweet' bullshit couldn't be for real."

"Oh, Josie, honey," Priscilla said. "We're sorry for that, we really are, aren't we, Jonathon? We didn't really mean you any harm."

"Really?" Josie tried to stay calm. "You really didn't mean me any harm?" She shook her head in wonder.

"Are we?" he said. "Are we really sorry? Yeah, sure, we're sorry. Sorry that we ever met your sorry ass."

"And I'm sorry you feel that way," Josie replied. *Don't let him get a rise out of you, no matter what*, she thought.

"Here we go with all that Program bullshit," he snarled. "Gee, I'm so sorry you feel that way." He imitated her voice. "What a load of crap." Josie looked down at her feet, which were shod in her old Manolo Blahnik boots. She didn't know what to say. He was definitely exasperating, and definitely pushing her. She took a deep breath and prayed for guidance.

"Did you buy those boots with my money?" he said.

She had to think for a second. "No. I, uh, I . . . I'd already spent all that money when I bought these." She was mortified that she'd taken the money in the first place, and even more mortified that it had all gone. She'd been a complete idiot. She should have kept some. It would have come in handy right about now.

"Spent it! How could you go through three hundred thousand in a year?"

"I don't know, really. I guess, well, I, uh, gave most of it away," she said softly, still staring at the boots.

"Gave it away?" He came closer to her now and she could smell his Armani aftershave and she felt herself swooning inside. *Stop!* "Who to? Bergdorf's? Barneys? Buy ourselves a few trinkets at Bulgari?"

She had to admit she had bought herself a nice watch, to replace the one he'd given her and then taken back when they broke up. But she'd lost it soon after. It was as if the money was cursed, or at least she felt like it had been. She couldn't wait to get it away from her. It was black money, there to remind her of what she'd done.

"It didn't feel right, so I gave most of it away," she said, looking at him, feeling like she wasn't free of him at all now, that he'd managed to draw her in yet again.

"Oh, so your conscience got the better of you, did it, Pookie? Yeah, sure."

"Jonathon, it wasn't about the money. Do you understand that?"

"Bull. You're one the most avaricious bitches I've ever met. Apart from my mother, that is."

"Jonathon, I was angry and hurt. I loved you. All I wanted was for you to be nice to me, to be there for me. I would have gone quietly and done anything you wanted. But you weren't. Not only were you not there for me at all, but you were stalking me, phoning me up in the middle of the night and threatening me. Following me. I was pregnant with your baby. I wanted to have it more than anything else in the world. But your father—"

"Don't bring my father into this! He looked after you very well."

She took a few deep breaths and tried to calm herself before she got out of control. "Your father called me," she continued, "I guess right after you told him I was pregnant. It was a Sunday evening. He called me from his car, on his way back to the city from Southampton. He asked me what I intended to do. And I told him I didn't know, that I needed some time to think. And do you know what he said, Jonathon? He said, 'Well you have a think. I'll be back in the city in a couple of hours, and by then you can tell me what you've decided. And tomorrow I'll have my lawyer call yours and we'll get this over and done with.' That's what he said. Like I was some piece of dust to be brushed under a rug. I'd been with you four and a half years, for God's sake!

"So, I told him I didn't have a lawyer, that this wasn't some kind of business deal, that we were talking about a life here. So he says to me, 'Yes. My son's life. I can't have him siring children all over the place.' He just didn't get it.

"That's when I started to get really angry. And, yes, then I finally did hire a lawyer. I never wanted your money. If you or he had been even remotely civilized I never would have hired a lawyer!"

"I don't remember any of this," Jonathon said.

"I don't suppose you would. You were insane. Look, I know you adore your father. That he'd do anything to protect you. But he's the one, Jonathon, the one who's made it so hard for you! He's never let you grow up and stand on your own two feet! He shouldn't have been the one to look after me in a situation like that—it should have been you! That's why I was so angry. You were all so dismissive of me!"

He sat back down on the couch, facing her, and lit up another cigarette. Their eyes met and she could see the pain in his and feel it in hers.

"It was the most difficult decision I've ever made."

"Which part?"

"All of it. The lawyer, the baby—our baby—growing inside of me like a ticking time bomb, and every day that went by it became even more difficult. I tried to talk to you, but you were out of control. It was useless. Your mother took me to your sister's gynecologist, Dr. Frederick."

"The Nazi who delivered Joni's kids?"

"Yeah," she smiled. "He sure looks and sounds like a Nazi. But he was really sweet. Your mother told him that you had been shooting heroin the whole time we were together."

"She what?!"

"I guess she was trying to make him convince me that the baby would be born with some sort of deformity or addiction, or something. She even mentioned AIDS. I told him that was a complete lie. That you were just drunk all the time."

"Gee, thanks. That bitch. I'm gonna get her for that."

"Oh, let it ride, will you? It's gone, over with."

He glared at her. "So you killed our baby."

"Yes. Yes I did. That's what they wanted me to do. They told me I'd have to file a paternity suit if I kept the baby. What an insult."

"All I remember is you wanting my money. Grabbing for it like some mercenary whore."

Josie ignored him. "And you told me you'd have nothing to do with the baby if I kept it. So, I finally did it. Yes, I took the money, but I was so angry with you. I thought it would be the only way I could get at you. Through your wallet." She sighed.

"Dr. Frederick took me to his clinic. I got down on my hands and knees and prayed for guidance. I still couldn't make up my mind. So, you know what I did? I flipped a coin. If it was heads I'd keep the baby and screw you all. If it was tails I'd do as you all wanted. Can you believe I decided the fate of a life by the toss of a quarter? Do you think I feel good about doing what I did?" The tears were flowing down her face now like two rivers. She didn't bother trying to hold them back.

"And after I did it, you called my parents in Australia and told them I was a murderer. You harassed them at all hours of the day and night. You called my brother and his wife and kids and cursed them out. You called all my friends and tried to hunt me down. I was petrified. I went to L.A. and you somehow found me there. You wouldn't leave me alone. And yet I'd never felt so alone in my whole life." She felt wrung out, just remembering half of the stuff that had gone on. And she looked over at him again and he was crying too. He wiped his eyes in a hasty swipe and sniffed back a sob.

"I'm sorry," he said softly.

"I'm sorry too," she sobbed. "You don't know how sorry I am. Every day I'm sorry for the decision I made. It had just started to fade some and now all of it comes back up again. For everyone to read. I guess it'll haunt me forever."

To her surprise he got up, crossed the rug, and sat down next to her. "So it was you. You gave all that money to those charities?" he said and softly wiped the tears off her face with his strong fingers.

"In your name. A lot of it, yes." She shrugged. "I really didn't want to keep it. It felt dirty. And wrong."

"I thought you were trying to harrass me. They've never left me alone, you know. I could kill you for that."

"I guess I was, really," she smiled. "Get you going and coming back." He hugged her then, and she knew how much he meant to her, how much this meant to her. Finally. Some kind of resolution. Closure. She felt herself sobbing again and she hugged him harder.

"Oh, how wonderful!" Priscilla chimed. "You've made up! Let's celebrate! Champai—uh, tea, anyone?"

"Tea's fine," Josie laughed through her tears.

"I'm gonna do it this time," he said to her after Priscilla left the room. "I'm gonna stay sober. Time I grew up."

"That's great. I believe you will," she said. "I truly believe you will. But right now our friend Priscilla could use our help."

49

Hamish sat on the toilet in his newly rented Tribeca loft and perused the morning's paper. Actually, he flicked immediately to the gossip pages. "Ah, the viper has made a complete asp of herself once again," Hamish sneered at the picture of his ex-wife. "God, I'm amusing." He curled his lips up in glee at his play on words. There she was, looking ridiculous, as always, with that hideous collagen-pumped Mona Lisa smile she stupidly thought was God's gift to men. She gave the worst blow job he'd ever had, no matter how puffed up those fat lips got. Dressed in some catastrophic combo of black and white fur. "Probably shaved rat," he said and smiled again at his talent to amuse himself.

The words beneath her picture held more interest than her pathetic taste in clothes. FEUDING KENTS KICK KAKA IN EACH OTHER'S KISSERS, the opener read.

> While Antonia, queen of the photographers' agents, hammed it up at Lot 61 with a bevy of hunky male models last night, we hear she is less

than amused at the multi-million-dollar lawsuit her ex has filed against her. Hamish Kent, famous for those celebrity portraits in the hugely successful Saint James campaign we see plastered everywhere, claims she is trying to steal the account for her newest protégé and paramour du jour, hunky Marcus Ashland. Mr. Kent says it's his account and has been for years. Mrs. Kent claims that by deserting her stable of world-famous fashion photographers her ex-hubby hasn't fulfilled his obligations to the campaign or the contract, which she created and brokered. No word yet from the folks at Saint James, but the fur is sure to keep flying between the two former partners and best pals until one of them skins the other.

He was slightly peeved there was no photograph of him.

"Piffle!" he said, tossing the newspaper down. "Just try to get me, you winched-up old lizard. You won't be able to tell those lips from your arshole by the time I finish with you." He started concentrating on more urgent matters and was in the middle of a particularly face-reddening squeeze when a staccato buzzing on the intercom distracted him.

Chris buzzed again. He knew the guy was at home, because he'd watched him arrive just ten minutes earlier. He should've caught him on the street, before he went inside, but he wasn't sure it was the right guy. By the time he found the photo of him in among the muck on the front seat of his car, the guy had disappeared inside the building.

"Who is it?" came an agitated voice from the interior.

"I'm Chris, your new assistant."

"Chris? I don't know any Chris. Doug's my assistant." The voice sounded very irritated.

"Doug's sick. He asked me to come instead."

"Well the little shit should have called first. How dare he be sick." The door buzzed open and Chris bounded up the stairs to the third floor. He rapped hard and the door opened an inch. Chris stuck his big foot in the opening and pushed hard.

"Process server. You're being sued."

"Buggering bollocks!" said the guy. He had a shaved head, a black eye, and his mug was red as a hot dog. Chris shoved the papers in the guy's hand before he had a chance to try to stop him. "That cunt," he snarled, and his face twisted up in the tightest, meanest look Chris had seen in a while, and that was saying something, considering what he did for a crust.

"Bugger off, you bloody weasel," the guy snapped at him.

"Sorry, sir. I'm just the messenger." Chris smiled at him, and it was then that he noticed the guy was naked from the waist down.

"And this is what I think of your bloody message." The guy turned, bent over, and farted loudly before he slammed the door in his face. Ah, another great morning in Manhattan!

50

Josie glanced across the limo at Andy, who sat nonchalantly reading the *Journal*. No big deal for him; this was potentially the most important day of her life. They were meeting with Marv and his family and it could get ugly. William had launched his own takeover campaign of Great Gams. Since he'd found out about Andy's bid, he'd been pushing to have Marv institutionalized and seize control of the corporation.

"Oh, my God." She read the same piece in the gossip column that had so enthralled Hamish that morning. "It's working! I can't believe it!" She put her hand up to her mouth and covered her giggle. "Oh dear. Ooh."

"What have you done now?" he asked, without even looking up from the *Journal*.

"I've been very naughty," she said, handing him the newspaper, giggling again. She watched his face as he read and was pleased to see him smile.

"You leaked this?"

"No, not leaked. Let's just say I sort of, um, started the ball rolling—with some help, of course." She felt guilty, in a way. But not too guilty, considering what those two had done to her. They could kill each other for all she cared now. She had much more important things happening. "They leaked it themselves, I guess. She loves seeing her name in print, even if it's not flattering."

"Jest like most of this town." Andy looked at her in such a way that she felt the blush rising from her toes. What on earth was going on? Was she imagining this?

"What?" she said. "What's the matter?"

He smiled and shook his head at her. "You're an amazing woman, Josephine Vaughn, that's what." He shook his head again and laughed, like he was in on some secret joke of his own.

"Oh. Thanks." She shrugged her shoulders and giggled again. "I probably shouldn't have done it, but . . . what the heck. They sure as hell don't look like they need sympathy from anyone."

He glanced at the article again, then looked back at her. "They been giving you a hard time, ain't they?"

"Hello! You only just noticed?" She laughed at the preposterousness of his comment. "Between those two and my ex and my best friend, Priscilla, my career as a Great Gams girl was more short-lived than an ice cube in hell. I'd still be stalking over Times Square if it hadn't been for those two. So the answer to your question is yes. Yes! They spread awful rumors about me. And I'm broke because of them."

"You shoulda told me, darlin'. Ah woulda taken care of them. Got my lawyers on to them and that rag."

"You know, I went and saw a lawyer, but I just couldn't be bothered going through the hassle and further embarrassment." She shook her head. "It just wasn't worth it. Besides. I figured out a way to get back at them, and this"—she pointed at the newspaper—"is the result. I think it's much more fun, don't you?"

"Hell," he laughed, "remind me never to get on your bad side."

"I could say the same about you, darlin'," she said. *Ohmygod! I'm saying "darlin'" now!*

"And what about your ex? You mean that lily-livered kid from the restaurant that night? Ah can sure 'nuf take care of him. All's Ah gotta do is call his daddy."

"Oh, it's okay. We made up. It's Priscilla I'm worried about."

"What in the hell is going on with her?"

"In a word, her husband."

"That's two words."

"Oh, shut up," she laughed. "You know what I mean. Look, he's a weirdo. Into young boys, that kind of thing."

"Yeah," he said and looked out the window.

"You knew?" She was stunned. "You knew all this time and you didn't say anything?" She felt like kicking him.

"Ah didn't feel it was my place to say anything. You never know what goes on behind closed doors in a marriage. For all Ah knew she coulda been into that type a thing too. Keep my nose outa other folks' business."

"But how did you know?"

"My brother. Word gets around in the velvet mafia."

"So you've known about Richard for ages! I'm sorry, but I just find it so shocking! Call me old-fashioned, but, you know, I figure by the time you marry it'd be kind of a good idea to have your sexuality figured out. Don't you?"

"Happens all the time these days." He shrugged, like it was no big deal. "Case in point." He pointed at the picture of Antonia. "Your British pals like a bit of 'swinging London,' from alls Ah hear."

"Her, too?" Josie was dumbstruck. "No. I don't believe it. She likes young boys." *My young boy,* she thought, as

Marcus's beautiful face flashed before her. "And how do you know all this? What are you—the gay gossip hotline?" she laughed.

Oh, no! Maybe he's gay too. Cripes. I've put my foot in it again. But what about the bimbo at Christmas? Gotta find out.

"How's your girlfiend?"

"Girlfriend?" He looked quizzically at her.

"Heidi? Isn't that her name?"

"Oh, Heidi's not my girlfriend." He shrugged. "She needed work, so Ah hired her as my personal assistant over the holidays. She's a sweet kid."

Yeah, right. Blow job all over your face. "So, you aren't seeing her?"

"Hell, no. Darlin', ah never have girlfriends."

Huh? Oh, so there you have it. Gay mafia. And all this time I thought he fancied me. What an idiot! How could I be so naive? Duh. He's got to be over fifty and he's never been married.

"So it's true!" she blurted out, then gasped.

"What's true?" He frowned.

"Oh, nothing," she smiled wanly. *Oh well. Another one bites the dust. Thank God I never threw myself at him.* "Look! We're here."

The limo pulled up outside the Great Gams building. Andy shook his head at her. "You're sumthin', you know that? Now, remember. Let me do the talking."

"My lips are sealed," she said, zipping them and turning the key.

Andy's attorneys greeted them and formed a phalanx around them like bodyguards as they entered the white-on-white foyer. Josie wondered what on earth would happen next. How many shocks could a girl take in one morning?

* * *

William had on another pair of overly tasseled and fringed loafers. The very expensive, crocodile jobs Josie had seen in places like that store . . . what was the name? That Arab place on Fifth Avenue. The one you had to be invited to get in. Actually, she remembered it had gone out of business. Or, at least it should have. Anyway, his shoes were hideous. *Such a shame,* she thought, *'cause he's so cute. But shoes maketh the man. And he's definitely proved that to be true, so far.*

His suit was hand-tailored. She could tell by the stitching on the lapels and buttonholes. His blue eyes averted hers when they landed on his tanned craggy face, and she realized, for the first time, that in fact she probably intimidated him. It wasn't that he was a jerk. Not at all. She had a way of looking somebody up and down, clocking them in a flash, and making judgments solely based upon what they were wearing. She was the one being the jerk. But she could never stop herself.

She smiled at him. "How's things?" And although she meant it, in all likelihood he thought she was being sarcastic. They were, after all, vying for control of his company. A business he'd undoubtedly slaved at since he'd finished college.

"Fine," he said, looking at his shoes, as she had just done. "You?"

"Never better," she lied, although she did feel a certain confidence today. She had Andy with her. And even though he'd just been struck off the ever-dwindling "available straight men" list, she felt safe with him. *Well, duh. Of course I'd feel safe with a gay guy! It's the straight blokes you have to worry about.*

"Shall we?" he said, politely, and ushered them into the conference room.

Marv was already seated at the head of the table. Josie smiled when she saw he had on a superbly gross leg-shaped tie. He smiled and winked at her through his thick glasses. "Hello, young lady," he cackled.

"You're back," she said, as Andy held a chair out for her and she sat next to Marv.

"Back to my old fighting self," Marv smiled.

"So we noticed," William mumbled.

One of the lawyers called the meeting to order.

"Now," Marv croaked, "before this turns into a big megillah I just want to say one thing. On behalf of Great Gams I want to apologize to this beautiful young lady." He held his hand out to Josie. "For all the nonsense we've put her through. She deserved our support. We should have stood behind her when those ridiculous rumors spread and instead she was ostracized." He leaned onto the table.

"If she and Mr. Wyatt can show me they will continue the Great Gams 'leg-acy'"—he chuckled at his little pun—"I will sell them *my* company. I will *not* allow it to be bastardized. Cut up and sold off to cover the mountain of debt all you corporate raiders are so fond of piling up. What do you say to that, Mr. Wyatt? Are you up for the challenge of running a real, honest corporation?"

"We have no intention of selling off Great Gams. Quite the contrary. We want to build it up, so its brand name and market share are the largest worldwide."

"Good." Marv smiled at Josie. "Then there really isn't much more to discuss. Let the bloodsuckers"—he waved his hand at the barrage of attorneys—"take care of the details."

"But Grandfather!" William rose, his face contorted with fury. "I own twenty-four percent of this company! Fred here, your other grandson, your flesh and blood, owns another twenty-four! We don't want to sell! We want to run it. Surely you can't dismiss your own family!"

"Forty-eight percent is still less than fifty-two, last time I counted," Marv said. "And if you two hadn't been such back-stabbing ingrates we wouldn't be sitting here today. Stop with your whining. You're going to be fabulously rich anyway you look at it. Maybe not as rich as if you'd had me bumped off, or worse, shoved me in that funny farm you tried to sell me on, but still a hefty sum. So stop kvetching. If you're lucky maybe these nice people might even want to keep you on."

And with that he rose, shook Andy's, then Josie's hand, and shuffled out. Josie looked at Andy in stunned elation. She was about to become William's boss.

"Congratulations, partner," Andy said, after they'd climbed back into the limo.

"Partners! Heee!" Josie grinned at him, elated. "I can't believe it!"

"Shake?"

"Shake, partner." They squeezed each other's mitts earnestly, then burst out laughing and hugged each other.

"Did you get a load of William's face?"

"Ah think he busted a nut," Andy chuckled.

"I kind of feel bad."

"He's gonna be jest fine. Now, there's just a couple more things for us to do today, kid." He picked up the phone and had his secretary connect him to "Page Six."

51

Richard Saunders didn't like losing. Anything. Especially face. So when he saw the article about him in the next morning's newspaper, his first reaction was shame. His second was to hit the roof.

His secretary, Doris, was used to hearing him screaming. But this morning she blushed at the obscenities coming from the other side of his office door. That and the shattering of glass. He was probably hurling his Baccarat scotch glasses again. She flicked through her Rolodex until she found Baccarat, dialed its number, counting the number of smashes as she did so.

"Hi, it's Doris over at Whiterock. Yes, I think we'll need another half dozen. Same design. Thanks, Mr. Grant. Have a good one."

Mr. Saunders strode out, slammed the door behind him, and walked past her, down the hallway. She picked up the phone again. "Incoming," she said to Jessica, his partner's secretary, "and in a blind rage."

"I'm not surprised," said Jessica. "You seen the morning's gossip page?" She hung up. Doris called the janitor, then went into her boss's office to assess the damage.

She tiptoed over the smashed crystal that covered the entire floor, reached for the paper that he must've flung at the wall, and flipped to "Page Six."

> Heavy hitter investment banker Richard Saunders is in a very tight spot. His wife of eleven years, Priscilla, has filed for divorce. Our sources provided us with copies of his arrest record, two months ago, for alleged sexual misconduct with a male prostitute. Priscilla Saunders called Page Six personally and asked us to retract our previous stories incriminating former Great Gams Gal Josephine Vaughn as her husband's mistress. Apparently Mr. Saunders kept a male "companion" for over four years during his marriage, unbeknownst to his wife. "I feel awful about Josie. None of those stories are true," she said. "I ruined her career. The press has vilified her. I'm truly sorry. We've made up and now we're best friends again." She is asking for half of her spouse's estate, worth an approximate $2 billion. This, folks, will be one nasty battle. Meanwhile, leggy Josie Vaughn has the last laugh. She and new partner Andy Wyatt have bought out her former employer Great Gams. Will we soon see the Empress's luscious legs and killer spikes striding over Times Square again?

Underneath was a picture of Josie Vaughn and Mr. and Mrs. Saunders, dressed to the nines, smiling and happy, like they hadn't a care in the world. *Poor Mrs. S.*, thought Doris. *She always seemed like such a nice woman. A little batty, but nice.*

She folded the newspaper and neatly placed it back on her boss's desk, then turned to look out across the Manhattan skyline.

"What the hell is goin' on 'round here?" came Eddy, the janitor's, voice from behind her, startling her out of her reverie. "Everyone's nuts this morning! Look at this mess!" He dragged the vacuum cleaner in behind him. "Fucking faggot," he mumbled under his breath.

"Eddy!" Doris glared at him. "That's not nice."

"It ain't too soon for this to come out, for my taste," he said.

"You knew?"

"Found 'im and that Lopez boy in my closet one afternoon. Goin' at it like animals. Nearly made me sick. It ain't natural."

52

Josie looked out her window. She could see the toddler in the building across from hers. She'd heard him wailing as a baby, seen his first steps, and watched him grow. She felt like she knew him, yet she had no idea who he was, or who his parents were or what they did. She wondered if they watched her too.

She picked up the newspaper and reread the bit about Richard and Priscilla and her. It seemed that no one knew anyone anymore, except for what they read in tabloids about each other, or saw from a distance, voyeurs of each other's lives, dislocated by the close proximity of an overpopulated metropolis. Immune to others feasting on their bad habits in plain sight. Perhaps those people had seen her walking around naked, picking her nose. When she'd first moved there, she'd been very conscious of things like that. Now she didn't care, and probably they didn't either.

She almost felt sorry for Richard. The poor guy had been living a lie. Probably all his life. Certainly during his long marriage to Priscilla. How could she not have known? Not a single inkling, so she claimed. Perhaps she'd chosen not to notice. Had wrapped the soft blanket of denial close around her, cocooned in its aura of wealth and safety. Appearances were everything, and they'd both put on a marvelous front. God, the guy must have been so tortured for so long. And now his insides had been blown out, aired for all to see. As had his wife's, and her own.

It made her sad, all of this, sad and alone, despite the fact that she had just pulled off the biggest coup of her life. To actually be part owner of a huge company, have a say in how it was run. Well, she'd leave the boring stuff to the suits. She knew her limits. She would be the creative head. The marketing genius. Ha! And although she was thrilled and flushed with excitement over it all, she still felt flat. The gnawing feeling that she'd spend the rest of her life observing other people's families, marriages, babies from afar. That she'd have nobody to share her successes and failures with. That nobody would ever truly love her. That she wasn't worthy. *No! Don't think like that! Have faith.*

She finished off her toast and was on her way to the shower when the doorbell rang. Thinking it must be the doorman with a parcel or something, she crossed the tiny living room and opened the door, without even bothering to check through the peephole. To her amazement, there stood Andy, dressed in a Ralph Lauren suede jacket, cashmere polo shirt, and corduroys, his feet in a pair of suede Tod's loafers, which she remembered she'd helped him choose. God, what a transformation he'd gone through in the past few months.

"Hi," she said, "what are you doing here? And why are you dressed like that? Aren't you going to the office?"

"You gonna stand there and talk about my clothes or you gonna ask me in?"

"Oh, sorry, yeah, sure, come on in," she said, nervous.

"Is anything the matter? Has the deal fallen through? What's wrong?"

"Will you jest relax? Nothing's wrong. Ah just wanted to come see you, is all."

"But why? What's the matter?"

"Do Ah need a reason? Can't a guy come and visit with his new partner?"

"Well, sure . . . I guess . . . but at seven in the morning? I mean, just look at me. I'm a mess."

"You look jest fine." He smiled and barged past her into the kitchen. "Y'all got some coffee?"

"Sure," she said, scratching through her matted hair. "It's right there. Let me get you a cup." What the hell was going on?

She handed him a mug, pulled some cream out of the fridge, and watched as he filled himself a cup. She noticed he was shaking a little. Uh, oh. Something was up. She knew it. He was firing her. He was going to get rid of her. Of course. Maybe he was going to out himself. Yes! That was it. He'd probably read the piece about Richard and figured it was time to come clean. Not that it made any difference at all.

"Come sit down," she said, in her most soothing, maternal voice. Now they were partners, she'd also be his confidant.

He sat nervously on the edge of the couch and looked at her. She really was a wreck, she knew, but she didn't care. *A gay guy isn't going to care whether I have on a flannel nightie and the ugliest slippers on the planet. He'll just make jokes about it.*

"Josephine, Ah had to talk to you," he said, slurping his coffee. "Had to set you straight about something."

"Yeah, I figured. Look, Andy, I don't care what kind of lifestyle you choose. You know I adore you no matter what. And now that we're partners—God, do I love the sound of that—you can tell me anythi—"

"Ah'm in love with you."

"You can tell me anything, it's oka—what?"

"Ah'm in love with you, Josie," he said, breathing deeply.

"But you can't be!"

"Why the hell not?"

"Because you can't love me!" she said indignantly.

"Why? You still in love with that young photographer? Or is it your old fiancé?"

"No! Of course not! But you should just accept who you are! It's fine. I have the greatest respect for you, Andy."

"You mean you could never love me, is that it?"

"No, that's not it. I'm mad about you, but what's the point? We're partners, and friends, and you have to go your way and leave me go mine."

"So you're saying that 'cause we work together, we have to stay friends."

"Yes. Yes, that is what I'm saying . . . I guess." She shook her head. "I'm confused. What do you mean?"

"Do Ah have to spell it out? Ah love you."

"But why?"

"How the hell do Ah know?" He stood and started pacing. "Do you think I had a choice? I was a goner from the minute I set eyes on you."

"So . . . you're saying . . . you're switching?"

"Switching what?"

"You know, changing teams. Hitting for the other side."

"What?" He stopped pacing and stared at her, completely perplexed. She felt like a complete dolt. Then he suddenly burst out laughing. "Jesus H!" he guffawed. "You think Ah'm a pansy!"

He roared with laughter and pulled her up from the couch and before she knew it he was kissing her neck and cheeks, nuzzling her with kisses. She froze at first, astonished, and then his mouth moved softly onto hers. "Ah love you," he whispered, his arms cradling her. "Ah want to love you forever." And he kissed her deeply and she let go, not worrying about her morning breath and the flannel nightie and the dirty pink slippers. Nothing else mattered anymore.

EPILOGUE

"Page Six" two months later carried several juicy tidbits on the same day:

Partygoers at Glo on Thursday night had more than just celebrity sightings to keep them entertained. Both champagne and fur flew as sparring exes Antonia and Hamish Kent gave the term "horizontal slam dancing" an entirely new meaning. On spying shutterbug and former client Hamish enter the club with his new squeeze, Juan Lopez, Antonia, still fuming at her ex-hubby's defection from her star-studded roster of photographers, swung a bottle of Veuve Clicquot in his direction, and she wasn't just offering him a cocktail. The bottle narrowly missed his shaved pate, drenching Sean P. Diddy Combs and his posse, who just happened to be in the flight path. One of Puffy's bodyguards, thinking the attack was aimed at his boss, threw the chinchilla-clad Antonia to the floor and held her down with a combat-booted foot, while she kicked her red-soled Louboutins at him and screamed obscenities. Our source tells us Hamish walked over and told her how classless she was to have thrown Veuve in Puff's direction. "At the very least it should have been Cristal," he scoffed. "And a jeroboam at that," said Puffy, while his aides wiped the "classless" brew off his white jacket. Hamish then ripped his former wife and agent's furry stole from her body and started whipping her with it. Unfortunately for him, he tripped and fell on top of her in the process, whereupon the "ex-Mrs.-K" bit viciously into his neck, drawing blood. The police were called and both of them were hauled out in handcuffs. No end in sight for this couple's feud. Both have filed lawsuits for the attack, adding fuel to the pending multi-million-dollar suits they already have against each other for the demise of their business partnership.

Meanwhile, Juan Lopez has had his former lover, billionaire bad boy Richard Saunders, arrested for statutory rape. Lopez, now twenty-two years old, claims he was only sixteen when first seduced by Saunders, who has denied all charges. Richard Saunders is up to his finely tailored lapels in lawsuits these days. Apart from the Lopez suit, which could result in jail time, his estranged wife, Priscilla, hired famed divorce attorney Melvin Shernofsky to lead her into battle. She has taken possession of their twenty-three room Park Avenue spread, along with the museum-quality modern art adorning its walls, as well as the Southampton estate and the Palm Beach mansion they once shared. She is reported to have become friends with Juan Lopez and encouraged him to contact the police over the alleged rape. Added to all this, famous interior designer Colbert

Constable has sued Saunders for money owed in the renovation of the apartment Lopez and he used as a "love nest." Richard Saunders, holed up at the Carlyle indefinitely, certainly has the fight of his life on his manicured hands, but even if Priscilla gets half of his vast estate, he'll still be sitting pretty on a cool billion or two. Which won't be much use to him if he's thrown in the slammer.

Priscilla Saunders has not wasted much time. She's floating around Saint Bart's with celebrity coiffure Pierre Parau, and romance is sizzling hot between them, as it is for their friends and travel companions, Great Gams' new owners, Josie Vaughn and Andy Wyatt. Also on the island is photographer Marcus Ashland, to shoot the newly refurbished Great Gams campaign. Parau, naturally, is doing the hair for the photo shoot; Vaughn is styling and modeling; while proud Andy and Priscilla sit back and admire their paramours. Who said work and play don't mix well?